I0721902

SHADOW PAWN

A MILITARY SPACE OPERA TALE

P. R. ADAMS

PROMETHEAN TALES

This is a work of fiction. Names, characters, places and incidents are used fictitiously. Any resemblance to actual events, or persons, living or dead, is coincidental. All rights reserved. No part of this publication may be reproduced, or transmitted in any form or by any means, electronic or otherwise, without written permission from the author.

SHADOW PAWN

Copyright © 2020 P R Adams

All rights reserved, including the right to reproduce this book, or portions thereof, in any form.

Illustration © Tom Edwards
TomEdwardsDesign.com

❀ Created with Vellum

ALSO BY P. R. ADAMS

For updates on new releases and news on other series, visit my website and sign up for my mailing list at:

http://www.p-r-adams.com

The War in Shadow

Shadow Moves

Shadow Play

Shadow Strike

Shadow Talk

Shadow Pawn

Shadow Fall

Books in the On The Brink Universe

The Stefan Mendoza Trilogy

Into Twilight

Gone Dark

End State

Stefan Mendoza: The Human Deception Trilogy

Split Image

Hard Burn

Null Point

The Rimes Trilogy

Momentary Stasis

Transition of Order

Awakening to Judgment

The ERF Series

Turning Point

Valley of Death

Jungle Dark

Chariot Bright

Dawn Fire

The Lancers Series

Deep Descent

Deadly Game

Dire Straits

Dark Secrets

<u>The Burning Sands Trilogy</u>

Beneath Burning Sands

Across Burning Sands

Beyond Burning Sands

<u>The Second Burning Sands Trilogy</u>

Inside Burning Sands

Over Burning Sands

War for Burning Sands

<u>**Books in The Chain Series**</u>

The Chain: Shattered

The Journey Home

Rock of Salvation

From the Depths

Ever Shining

1

———

Captain Faith Benson couldn't remember ever seeing a stranger mix of people. If she had, it certainly hadn't been in a conference room aboard the *Valor*, which was where she was now. She sat at the end of the table that anchored the room, looking at the wall display at the other end. To her right, Commander Alexander Tuleyev scratched the loose jowls of his face, nails rasping against the beginnings of scruff. He was the sort who probably needed to shave twice a day when he was young, and his whiskers weren't yet silver. Beyond him sat Lieutenant Clive Halliwell. A few weeks of healing had done wonders, restoring color and vibrancy that was clearly on display in his erect posture. Unlike her and Tuleyev's dress whites, Halliwell wore his Marine dress uniform, and he looked handsome.

Far too handsome.

To Benson's left, Captain Floyd Thiessen—her counterpart in the Gulmar Security Forces—coughed. His uniform was far less formal than those of the Kedraalian Navy. In fact, what he wore was closer to a business suit, really—a coat and pants of deep blue approaching black, with only silver along the cuffs to indicate rank. The shirt was a crisp white. She envied how comfortable it looked.

The man to Thiessen's left leaned forward and offered a reassuring smile that seemed right at home with his crumpled charcoal jacket and pants. Anders Manshaus had been the Azoren ambassador to Gulmar. Now he was their liaison to the Azoren powers on the home world of Himmel. "I assure you, Captain—this sort of delay is quite uncommon."

She straightened her back and sucked in the air, which had taken on their heat and scents in the two hours of waiting. Two hours of coffee and sugary pastries. Two hours of small talk about how well the trip through Fold Space had gone, all things considered, and how good it was to receive word from the Gulmar home world shortly after re-entering normal space that—at least in the time before the message had been sent through a Fold Space transmitter shortly after their departure—things were still okay. Two hours of the soft hiss of audio coming off the filtered channel piped in from the *Valor*'s bridge.

The whole time, she waited with dry mouth and sweaty palms for the reassurances of the Azoren High Command that the combined Kedraalian Republic and Gulmar Union task force was welcome to proceed to Himmel to begin their diplomatic mission.

Because without that message, their presence in the Azoren home star system all but amounted to an act of war.

Thiessen stroked the close-trimmed beard that traced his ever-so-slightly prominent chin. "What's the round trip to Himmel from here?"

Benson checked her data pad, just to be sure. Thiessen was a stickler for details. "Forty minutes."

"They could be having problems rousing someone."

Manshaus's head bobbed at the Gulmar captain's suggestion. Not a single strand of the ambassador's wispy, silver-blond hair shifted from its haphazard shape, which must have been crafted by disinterested strokes from a thick-toothed comb. His ice-blue eyes bugged out even more than normal. "Actually, this is quite possible. Without the appropriate people in attendance, the High Command will not operate. They are strict to a fault about this. Appearances, you see. It matters."

"It should be—" Once again, Benson checked her data pad to be sure. "—close to midday in your capital, Ambassador."

"Yes. The problem is that we are in a war posture, Captain."

"You've been in a war posture for decades." *Since you started the war that tore us all apart.*

"And we have adapted. Perhaps this is just that. A member of the staff—"

Halliwell groaned and pinched the bridge of his nose just above the notch where it had been broken some years before. "Or it could be an excuse to position forces to attack us."

Manshaus blinked. "The diplomatic mission was approved, Lieutenant."

"Sure. Approved by the same people who approved an attack on the Kedraalian Republic. Right?"

Tuleyev pulled a grimy handkerchief from his pocket and sniffled. "Lieutenant Halliwell, it is now our intent to seek out allies, yes?"

"I guess. Not my call."

"And we are now focused on a threat greater than the Azoren, yes?"

The Marine officer leaned forward, thudding an elbow against the tabletop and resting his chin on the upraised palm. "Are you asking for my assessment of our strategy, Commander? Because that would be a first."

"I only point out that we have such a strategy. You and I, well, this we must follow. Our role is not to form policy but see it through." The portly man sneezed into the cloth, then folded it back up.

Thiessen's face was stretched by a forced smile. "I don't believe I've ever heard of a strategy or policy in wartime that was truly palatable."

Halliwell's eyes swung from Tuleyev to the Gulmar officer. "Is that from Gulmar War College training?"

"History, actually. We don't have a War College."

"Too focused on profits, right?"

"Perhaps. But my point is that war is always about the least bad option."

The Azoren ambassador chuckled. "Other explanations are possible. A communications system failure. That is something that happens, even to the grand Azoren Federation."

Benson set her hands, palms down, on the table. "Redundant systems should prevent that."

"Yes." Manshaus seemed to sink in on his bony frame. "This is true."

"Our sensors are at full power. Weapons and shields are powered down."

"Good, good."

"We're not even moving toward Himmel anymore. Below the ecliptic, far enough out that none of our weapons pose a real threat…"

"Of course. Then, perhaps—" The skinny little man's bug eyes went around the room. "—we should continue our patient waiting? Answers are sure to come, don't you agree? Eventually, that is."

Halliwell rubbed his left shoulder. That's where he'd been grazed not all that long ago. Grazed by a rail gun round—it was the sort of thing that could turn you into a twisted, bloody smear. Benson hadn't seen the scar the weapon had left. His other scars? Those she'd traced fingers over.

All of them. Every centimeter of him.

But things had changed between the two of them. Sergeant Grier—Halliwell's senior NCO—had probably seen the new scar. And now *she'd* probably traced her fingers over every centimeter of his body.

And there was nothing Benson could do about that.

She cleared her throat. "Well, I think—"

The hum from the open channel to the Azoren disappeared, replaced by a crisp connection from within the ship. "Captain Benson?" It was Chopra—her executive officer.

"Go ahead, Dinesh."

"We're getting movement. At the edge of sensor range."

"On the screen down here, please."

After a second, the display broke into two windows, and the new window expanded, until the old window barely held a small corner. The black of space filled the new window, with a planet hanging dead center in the distance.

Himmel.

Computer imagery painted more details into that darkness, including a clump of red dots: the movement.

Benson's palms felt clammy. "How long until we have a sense of numbers?"

"It's all heat signatures at this distance. The computer's putting together ship profiles as we gain confidence in the details."

"Estimated time for them to reach us?"

"We've got time."

Time to plan. "But to pick up that much information, it has to be a big force."

"It does."

"As big as ours?"

Chopra's breathing grew louder. "By current estimates."

Tuleyev frowned. "A home defense fleet. They would not have the composition we do."

They wouldn't. But it would still be a problem. And intelligence reports had indicated the Azoren Home Defense Fleet was maybe fifteen ships. Something must have changed recently. Continued Azoren militarization? Or was this just another intelligence failure? The various Kedraalian agencies seemed to be more focused on fighting among themselves than on external threats, so stale intelligence was a real risk.

So was the possibility of infiltration by enemy agents. The reinforcements that had joined the task force over the Gulmar capital world of Radetta had brought word of a likely defector on Prime Minister Mengitsu Zenawi's staff. Benson had actually met the woman: Denise Gallo.

But Gallo hadn't seemed the type to work for the Azoren. They had a very strict definition of the ideal human in their crazed ideology: blond, pale-skinned, light-eyed. Gallo was a black woman.

"Captain Benson?" Chopra's voice tugged Benson out of her thoughts.

"Yes?"

"We're getting a better angle from the signals ships."

"A better estimate of numbers?"

"Well…soon. It's what we're seeing in orbit around Himmel that's more interesting."

"You know I'm not a fan of *interesting.*"

"I understand, Captain."

"All right. What is it?"

"Well, there are something like twenty ships still in orbit."

"Around Himmel?"

"Around Himmel."

"Configuration? Profiles?"

"At this distance—"

All eyes were on Benson now. "I need something, Dinesh."

"I— The configurations… They could be troop transports."

Manshaus's eyes looked ready to pop out of his head when he heard that. He was easily the most stunned.

Benson filed that away. "What about the closing ships?"

Chopra's voice turned muddy—the microphone turned down or covered by his hand. Then he was back. "There are several smaller escorts mixed in with what look like more conventional defense fleet vessels."

Escort ships. Troop transports. Had they stumbled into the beginnings of a planetary assault effort? Who would that have targeted?

"What about—?" Her eyes drifted to the ambassador. It would be so much easier if he weren't in the conference room with them. "What about shadow technology?"

"Stealth ships?" Chopra sounded surprised. "One moment."

He hadn't thought of that. A single victory against the Azoren sneak attack fleet, and everyone seemed ready to discount the idea that such an obstinate enemy was still a threat. What if they were only seeing the ships the Azoren wanted them to see? It was one thing to keep a potential ally happy by not powering up advanced sensor systems. But if that ally had a history of using the technology those advanced sensor systems countered…?

It sounded like Chopra was moving among the bridge crew—soft voices coming through with authority. Then he coughed. "Captain Benson?"

"Go ahead."

"No sign of stealth ships. But at this range…"

She licked her lips. "Keep me updated."

Her XO's voice was there, wordless. Then— "Will do, Captain."

What sort of advancements had the Azoren managed since the destruction of their stealth fleet? They were too ambitious and fanatical to settle for frightening their rivals. Another shadow fleet, another sneak attack—it would happen eventually. It's why Benson had been sent to the Gulmar in the first place: Develop an alliance and break this threat.

Except now a greater threat existed.

The Azoren ambassador squirmed. "Something such as a fleet of advanced spacecraft as you suspect—this requires substantial outlays, Captain."

Thiessen cocked an eyebrow. "That didn't stop the Khanate."

"This is true. But the Khanate has not suffered the strain of an ongoing war with the Moskav."

Benson clasped her hands in front of her. "We'd been told for years the Khanate was a non-issue, Ambassador. Your people and the Moskav had supposedly seen to that. Yet here we are, ready to negotiate an alliance with the Azoren leadership to actually do what your military supposedly already has done."

Manshaus shrugged. "The Moskav became the greater threat in Supreme Commander Graf's eyes. This struggle has stretched our resources to their limit. What more proof is necessary than exactly that?"

"Yet your government found the resources to launch a fleet of advanced spacecraft at Kedraalian space."

"But not...troop transports, Captain. Most of those have been committed to the Moskav front for years now."

It was what Benson's intelligence briefings had said. It was what Thiessen's briefings had told him. The Azoren were in a stalemate with the Moskav in the fight for control of the colony worlds that group had stolen from the Kedraalian Republic when the War of Separation had begun. In fact, Thiessen had said he believed the Azoren were actually losing ground on the Moskav worlds, that the Azoren held the sky, but the desperate determination of the Moskav people meant Azoren soldiers faced a soul-draining meat grinder.

These wars—they were all a terrible, stupid waste of life. No one needed the planets controlled by the other powers. They wouldn't for centuries, if ever. The wars weren't about resources but about silencing other thoughts and ideas.

How human.

The Azoren ambassador sank in on himself a little more. "The tragedy of that fleet, Captain Benson? At times, there can be disagreements among the members of the High Command. You understand?"

"What about Supreme Leader Graf? Doesn't he have the final say?"

"Ah, but he oversees the vast Azoren holdings. He leads the great march toward our utopia. Even as magnificent as he is, there are times when he might be deceived."

"Thank you, Ambassador."

Halliwell glared at her, then turned his attention to the ships approaching on the conference room display. He was having none of the ambassador's excuses.

It was a perfectly rational position. Waiting longer for the Azoren leadership to respond put the fleet—her people—at unnecessary risk.

She connected back to the bridge. "Commander Chopra?"

Her XO's face appeared on her data pad, the light of the helm console shining off his bald head. "Captain?"

"The high command has had plenty of time to respond."

"I agree."

"This feels…unnecessarily dangerous."

"Are you thinking of a change in posture?"

"If we power up weapons and shields to defend ourselves, it risks projecting offensive intent, even without moving closer to Himmel."

"This is true."

"Send another transmission to Azoren High Command. Emphasize that we're here on a diplomatic mission."

Halliwell twisted around in his chair. "We could take them."

Benson stiffened. "Excuse me?"

"The Azoren. This fleet. Draw them in, then hit these light escort ships with energy weapons. Launch missiles at the heavier ships. You do that, half their numbers are gone before they know what's happened."

Manshaus's jaw dropped. "Lieutenant, those you propose to slaughter in ambush are sailors, not doctrine officers."

"Yeah, well, they're serving aboard those ships that are threatening us."

"As conscripts. Service is not voluntary for us, you see?"

Thiessen straightened his coat. "Our service is voluntary, but…"

"It is also your only way out of squalor." Something touched the ambassador's ugly smile. Pity? "These ways into service, they are quite similar. Rounded up at gunpoint or facing a life of starvation and hopelessness."

The Gulmar captain glanced at Benson. "I hope it's clear that my people aren't ideologues."

Halliwell scowled. "I don't think it matters whether a bullet is fired by a zealot or someone desperate. People die either way."

"Doesn't that diminish your own Marines, Lieutenant?"

"How's that?"

Thiessen shrugged. "They train to be the best. Isn't there a belief in there? Doesn't that show loyalty and dedication?"

"Loyalty and dedication can't stop a rail gun round from tearing a body apart."

"But your commitment sets you apart."

"We're not zealots, if that's what you're saying." Halliwell shifted so that his body was fully facing Benson. "We don't need the Azoren to take out the Khanate. The reinforcements we received and the Gulmar task force—we can take that Khanate fleet on our own."

It was the same argument the Marine had made before, and there was truth to it. But she needed this alliance, or she would leave Kedraal exposed to Azoren treachery again. "If we've received reinforcements, the Khanate fleet probably has, too."

"But we know their tactics now."

"And they know ours."

Thiessen pointed to the large wall display. "Lieutenant, we share the same desire to see the Khanate removed as a threat. But imagine what those ships could do if dedicated to helping us."

Tuleyev harrumphed. "Unfortunately, it is flying toward us, not helping."

"But it hasn't done anything aggressive yet."

"And still—" The commander clasped his hands on top of his protruding belly. "I would prefer we be at least prepared for things going wrong. Captain?"

Benson caught the desperate look of the Azoren ambassador. The closest he had to an ally was Theissen, but the Gulmar captain's eyes were downcast now. She bit her lip. "Commander Tuleyev, I'd like to think we *are* prepared. Our missile inventory is at full capacity. We're ready to fab more immediately."

"But those could be missile platforms."

"They could. And we'd have to deal with them if so. But the way that group of ships is moving toward us—clumped together to make it harder to read their signatures—it would be easy to seriously damage them."

A soft groan slipped from Manshaus. "Captain Benson, please."

Thiessen's head came up. "Perhaps if I moved my ships back and out wide of yours, we might present less of an impression of…aggression?"

Aggression? They didn't even have shields powered up! Benson fought back rising annoyance at the way everyone seemed bent on being so difficult. Had they all forgotten they were facing an existential threat?

She counted to ten. "All right. Captain Thiessen, let's split your ships out."

His back straightened, then he relaxed. "I'll have them on alert."

"Good." Benson turned to Tuleyev. "As for our own readiness, I think we've briefed everyone that we're one second away from general quarters?"

The commander ran thick fingers over the unmoving mass of gray hair atop his head. "This is not the same as—"

Benson held a hand up to stop him. "We'll go to general quarters when those ships reach maximum effective weapons range, *if* they haven't contacted us or the high command hasn't responded by then."

"And maneuvers?"

"We already have our defensive maneuvering queued. We'll begin when we go to general quarters."

There was the look of ready argument on the portly officer's face, but after a second, he nodded.

Next, Benson turned to the ambassador, who was fidgeting. "Ambassador?"

"This is a very bad idea, Captain—a terrible mistake."

"We're not attacking."

"This I understand, yes. But going to general quarters—this is provocative."

"If you could somehow secure reassurances? I need to be able to not only tell my people they aren't at risk but believe that myself."

His mouth opened, and his lips seemed ready to form those assurances, then he sank back in his chair. "The High Command…"

"It's the same High Command behind the sneak attack that nearly destroyed Kedraal. Lots of my comrades died fighting against that attack." The sting of memories—lost *friends*—was still fresh in her mind.

The ambassador's eyes dropped to the tabletop. "My role is as a diplomat, Captain. I am not a military officer."

"I understand." She stiffened her back. "For now, I think we have our marching orders."

Tuleyev pushed up from the table. "I will return to the *Lyon*."

Thiessen shot a glance at the big display again, then stood. "I'll get my task force into position, Captain."

"And I—" The ambassador got to his feet slowly. "—will return to my quarters."

The little man slouched to the exit at the side of the broad-shouldered Gulmar captain.

The hatch closed, leaving only her and Halliwell.

Benson wasn't ready for a talk with the Marine about his behavior, but it needed to be discussed. His temperament had always been…fiery. As one of her key officers, she'd asked him to work on that. He'd made progress, but it had disappeared since his recovery from the injuries sustained boarding the Khanate ship.

She sucked in a breath, telling herself it was time—

Only to be rescued by Commander Chopra's face appearing on the display. "Captain?"

Let this be good news. Please. "Yes?"

"We have a message from Azoren High Command."

"Put it through, please."

A room appeared on the screen. Gray concrete walls that gave the impression of solidity and mass. Flags and bunting of black, red, and white. Angular, heavy furnishings with gold accents and polished surfaces. A table full of uniformed men with their heads turned toward the camera. An empty chair—almost a throne—at the head of that table.

She ran a quick tally—fourteen men. Only six showed the signs of age —pudgy faces, doughy bodies, sunken cheeks and wrinkles, gray or thinning hair—that matched the senior ranks she recognized on their shoulders. The rest had the appearance of what Thiessen called Golden Children.

In the sea of blue eyes, alabaster skin, and flaxen hair, she saw only youthful vigor and cold hatred.

Franz Graf wasn't sitting atop his throne. Only the oldest of the officers seemed familiar: General Erwin Guderian. Stone-faced, short, and slender, now with only a crown of white hair and blue eyes that were nearly gray. He'd been Graf's right-hand man for a couple decades, the most senior military officer. The others?

Guderian nodded toward the camera. "Captain Benson, please accept our sincerest apologies. Your diplomatic mission is, of course, welcome to proceed into Himmel space. Under escort. Please bring down your senior staff and Ambassador Manshaus for a meeting with the High Command at your earliest convenience. We look forward to meeting you."

The message ended abruptly, and the screen blacked out.

Benson blinked at Halliwell and saw on his face the same thoughts she was feeling: Something had changed.

2

Finally, Benson's breath came back to her. It sounded like a bullhorn-amplified sucking sound, booming off the conference room walls. How long had she held everything in after the message ended? Long enough to make it sound like a desperate gulp when she breathed. Being shocked like that really was like being kicked in the chest, having every muscle in your body tense up while your lungs tried to come back online.

Her palms were thoroughly damp now. When she licked her lips, a little bit of sugar from the pastries came away. She reached for her cup, which held the last of cool, black coffee that now smelled wicked. To talk, she needed *something* to wet her throat.

She swallowed the drink, then set the cup back on the table with a shaking hand.

Another look at the display, a hope that maybe the High Command would be there, laughing. "A good joke, Captain Benson—don't you agree?"

Ha-ha-ha!

No joke. It was just her and Halliwell and his scowl and her jagged breathing and her armpits growing damp and her crazy heart racing anxiously.

What had just happened?

Halliwell slapped a hand against the table. It was like a lightning strike —the instant of light flickering just before the boom.

That was just her blinking at the sudden movement, then getting caught up in the silence before the sudden thump.

All the same, she jumped, exactly as if it had been thunder.

The Marine's scowl deepened. "You're not falling for that, right?"

"Falling…?"

"An escort? They send a *fleet* as escort?"

Oh. *That.* "Something's changed."

He snorted. "You think?"

"Clive. Stop it."

"Stop what? They're asking you to put all of us right in their crosshairs and then smile while they turn us into twisting wreckage they can salvage at their leisure."

She ground a knuckle into her chin. "Think about it for a minute."

"Think about—?" He shook his head. "You're actually considering doing this?"

"Clive—"

"No. Seriously? You want to let them tell us what to do? They can sneak in nice and close. We can keep our shields down. Maybe we can send them some targeting information, just in case they can't get a clean lock-on."

The knuckle ground harder, pinching flesh against bone. "Your anger is taking away your objectivity."

"Oh, so this is a *me* problem? *I'm* the one making a mistake? *I'm* the one about to stick the fleet's ass up in the air for a free shot?"

"Let's keep this professional."

His face turned red. "A professional wouldn't risk her fleet."

The intensity and heat coming off of him—things weren't resolved between them. "This isn't the right time to let things become…personal, Clive."

"Really? When is that then, Faith? Maybe you could talk to Floyd, see if you can get on his calendar to work out whatever scheduling you two need before you slot me in for a good talking to?"

This is about Thiessen? "I... We need to focus on the matter at hand. Please."

"The matter at hand is you making bad decisions because you're too distracted by impressing your Gulmar boyfriend."

"Clive—"

"You don't care enough about your people—"

"Clive—"

"—to do your job and blow the hell out of—"

"Lieutenant Halliwell!"

His teeth clacked together, then he leaned back in his chair. "We could end this threat right now." His voice was soft and shaky. "You saw the latest update on that fleet. We outgun it."

"We can't afford to lose ships we'll need against the Khanate."

"This is our chance to repay the Azoren—do to them what they did to us."

"We're better than that."

He dug a necklace out from inside his shirt. A polished piece of shrapnel dangled from the end. That chunk of metal should have killed him long ago, when most of his battalion had died in a bungled training exercise on Dramora. It was a planet now entangled in an effort to leave the Kedraalian Republic for the Azoren Federation.

That betrayal, that crass need to play at political divisiveness—it had to hurt, to burn where the memories of dead comrades felt like empty shadow.

The Marine stared at his metal talisman. "Is there really any value in it?"

"In...?"

"Being better? You know: Not being the one to pull the trigger first? Letting your people die nobly and giving them ribbons and medals in memory? Taking the more merciful option, even if it means more coffins shipped home after the engagement? Letting someone who just killed a platoon with a dirty bomb walk away with a light sentence in a cushy prison? I think if you asked the dead, they might disagree."

Sweat trickled down her side. She hated fighting with him. Inside, everything twisted and ached not just because of his passion but because he was right. No one had a problem asking the military—especially his Marines—to make sacrifices. None of the politicians who formed the policies that put her and him on the front line, at risk every minute of the day, had even served. They had no idea what they were asking, what even a second under fire felt like.

But in this one instance, the policy was meaningful. She had skin in the game because she'd helped craft this.

She fought back the urge to reach for his hand. "This is the right thing."

"What if it isn't? What if they're coming in for a strike?"

"Then they'll be dead not long after us. And maybe we'll be dead not long after we kill them. Clive, this is about survival. Right now, somewhere out there, that Khanate fleet is moving to its next target. If we can't pull together a big enough force to go after their home world and force them to engage us, millions of innocent people could die."

"I don't know if there are millions of innocent people left, Faith."

"When I was on Radetta, Floyd took me to the...city where he grew up."

"Touching."

She shook her head. "It wasn't touching at all. It was filthy and poor and hopeless. Like the ambassador said, it was squalor. There's nothing like it in the Republic. Even our poor are treated with some level of dignity. Those helpless and powerless people were incinerated. The Khanate force launched missiles into a bunch of tin shacks."

Halliwell looked away. "They're just another form of scum."

"They're the type of people who won't quit. They have no tolerance for anyone who doesn't embrace their beliefs."

"Convert or die. I know."

"I don't think they're concerned about converting anymore. They've gone mad."

He leaned toward her. "They all went mad—the Azoren and Moskav, too."

"It's a different madness. I think there's a grain of sanity in the Azoren. Maybe it's not *sanity*. Maybe it's self-preservation. If Manshaus is right, it sounds like some people are growing tired of the war with the Moskav."

"Or they're just running out of people."

She waved that away. "If we can convince the High Command that the Khanate is the greatest threat, we can use that fleet out there or one like it. We can reduce the losses we'll suffer in this fight to survive. Isn't that what you want?"

"I want to do the right thing."

"Destroy the Azoren?"

"Wipe them out. Hit them now. Don't let *them* be the ones to trick and lie. Even if this isn't an ambush, you know they'll turn on us the second they get the chance."

"And if we don't wipe the fleet out? If we sustain heavy casualties in the fight?"

"We can outproduce these people. We can win this war. It just takes commitment."

"Commitment to what?"

"To doing whatever it takes."

Benson set her hands on her lap. "I don't have that commitment, Clive."

"I know." He stood, face twisted down in a sulk. "I had to try."

He stomped out.

Stopping him would have done neither of them any good. She sucked in a deep breath and counted again, this time to twenty. Then she used her data pad to connect to Thiessen.

He accepted. "Captain Benson?"

"Floyd, are you still aboard the *Valor*?" He was. She showed him in the lift, headed down to the hangar deck.

"Yes."

"Are you alone?"

"I'm the only one in the lift."

"Can you—" She blushed, feeling like a schoolgirl talking to a boy in the hallway. "I'll meet you at your shuttle. If you get a moment, please give the Azoren High Command response video a look."

"They finally responded?"

"A recording. I'm forwarding it to everyone now."

"All right."

Thiessen was pacing at the bottom of the ramp, head down, tugging at the fine whiskers of his beard. Behind him, the airlock light was a soft amber that was like a distant sun. His head came up when she stepped back from the viewing porthole, and the inner hatch opened.

"Captain Benson." His eyes darted to the other ships in the hangar.

She nodded toward his airlock. "Mind if we talk inside?"

Tension eased from his body as they strode up the ramp. When the outer airlock door closed, he leaned against it. "Is this about your lieutenant's outburst?"

Her head sagged. "Clive… He's complicated. His situation is messy."

"I don't think there's a person who's actually lived life who doesn't have messy complications. That doesn't mean they talk about ambushing potential allies in front of a diplomat."

"I know."

"Not that I disagree with him."

That brought her head up. "What?"

"It *is* the perfect time to hit them. Anders knows that, too. I think at some level, he's expecting it."

"But we're here to negotiate the terms of an alliance."

"And you catch them with their pants around their ankles if you attack. That's why they've scrambled that fleet. They know they're vulnerable. They're thinking it's the kind of thing they'd do. You could see it in their eyes in that video."

"We're not them."

He scratched the back of his head, where shrapnel had cracked his skull not two months ago. "People have a hard time seeing the world with eyes other than their own. *They* would use a maneuver like this to launch a sneak attack, therefore *everyone* would. That's why the Gulmar leadership behaves the way it does."

"Like bloodless psychopaths?"

"As far as they're concerned, *everyone* is a bloodless psychopath, all willing to knife their parents for a couple dollars."

"I…don't think I could make a career in service to people like that."

"You sure?"

"My government's not…" Could she really draw a bold enough line of distinction? Yes. Yes she could. "We're not *that* bad."

"Maybe they aren't. Anyway, moot point. My career's done when this contract's up."

"Had your fill?"

He blushed. "Actually, I'm probably looking at doing time on one of the penal colony stations."

"Prison?"

"That's a nice way of describing it."

"What for?"

"I participated in an act of coercion against the provisional leadership council. Wouldn't that get *you* put in prison?"

"I—" He was right. The Gulmar leadership couldn't touch her for the actions she'd forced them to take. But Thiessen? He had no such protection. And if she'd tried something like she'd done with her own prime minister? But... "Won't you have the security forces at your command when this is all over?"

"It's a temporary position."

"But you hold it right now. Couldn't you...change things?"

He folded his arms over his chest and pinched his chin. "That would prove their point about the danger of giving so much power to someone without proper vetting."

"Or it would prove that anyone can break when pushed too far."

Thiessen shoved off the outer airlock door. "I suppose there will always be two ways of looking at anything. Was that what you needed to talk to me about—your lieutenant? See him in a different light?"

"No. I wanted to get your thoughts about the Azoren."

"My thoughts about whether this is an ambush on their part?"

"Yes."

His eyelids narrowed in concentration. "If we play it cool, we should be fine. I don't think they're looking for a fight right now. Not with the Khanate fleet hidden somewhere out there."

"So they understand that this is a real danger?"

"Anders does, and he assured me that—" Thiessen sucked in air with a hiss. "Well, he assured me that the people who used to be in the High Command believed him."

"But all that changed. I didn't recognize half of the people around that table."

"Looks like." Thiessen tugged on the hem of his jacket. "I need to get back to my ship."

Benson smiled, but it felt awkward. She wanted to say more but couldn't think of what. Maybe it was just a mention of how much she enjoyed his attention to detail and calm, something she really respected and needed. Or maybe it was the way being so close to him and taking in his warmth and the gentle grassy sweetness of his cologne made her tingle.

The outer airlock door hissed open, sucking out that heat and aroma, and she followed after it down the ramp, saying nothing more but glancing back when she reached the bottom. At the top of the ramp, he stood stiffly, brow bunched, as if he were angry.

Had she crossed a line—perhaps with her suggestion of a coup? She hoped not. Allies were hard to come by, and he seemed so promising.

Then the airlock hatch hissed shut, the ramp rose, and she was alone.

For the last two years, Colonel Avis McLeod had spent more hours at work in his Group for Strategic Assessment office than home. In fact, to him, home had become a nebulous idea. It was a house, certainly—big, empty, an hour outside the city, surrounded by an immaculate broad lawn. But eating a meal alone there was no different than grabbing a bite in the commissary and reading over unclassified reports. If anything, wandering the halls of the sprawling GSA building was more relaxing and better helped him find the focus he needed. People didn't actively *watch* him here like they did when he was away.

He had a job. He had responsibilities. He delivered.

That's what mattered to his superiors. That's what mattered to the Republic of Kedraal. It's what kept people alive.

So, he finished off a dry chicken breast topped with a slice of white cheese that could have passed for the wax paper separator. The meat was drenched in garlic and salt and floated in wine sauce, but none of that could hide the stale, papery cheese. While he ate in the empty corner of the quiet and dark commissary, he read an analysis on the value of transferring more planetary naval personnel to the space fleet as part of the continuing ramp-up of forces.

People were slowly coming around to the realization that the current struggle wasn't about right or wrong or saving money or appeasing a mineral-rich planet where hotheads were making outrageous demands because, dammit, they felt more important than their population actually made them. This fight against the dark things that moved in shadow was about survival.

Not *their* survival. The survival of the species.

Good.

The message was old. It predated the current situation by decades, going back to a time before the Azoren and Gulmar and Moskav and Khanate were nothing more than embarrassing thorns in the side of human decency. It was hard to get people to hear that message, though. Most were busy listening to themselves blabber about the importance of tolerance and decency and acceptance. And freedom. They always pointed to freedom.

Those were great concepts. They were the sort of ideals people could feel proud dying for.

But those concepts had led them down this dark path.

What had been the great human experiment, the republic that would be home to humans after they'd taken a crap all over their first home—that was all over now. The samples had been tampered with, spoiled. Unwanted cultures had been allowed into the Petri dish, and fouled the experiment. What good was there in spending centuries terraforming new worlds if they were just going to act as a new toilet for all the poison and pollution of Earth?

He clomped through the tunnels beneath the main building, checking in at the various security stations and engaging in small talk with the bored guards. Then he slipped into his office, closed the door, and settled at his desk.

There were spies within the government. And there was corruption. Worse, there was rank incompetence.

In that stack of problems, where would he put the uncompromising dogmatists like Representative Sargota Benson?

Harmless. Too rigid and brittle to understand the ways of governing.

McLeod tapped the desktop terminal to life and pulled up the latest classified reports on the spy network that was being uncovered, largely thanks to the work of Brianna Stiles. She'd missed Denise Gallo, but that little fish had been tagged long ago, and now that her use had played out, she'd been let go. But the others? The Patel network Stiles had started to map out?

Priceless.

And yet...

Stiles was late reporting in. Her trip to Dramora should have produced a news report of the unfortunate death of Devanshi Patel. Plucking out that linchpin of the powerful family should have led to a catastrophic collapse within the Dramoran Independence Movement and cut off a lifeline to the Khanate and to the Azoren.

For the third time that day, McLeod accessed the GSA Fold Space transmitter station on Kedraal's moon and typed in RCL. It was the same recall code he'd issued each time before. At the very least, Agent Stiles should have received the notice to report in. She had codes of her own, all of them three-character combinations, ranging from MSR (Message Received) to ENR (En Route) or MNA (Mission Abort). They were the sort of codes she could send with minimal effort, even when bound. It might take time, what with the low-power transmitter embedded at the base of her neck having to not only find a device within range but also to seek out a network undetected and ride that to the nearest Fold Space transmitter.

But it should reply. Eventually.

It just wasn't like her to be offline for so long. Had she found something that took her deep? The Patel network was intricate; the people they ran with were masters of byzantine twists and turns.

But when McLeod was honest with himself, it was Stiles's behavior that was truly worrisome. She'd become too aggressive, too prone to take risks.

She was feeling the pressure. How could she not? Everything around her was slowly coming undone, with each brick she pulled leading to collapses big and small.

Shadows didn't like the light, he reminded himself.

His terminal buzzed: A message…from Stiles.

Finally! He would have to talk to her about promptness and—

The message blinked at him on the terminal: NLA.

No Longer Available. Dead. Flatlined. Exterminated.

How? She was his best. Even better than her brother by all accounts.

McLeod's fingers hovered over the virtual keyboard glowing on his desktop. Shaking. He was shaking. Every asset was valuable, and every asset was expendable, but Stiles…

His heart pounded. There was so much work still to do, and he'd been counting on her.

Another buzz as a second message came in, also from her. It had been hung up in the delay between the orbiting Fold Space transmitter and the processing center in the building.

He stared at the three letters: RSC. After a second, he frowned, then opened another window and began typing, arranging for a priority trip to Dramoran.

There was still work to do.

3

Darien Caville wasn't a sailor, but he had enough experience in deep space operations to know when a ship had come out of Fold Space, and the *Ollie* had just done exactly that about three weeks early. Subtle sensations washed over him, like ripples of water spreading out. The bow of the ship was the center point of the ripple, where residual energy from the jump between dimensions first struck. They were coming out of the place where physics took a hike and left the matter of defining the meaning of distance to the ship's strange Fold Space drive. Now that they were back in real space, his stride really was nearly a meter long as he headed forward.

Apparently, Lev Goldman was ready for the confusion. The captain of the *Ollie* was waiting amidships, arms crossed enough to hide some of the scars, cybernetic eye glowing a dull green. The muscles of his thick neck were tensed, and that tension informed his odor—ripe and sharp. "Far enough."

Caville was nearly as tall as the other man but built rangy. His dark eyes caught activity beyond Goldman's position: crew in a hurry. They were rattling and stomping—moving crates from the cargo area toward the airlock. "What's going on?"

"We have a rendezvous. You know how it is."

"You said we were heading to Azh Shivan."

"We are. This is a minor detour."

"You didn't tell me—"

"I'm the captain. I'm the only one who needs to know. That's how our operations go. Remember?" The older man shifted subtly, his arms less firmly crossed. His hand could quickly pull out the pistol he'd given Caville to shoot Stiles.

The young man's shoulders slumped. "I thought you trusted me."

"More than most of my crew, sure. But I don't trust anyone. Not really."

"That's how pirates die."

"Exactly." Goldman smiled. "Why don't you cool down?"

"I am cool. I was worried—"

"Don't be. Everything is under control. Hey, go spend some time with Denise. It's been a long trip, and I don't think she's enjoying it."

"We've been talking."

"She needs more than talking. Look, she's a fugitive. Until she gets back to Khanate space, she's going to feel threatened. That sort of vulnerability—you can really take advantage of it."

"Sure." Caville smiled. "Make her feel safe. I've been doing that."

"Good. It's not like she's unattractive."

"Not at all. I'll swing by and check in on her."

"See? That's the right approach." Goldman's legs didn't budge from their wide spread, nor did his arms unfold, but the dull, green glow left his eye.

Threat averted.

Being perceived as a threat was the last thing Caville wanted. Before Stiles had inserted herself into the situation, he'd been a trusted some-times member of the *Ollie*'s crew, a hired gun for pirates. He'd done terrible things to prove himself. Now it felt like he'd fallen down a couple pegs, despite being the one to shoot Stiles in the head.

Caville headed aft, toward the Khanate spy's quarters. They'd spent a few nights together and had a good relationship despite her odd religious views.

Halfhearted views. She wasn't a zealot.

The young woman hadn't yet slipped into the ugly, concealing robes of her people. Actually, she had, but she'd also slipped out of them after a few drinks and some laughter. She apparently wasn't ready for the whole repressed lifestyle thing. Or maybe she was, and she saw this flight back as her best chance to enjoy one last fling with freedom.

That was fine. A total lack of inhibition made her great in the sack and took some of the sting off what he'd had to do to Stiles.

He stopped at a small, semicircular recess in the bulkhead, where a ladder connected the decks. The rest of the crew were back in the cargo hold area, moving crates to the airlock.

Supporting the rendezvous.

The rendezvous with whom? Transferring what?

Stiles had risked her life getting a look at the crates that had been transferred onto the *Ollie* by Devanshi Patel's people. Caville already had a good idea of what was onboard. Goldman was a Security and Intelligence Directorate operative, and SAID was all about spreading chaos. They were moving advanced technology and weapons to the Khanate in exchange for freeing hostages. It was an operation that stretched back decades, something cooked up long ago by Mengitsu Zenawi before he was prime minister as a means to solidify his political power. Aside from a bungled rescue operation that had left eight Marines and Navy pilots dead, none of Zenawi's predecessors had ever done a thing about the hostages. Now, with a crumbling coalition, the rookie prime minister was ready to push all his chips in and declare himself a hero. How better to distract everyone from his checkered past?

But this felt different, like a shadow within a shadow, a compartment Goldman wanted to hide from prying eyes.

Was the Patel family behind it? They weren't really Zenawi people.

A quick glance up and down the passageway confirmed Caville was alone. His computing pad wasn't picking up cameras or other sensors in the area, and he couldn't see anything in the recess or on the ladder rungs.

He stepped onto the ladder, then scampered up to the top deck, stopping a meter short of the opening and listening: quiet. When he poked his head up and glanced around, the passageway was as empty as the deck below.

What he wanted was the cockpit, where the pilot and engineer on duty ran things. It was all the way forward, where the upper deck extended past the lower sections. All the sensor and control systems were there. He would be able to get a look at what was going on in the cargo hold and airlock using those control systems. It might not give him the details he wanted, but it was better than the blind eye he had at the moment.

He hated being blind. It meant he was failing at his job.

Other than the soft pad of his steps and the hum of systems, it was quiet. If he stood still, held his breath, and strained, he could hear the clump and clatter of the ship's infrastructure—air and water recycling; power systems; the *thwip* of shields that protected against asteroid impacts and acted as a magnetosphere for the ship, keeping out otherwise lethal doses of radiation.

Caville stopped at the point where the stairs led up from the cargo hold. The grunting and shouting was still in full swing. Crates would be clasped into place on dollies, and maybe those dollies were already being lugged into the airlock.

That meant it was still clear.

It wasn't like Goldman to leave the cockpit without a guard. Someone would be in the area. The hatch would be locked.

Getting through the hatch was easy enough. But a guard?

That was exactly what Caville had trained his entire life for: assessing risk, taking chances.

Then again, Stiles had trained the same way.

It's the job. You did what you had to do. Now it's up to others.

Caville padded forward, slowing as he approached the poorly lit forward section of the ship, which held the areas that were actually monitored. He was in a starboard side narrow passageway, which ran parallel to another narrow passageway on the port side before they came together several meters ahead. Goldman's cabin was up in that area, as were those of the two pilots and engineers plus the common bathroom—head—they all shared.

There were cameras and movement sensors in both passageways. In the intersection where a passageway led to port and starboard emergency airlocks, someone had recently installed a heat sensor. That area was usually the coolest spot in the ship. Passing through there would register a heat blip that would fire an alert in the cockpit.

But if there was a guard on duty…

There were simple routines built into Caville's data pad. Those routines were more than enough to overcome the cameras, which were unreliable to begin with. It wasn't that the ship was broken down and ancient, but Goldman had to compromise on who he hired. People didn't line up by the thousands to sign up for murder, and he especially didn't want anyone too bright or too curious. That meant the engineers might not do everything they could to keep things running.

The data pad flashed green, telling Caville the cameras were compromised.

Next came the movement sensors. These were set up about knee and waist high. You could belly crawl under them, or you could make a high jump. The high jump would make a racket on the loose deck tiles. That was by design.

Caville blinked contact lenses into place and located the infrared lines crisscrossing the passage. He crawled under the first two sensors, but someone had modified the third, dropping it down to ankle height. That and the heat sensor…

Had someone been caught trying to access the cockpit?

Heavy steps echoed from the cockpit area just ahead of a belch: the guard!

Crawling back under the movement sensors would take too long. Caville hadn't figured out how to defeat the heat sensor yet, but he now had his answer about whether there was a guard or not. That meant triggering the sensor wasn't a crisis.

The GSA agent tumbled between the lower line of the last movement sensor and the waist-high line, tucked into a ball, and rolled over the loose deck tiles with as little noise as was humanly possible.

It was still a clatter.

That caught the guard's attention, and the heavy thud of booted feet raced closer.

Coming from the starboard side.

Caville hurried to his left and slipped into the narrow passageway that carried him forward. To his right was an engineer's cabin. If all hands were involved in moving the crates, the cabin should be empty. But unlocked?

He tried the access panel: locked.

The booted feet were behind him now, back in the intersection.

Up ahead, the passageway took a sharp turn to the right, then merged into a single way forward. The pilots had cabins off that, one to either side. Goldman's cabin was opposite the cockpit itself, the hatch looking onto that single passageway.

It was past the point of finding an optimal hiding place, so Caville tested each hatch as he ran past. The two pilot hatches were locked, but…

Had Goldman's flashed red, too?

"Someone there?" There was no mistaking the voice: Theo. The big man was probably halfway to drunk already. He had paused rather than come forward into the passageway.

The options at that moment were brutally simple: run back and test Goldman's hatch, or go for the cockpit. Caville had the codes for the cockpit, but Theo was almost guaranteed to check the cockpit.

Then again, he might check all the cabins.

Or he might call Goldman.

Which pointed to the third option: get the hell out of the forward section of the ship before Theo realized there really was someone there. He was a big man and slow, even when he was sober. Outrunning him was a real possibility, but not if Caville got trapped.

Taking risks had forced Caville to shoot Stiles. But those were bad risks. *Stiles's* risks.

But something had changed aboard the *Ollie*.

There would never be as good a chance to uncover what was going on.

Caville dashed back to Goldman's hatch and tested it again: green.

He popped it open, but instead of going inside, he pulled something out of his pocket, dropped it to the deck, and skittered back to the cockpit and opened that hatch, too.

As it closed, Theo's voice boomed. "Hello?"

The cockpit was a fairly tight space: the pilot's station fully forward, looking onto a bank of displays; one engineer station to the right with its own set of displays; a second engineer or co-pilot station on the left mirroring the others. Each station had a swivel chair anchored into a slot in the floor, allowing the seats to move in close to consoles or push out.

At that moment, the room was lit by a few dimmed displays, leaving shadow in the corners.

Caville pushed the starboard engineering station seat in, then slipped beneath the port engineering station before pulling its seat in, too. It was crude and hopelessly bad cover. Anyone would think to look in the shadows. That would force the fourth option: killing Theo.

After several long breaths, the cockpit hatch hissed open.

"Hey! You in there?"

Boots thudded, and in between each step was a heavy, beer-tinted breath. The wide man shuffled to a stop just past the engineering stations. His thumb and forefinger rubbed something that reflected the light from the displays: a bullet. Was it the one Caville had dropped in Goldman's room?

In the dim light, the big man's olive skin tilted toward dusky. He shoved the bullet into a pocket, then brushed the back of a thick hand over his big nose while he scanned the cockpit with bloodshot eyes. His left arm was draped at his side, and a shotgun was clenched by the stock.

His head turned slowly to the starboard engineering station, and he staggered that way, then pulled out the chair.

"Huh."

He swayed.

Then he twisted around and stared right at the port engineering station.

"Could've sworn I heard..."

The big man let out another belch, then staggered back out of the cockpit.

When the hatch hissed closed, Caville slid out from his cover. He would panic later, when he had time. Right then, he needed to know what was going on, or the whole effort was a waste of time.

At the pilot station, he powered on the console and accessed the external cameras. An umbilical connected the *Ollie* to another ship. The design was familiar enough, a smaller version of the *Ollie* but older. It was a privateer ship, something built by the Azoren and put into space to plunder and terrorize Gulmar shipping.

Crewed by Gulmar, too. The bastards were as greedy and desperate as anyone. So, was Goldman selling technology to the Azoren, or was there something more at play? There were the occasional Gulmar privateers who actually operated for themselves, screwing the Azoren over.

Without getting aboard that privateer ship and checking those crates, Caville would never know.

He powered the console back down and tiptoed back to the hatch. Waiting in the claustrophobic bridge space wasn't an option. The cargo transfer would finish. The crew would return to their stations.

Caville had to get out.

A calming breath, a centering focus, then he pushed the button.

The hatch opened. He stepped into an empty passage and listened. Boots clomped somewhere back closer to the intersection. It sounded closer to port than starboard.

When the cockpit hatch hissed shut, Caville cut left, hurrying down the starboard passage. Off to the right, Theo's heavy steps thundered. He snarled.

In the intersection passageway, Caville rushed to port and retraced his path through the motion sensors. Behind him, the drunken pirate roared in frustration and hurried aft.

It seemed like Caville's feet were glue. They wouldn't move fast enough. He almost fell when he reached the stairs that led down to the cargo area and darted to starboard again. Sounds of pursuit were coming down the port passageway now.

Once down the passageway a few meters, Caville stopped, exhaled, turned back around, and headed forward again.

Theo burst into the open area and grabbed onto the stairway railing. "Hey!"

Caville's eyes widened, and he threw up his hands, as if startled. "Whoa!"

The big man's shotgun wavered as he pointed it. "You see anyone come through here?"

"N-no! I—" The GSA agent pointed back down the passageway. "I've been kind of distracted."

"Distracted?" Theo lowered the weapon. His thick chest rose and fell.

"Working up the nerve to check in on Denise. The Khanate gal?"

A smile split the pirate's face, exposing grimy teeth. "Yeah? She's a good one. Not like that sweetie you brought on." He chuckled.

Caville joined in the laughter. Remembering how the pirate had talked about raping Stiles, remembering how he had done exactly that to other women before... It took a lot of effort for the GSA agent to keep his feet planted rather than charging across the open space and snapping the beefy pirate's neck.

Theo shuffled closer. "So, does she give it up?"

"Well..." Caville shrugged. "We talk about it."

"Yeah. See, I'm not much for talk. Someone like that, walking around in her robes, hiding the goodies..." The big man's breath was sour and rotten—a brewery gone without attention for too long. "I've thought about checking on her at night. Y'know."

"I think she's under Goldman's protection."

"Pfft." The fat man waved the idea away. "She *thinks* she's safe. But uppity women like her, a couple good slaps, maybe a punch in the gut. Yeah, she understands she better not talk about what I do."

Caville's eyes drifted to the stairs. There was still a little scraping and shouting coming from below. People were busy. No one was on the upper deck but him and Theo. The big man was drunk, swaying, his speech close to slurring. A strike to the belly, another to the solar plexus, and it would be easy to put together a convincing fall down the stairs and a broken neck.

But someone could be below. They could look up before there was a chance to pull back out of sight.

Instead, Caville put a hand on the other man's shoulder. "Aren't you supposed to be on watch up here?"

"Huh? Oh, yeah. Thought I heard someone—"

"Might want to lay off the beer for a little bit, right?"

Theo scowled, and color flashed through his cheeks. "I know what I'm doing."

"Oh, *I* know that. I'd be worried about someone else saying something, that's all."

The fat man made a sound that was half snort, half grunt. "Yeah."

Caville looked back down the passageway he'd come out of. "I won't say anything if anyone asks. You know."

"Okay. Yeah." Theo's features brightened. He nodded, nearly fell.

"Whoa!" Caville caught the other man and helped him keep his balance.

"Thanks."

"Sure. Hey, um, if you wouldn't mind—I'd rather no one know I'm nervous about things with Denise."

"Huh? Oh! Yeah." The big man tugged an imaginary zipper across his mouth.

"Appreciate it." Caville straightened. "Wish me luck."

"Give her an extra shot for me, huh?" Theo thrust his hips clumsily, then turned and took a step forward before stopping, as if confused by having two passageways to choose from.

Caville coughed. "You came down that side." He pointed to port when the big man turned.

"Right." Theo staggered out of sight.

Once Caville's heartbeat was back to normal, he made his way to the ladder and returned to the passenger cabin deck. The last bit of noise coming from the cargo area died off, and he imagined the Gulmar privateer was pulling away.

A minute later, he tapped on Denise's hatch. It hissed open, revealing a woman a little shorter than Stiles, with darker skin but pale brown eyes. Gallo's features were soft, closer to cute than pretty. Her lips were full, and they curled up as she looked him over. "I was wondering if you might visit me again."

She moved aside with a soft rustle of the concealing robes she'd taken to wearing since settling aboard. They were a dull, cream color and heavy, cinched at the waist by a gold sash, which she was undoing as she crossed to her bunk.

Then the robes slipped to the deck, and her eyes twinkled. "Can you stay for a while?"

He grinned. "I've got all day."

4

The capital city of Paradies was almost nothing like the historical videos Benson had reviewed back on Kedraal. There were, of course, newer intelligence images, but they were of building interiors and limited street views. What had once been the city of Lagos, with its early-state high-rises and simple wooden structures, was now row upon row of hulking, gray granite block buildings with sharp edges and smooth, swooping eaves. Everything exuded a feel of bunkers and bomb shelters. The landing pad designated for the shuttle to set down on was inside a high-walled compound lined with machinegun turrets. It was accessible on the ground through only one long, gray road that had nothing on either side for a kilometer or more.

The shuttle engines cranked louder—dull and distant as Benson popped her ears.

Thiessen leaned closer from the seat to her right, his breath surprisingly pleasant after so long breathing the recycled, dry air. He seemed immune to the stiffness that should have come from such a long flight. "It's like a race track."

She sipped from the bottle that had followed her from the *Pandora*. "What?"

"That road." He nodded toward the strip of gray now disappearing as the shuttle dropped below the top of the wall. "It seems built for high-speed vehicles."

Across the aisle, Ambassador Manshaus's head came up from the data pad he'd been studying. "You refer to the airfield avenue?"

"Yes." The Gulmar captain leaned back in his seat as the shuttle engines roared for the final stretch of the landing.

"There are minefields on either side, but high-powered rifles still can sight in on vehicles."

Benson flinched. "You have terrorists?"

"We—" Manshaus winced as the spacecraft settled hard. "—have aggressive policy discussions."

With the spacecraft settled on the airfield, the engine whine dropped into the slow tapering that would lead it to rest. Behind Benson's row, belts and harnesses popped, and the murmur of voices began. Dietrich and Kohn had taken seats on opposite sides of the aisle and were already diving into vigorous debate over who should pull their luggage from the storage racks at the rear first.

Like children.

They were both brilliant and inclined to idiosyncratic behavior. It was a small price to pay for what they offered.

Thiessen smiled, maybe in sympathy. "Your Marine lieutenant couldn't make it?"

"I was worried it might send a bad signal to have someone so…junior in the assembly."

"But your doctor's assistant—isn't he also junior?"

She stretched to glance over her seat at the two men, who were now whispering excitedly about something else. They seemed seconds from throwing punches. "Commander Dietrich felt having a prodigy accompany us might send a different sort of signal."

"The ensign is a prodigy?"

Was Kohn a prodigy, or was he just a particularly flawed yet accomplished genius? "I think it's more accurate to say that he makes a point."

"He does?"

"The people the Azoren model their ideology off of—the Nazis. They had a problem with Jews."

"They did?"

There was no hint of teasing or incredulity on the captain's face. History, she reminded herself. It was always one of the first victims of tyrants. When *she* thought of tyrants, she thought of the rulers of the other powers—the Azoren, Khanate, and Moskav—but corporations had their own way of reshaping perceptions. Or, more likely, they simply didn't see the value in actually educating their poor.

She drifted toward the luggage rack. "We'll need to have a chat."

"About these Nazis?"

"At the very least."

Thiessen frowned. "Where I grew up, history wasn't really considered that important. You learned to fix things—machines or people. If you couldn't do that, you put your back into hard labor. If you couldn't do that, you…"

"Fell into crime?"

His face compressed as he pulled her luggage out and handed it to her. "We weren't proud of it. It was survival."

"You were fortunate to get out." It was as if he needed to be reminded.

They shuffled to the airlock, down the ramp, then spilled out onto the concrete beneath purplish-gray skies that did their best to hide the sun. Soldiers watched them from the glass-shielded weapons towers. A faintly woodsy and refreshing scent rode in on a breeze as a couple of young men stepped out of a low, concrete structure and headed toward a gray-black armored vehicle. An empty weapons mount rested on the rooftop, and when a diesel engine rumbled to life, lights bloomed on the front.

Manshaus's back lost a little of its curve. "The Night Leopard AAV."

Thiessen cocked his head. "AAV. Armored?"

"Armored Assault Vehicle, yes. These have undergone modifications. Heavier armor, a high-performance engine."

Benson scowled. "And no gun."

The ambassador sank slightly. "Weapons do not stop other weapons. Getting into Paradies is our objective. These Night Leopards will do that."

There was only one vehicle, which made Benson wonder—

A second rumble came from beyond the low concrete structure, and another of the Night Leopards rumbled toward them. There was no discernible difference between the two other than a small series of alphanumeric markings that would be almost impossible for someone to read from a distance.

Unless they had a high-powered scope.

The second vehicle came to a stop, and a man who must have been as old as the ambassador nodded at them from behind thick glass. This man and his significantly younger comrade wore uniforms that matched the vehicle. Both had sunken cheeks, as if malnourished, but they had alert eyes. It wasn't until the ambassador waved Benson toward the rear and the old soldier turned to watch that the jagged scar on the right side of his face became visible. The back half of his cheek and his right ear were…gone.

A veteran, then. Maybe from the Moskav front. No wonder he didn't want to get out.

Benson stopped at the rear doors, which Manshaus had wrestled open, then studied the other armored vehicle. "Who goes into which one, Ambassador?"

"Hm?" The old man followed her eyes. "Oh. No one."

"They're our escort? Without a gun?"

Thiessen leaned in, voice a whisper. "They're the decoy."

"Decoy—?"

It hadn't really registered for her until that moment just how serious their situation was. They needed a *decoy* to better their chances of reaching the capital city.

She went into the rear of the vehicle first, getting a mouthful of sour sweat and the faint hint of rancid gore. A metal plate with a small door in it separated the passenger section from the forward compartment. Dark stains covered the walls and floor, and a few of the seats had holes in them where the blackened padding seemed ready to ooze out. Discolored metal marked where rounds had punched through the armor and it had been patched.

Not painted over. Not cleaned. This was a message to the occupants: Hold on; it's going to be bumpy.

The seat closest to the driver's side at the front was new. She took that.

Kohn blanched as he ducked into the passenger space, then settled across from her.

Only Manshaus seemed completely unaffected. "Do not be discouraged."

His crooked smile set Benson's teeth on edge. "Why's that?"

"Everything in the process has improved since the assassination attempts began—the armor, the engines, even the hunt for the rebels."

Rebels. Not terrorists. "What's the rebellion about?"

The corners of the little man's mouth twisted—smile, frown, smirk, then finally a resolved and tired wince. "Such things are never easily understood, Captain. Many complain about the food shortages caused by feeding the war machine; others complain about the lack of heat in the winter. Some are unhappy about limits to how many children they may have. Rumors abound of people refusing conscription and slipping into the forest. Those rumors say that such people would rather fight for an end to the war than actually fight in that war."

Dietrich blinked and turned to Kohn sitting to the right. "What a novel idea: a war to end war."

"It is at our heart to wish for peace, Doctor."

"I see. For as far back as I can remember, it was your people who agitated the hardest for conflict of one sort or another."

"Wishing for peace has no guarantees of finding it. Our leadership will not accept the risk of the Azoren way of life being compromised by those outside."

"So you kill anyone who opposes you?"

"The leadership sees threats and resists."

Benson shook her head at Dietrich, who was growing red. A grinding sound—like giant, straining gears—leaked in through the armor, and the engine growled a throaty challenge. Another engine replied, then the chirp of tires clawing at concrete announced the first Night Leopard's launch. A few heartbeats later, their own shot forward, and she was almost thrown into Thiessen's lap.

They picked up speed, felt mostly by the tug that pressed her against the Gulmar captain. He was in turn being tugged toward the little ambassador, who seemed genuinely entertained by the rocketing vehicles.

Distant thunder resolved into gunfire, which was answered by the stutter of machinegun fire. She looked past Thiessen at the ambassador.

Something plunked off the armor, maybe toward the rear, behind everyone.

Then came a second plunk.

And a third.

Her ears were still dull from the shuttle flight down, but she thought maybe she'd heard glass break somewhere far away. At that moment, she wished they had simply taken the shuttle directly into the city. Manshaus had assured her that was far too dangerous, as most rooftops were now mined to prevent aerial assault.

Who could conduct aerial assault other than trained commandos? Rebellions made up of angry and terrified civilians couldn't do that.

Could they?

The sound of gunfire died off, the plunking ceased, and Kohn slumped forward, head pressing against open hands. "This was a bad idea."

Dietrich snorted. "We have to show them."

Kohn looked up at the doctor. "Show them?"

"You're quite the display of what we're capable of."

"I'd rather not be considered a display."

"That was a poor choice of words." The doctor stretched his neck out.

It wasn't an apology, of course. Dietrich wasn't much for apologizing. He was annoyed that he'd diminish Kohn, or at least that he'd made the young man more aware of his role. But apologize? It was on the older man's face: This was personal. He had a message for the Azoren.

You are not the superior race. You are an embarrassment.

The vehicle slowed, and the tenor of the engine changed. It sounded like echoes curling up and rolling back over. The frame shuddered.

When they braked hard, she realized that they were inside the city. A moment later, they turned, and the echoes changed again. There was no constant gurgle and hum of vehicles around them. Traffic on the orderly and neat avenue and whatever had brought them into the city had been light or nonexistent. Maybe that was the norm.

Another deceleration, another turn, more acceleration, then they came to a stop.

They were at the High Command Headquarters.

The back door opened, and a squad of big men in black uniforms filled the space. They reminded her of some of the corpses she'd seen on Jotun: the soft, pink features of youth hidden from the sun; a sameness in their pale eyes and faces that seemed caught in the gravity of childhood androgyny rather than the hyper-masculine sharpness of a super soldier.

But they were almost handsome, if you were one for a cold, soft look.

She wasn't.

One of the men waved them out, and the way his coat moved, she realized their bulk must come from segmented armor.

Outside of the vehicle, the air inside the city wasn't much better than that inside the passenger compartment. A dull haze hung over everything with the sun now setting, and that haze carried a sharp, metallic tang that scratched at the throat. Apparently, the haze also left its mark on the buildings, which looked more grungy and tired close up.

As they were led away from the vehicle, the driver's door opened, and the scarred, old man lurched out. He doubled over and retched over a gutter, shivering.

The black-uniformed men led them past the front of the vehicle, and Benson realized what had gotten to the driver. What remained of the shattered passenger window was sprayed red and black. A form slumped in the seat, and she had a sense of the shape before looking away: The top of the young man's head was gone, and one of his eyes dangled down.

There was no time to dwell on that, as their escort rushed them up wide steps that ended where statues of stern men riding horses thrust sabers heavenward in unison. The stern men didn't look like the black-suited escorts.

More guards in different uniforms waited at the building entry. These were regular people, with darker hair and the hint of a day's growth.

As fierce as these guards looked, the escort didn't even acknowledge them. Inside the building, the impression of a giant bunker settled in almost immediately. The floors were marble that had lost its polish and gone dull and dusty. A diesel-like smell clung to the concrete walls, staining framed portraits—physical portraits—of old men in a variety of uniforms. There was a deadness to the men's eyes that couldn't be attributed to the accumulation of time. Oddly, several of the frames were empty.

Benson recognized the faces still in frames—the High Command. Six of them. There were eight empty frames.

No doubt by design, their escort's booted steps were like syncopated hammering. She found herself matching their cadence by habit and fought it only to fall back into the beat.

They descended narrow stairs and passed through heavy steel doors into a hallway maybe two meters across. It forced her in closer to the Azoren man-children. They might appear youthful and free of puberty's touch, but they had body odor. Beneath their helmets, their hair was greasy.

Power cables strung on heavy hooks just below the ceiling, and hanging lights added even more of a sense of a giant, desperate bunker to the building. Another heavy steel door—this one partially closed— blocked their way.

More guards, more disdain for those guards from the escort group.

And then they were in a familiar, big room. It had a lived-in smell the video couldn't have captured, like a cafeteria and locker room had produced an unwanted child. The heavy wooden table and chairs, the sagging flags of black and red, the bunting of the same colors but with white striping—it was all here. They were inside the High Command meeting area. This was where the supreme leader and his senior command staff set policy.

Dietrich whispered behind her, probably to Kohn, but she caught it. "Cheery."

Thiessen cleared his throat. "They had tanks back there. In the street."

Benson's eyes were drawn to the gargantuan concrete support beams running overhead. "I didn't see them."

"Hidden between buildings."

It felt like the short-lived coup they'd broken up on Kedraal, but this seemed…perpetual.

Kohn blew out a burst of air. "There was gunfire. Automatic."

Manshaus scraped past them but only just. "Firing squads, usually."

"Firing squads?"

"Yes. Even a military as devastating as ours faces failure."

"You mean…a coup?"

"Confusion. Disagreements. Disappointment, perhaps. Quite possibly, a large enough group of dissidents has been rounded up." The ambassador's cheek twitched.

She hadn't seen that before. Was he nervous being home?

Before she could ask if everything was all right, their escort melted back out through the heavy door, and more stomping boots echoed in the hall. Another large group was coming.

Benson smiled hopefully. "Ambassador, this is a little embarrassing, but you must know that diplomatic connections between our people aren't very good."

"Not good at all, no."

"Well, I *did* try to read up on your power structure, but our information is obviously out of date. I was—"

He looked her up and down. "The High Command, you mean?"

"What—?"

"The men you saw in the video, yes?"

"Oh. Yes." She'd given him a copy of the video. "We have a rough idea who your supreme leader is, although the images are old. Your second-in-command… Well, no one knows, really. But the senior officers—"

"Were not in that video. Most, at least."

"No. Several were recognizable. General Guderian was there."

The little man bit into his bottom lip. "Neither the supreme leader nor his second were in that communique. Normally, one or the other must be present in all meetings of significance. That message qualifies as significant, should you feel uncertain."

"Good. Thank you."

"Less than a month ago, most of those on the call were not members."

"Oh?"

Manshaus bowed. "The meaning is not so easy to derive from just this. Perhaps both the supreme leader and his second are dead. It is also possible neither are. Then again—" The ambassador glanced around the huge room. "—possibly something of great importance has happened."

"Something of great importance, meaning...?"

"All of those Children? You must have noticed? The youths at the table?"

"Yes."

"In matters of prosecution of the war, they have been spoiling for a greater say. A seat at the table, as some would say."

"You think they...replaced their predecessors."

"Leaders such as ours do not go quietly into the night, Captain."

The booted stomp grew louder, drawing Benson and the others around. Through the door marched a thick procession of soldiers and men in uniforms riddled with decorations, braided ropes, and other finery. The senior officers were the men from the video, and their escort was surprisingly in uniforms like those guarding the building.

Why had their own black-uniformed escort acted so cold toward the others if these were what amounted to bodyguards? Was it just that these were normal people like her? They seemed as imposing and competent. If she were honest, they seemed *more* imposing, as most were older and looked more masculine.

A smaller group came in, these in the same black uniforms as the group that had escorted her but lacking the soft, boyish features. In their midst was a vaguely familiar man. He had a soft face and wore something more like a business suit than even Thiessen's uniform.

The soft man waved at Manshaus and hurried over. "Ambassador Manshaus! So good you have come."

"With heavy heart, Minister Potthast."

"Yes, yes. The loss of our good friends on Radetta." When this Potthast tut-tutted and shook his head, the waddle beneath his weak chin shook.

Manshaus indicated Benson with another subtle bow. "As you must know, Captain Benson was there."

Potthast smiled, and his heavy-lidded eyes slitted like a snake's. "Captain. Welcome to Himmel."

Benson shivered. She wanted to keep her hand free of the man's touch but extended her arm for a shake anyway. "Minister Potthast. You manage…?"

"Communications." His palm was clammy and cool, reinforcing her sense that he was a snake. "Recently, my role has expanded, you see? Supreme Leader Graf asked me to step in while our chief scientist rededicated himself to the Golden Child program."

"Then Supreme Leader Graf is well?"

"Oh, yes! Quite well. There was a minor automobile accident, nothing more."

"And he'll be participating in our meeting?"

"Soon now, indeed. He asked me to meet with you and to reassure you that the delays were naught but a necessary inconvenience. Some might feel compelled to show their superiority by imposition of annoyance. Not Supreme Leader Graf."

Someone cleared his throat, and Benson realized one of the younger members of the High Command had crept up. He wore a black uniform like the escort group, but his had several ostentatious badges and ribbons. There was a silver wolf's head emblem on his pocket. His back was straight, his gold hair clean and fresh. There was maybe a little more of a pronounced jawline, as a teenage boy might have as he shed the fat of youth.

An older woman hovered behind him, glaring from the corner. Her uniform didn't quite match any of those in the room. She was as tall as Benson but pale and thin. Silver-blonde hair framed a face set in…

Jealousy? Hatred?

Benson focused on the young officer, who flashed gray eyes at her. "Minister Potthast, many would consider it rude not to make introductions."

The smaller man chuckled and threw a look of complete adulation at the young officer. "Of course, of course. Captain Benson, might I introduce to you Field Marshal Dietmar Faulk?"

With a snap of boot heels, Faulk tipped forward. "Captain."

Despite herself, Benson smiled. "Field Marshal." Was that senior to a general? "I'm not sure… We don't use that rank…"

"I am in command of the Moskav front."

"The Moskav—" She swallowed. He looked like he might still be in his twenties. "Congratulations."

"We will be working together, you and I. I look forward to sharing my ideas with you."

"Thank…you."

The stern woman scowled. Her hands were clasped around what looked like an old, leather valise.

More stomping boots killed the rising murmur of conversations within the room. One of the minister of communications' escorts scampered forward and touched his superior's elbow, and they stepped away to whisper.

Manshaus leaned in closer to Benson. "That would be Supreme Leader Graf coming."

"Meaning the communications minister must leave?"

"For security reasons, only one should be here at a time."

"But not General Guderian?"

"He is less important. Officers of the military are replaceable."

A group of the same black-uniformed Golden Children came through the opening. No, not the same—they had red skull emblems on their pockets. Moving slower and with an obvious limp came Franz Graf—older even than Benson had expected, and sporting bandages, bruises, and scrapes. The man's left arm was in a cast. His dark eyes scanned the room; his bodyguards did the same.

Potthast threw his arms wide. "Supreme Leader! You look robust and youthful!"

The old man shuffled close, squinting at Benson. There was a medicinal smell about him, along with a sense of age and fragility. "This is the Kedraalian? She's pretty enough."

"It is! Ambassador Manshaus has brought her and—"

"A Jewish dog."

The communications minister chuckled. "There is no escaping their influence."

Benson's guts twisted. She'd been prepared for the sick minds, or at least she'd told herself so. Actually being in the man's presence and hearing his poison made it clear that she could never be ready. "If we might start our discussions—"

"Not with the Jewish dog here."

"But—"

Graf grunted and turned back to his crowd of bodyguards as heat rushed into Benson's cheeks. She took a step back and sucked in a breath, then held it. If she'd had a pistol at that moment, she doubted she could have resisted shooting the old bastard.

Manshaus disappeared behind her and began apologizing softly to Kohn and Dietrich, who were among the larger clump of officers farther back in the room.

The young field marshal scooted up to her. "You are troubled by his words?"

"I..." She tried to smile, failed. "We don't share these views."

"Of course not. This is why you are weak." He stared into her eyes.

In the corner, the only other woman in the room scowled even harder. Did she and the field marshal have some sort of relationship? She wasn't quite homely, but with her hair pulled back so severely and her pale, angular face, she seemed—

There were calls from outside the heavy steel door: voices demanding someone stop.

"I must see Minister Potthast!" The voice sounded high and strained. "An emergency!"

A little, mousy man burst through the opening.

Potthast turned. "Heiko? What is this about?"

Something about the little man—the way his hair matted against his head; the way he squeezed an attaché case to his chest; the way his bulging eyes searched and locked on to the supreme leader...

Benson froze. "Bomb."

In that instant, Graf's bodyguards came to the same conclusion. Three tackled the supreme leader to the floor. Another three created a wall between those on the ground and the mousy man with the case. The rest pulled pistols.

The mousy man's eyes bugged out even more.

Potthast stepped closer. "Heiko!"

"F-f-freedom!"

Pistol fire.

The mousy man's eyes going impossibly wide. His body twitching.

Potthast quivering in disbelief.

It was enough to shake Benson free of her terror. Without meaning to, she grabbed Faulk and took him down.

Then an explosion tore through the room, and she blacked out.

5

Faulk was choking on the concrete dust that was suspended in the air like a thick, dry fog. He shifted out from under the pretty Kedraalian captain, who had apparently been killed in the explosion. Blood trickled from a gash in her scalp, and a large chunk of gray concrete rested on her right arm, which was bent at a bad angle. Perhaps the shock from the explosion had been merciful and quick. That would be nice. She had seemed…intriguing.

For a Kedraalian.

His ears rang so that he didn't even hear the crack of another block of concrete when it fell not a meter away, trailing a fine stream of the dust he was gagging on.

He rolled onto his hip, then onto his knees, fighting against a horrific headache. In all his movement, nothing signaled failure in a limb or the collapse of an organ. Breathing was a little labored, his elbows were tender from the fall, and when he coughed and spat out the dust, there was red in the gray saliva slurry.

A glance up told him that the blast had shattered one of the support beams overhead, and that in turn had dragged down a sheet of the concrete ceiling. The giant room was now split almost in half down its length.

The door? Warped. Knocked off its heavy frame. Cracks ran through the wall.

No one else was up yet, although the Jew and his comrade were stirring. Just seeing the dark hair and swarthy flesh among all the dead Children was nauseating. There should have been a fairer allocation of death and injury, sparing none of the Kedraalians, except maybe the captain. The supreme leader's bodyguards—some of them mere gory chunks of meat now—should have been spared.

Movement in that pile of shredded ruin caught Faulk's eye.

Supreme Leader Graf's head came up from around one of the corpses. Somehow, the ancient bastard had survived *another* attempt on his life.

And now it was clear that there were other survivors, two of them brothers who had only just found their way to the table alongside Faulk. But they were maimed, the beauty and vigor of their genetic perfection would be forever gone thanks to the freakish nature of explosives. Had the Kedraalian captain not taken him down, he, too, might be a broken shell of perfection gifted by the engineer of life.

Out of the corner of his eye, his fuzzy peripheral vision spied the Jew and the older Kedraalian officer crawling along the wall created by the caved-in ceiling. They were checking the wounded and dead.

Triage, Faulk realized. He remembered then that the older officer was a celebrated surgeon, and both men had served aboard a search-and-rescue vessel.

That was inconvenient.

Faulk stumbled over to the legs of one of the supreme leader's bodyguards and searched for a hip holster. The hard, black case had nearly been torn from the matching belt but was still secure.

The field marshal pulled the dead bodyguard's pistol and checked the weapon. It took three tries to work through the simple process of popping the magazine out to confirm there were bullets and that the receiver would accept the magazine without trouble. Cycling a round also took a few tries.

The weapon was fine, but Faulk's hands shook dangerously.

Where had the Kedraalians gone?

A bright spark off to his left turned into a flash, then a flame.

What had been in that area of the room that might cause an open flame? Maybe there had been more than one person involved in the assassination attempt. Someone sneaking a bomb into the building...it was almost unthinkable. There would be more guards sent to the firing squad for failure or complicity, yes, but the reality was someone had probably sneaked the explosives in and hidden them somewhere for the sniveling little bureaucrat to grab before charging into the room.

Supreme Leader Graf had become wildly unpopular in the last few years.

The Federation had lost sight of its goals. Potthast had lost his touch with his messaging. Fear had replaced fervency. Humans could feel in their ancient bones that they had been obsoleted by those who now ascended the ranks of the military, first to oversee the use of the remaining human military cogs, then to displace them from the machine of war completely.

Midway down the length of the crumpled ceiling sheet, the two Kedraalians now worked on one of the surviving Children. They pointed at the mangled body, mouthed words, nodded. Maybe they were speaking. It seemed the ringing in Faulk's ears had grown less painful.

The fire. There was a fire. Where...?

Faulk shook his head to clear it, then remembered what had likely caused the flame. It was common now for the members of the high command to eat meals together while arguing their strategies and resource management. Shared food wouldn't be poisoned, after all, and Supreme Leader Graf commented wryly that it built camaraderie. The fire was merely one of the heating elements that had been shattered and ignited. It would burn out quickly.

Now the Kedraalian doctors split up, the Jew crawling toward his dead captain while the older one made his way to the supreme leader.

There had been an opportunity, Faulk realized, but it was now lost.

Eliminate the wounded.

He staggered past the dazed ambassador—no threat—and came to a stop next to a brother who had been propped up against the ceiling-turned-wall. Deep fissures spiderwebbed through the gray material. Powder covered the young man's pale blue uniform, which marked him as the commander of logistics, part of the fleet. He had actually been quite competent at the job, quickly absorbing and improving upon the work of his human predecessor.

The other man's eyes seemed to have a hard time focusing. He mouthed Faulk's name, then reached for an empty holster with a hand that wouldn't have been able to hold a pistol much less shoot it.

Faulk sneered, then fired.

He almost jumped at the sound of the gunshot, which slashed through the ringing.

That brought the older doctor's head around. His face was ridiculously caked in dust and blood, but his eyes were alert. He'd already pulled the dead bodyguards off the supreme leader and had begun doing something with the old man's arm.

Left arm. The broken one. The cast looked as if it might have cracked. Blood smeared the end where his fingers should have been.

Despite Faulk having a pistol and the doctor having nothing, the older man shouted something. It was dull and far away, but there was intensity behind it.

Another of the wounded generals—an old one—began pulling himself toward the mass of dead bodyguard parts, dragging himself on his belly with his elbows. His jowls shook desperately as he propelled himself with grunts and snorts, the deep bass of which got through the ringing.

At the edge of the pile of body parts, the old man plunged a hand in and searched around.

Faulk fought to keep his balance as he shuffled forward, pistol raised. When the old man pulled something that might be a weapon from the mound, the field marshal fired.

The old man's arms thrust out stiffly, then he dropped his ghastly prize.

Another pistol.

Once again, the Kedraalian surgeon screamed. This time, a few words came through: Savage. Murderer. Animal.

Of course it would seem that way. To Faulk, though, this was not only opportunism but necessity. "Our oxygen." His voice was far away.

Air was a precious resource, and useless consumers were no longer worthy of things so valuable.

He twisted slowly and put a bullet through the youthful brother the two doctors had tended to not even a minute before. Dead, gray eyes stared back as blood dribbled from a hole in the young man's forehead.

From the corner, Faulk's aide watched. Her head was twisted to the side, and a long sheet of scalp dangled from her brow where debris had crushed her skull. Even in death, though, her eyes seemed locked on to him. She would want to talk to him about doctrine and his loyalty to the supreme leader.

"All hail the supreme leader." He choked back a sob.

Where had the Jew gone? Faulk turned around, trying to reorient himself in the swaying room.

There. The young man's dark hair was unmistakable. His strong nose and almost black eyes—

He was working on the Kedraalian captain. How stupid. She was dead. She—

The young doctor didn't look up, but he shifted so that his back was between Faulk and the fallen captain. The clump of concrete that had pinned an arm down awkwardly was gone. He'd torn a sleeve off her shirt and wrapped that around her head.

Her eyes fluttered open. "My arm."

"Dislocated elbow. I've put the bones back into the joint. I'll make you a sling."

"Floyd? Commander Dietrich? The ambassador?"

"The ambassador's all right. So is Commander Dietrich."

She had been dead. Faulk was sure of it.

Could he shoot her? *Would* he shoot her?

Her eyes passed over him, took in the rest of the room, fixated on the new wall. She pushed up with her good arm. "They're trapped."

Yes. Obviously, she was dead. Or dying. Her brain was mush. How could she concern herself with the others beyond the wall if she were alive? All that mattered was survival. She would collapse and die again. Tragic but inevitable.

But the Jew? Faulk could clean that mess up after she slipped away.

He turned back to Supreme Leader Graf. The impossible was within reach. Eliminating the old man was more than a natural progression delayed far too long by the benefits of incumbency and the fierce attention of Purity Minister King, the father of all science. Fresh blood was needed to salvage the Azoren ideals from the scrap heap, which was their current destination under the failing leadership.

The Kedraalian surgeon looked up from working on Graf. "Don't come another step closer."

Not a plea but an order—a very angry order, even.

Faulk stopped without meaning to. He hesitated while raising the weapon. "The old man can't survive."

"I've already stabilized him. He'll live."

"Surgeons have a God complex. There is no saving him."

The Kedraalian's head came around, but he kept his body between Faulk and his target. "That's your assessment? That's all they teach you and your kind when they drag you from your synthetic wombs—your predecessors can't survive?"

"Everything born dies."

"Of course. We all die. That doesn't mean some savage spat out of a vat has the right to name the time and place."

"You are poorly positioned to be hurling insults at me, Doctor."

"They're long overdue, based on your brutish behavior."

Faulk raised the pistol. "Power resides in my hands. The power of life and death. You should consider that before you speak again."

"Not life, you cold-blooded monster. All you hold is death."

Something scraped dully at Faulk's side; he whipped around.

The Jew stumbled past a couple meters away, both hands raised. He stopped beside the other doctor. "We only want to save lives."

A dark laugh burst from the field marshal. "Have you any idea whose life you try to save? Hm? The policies we embrace? His. My creation and that of my brothers? His work."

"What matters is that he's human. Our oath requires that we do no harm."

"It would be the work of a bullet to harm him, not you."

Neither doctor budged. Behind them, the old man lay on the floor, eyes closed, breathing shallowly.

A cracking pop came from far back in the room. Faulk stepped away from the Kedraalians and brought his pistol around to point it at the source of the sound, freezing when he saw the tall captain with a chunk of concrete in her good hand. She was centimeters from the section of ceiling splitting the room. Where the concrete had cracked against that new wall, there was a white impact point.

The damage to her brain was becoming more obvious with each second. A pity. He checked to make sure the doctors hadn't come closer, then backed toward her. "What are you doing?"

She scraped the rock down the wall. "There must be survivors."

"They've all been crushed."

"No. The ceiling gave along that central beam. If it had done more than drop this section, we would've been crushed, too."

"Nonsense."

Crack!

She swung the big chunk of concrete with one hand. She had been knocked out by something—the fall or whatever had hit her in the head. Blood trickled from the improvised bandage wrapping her hair tight.

And she only cared about survivors.

"Stop!"

She turned her attention to him, confused. "We have friends in there."

"I have no friends."

Her brow bunched even more. "Comrades in uniform. Humans. Help me."

He didn't move, even though he felt foolish with the pistol pointed at her.

Pointed in her general direction, not at her.

Actually pointing the weapon at her seemed… Why couldn't he point it at her?

Crack! She pressed her ear against the wall. "Hello! Can you hear me?"

He stepped closer to her, admiring the firmness of her exposed arms and the exotic look of her eyes, which were a jade like he had never seen before. The slightest hint of an epicanthic fold made those eyes even more exotic. There was color to her face, a richness of tone that seemed to promise health and strength. And she was tall, filling out her tattered uniform in a way that drew the eye.

Women were uncommon in the Azoren military. Here and there, someone influential pressed to allow a sister or daughter or some more distant relative into the ranks. They were generally shuffled off to remote posts to serve quietly—out of sight and away from harm.

A naval captain? A naval captain sent as a diplomat on what had to be a mission of tremendous importance?

She must know things about her superiors. Perhaps she slept her way through the ranks and leveraged that to blackmail those above her.

Except…

Except the communique from Kedraal had very clearly stated that she was a representative appointed by the prime minister and approved by the Kedraalian Republic's parliament and senior military staff. Would they all agree to send someone incapable for such a job? It wasn't possible she could sleep with enough people to bring about that sort of blackmail.

Was it?

The pistol dropped to his side. His head ached.

Something hissed and popped: the fire, now dying.

"Oxygen." He sniffled, tasted the air. "We'll all suffocate. The more people breathing—"

Crack!

Her face was even prettier when she was angry. "Your people should be rescuing us soon." She twisted around to nod toward the heavy steel door that was crumpled in its doorframe. "A few support braces, some cutting torches. Not even two hours."

Faulk stiffened. She couldn't possibly know what was involved in the intricacies of rescue operation—

Of course. She had been on the staff of the search-and-rescue ship.

What had he read? That ship had most likely penetrated deep into Azoren space at least once. It was believed that she had been involved in the action on Jotun, although the records from that outpost were still incomplete.

He took a step closer. "Rescue operations here are complicated, Captain."

Crack! Crack!

"Hello!" She scowled at him. "Are they all as helpful as you?"

The field marshal tried to holster the pistol, then realized he wasn't wearing a holster. Unlike some of the others, he felt that policies forbidding carrying sidearms into the high command building made holsters ridiculous.

He set the weapon on the floor. "The bomb that did all this. Someone in the ranks sent it down here."

That seemed to get her attention. "You have so many layers of security…"

"Not everyone views the federation's agenda the same way."

"Ambassador Manshaus mentioned the rebellion."

Faulk considered the little man, who bowed where he sat. "He did, did he?"

"One of the men in our armored vehicle was shot."

"I see." The field marshal gathered a large piece of concrete. It was surprisingly heavy. How was she wielding such a thing so easily in her off hand? "The threat of a rebellion member sneaking a bomb into this building is negligible."

"Then…?"

"As I said: someone within our own ranks."

She shook her head and seemed to wobble slightly. "I wasn't briefed on there being dysfunction of such a level—"

A dull *crack* slipped through the wall.

The captain blinked dully. "Did you just hear—?"

"Yes." Faulk moved close to her side, caught the scent of her even over the sharp chemical remnant of the explosive. There was a sweet perfume, maybe something similar in her hair. Luxuries like that were rare among his people.

Crack!

He struck the wall with his own bit of concrete.

Far, far away, it sounded like someone was calling out through a very small hole.

He leaned in and squinted through a seam that ran most of the length of the collapsed ceiling piece. Perhaps there actually was something on the other side of the wall.

A finger could slip into the seam. Another. He pried at that crack, and concrete came away in a hand-sized clump that rolled and popped down the wall and over the floor.

The captain smiled—far more glorious than her anger. She tossed her own rock and pushed her hand into the same opening and pulled more away, widening the crack.

They pulled together, their flesh sometimes rubbing, and more of the wall came away.

"Hello?" There was no mistaking it: Someone was alive on the other side.

She smiled at Faulk, eyes slightly unfocused. "See?"

He grunted and continued pulling out bits of concrete. Being so close to her, feeling her warmth and sometimes even having her brush against him—how could he resist? There had been no intent to engage in rescue operations, but she had dragged it out of him. Now the sparkle of her joyous laugh almost drew a smile from him.

Losing control and discipline was dangerous. It wasn't like him at all. It was this captain, this Kedraalian.

This one was going to be a problem.

6

By the time the scrape and grind of rescue gear stopped, signaling that the Azoren had finally broken through the warped, metal door, Benson's headache had turned into a pounding behind her eyes that matched the beat of accompanying sledgehammers. Concrete dust hung in the air and coated her uniform and face. She and the Azoren field marshal—Faulk, although his name should have been butcher—had cleared a hole in the fallen ceiling slab big enough to squeeze a shoulder through. There were survivors, just as she'd said.

A giant hammer rang against the metal door until it groaned and shuddered, then fell free of the frame. It slammed against the floor with a deafening crash, then wobbled with smaller slaps that kicked up even more of the bitter, choking dust.

She slid down the wall on jelly legs, giving herself permission to cry. It had grown almost impossible to breathe within the chamber, something that she hadn't realized until fresh air rushed in.

In an instant, the horrible stench of shattered bodies registered. How had she not noticed it before?

Shock. Shakes from that hit her now—delayed and coming on with a vengeance.

With that air came first the building guards—wild-eyed and frantic as they rushed from slushy and tacky puddles of the dead to where Dietrich and Kohn now hunched over Supreme Leader Graf. More of the black-suited bodyguards followed. They seemed ready to gun everyone down.

Dietrich waved them off with a bloody hand. "If you move this man without stabilizing his spine, you'll kill him!"

The bodyguards froze, submachine guns still pointed at the doctor, as if they thought they might be able to intimidate the injuries he was talking about into slinking away.

When all you have is a hammer...

Kohn followed a group of men stripped down to sweat-soaked, grungy T-shirts over to the opening that had been dug into the ceiling-wall. "There are six survivors, but four of them are near death."

The men in T-shirts nodded, muscles working in their jaws. They went to work with the hammers and were quickly joined by comrades with hydraulic supports.

Faulk chuckled, then backed away from the area, staring at the gash in the ceiling above. "How close we came to being crushed."

Someone tapped Benson on the shoulder, then knelt at her side. "Captain?"

She turned into stale breath and reared back from Ambassador Manshaus's ghastly face. "What—?"

"The ceiling." He pointed over them, to where the jacks were pressing iron beams. "It could give at any time."

"But Commander Dietrich..."

The doctor was glued to the floor next to the fallen Azoren leader, lips compressed and bloodless. Somewhere far, far away, it sounded like squeaky wheels were rumbling through a broad hallway.

Then a gurney was lifted over the big steel door. Youthful soldiers with medical insignia rushed forward with a hard, plastic board adorned with straps.

Manshaus tugged on her good arm. "Please, Captain. The hallway..."

She tried to get to her feet, stumbled, then felt his hands around her ribs, lifting just enough that she finally found the strength and balance to rise. It was hard to speak, but she wanted to demand that they get the other survivors out. She'd come down with—

Their faces appeared in front of her, but she couldn't remember their names.

Dietrich. Kohn. Thiessen. And Ambassador Manshaus.

Was Thiessen still alive? Hadn't she heard his voice on the other side of the wall? Hadn't she seen him and held his hand at one point once the hole was large enough to reach through?

Yes. Faulk had made an angry face for some reason.

He hates us. He wants this operation to fail.

The sledgehammers thundered against the concrete while the other engineers erected support beams. In between the cracking and popping of concrete, shouts went from one group to another. They were making progress so quickly: The meager hole she and Faulk had dug was now wide enough for a small person to slip through.

Sometime during that work, the medical team had gotten the supreme commander onto the gurney. Now they were moving him over the metal door and into the hallway under Dietrich's gentle guidance.

"Hold that tight!" The doctor hovered over the old man's head, which was covered by an oxygen mask. "Don't you dare slip!"

The ceiling issued a groan that could only have come from the bowels of the earth, and dust rained down, followed by a couple of concrete chunks as big as a head.

Kohn was among the rescue team, shouting encouragement into the other section of the room. "Just another minute! Hold on!"

Her team from the *Pandora* would have sprayed an adhesive-cement onto the ceiling. They would have planted shaped charges on the wall. Once a hole was punched, they would have run a tube of flimsy plastic through to the other side and then hardened it with bonding agents. In space, operations had to be speedy. You used tried-and-true methods. There was no concern about reclaiming the ships or stations, only about the people being rescued.

Another section of concrete fell beneath the sledgehammers, and Kohn waved two of the engineers away. "I can fit through there."

They backed off, and he scampered through, squatting and twisting.

He wasn't gone long, returning to squeeze back out. Someone on the other side helped him get a body through. An old officer Benson recognized.

Bloody, ashen-faced, hacking between moans.

Kohn tapped one of the engineers, who grabbed the older man's legs and helped him carry the old man out to where more medical technicians waited.

When Kohn and the engineer returned, the intern scowled at Faulk. The field marshal cackled. "Do you know this man you just saved?"

Kohn muttered a thank you to the engineer, who returned to the wall, then scowled at the Azoren field marshal again. "No."

"He would have someone like you shoved into a furnace and burned alive."

"That makes *him* a monster, not me."

"Not you? What is it, then, when someone saves a monster? Hm? What are you when you enable your enemy to continue his butchery?"

The only answer Kohn managed was to grind his teeth.

Manshaus bowed his head. "What you have seen, Captain..." He made a soft, sad sound. "I apologize."

More hammering, more sections of the fallen ceiling crumbled away, then Kohn squeezed through again. Once more, he returned with a wounded man, but the next three were the youthful, golden-haired creations, like Faulk.

At some point during the operations, the field marshal had dropped his weapon. Now he sneered at each body taken out.

Benson wanted to stop Kohn, to ask where Thiessen was. It wouldn't sound unprofessional—the Gulmar captain was part of her team. She was his protector, his ally. He was the only one still unaccounted for.

And then the tall, handsome man came through, crawling after Kohn, standing and brushing dust from beard and hair.

Thiessen smiled, embarrassed. "That's one ruined uniform."

As she reached out for him, the room filled again with more of the black-uniformed soldiers. There were minor differences in their outfits— silver wolf heads on breasts; lightning bolts; white hammers; Graf's red skulls. These were the silver wolf heads like Faulk's. Hadn't they been their escorts into the building?

That seemed right.

"Come with us." It came from the one with the most masculine face. It wasn't a request.

She did as directed, and Kohn and Thiessen fell in behind her. The hallway was clear except for medical teams, but they didn't seem to be in a hurry now. They were pulling on heavy-duty rubber gloves and unfolding black bags of the same material.

Body bags. Just gather the parts. Sort them later. Or throw them into a pit.

Dietrich was nowhere to be seen. Farther down the gray hallway, a group of the building guards stood rigid, backs to the tableau.

Faulk was gone now, too.

Their Silver Wolf escorts hurried the three of them down the hall, up a flight of stairs, and into the night. More soldiers—these in a broad array of uniforms—formed a perimeter around the front of the building. The tanks she hadn't seen earlier now poked out of the alleys.

Benson was led along the front of the building rather than down the steps toward the street. She shivered in the cool night air as they turned right and down the side of the building. Her arm throbbed, but it wasn't enough that she couldn't keep up.

Shouted challenges didn't slow their escort, either. The hard-faced leader barked back code words or esoteric orders, and the challengers parted.

Then they headed down broad steps like those at the building front.

Diesel engines coughed and growled to life. Lights flared.

Night Leopards again. With them, a couple cars—simple in the night.

Their escort broke into smaller teams, then Benson was ushered into one of the armored vehicles with a trio of Silver Wolf soldiers. The door slammed, and she realized she'd lost her team. Before she could point this out, tires squealed, and they lumbered forward.

These Night Leopards weren't built for speed or comfort. The seats were wood with minimal padding and a heavy-duty cloth cover—black or a dark enough to appear that color in the dark. It was still cold inside the vehicle, but at least it smelled cleaner, less heavily used.

Several minutes passed with the bass gurgle of the engines rising and falling away, the slow shift of the transmission murmuring beneath her feet, and the shake and jerk of sudden turns.

Her escort murmured to each other without looking at her. One pulled a data pad out, and in the bright light, it seemed as if he had no iris.

She shivered. Was she being kidnapped? Taken out to be shot?

Earlier, her head had felt fuzzy, and a headache had throbbed. Those both grew worse and nausea threw its hat in the ring. "I don't feel well."

"We are nearly there." It was clipped and cold.

She nodded. *Just hold it in.*

But whoever had spoken was right. They stopped a couple minutes later, and the three Silver Wolf soldiers hopped out.

It was gray, with only distant building lights providing any way to figure out where she was. She had the sense of a courtyard or a parking lot. The cars and armored vehicles were there, spewing diesel exhaust.

What did it say for vehicles to have such engines?

The planet had petroleum reserves. They were relatively cheap and easy to maintain. Maybe the designs were new and efficient. Maybe the vehicles were simply all that could be fielded at the moment.

"Captain?" It was Kohn's voice.

Flashlights flicked to life around her, and two other clumps of soldiers added theirs to the mix. Kohn and Thiessen were surrounded by three of the Silver Wolf soldiers, just like her.

Then a dark form stomped between the three clumps, and the man who had told her they were almost at their destination said something again.

She swayed. "What?"

"Not long now. Come."

Nausea hammered her, but it was actually manageable once they started moving. A door opened ahead of them, and light spilled out, providing even more detail: a wall that rose up; a heavy, wrought iron fence with a concrete foundation; what might be a street beyond that fence; a set of steps that led down to a pool of darkness to the right of the door.

Then the interior light went out.

Her guides hurried her through the door, into a hall with a high ceiling and a floor that made the slap of everyone's steps a thunderclap. There were faint traces of gunpowder or something similar in the air, riding on the tail of must and mildew.

Whispers rose up, distorting in the open space above.

A door clacked and clanked, then squealed on forgotten hinges and groaned open.

She was guided to her left, and somewhere to her right, a match scratched across a pad and coughed to life. The flame guttered, then caught, then the sharp smell of kerosene filled the air.

A lamp. Glass, with a metal base painted green.

In the yellow light of the flame, the room she'd been guided into turned out to be a large barracks room lined with bunks that had no mattresses. Her three escorts backed out of the room as more doors clattered opened in the hallway.

Masculine Silver Wolf stood in the doorway. "The bathroom is across the hall. Water runs. Keep the lights off. Heat will slowly return. It is an old building."

She shivered. "Are we staying here?"

"It is the safest place. For now."

The man didn't close the door but stepped out of sight. "Fall in!"

Boots clomped down the hallway much faster than they had coming in, leaving her with her lamp and the cold and mildew.

She squeezed two fingers of her good hand inside the carrier ring of the lantern and headed into the hallway. Directly across from her room, another door was open, revealing a row of sinks and stalls. Everything was a dull white in the light. At the end of the hallway, the outer door banged open, and the Silver Wolf guards stomped out into the night. Then the outer doors slammed shut again.

Another kerosene lamp poked out from around a hallway Benson hadn't even noticed, off to her left. Thiessen stood there, blinking in disbelief. "I think I would feel like an ass for complaining about the accommodations, but..."

From behind him, steps scraped, then Kohn appeared. "I think there's actually a...kitchen back this way."

"I don't think I'm hungry." The Gulmar captain leaned toward Benson. "Are you…?"

"Not hungry, no. A little nauseated, actually."

Kohn took her lamp. "Can I see the back of your head? You took a blow."

She held still while he unwrapped the improvised bandage.

While he prodded back there, Thiessen frowned. "We really stepped into a mess."

"That bomb…"

"General Weber said it was the third attempt in as many months."

"Weber."

"One of the old guard."

"Are months really long here?"

"No."

Benson hissed when Kohn's probing produced a sharp pain.

"Sorry, ma'am. We need to stitch this up. I think the kitchen might have supplies. There were boxes on a table in there."

She followed the intern into the hallway she hadn't noticed before, then through an open door on the right. Long tables with benches pressed underneath filled an area three or four times the size of her room. Piled against the wall to the right, about halfway into the room, were plastic-wrapped sleeping bags. Brown boxes of several sizes rested on the closest table. In Kohn's light, labels became clear: food, medicine, field supplies.

He tore open one of the field supplies boxes and pulled a smaller box out. Thiessen took that and unfolded the flaps, removing a paper cube labeled *soap*, then a tube labeled *shampoo*. "All right. At least we can get this grime off of us."

There were boxes with towels and undergarments as well—all dull white and of a functional nature. They sorted out what would fit.

Then Kohn laid out a basic medical kit. "Alcohol, a needle and thread, anesthetic and antiseptic spray, and a coagulant seal. Are you up for this, ma'am?"

Benson nodded. "I think I'd like to shower after."

"You can wash your hair. The sealant's rated for it." He went to work on her scalp, starting with the alcohol swabs to clean around the wound. "Um, that bomb wasn't from a bunch of rebels."

"It wasn't."

Thiessen pulled the nearer bench out and patted it for Benson to sit down. "I got the sense from Weber that the Golden Children have become pretty aggressive about eliminating rivals."

She took the proffered seat. "Thanks."

He stared for a moment. "You think things are falling apart?"

The pain that had been throbbing at the back of Benson's head subsided slightly, taking the nausea with it. She hadn't made the connection before, probably because she hadn't realized how intense the pain was until it faded. "My briefings indicated there was a constant shuffle. I had no idea they were going after Graf."

"That bomb could have taken us all out if that little bastard had come deeper into the room."

Kohn showed Benson the stitching needle. "You shouldn't feel this, but—"

She sighed. "Don't move. I know."

A dull tugging came from the back of her head. "I had to shave some hair away."

"I'm sure I've paid a lot of money for worse hairdos, Ensign."

Thiessen pulled the other bench out and sat down, still frowning. "That was their second in command."

"Potthast?"

"Yes. Temporary, Weber said. They've got the normal second working on a big project."

Benson let that settle in. She'd heard it before, she was pretty sure. "They took Dietrich with Graf. That doesn't sound like they're trying to kill the old man."

"But it does sound like things have become complicated. General Weber was absolutely terrified of the wounded Golden Children."

The sound of the outer door banging open made Kohn jump. "Sorry, ma'am."

She almost pushed up from the table. "I'll keep still."

Booted feet echoed, growing rapidly closer. Benson saw the beam of a flashlight in the hall a few seconds before Field Marshal Faulk appeared in the doorway, smirking.

She closed her eyes. "Field Marshal."

"Captain Benson." He stomped into the room.

"I see you've had a chance to change into a new uniform. Could we have our ships send us down a change as well?"

"This is hardly something to be concerned about." He squinted at Kohn's work.

A woman stood in the hallway, watching the young man. She looked familiar.

Benson stifled a gasp. It was the woman killed in the bunker blast. There wasn't a hint of injury.

Twin?

Faulk took a step back, and his eyes went from Benson to the woman before he thrust his chin up defiantly. "Tell me, Captain Benson: Your role here was to sell me on an alliance."

"We're still looking forward to it."

"Yes, of course you are. So, sell me on this entirely new front for the Azoren Federation. Diplomat me. Explain why I shouldn't have you and your people executed at dawn."

Executed? "I—I don't understand. You think we were behind the assassination attempt?"

"That has no bearing on the question."

"Well…" She swallowed. "There's not much to add to what we sent in the initial briefing. The Khanate threat extends far beyond anything any one power—"

"Captain, the Azoren don't need you, and they certainly don't need this gutter rat—" Faulk waved dismissively at Thiessen, who flinched. "—to destroy an enemy. We have the most capable navy in space."

"Maybe you do." Seeing the pain in Thiessen's eyes had rattled Benson more than the threat of execution. She pressed her good hand against the tabletop. "The question is whether or not you have the resources to match the Khanate."

"Without a doubt we do. They are savages barely able to reach space. Our fleet destroyed everything they had in the sky years ago."

"Yes, well now they have a fleet not only as big as anything any of us have ever launched but with technology to match."

"This is hardly a problem for the Azoren."

"Because…?"

"Our focus has been and remains the Moskav, Captain."

"I understand that. We wouldn't ask you to leave that threat on your flank."

"Ah! Then you propose we remove the Moskav threat before turning our attention to the Khanate."

"That was the plan."

The Azoren officer grinned. "Good! The firing squad can wait. For now."

He spun on a heel and almost skipped out, speeding out of sight with the ease of someone who hadn't just survived a bomb blast a few hours before. The Gulmar captain's eyes blazed at the doorway.

Kohn set the needle down on the tabletop next to her hand. "At least he didn't call me 'the Jew' this time."

Thiessen chuckled. "That's something."

"You're good to go, Captain."

She gathered the towel, undergarments, and cleaning supplies she'd set aside earlier. "Thank you. If you'll excuse me, I need to wash some slime away."

7

———

Caville liked the *Ollie*'s galley. In the early hours, it was empty of anything but the residue from the previous night's dinner and the lasting impressions of significant meals in its history. There was a burn spot on the splash panel beside the oven where someone had overcooked a pizza and fire had broken out. On the stovetop, someone had sloshed a garlic sauce onto a glass burner and created a permanent black film nothing had peeled off. A brown stain spread from the center of the bolt-down table plastic top to the starboard edge, where someone had spilled coffee or tea that had been far too hot and too strong.

These were the signatures of the crew from before and since Goldman had taken possession of the ship and become the dreaded, bloodthirsty pirate who terrorized the mining and commerce lanes.

How many years had he been operating, Caville wondered. All he had was what Goldman shared: stories, insights.

The hard bench built into the table pressed against the GSA agent's butt as he sucked on a sweet drink he'd taken from the chiller. He breathed in the turmeric, garlic, and thyme—remnants not just of the night before but of Earth, the place that had birthed these people and, ulti-mately, his own. Accompanied by the soft thrum and scrape of the ship's recycling systems, he sang a song he'd learned as a child—in training. It was tuneless and whispered, because even alone, he didn't want anyone to hear him.

Soft steps padded toward the galley, and he took another sip, letting the song die.

No one would have a problem with him being here. They had sufficient stores for anyone to grab a midnight snack or an early breakfast. After all, the *Ollie* was a successful ship. It didn't even need funding from its true benefactors to operate. That probably made it even more appealing to keep around, maybe even beyond its mission.

And that was what had Caville up at such an ugly hour: the mission.

The *real* mission.

What had Goldman been up to, offloading gear to Gulmar privateers? Was that just for money, a way to legitimize the ship as a successful pirate? Or was there something more behind the SAID operation than what the GSA knew?

Whoever was coming to the galley stopped, belched, then shambled forward.

It was the captain himself, swaying slightly, empty beer bottle in hand. He looked disheveled, bloated, as if he'd done nothing but drink for the last couple days. "Darien?"

Caville threw a leg over the bench. "Sorry. I was trying to clear my head."

"Nah. Don't go." A dull green light leaked from the pirate's cybernetic eye.

"I've got watch duty—"

"Stay."

"I haven't been getting much sleep."

"It's a glorious club, isn't it? Our fugitive passenger working you hard?"

"Not really. Is that what you're missing? I thought you and Talia—"

"That's not the problem." The pirate dropped the bottle down a recycle chute, then opened the chiller to pull another from its silicone brace. He dropped onto the opposite bench, staring at the bottle. "It's the memories. There are nights where you can't sleep because of the voices and the eyes."

"The eyes?"

"That look. You know—like your friend had just before you shot her?"

That doomed, helpless look. "People deal with death differently."

"Sure." The pirate twisted the top off. "Until that last second, then we're all the same."

Caville's gut knotted. Had Theo talked? Had Goldman come to eliminate his mysterious mercenary because someone might have broken into the cockpit?

It wasn't that Caville was frightened of the pirate. The man had some modifications, and there was no doubt he was deadly, but in a straight-up fight? No human was a threat to a Genesis.

"What—?" Caville tried to relax. "What do you see in those eyes?"

"You mean besides the fear?"

"There has to be more."

"Sometimes." Goldman took a long, slow drink. "I've never had the chance to do what you did for your friend. That was classy. I really respected it."

There wasn't much to do but look away. "We were tight once."

"I could imagine. She was easy on the eyes."

The words made Caville tense. "Professionally."

"Oh. Yeah. I get it. But the way she handled it—ice. Tough."

"I'm sure she was afraid. We're all afraid of dying."

"Tell me about it. This line of work, what I've had to do for so long… It's all lethal, y'know? Everyone. Everything. You could get caught in the blast from a heat exhaust line and have your skin boiled off. You could get sucked out an airlock. You could get knifed in the back by a greedy son of a bitch who wants that extra half a percent."

Okay—this isn't about me. Caville shrugged. "You'd rather die as an old man in your bed?"

"Fuck yeah." The pirate took another sip, then snorted. "Nah."

"What you're doing has meaning, don't you think?"

Goldman's head jerked up as a series of shuddering clanks ran the length of the ship, then looked back down. "Does it?"

"I think so."

"Hauling this shit out to a bunch of psychotic—" The pirate winced and bowed his head. "You said you've done work for intelligence agencies before."

"GSA. At least I'm pretty sure. And another group. They said they were SAID."

"Wet work?"

"Not me personally, but they did. I managed the escape and surveillance."

"That checks out."

Caville tensed, but it was more for show. "You checked me out?"

"A little background query. Everyone does it. They gave you high marks."

"And you trust them?"

"The ones who're still alive."

"What happened?"

The pirate studied the beer bottle. "Something that never should. You remember that dustup after Zenawi took power? That representative who screamed bloody murder about SAID fabricating evidence about Azoren weapons testing?"

"A little." It had been a big story for a month or so. Everyone knew.

"That representative? Novak? Her husband was SAID. He ran an operation on Himmel—a Gulmar trade office. One of Zenawi's stooges leaked that information to the press. Novak's husband was en route to Gulmar space right around the time word reached the Azoren worlds. He turned around when his ship exited Fold Space and got the fuck out. None of his team did."

"Is that what you are? SAID?"

Goldman took another pull. "Does it matter? What I'm not is—" He pointed all around him with his bottle. "—this. This thing we have to do."

"It's just a job to get the real task done."

"Sure. But if I put a bullet between the eyes of an Azoren spy, I don't lose sleep over it. Not much. That's part of what I signed on for. Doing this? Maybe accidentally killing someone's mother? Maybe giving someone the materials to build a bomb that blows up a bunch of innocent kids?"

"Someone has to do it."

"I know." The pirate captain got up with a wobble and pushed the beer bottle into the recycler. He opened the chiller for another, then closed it and plopped back on the bench.

"You okay?"

"No. I wouldn't be human if I were."

"That's not being fair to yourself. Your job—"

"Don't. You can't make excuses. Not for…some things."

The look of resignation in Stiles's eyes burned a hole in Caville's heart. "I…guess not."

Goldman chuckled and pulled a battered data pad from his pants pocket. He plunked the device on the table, right in the middle of the brown stain, then powered it on and flipped through a few interfaces until he'd settled on something, then turned the display around for the young man to see. Two kids—a boy and girl who seemed on fast approach to their teenage years—smiled out. "Saul and Ruth."

"How old are they?"

"Twelve and ten. They think I'm on a far trader running rare earth minerals around the Kedraalian systems." He clinched his hand into a fist. "I'm so sick of all the lies. They deserve better."

"You're doing what you have to."

The pirate took the data pad back. "You ever hear about the hostage rescue mission? The failed one?"

Caville nodded. Everyone knew about it. "Embarrassing."

"When I joined SAID, they assigned me this lady as a mentor. She had twenty years under her belt, a lot of that in the field. Her mentor had been in the original Directorate, back on Earth. She told me some of the stories, some of the things they'd had to do back then. Terrible stuff."

"I'd bet."

"She was on that rescue mission with her mentor. He was one of the ones who didn't make it out."

"That had to be something."

"Worse than any of the stories he'd told her about his job on Earth."

"So, what's the real story? How'd it go so wrong? I heard it was weather—"

"It was everything. The planning, the timing, the execution—everything. Political idiocy, mostly. They bungled it from the start."

"Yeah?" Caville leaned back.

"From the first meeting, she said the planning was built around not offending the wrong people. Generals, admirals, politicians…" Goldman flexed the arm that sported scars from surgeries and battle. "It was more important to cross and dot than to get the job done right, know what I mean?"

"Political pressure?"

"Not just from Parliament. The military, too. Hell, even the Azoren and Moskav couldn't be offended, and they were already balls deep with their own wars against the Khanate. So many people running around, covering their asses instead of thinking about the objective."

"That's survival. Everyone wants to avoid risk. They use people like you for that."

"Yeah. Risk. We left a lot behind that day. That risk shouldn't include burning alive inside a shuttle with seals that've gummed up because you shipped the wrong parts and brought along maintenance crews who've never worked those shuttle models."

"They…burned alive?"

"One of the big gunships had a malfunction as they were maneuvering for landing, lost tracking on a shuttle because they were from different branches of service with different systems, and hit them with rocket backwash."

"That shouldn't have set them on fire."

"They were refueling, prepping for the extract."

Caville rubbed his eyes. "These Khanate guys—they're animals."

"They're all animals—Azoren, Moskav. Khanate's just the worst is all. Everyone knows it. Or they should."

"Then why are we giving them this technology?"

Goldman's cheeks puffed out, as if he might vomit, then he seemed to get himself under control. "Orders."

"But—"

"I think…" He shook his head. "This is my last job. I—I can't do it anymore."

"You have something else lined up?"

"Maybe an office gig. Maybe something that doesn't make me hate myself. Anything is better. I just don't—" The pirate's hand shook as he squinted at it. "You know that burning alive thing? Pounding on the hatch to try to get out as the fire cooks the inside of the ship and cooks your skin off?"

Caville couldn't do much more than grunt.

The pirate's cybernetic eye glowed a little brighter, as if the system were shedding an electronic tear. "What the Khanate does to victims—the constant torture, public humiliation, sawing your head off? I think it could be worse."

Realization wormed its way through Caville's head. Goldman was asking to be killed if the Khanate people took him. "I won't let them do that to you."

Once again, the SAID agent's cheeks puffed out, but this time it wasn't the precursor to illness. He released a relieved gust of beer breath. "Thanks."

"I don't believe in that kind of thing."

"Yeah. How could you? And, look, I'll take care of you the same way."

"I appreciate it."

Goldman scratched his scalp, then got back to his feet. "One human to another, right?"

He stumbled out of the galley, and his heavy steps slowly retreated.

Caville folded in on himself just a little. What he'd done with Stiles— what he'd let happen to her—was its own sort of pile of lies in the name of the mission. It should have hollowed him out and left him like Goldman: barely held together, fighting the gravity of fear, despair, and self-loathing.

She knew what she signed on for. She was sloppy. I warned her.

It didn't really justify what had happened, what he'd done. A part of him that wasn't capable of swallowing the lies whispered that he was being pulled into the shadows, becoming just another strip of darkness and corruption that pointed to the surrounding dark and swore that it wasn't like that.

If the SAID agent failed and fell into Khanate hands, could Caville deliver on his promise to put the other man down before he went through all that?

Not if it put the mission at risk. Nothing came before the mission.

8

———————

It was a crisp, autumn morning, complete with gray sky, chill winds, and the slightest residue of frost on the opalescent indigo skin of the Gazelle roadster borrowed from Supreme Leader Graf's collection. Brown grass whipped past as Faulk entered a long straightaway and floored the accelerator. He smiled at the feel of the vehicle's power, radiating up from the steering wheel and the sturdy, leather seat. How many megacredits had been spent purchasing the designs and eventually many of the parts? All to appease the old man's vanity.

Still, it felt thrilling to drive down the open roads connecting Graf's rustic manor to Paradies, the taste of bitter espresso still fresh, the aroma of morning fires rising from the valley to the north.

At his right, the Gazelle's passenger frowned. Her crystal blue eyes carried a little more color than his, and her alabaster skin might seem a little warmer. A black peaked cap pressed down spiky, straw gold hair that bordered on white. She wore the same black jacket as him, but where his Silver Wolf patch should have been, a red circle around a bird bent over the slight swell of a breast.

The doctrine officer twisted around in her seat. "The Night Leopards have fallen back several kilometers."

Faulk smirked. "They can catch up when we reach the edge of the city."

"Rebels have been known to prowl the woods."

"It would take a sniper of incredible skill to threaten us here."

"The enemy has snipers."

"Not as good as mine. I have the best."

She had a leather case pressed against her narrow chest. She set the case on her lap and opened it, pulling out a small binder. It opened with a soft tap against the seal, revealing a digital pad. It flared to life, washing away any last hint of color from her face. "Why did you move in to the supreme leader's manor?"

"Analyzing me on such a beautiful morning? How tragic, Colonel."

"Duty does not concern itself with weather or the pleasure of a fast car."

"If you were to understand the thrill of being alive, you would question such a belief."

"Your attempts to avoid the question will not prevent me from asking it."

He smiled as he braked to enter a wide turn. "Very well. Best I answer. I moved into the old man's favorite property for the same reason I borrowed the car this morning: It needed to be done."

"Needed to be done?" She tapped on the digital pad screen. "Could you explain that, please?"

"I can try, yes." He let up on the brake. "Do you believe Supreme Commander Graf will survive his current situation?"

"The call this morning indicated he was stable."

"Stable, yes. After a night of our best doctors hovering over him."

"And the Kedraalian doctor. This surgeon apparently has years of experience with battlefield trauma."

"So it would appear. But even the greatest surgeon might struggle with an old man so recently come off a life-threatening injury. Graf *is* an old man. He is fragile, even in the best of times."

"The supreme leader has managed his health despite the years."

"He has, hasn't he?" The field marshal frowned. "Youth resents the resiliency of the old. That's another truth you wouldn't understand, what with your synthetic immortality. It desensitizes you to what it means to be young and hungry. We feel chained and denied our right to ascend."

"You resent Supreme Leader Graf?"

"No, no. It's more impersonal than that. I resent anything that stands between me and my destiny. We Children were told from birth that our right was the throne of the stars."

"Throne?"

"Not literally. Truly, you must work on this inability to appreciate figurative speech."

"You and your brothers have shown just as much of a deficiency with this."

The Gazelle's engine growled, but it couldn't drown the frustration rumbling in Faulk's chest. He hated the doctrine officers and their inhuman oversight. How was it they could be even more a creation than he and his brothers, yet act as Graf's evaluation of the worthiness and wellness of his progeny?

She looked up from her digital pad. "Would you say that the promise of destiny is at the root of your hostility, Field Marshal Faulk?"

"I'm not so sure *hostility* is the right word, is it, Colonel?"

"Did you shed a tear when I was killed in the bomb blast?"

"Not a single tear. Should I?"

"I have been at your side for nearly ten years now."

"And you have returned from death three times before. Why should I cry?" *And why* would *I?*

Even more than the civilian populace, those in the military saw Faulk and his brothers as inhuman monsters. How could they embrace such a belief when the Children were managed by...things like Colonel Amanda Karlson? At least Faulk bled. He had the hungers and needs of a human. Being blessed with superior capabilities didn't remove his humanity.

But Karlson and her sisters? They weren't human at all.

She inhaled, an affectation rather than a necessity. "Do the Kedraalians realize the depths of our challenges?"

"You mean, do they realize how desperate our situation is? How greatly diminished our military has become? How our control of our resources is strained? Is that what you mean?"

The colonel nodded.

Faulk smiled coolly. "Not yet. It is only a matter of time, of course. No purge is ever complete. Spies survive. They plan and prepare."

"Do you mean to indicate that we do not?"

"Perhaps we don't plan and prepare *adequately*."

"Yourself included?"

"Would I be in this car with you if that were the case?" He laughed.

Ahead, the road gently sloped toward the outskirts of the city, where the buildings were a mix of the old wooden shacks and low, stone structures that had been in place when the Azoren had rechristened the world Himmel. The old buildings—like the old residents—should have been burned to the ground, bulldozed, and replaced by the superior architecture and design of the conquerors. Instead, resources had been immediately thrown into constructing a war machine that could withstand the intrusions of their former Kedraalian masters.

Turn your eyes outward too quickly, and you will ever have a knife at your back.

It was a lesson a child should have known, but not Supreme Leader Graf. Maybe he had assumed a few generations of Azoren believers would be enough to eliminate the stain of the original settlers. Instead, the old occupants of the planet poisoned and corrupted the blood and minds of the Azoren. And yet it wasn't just the fiercely independent and stubborn settlers of old living in the woods but the grandchildren of those who had claimed this planet for Graf.

Faulk slowed now that he had the city within clear sight. Beyond the few kilometers still cluttered with these old buildings, the thick, bulky buildings of his people held an even greater threat: his rivals.

Colonel Karlson continued to tap the screen of her digital pad, absorbed in whatever analysis she was conducting. When she did look up, it was to study his profile or perhaps to stare at the gloved hands with which he held the steering wheel.

As they passed the first sagging buildings lining the narrow, concrete roads, the field marshal chuckled. "You can relax now, Colonel. Your precious escort is nearly upon us."

Once again, she turned around in her seat to check on the armored assault vehicles. "One of them should always be ahead of us."

"I would have nowhere to drive with—"

A gray form rose on a squat rooftop to his right, then a bright spark like a small fire obscured it. Almost immediately, a long, white trail sped toward the racing car. Then a bone-shaking explosion drowned out Faulk's heartbeat.

There was an instant to decide on his next course: fight or flight or freeze.

All he had on him was a knife and a sidearm—his 10mm Griffon pistol. The Gazelle could outrun anything on the road, and he could handle it, even in the city.

Another form rose up in his peripheral vision, and this time the spark made its true shape known: a plume of fire roaring parallel to the ground.

Backblast from a rocket launcher.

The colonel gasped an instant before the rocket exploded somewhere behind them.

The Night Leopards.

Faulk made the decision without any further thought, flooring the accelerator and leaning forward. Being in the Supreme Leader's collection, the vehicle would have bulletproof glass. There would be a reinforced undercarriage. The tires and side panels would be hardened.

And yet...

More of the gray forms resolved from the autumn gloom, hurrying out from between buildings, weapons raised. Automatic gunfire clapped all around them, and the windows went white with multiple impacts. The side panels held, then Karlson grunted and dropped her digital pad.

They sped past the soldiers and the buildings, Faulk squinting to gain even a hint of an idea of their course.

Straight here, but ahead would be a turn when they came to a fountain. He would have to—

More gunfire. The windows cracked. A section broke in. Out of that small opening, it looked like someone jumped from a rooftop ahead of them.

Not someone jumping. Someone threw something in their path.

Faulk slammed on the brake and swerved. Metal screeched and the vehicle lurched as they ground along the side of a stone wall.

An explosion—this one closer—lifted the rear of the car.

The Gazelle shuddered, jerked, growled, then made a high, keening sound.

Everything became sluggish, and they slowed abruptly, throwing both of them forward.

Something has happened to the transmission.

They came to a stop, the sharp tang of burning oil riding on a white cloud gushing from the front of the vehicle.

Voices shouted, but they seemed distant in the dull headache ringing out from Faulk's ears. Karlson's glare cut through the haze, carrying with it all the scorn that a scream would have: *You should have stayed with your escort!*

Except, of course, that escort was probably a pile of burning wreckage half a kilometer back. Distance might have actually saved his life.

Metal scraped against metal, then with a terrible groan, his door opened. Men in gray uniforms pointed assault carbines at him—the same Blood Eagle weapons Faulk's men used, the best in the Azoren inventory.

"Out! Out! Or we shoot you where you are!"

Faulk raised his hands while one of the soldiers—an older man with a gaunt face—leaned in and unbuckled the seat belt. On the other side of the car, another man was doing the same for Karlson.

Then Faulk was hauled out by the lapels of his jacket and dragged over to a stone wall. Karlson was shoved against the wall to his right. Men in gray uniforms darted toward them, weapons at the ready. Black smoke rose in the distance: the burning wreckage of the Night Leopards. Stronger than the faint stench of the cooking bodies was the sharp smell of the expended gunpowder.

An even older man than the one who'd dragged Faulk out of the car, came around the front of the stone building, dragging a handkerchief across a long, narrow face that shook ever so slightly.

The man's green eyes twitched, then settled into a hard squint. "Field Marshal Faulk." It sounded like an accusation.

A smile stretched across Faulk's face. "Major Olbricht. Where is your master, General Weber?"

"Safe."

While keeping his hands raised, Faulk rubbed his face against his shoulder. "Your ambush was well executed."

Olbricht bowed slightly. "My men are exceptional soldiers—veterans from the Moskav front. Loyal."

"Ah. You *are* pointing weapons at the most senior officer in our military, Major. That might make someone question your assertion about loyalty."

"Our enemies are the Moskav dogs. Supreme Leader Graf understands this."

"Perhaps he does. If he survives his injuries, he might say as much."

"He would never involve us in this nonsense with the Khanate. One enemy at a time."

Faulk flashed a tight smile. "You might not have heard, but Supreme Leader Graf *did* approve a strike against Kedraal."

Olbricht frowned. "General Weber will set things right."

"General Weber will be dead before the week is out."

"He'll outlive you." Olbricht pulled a pistol from a hip holster.

"Major, what if I told you that in exchange for fighting the Khanate, we will see the Moskav animals turned into a bloody paste? Hm?"

"Thanks to all the distractions you and your brothers have caused, we no longer have the capability to do that."

"Oh, but we do, Major. It just means accepting that the vermin must be called out of the dark by treats and promises. *Then* they can be killed."

"Treats and promises?" Olbricht sneered.

"It can be an effective means to reach your desired result."

"What we lack at the moment is the proper leadership to accomplish our objectives." The major bowed his back and sucked in a breath. "General Weber will give us that once again."

"We will have the proper leadership, Major."

The major's sneer grew deeper. "You?"

"Yes. Me. Unfortunately, you won't live to see my successes."

"*I* won't live? Field Marshal Faulk, perhaps the grenade that took out your car rattled your brain. How else could you forget what just happened? I am the one holding a pistol in my hand, not you."

"True." Faulk grinned at the colonel sagging against the wall at his side.

She bowed her head, resigned. "It makes perfect sense to question your leadership."

"Does it?"

At the back of the crowd of Olbricht's soldiers gathered in a semicircle, one of his men collapsed. It was quiet compared to the explosions and gunfire from earlier. Only the men beside the fallen man even noticed. Then there was a distant crack a second before one of the other soldiers made a noise—the start of a shout—then collapsed as well.

Another distant crack was followed by silence.

Then another of the gray-jacketed soldiers crumpled.

A soldier at the back spun around, pointing deeper into the city. "Major! Snipers!"

Before anyone could act, gunfire erupted, and black-jacketed men with Silver Wolf patches rushed toward the stone house from deeper inside the city.

Another of Olbricht's soldiers doubled over and collapsed.

The major's eyes went wide. He pointed his pistol at Faulk and fired.

A bullet cracked off the wall next to the field marshal, and stone chips blew against his back, but he barely heard the pistol's report over the roar of Blood Eagle carbines—his men's and those of Olbricht's.

Realization settled over the major as he fell to the ground, clutching his shoulder. Blood oozed between his fingers. His men dashed to cover among the low houses and walls, but they, too, must have realized their situation.

Overhead, an orbital roared down, raining railgun fire on the houses providing cover, killing ambushers and occupants equally.

Where the rounds struck, gray-uniformed limbs fell away from ruined bodies.

Faulk ducked when a burst of rounds tore chunks out of the wall above his head. He drew his pistol and knelt beside Olbricht.

Tears dripped down the side of the major's face as the last of his men fell.

Then the battlefield went silent, and Faulk got back to his feet. His headache was a constant throbbing—the sort that would get worse throughout the day. For now, it could be managed.

Like Olbricht and his sort.

The field marshal glanced down. "You see, Major? How easy it is to draw out the vermin with offers of treats? Give them a chance at vengeance, for instance?"

Olbricht whimpered. "Your creation began the end."

"It did."

Faulk fired the pistol, putting a bullet between the major's eyes, and the old soldier stiffened, then relaxed.

One of Faulk's men waved, then rushed forward, pulling a black mask off his face. There was a strong, almost familial resemblance between them, although a discerning eye would be able to pick out the subtle signs of age that made the field marshal the older of the two. It was the work of Minister King: templating. Faulk's clones were imprinted, loyal.

He nudged the major's corpse with a booted toe. "Well done, Captain."

The younger man came to a stop, then snapped to attention. "Your assessment of the threat and how to draw them out was the key, Field Marshal."

"It was. Were you able to track any signals from them to Weber?"

"The general evaded us again."

"Tragic. Do keep after him."

"Of course, Field Marshal."

Karlson was at Faulk's side, staring down at Olbricht. "This was an ambush?"

Faulk shrugged. "What they did was an ambush. What I did was a trap."

"You stayed at the supreme leader's mansion and drove that car to draw them out?"

"To move forward with our plan requires a single focus."

"Yet your plan lacks exactly that."

Faulk considered his pistol. "My plan is focused, Colonel."

"No. You've allowed outside influences to corrupt your vision. This is something that must be discussed and analyzed. My counsel—"

"Your counsel—" Faulk brought the pistol up and shot her in the head, the same way he'd finished off the major. "—is no longer required, Colonel."

When she fell to the ground, he holstered the pistol.

The captain who'd led the ambush against Olbricht stared at the dead woman for a moment, then turned his attention back to Faulk. "Will you need another counselor, Field Marshal?"

"I think not. I've outgrown the need for a mother."

Deeper in the city, the rumble of Night Leopard engines grew louder. His new escort was coming for him. Good. A great deal of work remained to be done.

Perhaps no purge could be complete, but he was getting close.

When he was done, the Azoren would be positioned to rise above everyone.

9

———

The distant chatter of automatic weapons fire woke Benson. The sound leaked in through the open window of her room, riding on the chill breeze. From the position of the sun in the window, she guessed it was afternoon. The window—the room itself—gave off a comforting sense of antiquity. It wasn't that the window was particularly dusty, and the glass wasn't cracked. But the design of the thing—wooden jambs and frames, a manual lever—was rustic and simple. It would have seemed out of place almost anywhere else, but in the sturdy, old manor she, Kohn, and Thiessen had been transferred to a little before midday, the windows were right at home. In fact, anything else would have seemed out of place against the warm, dark wooden paneling inside her room. And from the outside, where the walls were rough-mortared stone, the windows were simply of a piece.

There was a knock at her bedroom door—dull through its heavy, dark wood. "Yes?"

"You hear it?" It was Thiessen, sounding far away.

She threw off her covers, then almost skipped to the door and opened it. The Gulmar captain's attention was far away, eyes raised to the heavy timber ceiling. Hearty herbs and spices still clung to his simple clothing from the rich stew they'd had for lunch. "More executions?"

"I don't know if we'd be able to hear gunfire from the city this far out."

"A fight in the woods? That's only a few kilometers, right?"

"They must be using heavy weapons. Machine guns."

She waved him in, searched up and down the long passage lit only by kerosene lanterns resting atop tables of a uniform mahogany to match the paneling, then closed the door again. "Feels to me that there's been some sort of development."

"A new justification for all the fighting?"

"I know. They don't seem to need justification."

"Bloodthirsty animals." Thiessen's eyes swept her room, darting over the wooden chairs that must have been fashioned by a master craftsman, to the door to the bathroom that was fashioned in pale rose and white tile, then to the fireplace crackling with the soft glow of a dying fire and the armoire opposite the door. Finally, his eyes settled on the bed—a glorious, four-poster beast of the same design and materials as the rest of the room. Deep crimson sheets, pillowcases, and matching patterned comforter punctuated the giant piece of furniture, giving it the totally unnecessary gravity that said *this is the center of the room.*

She smiled, embarrassed. "Did I get the nicest digs?"

"Mine looks like something cut from ancient Earth history, too. Like a prince might live here."

"I almost feel bad for preferring this to that old…barracks they had us in last night."

"Don't. We're still prisoners."

"You saw the guards?"

"Two inside, ten out on the lawn. I'm pretty sure those hedges aren't just for looks, either."

"Perimeter sensors?"

Thiessen nodded. "Just because everything runs on old fuels—" He nodded toward her fireplace and the lanterns on the mantel. "—doesn't mean there's no power here. When I was talking with Kohn after lunch, he saw one of the guards go through the kitchen door. There was another door open in there. He said it glowed like it was full of monitors."

Benson shivered. "One of the…servants said this is where Graf spends his winters."

"I'd imagine he's seen his last one."

"I wouldn't take that bet. He's apparently survived a lot of attempts."

"How's your head?"

She brushed her hair back from her face. "The headache's okay. My arm's worse."

"Do you need more than that brace?"

"I shouldn't." She extended her arm slowly, and the lamplight reflected off the tight, clear sleeve Kohn has put over her elbow. "It keeps everything in place."

Another knock at the door brought them both around. Thiessen slid over to where he'd be hidden when the door opened, then nodded.

Benson cleared her throat. "Yes?"

"Captain?" It was Kohn.

Thiessen relaxed, then opened the door and waved the ensign in. Once the younger man was in the room, the Gulmar officer repeated Benson's earlier search of the hallway.

If there was a security room on the first floor, her room was probably bugged. Memories of the images that had been floated around of her from earlier in her career in an attempt to humiliate her and derail her promotion left a burning sting on her cheeks. Those had probably been the work of some sick and angry member of the crew, maybe someone she'd rejected or someone who resented her looks and her rank. Who knew?

Would the Azoren take a sick pleasure in repeating something like that? Spying on her with that level of intimacy?

She pulled the loose flannel shirt she'd found in the armoire tighter around her. It smelled faintly of naphthalene, same as the heavy jeans she'd squeezed into, grunting at the stiff, blue material. They were real denim, sturdy, meant to last. Now she felt like she'd been robbing a grave, although she doubted the woman who'd used the room was dead.

Unless they killed the people who were associated with the deposed rulers? That sounded primitive and brutal, which fit the mold of the Azoren nicely.

Kohn crossed to the fireplace. The white shirt he wore almost glowed gold in the dying light. He rubbed his hands in front of the grate. "It's going to get cold tonight." When he twisted around, his dark eyes were wide.

Thiessen straightened, then crossed to the fireplace and warmed his hands as well. "It's cold already."

When Benson joined them, she chafed her arms. "Did something happen?"

The ensign turned back to the fire. "I went downstairs for a glass of water. The guard who's been wandering around the inside? He looked ready to shoot me. When the old woman who runs the kitchen saw that, she walked right between us and took me into the kitchen. I guess the staff don't much care for these Silver Wolf guys."

Thiessen snorted. "Who would?"

"Well, some of the staff are old settlers. Descendants of them, at least. She said they came here because the place had spots that were a lot like Earth. Well, back before everything went so bad. This area—it used to be a giant forest with lakes all around. Perfect for her grandparents and parents. She actually grew up in a log cabin about two hundred kilometers out. Before the Azoren came."

Locals. On the supreme leader's staff. Was that because those were the only people he could trust? "Is she loyal to Graf?"

"I didn't get the impression she was loyal to anyone. Her brother is, though. She said he bought into everything. He's not a bad man—at least that's what she said."

"I wonder why they didn't just leave when this happened?"

"I actually asked her that exact question. She said that by the time the new flag went up over the old capital, a lot of them were shocked and more were just sort of resigned."

"But they don't buy into the dogma?"

"Some might. I got the sense they were more feeling they could outlast it."

Benson remembered the dogged determination of the Azoren attackers on Jotun, the way they'd kept coming, even after her people had managed to set up decent defenses. Charging into the face of dug-in defenders, even creeping in with chameleon shadow tech to hide them—it wasn't the sort of thing she'd look at and think she could simply outlast.

What did that say about the original settlers?

A real shiver ran down her spine. "These commandos are like the ones from Jotun."

Thiessen grunted. "Commandos now. Is that what you're calling them?"

"We've seen the black uniforms. Our intelligence people say that almost all the elite units are made up of Children. They go through intense training from childhood."

"Brainwashing." The Gulmar captain scowled. "I've dealt with them before. They've showed up on Radetta: honor guards stuffed with pride and bluster. A couple wandered into the settlement where I grew up. They learned the difference between training and experience."

Benson's brow knotted. "That settlement was kilometers out."

"*Wander*'s the wrong word. They stole a vehicle and drove out to 'visit the zoo.'"

"Oh."

Kohn shoved his hands into the pockets of his dull gray cargo pants. "You do a good job hiding your bitterness."

Thiessen winced. "No better than you, I'd imagine."

"Well, we mostly use automated counseling systems and drugs to cope with all the damage. A combination of psychedelics and body chemistry regulators along with sleep therapy and objective assessment of the memories—"

"Okay, maybe we handle it differently."

"It makes sense that most cultures have different approaches."

The Gulmar captain relaxed. "It's just how we cope. For us, it's constant. You scab over. You scar. Our community acts—acted—as a healer. It was this gentle voice that reassured you that everything was going to be okay, even though we all knew it would never be okay."

That sense of hopelessness in Thiessen's voice—Benson could understand that. She touched his elbow. "Was it any better once you escaped?"

"Escaped? Oh. When I actually had a job?"

"The security forces—"

"That wasn't a job, really. The contracts were uncertain. You could go weeks without a paying gig, especially when the executives worried about their bonuses. When the privateers made things rough, Leona's people were just as likely to cut funding as they were to send a task force out to hunt the troublemakers down."

And now Leona Trang was a part of the ash pile back on Radetta, victims of the Khanate threat she'd refused to acknowledge.

Benson wondered if she might be the same sort of problem dressed in less regal clothes. Was the Azoren threat she was embracing as a potential ally really just an asp clutched to her bosom to avoid fallout for her previous acts? Was the alliance like the namesake of her old ship—the *Pandora*—a box that released peril into the world once opened?

That was ridiculous. Peril had been part of humanity from the moment of its birth. The instant a shuffling hominid had found a desirable place to hunt, another had felt envy. When the first ideal mate had been identified, there had been jealousy. Failings were hardwired in, like fuses meant to slow progress.

She sighed. "The piloting job you had—that's what you did between jobs?"

"Yeah. I flew bigwigs around to meetings, sometimes took them from planet to planet. Leona liked me. She had me under contract for a few years. I think she imagined she could understand the common people by —" He blushed. "Osmosis."

"I don't think I've ever heard that as a euphemism for sex."

His blushing grew more intense. "She never understood people at all, especially not mine. You never know what it means to be desperate and depressed unless you actually experience it."

Kohn glanced over his shoulder at the door. "I'm worried about Ernie."

Benson tensed. She should have been thinking the same thing but hadn't. "I was hoping them not saying anything about him might mean he was proving invaluable."

"That's probably how he's thinking about it, too, but with the way he treats people and the way these people just casually murder..."

"If he saves Graf, he'll be fine."

There was another knock at her door—loud and insistent. She pointed at the floor, indicating that the other two should stay there, at the fireplace. If she could have, she would have told them to just look casual, but the knock had made them all jump. Paradies was getting to them.

Halfway to the door, it opened, and two guards she didn't recognize stepped in. One of them stared at Kohn. "You. Come."

The ensign's jaw dropped slightly, then he smiled anxiously. "I…guess dinner plans have changed."

Benson let her fingers brush over the young man's forearm as he passed. She wanted to tell him to be strong and not to panic. They were diplomatic guests, after all. They'd come seeking an alliance. They weren't threats.

Yet Kohn was the one they'd singled out from the start—Dietrich's star pupil and poke in the eye.

Now the young man was being led away, and she couldn't stop it.

L ightning rippled through the clouds below McLeod's shuttle, casting them in a dark crimson that reminded him of boiling blood. It was Dramora's stormy season, a time where the southern hemisphere was assaulted by hurricane-force winds and floods and landlocked seas belched rotting mysteries onto their shores. Just across the equator, the storms were more manageable. Weeks of sandstorms turned everything red, then intermittent torrents flooded gulches and ravines and filled grottos and dry lake beds.

He truly hated the place. Of all the planets settled by humanity since leaving Earth, Dramora was most like a crude, unwelcoming wound. It was largely a dry rock washed in heat and misery.

But it was mineral rich, and only the sturdy and stubborn lived there.

Especially the stubborn.

The shuttle dropped through the clouds, the engines drowning out what almost certainly would have been the steady patter of rain. When he stepped down the ramp at the starport, he was drenched before he could reach the waiting car. It left him shivering despite the heater blowing. The rain had an almost sweet, metallic taste and smelled like blood. It stayed with him the entire drive past gauche storefronts lit by ridiculous neon signs.

At the hotel, he took a hot shower to shake the cold and switched to light pajamas, then sent his uniform out for cleaning. There were messages waiting for him when he settled on the bed.

Updates. Analyses. Queries.

"Colonel McLeod, we've received the latest on that lost shipment. Looks like it might have been inadvertently redirected to Persephone Station before being mixed into palettes meant for commercial shipping. We have people tracking it down from the last known location, but right now, everything points to it being lost to pirate activity."

Of course. It was the seventh such shipment in the last two years. Highly sensitive, mishandled through simple incompetence. Not espionage. It couldn't be. The military had cracked down on security. It was a brilliant lie that everyone loved to tell each other.

Where were the gaps? Someone was stealing military hardware and systems, but even when he found where it had gone to, he couldn't prove who was behind it.

"Colonel McLeod, we've taken a look at the debris gathered from that research ship—the *Loki?* Looks like you were right: It couldn't have been a cascading reactor failure. We've run some more tests, and there are trace amounts of explosives material. Looks like someone blew the reactor shielding and let the radioactive steam vent right into the circulation system. Not an accident after all."

It couldn't have been an accident. You'd have to be willing to allow an absurd set of details pass without question to accept that analysis. Yet people in the Data Acquisition Group had done exactly that. Why? He'd have to follow up on that. The DAG leadership had changed six months ago. Maybe the background checks hadn't been as thorough as he'd thought.

"Colonel McLeod, we had a request for follow-up from the prime minister's office. They—um— They'd like to have a look at your data on the Counter-Espionage Directorate before they consider granting access to the records. Would you be able to approve us sending those along? This comes from Prime Minister Zenawi himself."

Of course it would. Zenawi had considered the CED his own little toy for decades now. Probing the budgeting anomalies and other embarrassing data that would eventually bring down Kusno Saripado and his network of traitors ran the risk of snagging the prime minister, too.

McLeod thumbed approval of the data query, then specified that he wanted a tight audit log on the transfer. If a gnat crawled on the display terminal showing the data, that fact needed to be captured.

He flipped through the last of the queued messages, then paced, suddenly feeling very alone.

The room was small and looked down on a street lit bright red with the advertisements of local cuisine. They liked their spices hot on Dramora, like their summers. Maybe he'd have to try out some of the local dishes, once he had recovered from the rigors of travel.

His data pad buzzed: incoming call.

Who—?

An older woman with graying hair and dark gold skin. A pronounced nose dominated a round face.

Devanshi Patel.

Her smile was artfully inauthentic, the tilt of her head meant to be whimsical but coming across scolding. The mole on her left cheek had grown since the last time he'd seen her. "Avis! And ready for bed so early? What are you doing in Asilo? I thought you hated Dramora."

"It's nice to see you, too, Devanshi. I'm here on business."

"Really? I thought the GSA kept you tucked away in the dark like a vampire. You should have told me you were coming."

"It was sudden. Really. I barely had time to pack."

"Well, you must come for dinner while you're out here. Tomorrow night?"

"I think I could do that. My day is packed tomorrow, but my night is open."

"That would be lovely. Then again, I worry about you operating with an open schedule at night and away from home. That's always trouble for you, isn't it?"

"I'm a reformed man."

She snorted. "Men can't reform themselves."

"I'll see you tomorrow."

He disconnected and thumbed the data pad into low-power mode so it could recharge quickly off the hotel's power system.

Devanshi was alive. That meant Stiles hadn't been able to complete her mission.

Unfortunate. That would have been the easier solution, which was always preferable. Someone doing the dirty work behind the scenes meant staying clean and free of entanglements. At his age, in his position, risk was dangerous. It carried weight and substance, things he couldn't shake free of. Not easily.

Then again, it might be good to get his hands dirty again.

He paced for a bit, but his eyes were drawn to the intense red neon lights. What spices did they offer on a planet like this? What delicacies?

It took him a moment to realize he was rubbing his hands together.

Maybe it *was* too early to go to bed. Maybe there was time to walk the city streets and get a feel for the local flavor. He'd been too long without a taste of things that could truly satisfy him.

He unbuttoned his pajama top and rubbed where the bullet had struck him not so long ago.

Killed him.

He'd been lucky, preserved by the resuscitation ring.

His gut knotted, and he reached for the pajama top, then froze.

Devanshi was right. Men couldn't reform themselves. And maybe he didn't want to.

10

─────────

Toni Grier wasn't meant for calm. She was built for action, from the first memories she had as a child running around in the muddy yard around her modest home to her days as a Marine. There had been opportunities throughout her life to take the easy path, to let things wash around her. Every time she'd done that, she'd been swept away with the current.

Action was what she needed.

But hours out from Himmel, the only action the fleet was seeing were exercises and basic maintenance. It made people like Chief Parkinson happy—digging into problems that had been allowed to slide for weeks or months and finally putting solutions into place. But her? She was ready to scream.

She'd established a new routine, pushing her Marines to go beyond their regular workouts. And there were visible results—things to be proud of.

It wasn't enough to fill the dead time.

Now she was caught up in something far more challenging than the weights and cardio routines. On the display of her data pad propped up on the top of her bunk, Benson sat at a conference room table. She was surrounded by the handsome Gulmar captain, the grumpy and disheveled captain of the *Lyon*, the rodent-like Azoren ambassador, and Clive. Grier's commander.

She imagined herself sitting at the front of the table, back erect just enough not to look like it was in a brace, chest thrust out just so. She took a sip of bitter tea, pinky extended slightly. There was the faintest hint of perfume—sprayed on her T-shirt while searching through the captain's quarters.

Did that grand cabin, with its open space, private head, and polished desktop, contribute to who Benson was, or was it a reflection of her?

Grier straightened up her own cabin a bit, then returned to the display.

She resumed the video, listening to Benson's voice more than her words. The way Benson kept her calm or at least kept any obvious anger or fear hidden.

How did she do that? Was it voice training?

The sergeant cleared her throat. "Redundant systems should prevent that."

There was a waver to her voice. It sounded fragile and weak compared to Benson's. Simple facts. How did you get nervous over simple facts?

"Redundant systems should prevent that."

It was still there—a squeakiness where there should have been coolness.

Benson was sitting when she talked. Maybe that gave her more confidence. Going through the academy, she'd probably taken classes on speech and managing drama. Leadership. Knowing how to push buttons or to deescalate. Training videos existed in the *Valor*'s library. Educational courses, too. Marines and sailors finished degrees while deployed all the time.

But Grier wasn't smart enough for that. She'd resorted to the bottle for a lot of reasons, among them her recognition of all of her failings.

Not Benson. Pretty, smart, graceful, respected…

How could anyone compete with that?

Grier sucked in a breath and tried again. "Redundant systems should prevent that."

Even when she managed to keep her voice even, her accent leaked through. The lazy lack of enunciation, the inclination toward a drawl...

She sounded like the poor trash she was.

Benson's choice of words. They seemed precise and to the point. Grier knew most of the words, but they didn't come naturally. They didn't just roll off her tongue like they seemed to with the captain.

It's more than word choice and delivery. They make a difference, but...

Frustration and shame bubbled up, and her eyes watered. Did you have to be what you were born to? Was the bad luck of parenting something that stuck with you until you died, like a birth defect?

Money had to play a part. It *had* to. Benson came from...

Grier sent the video window to the background and pulled up the captain's record. There she was as a child, in an image that showed the parliamentary building in the background. She'd been recognized for some academic achievement and had toured the building where her mother worked. Tall, thin, cute. Holding a finger down on the image brought up more information: She was top of her class in testing.

And she'd had tutors.

Maybe a representative didn't make all that much money, but she'd spent what she could on her child. Maybe Benson didn't have a father to influence her, but her mother stepped in with discipline to spare.

And there were other images. All throughout her childhood, Benson rubbed elbows with kids from the same background—politicians' kids; wealthy kids; kids whose parents taught or performed research. That kind of association mattered. Grier had associated with other poor kids. She'd had a circle of friends who worried about the next bottle of beer they stole or the next time they got stoned. They couldn't spell *ambition*, much less make it a part of them.

"That's sophistication." Grier rolled that word out again, giving each syllable a chance to breathe. "So-phist-i-ca-tion."

She remembered hanging out in the basement of an abandoned building with a group of teens, passing around a bottle of cheap whiskey and some home-grown herbal drugs that left a taste like charcoal on the tongue.

"Sophistication."

A boy's hand on her breast, his tongue scraping around in her mouth.

Tears again, dammit. She couldn't undo a lifetime of bad choices, and it all seemed so unfair. All she wanted was—

Her hatch chimed, and she nearly choked sucking in a breath.

Who would be there at this hour? She'd waited until she'd had the cabin to herself to study Benson. It was almost 3 a.m.

She checked the data pad. It was Halliwell. *Shit.* She connected. "Yeah?"

"Hey. I know it's late. You…you got a minute?" He looked confused.

"Sure." Grier slid the data pad under her pillow and took a step toward the hatch, then froze. Her T-shirt. Would he smell the perfume? She pulled it off and stuffed it under the pillow, too.

"Toni?"

"J-just a sec."

She dug a clean T-shirt from her locker, dried her eyes with the soft material, then opened the hatch, trying to look like she'd just woken. Halliwell blinked, bleary-eyed and wobbly in the same black T-shirt, but he had on jeans. "Can I come in?"

"Sure." She stepped aside, heart racing. Had he discovered she'd gone into Benson's cabin? Just part of the terrorist sweeps. *I thought it'd be a good idea to make sure there wasn't a bomb hidden in there, y'know?* That's how she'd explain it away.

He staggered over to the bunk and leaned against it, turning, then sniffing the air, squinting. It looked like he might say something, but he shook his head. "Sorry. If you want me to come back later—"

"Nah. It's all good." She squeezed past him, punched him in the arm, then hauled herself up to her bunk. For a moment, she'd expected to maybe smell alcohol on him, but he smelled like soap and sleep. "What's up?"

The tall Marine shrugged. "I don't know. I was kind of hoping you might help me…figure some things out."

"Yeah. That's me: the detective."

He looked around. "Everyone else on duty?"

"Except for Yasmin. She's in the infirmary."

"Nausea problems again?"

"They're going to run a test tomorrow to see if there might be blockage."

"Okay. We'll need to work on a new rotation, I guess." He sniffed the air again.

"What, does it stink or something?"

"No. It's just…" He sunk in on himself. "I thought I smelled Faith's perfume."

Grier tried on a big smile and shifted closer to her pillow, then pressed a hand on top of it. "You must be missing her."

The lieutenant scowled. "Hardly."

"You two still fighting?"

"Not really fighting. She's all eyes for that Gulmar captain since she met him."

"Oh. He's pretty good looking."

"Thanks." Halliwell's eyes dropped from Grier's face for the first time, settling on her T-shirt and panties for a moment, then turning away. "Things were getting messy before that. I don't think I can ever do the right thing with her. Every decision I make is hotheaded or stubborn or… You know."

"That's what woke you up?"

"Huh? Yeah. I guess. I mean, I've been wanting to talk to her, but she's always busy."

"Avoiding you?"

"Not really. There's so much going on. You know how crazy it is for her."

"Being captain and all."

"How many hours did we commit to weeding out potential Khanate terrorists? Getting survivors from the other ships moved into new positions? Then it was the same thing all over again helping the Gulmar. There really wasn't time."

"I remember. I helped."

"I know. I probably didn't say thanks enough. Sorry."

Grier kicked her legs anxiously, realizing just how hopeless this all was. She'd wanted Halliwell since the day she saw him, and here he was sulking about the woman who made that desire even more of a burning hollowness in the chest. "You thought about maybe trying to call her down there?"

"On Himmel? Yeah. I tried. She's not accepting."

"Ouch."

"Well, they're going to be busy down there, too. I think. Maybe."

"Parties and meetings and all of that."

Halliwell shoved his hands in his pockets. "Yeah. Being around people like her."

Sophisticated. "Well, if you came here for cheering up, I don't know that I can help you much."

"I think I was looking more for…" His head came up, and he twisted at the waist a little, eyes narrowed as he looked at her. "You think I'm being stupid? Like I'm not worthy of her and she's just now figuring that out?"

That was a gut punch. It made Grier angry for what it said about the captain, but there was also a sense of connection and empathy with Halliwell and…hope. "Worthy doesn't sound right."

"You don't think so? She's a captain. She's running a task force."

"And she kept you around and got you a commission. Doesn't sound like she found you unworthy."

"I think I was convenient."

Grier snorted. "That's the *last* word I'd use to describe you, Clive."

"Thanks. I knew I could count on you to make me feel better." He turned for the hatch. "Let's work on the rotation tomorrow—"

She hopped off the bunk and grabbed his arm. "Wait!"

He sank lower. "Look, you're right. Okay? I'm a pain. I make bad decisions."

She shoved him. Just a little. "Cut it out."

"What?"

"This whole self-pity thing. You're a great guy. You're everything a gal could possibly want. Maybe she can't see that. Or maybe she's so caught up in this thing with the Azoren that she can't take your call. Or they could be blocking her device from using their network. You ever think about that?"

He winced. "No. I mean, she's a diplomat."

"On an enemy world."

He sighed. "You're right. They might have communications problems."

"Redundant systems should prevent that." Grier didn't even realize she was imitating Benson until Halliwell's face pinched up.

"Why'd you do that? The last thing I want to hear is her right now."

"Sorry."

He squeezed his eyes shut. "Don't apologize. I'm the one being stupid. Getting worked up over something that probably never should've been in the first place. Look, hit the sack. I think we could both use some sleep, right?"

Sleep. With him so close, it was the last thing she had on her mind. "Y'know, I was thinking earlier. Just sort of rolling ideas around in my head."

"Yeah? What about?"

"Well, sort of—" Her voice turned into a squeak. "Dammit. Sorry. Nothing."

He straightened. "You okay?"

"Sure. Better than I've ever been."

His eyes stayed on her, and somehow, it felt like he'd become a blast furnace. "I worry about you, y'know."

"You don't need…" But she wanted him to. Her body tingled at the thought of it. "I'm fine."

"Okay. It's just, we're both in more senior billets. I know the pressure—"

"I'm fine." She put a hand on his shoulder, something that was meant to be playful and a sign of camaraderie and reassurance, but he shifted or she misjudged or maybe there was a twitch in her shoulder, and her fingers drifted over his chest, trailing around his pectoral muscle, then up to the artillery round fragment he kept on a necklace. She traced its shape beneath the T-shirt, as shocked at what she was doing as him not brushing her hand away.

He held his breath for a moment, then sucked in deep. "Toni…"

Without realizing it, she tugged on his T-shirt. "Maybe you could…stay…"

"Toni…"

She pulled his T-shirt away from his belly and ran her hand up the flesh of his chest, almost clawing at him. "…just for a little…"

He pulled her hand free, but instead of pushing her away, he pulled her in closer. Muscles worked along the length of his jaw. "Toni…"

Grier kissed him—a peck on the lips at first, but it quickly grew intense and hot as a star, the sort of thing that would leave her lips tender later. Then his hands were on her and hers on him, and there was a frantic tug of clothes that quickly piled onto the deck with a whisper. He set her on her bunk, then climbed up after her, emotions flashing in his eyes.

Was that lust? Was it regret? Was it anger?

It didn't matter. She had him, and he had her. At least for that moment. Anything else could be worked out later.

Chief Will Parkinson tapped out the last few command sequences, then raised his head from the display. Sitting in a chair to his left, Chief Greta Taylor pinched her bottom lip, which looked discolored in the soft, blue glow coming off the display consoles. The dark hair framing her face merged into the black around her. She was making a soft, wet sucking sound, like she was slurping up her own saliva. That wasn't the problem, though. It was odd having another chief engineer in his shop—an invasion.

And then there was her perfume: abrasive, like a cherry syrup where there should have been grease and overheated electronics. Her bulk—and he couldn't see the big woman's form any other way—intruded into his space, despite the desk separating them.

But Taylor was necessary for his work, probably as close as he had to a peer among the engineers, at least now that Lana Tucci was dead.

Parkinson snorted at that idea.

Taylor's big eyes came up from her terminal, slow and annoyed. "Something funny, Will?"

"I—" He locked on to her big, brown eyes, which seemed to float in the darkness. The display washed out her olive complexion, leaving more of an impression of a computer-generated version of her. Big eyes, wide nose, full lips. "Just thinking about Lana."

"A good memory?"

"It was."

Taylor went back to her display. "So, we run this simulation based on the data you took from all the ships, and it tells us what again?"

"What those Khanate ships were running."

"But they were running the same stealth systems we are. It says so right here in the reports."

He sighed. Tucci would have understood. "Okay, so, let's go through this again. We know—"

Those dark eyes came up from the display again, but they were slitted now, and the ghostly, blue glow that had washed out Taylor's features turned white as she closed the analysis window. "Will?"

"Yes?"

"You haven't really worked with me before."

"No. Lana said—"

"Lana was a good person. Let's leave her out of this, okay?"

Parkinson's ears burned. It felt like Taylor was dressing him down. "I don't—"

The big woman pushed up from her seat, came around the desk, and settled against his desktop, her left thigh spreading out until the jumpsuit's gray fabric touched his keyboard. "You know why I came over here to help you out with this simulation? Right?"

The way she looked down at him and squeezed herself into his space was intimidating. She was a half a head taller and out-massed him by who knew how much. Closer up, he realized it wasn't that she was *fat*, there was just a lot of her. When he'd been brought on to be the *Valor*'s chief engineer—the *task force's* chief engineer—he'd given his team a review. That first day, he'd swiped through the files on his fellow chief engineers, but he'd only given Taylor a cursory look, shrugged, and swiped to the next engineer.

Parkinson didn't consider himself riddled with prejudices, but, really, *big* people weren't professional. Professionals took care of themselves.

He leaned back in his chair, fingers laced behind his head. "You're helping me out because I asked you to—"

She shook a finger at him. "Stop."

Stop? Did she really tell him to stop? "Chief—"

"You have to know we all talk, right?"

"You all…?"

"The chiefs. The women engineers. The people who work with you."

Of course they would talk. They probably spent all their free time talking. "And?"

"And you have a reputation. Someone might be protecting you, but there's talk."

He smiled. "Chief Taylor—"

"Let's keep it casual for now. *Will.* You call me Greta, okay?"

"You *do* realize I'm the chief engineer—"

"We all know who you are. Now, for the next few minutes, you need to listen to me. Understand?"

His smile drained away. "Greta—"

"A nod is good enough." Her lips spread into a grin that told him to shut up. "I came over here because everyone else told you to fuck off. They did that because you've been an abrasive ass since the day we launched. I've got a pile of shit backing up on the *Seattle* that needs my attention, but Commander Karras said to give you a hand, and since no one else is willing to put up with your bullshit, I came over. Are you reading me?"

Parkinson swallowed. He was in charge here, dammit! "Captain Benson—"

"Gave you a priority assignment, and now you're ready to run this simulation that will give her the answers she wants. I understand. What you need to understand is that you can't bully me around. And you can't impress me with your rank, like you try with some of the gals on the *Valor.* And you certainly can't impress me with your decorations or your scores from tech school or anything else you've tried with who knows how many women."

Ah! So Taylor swung that way. He'd never bothered to ask around. "I get where you're coming—"

She leaned forward and grabbed his knee, then squeezed. "No, Will, you don't. If you *got* where I was *coming from*, your mouth would still be closed. Let's try this again. You're working with me because I know I can handle you. Now, what you're going to get through your head—and I mean right now—is that we're not going to waste a lot of time with your whining or posturing or flashing your plumage. You're a smart guy, and you're a little cute, but I've met smarter, and I've fucked cuter. So, get over yourself, and let's get this stupid simulation done. Read me?"

Her fingers dug into his thigh.

Parkinson winced, then nodded.

The tall woman returned to her seat, and her display returned to a ghostly blue. "Here we go, then. We're going to run this simulation to see what?"

He cleared his throat. "So, um, when we were aboard the *Pandora*, we had what must have been a prototype of this stealth system. Someone had sneaked it onboard."

"Okay." She dragged out the word.

"It got us into the DMZ without being detected. A few months later, we used the system to sneak into Azoren space again, but we ran into personal stealth systems that…" He frowned, remembering the way the Azoren soldiers had crept in unseen. The pain of those injuries flashed anew. "They weren't quite comparable, but it was better than what we expected from the Azoren. I tore those systems apart. It was the same basic technology, only it operated at different scales."

"Ship scale and personal scale."

"Exactly. Then when we returned to Kedraal, we ran into a task force of ships with capabilities that nearly matched the *Pandora* system. That wasn't even six months, and that task force had to have been a couple years under construction. The Azoren don't have shipyards to match ours."

"And this Khanate data." She was pinching her bottom lip again. "You think they have a different technology path?"

"Well…no. But they shouldn't have this technology at all. They supposedly didn't have a fleet. Where did they get all those ships? Where did they get this technology we're just now fielding?"

"And the simulation?"

He scratched his scalp. "Maybe it gets us some answers. The signals ships were pulling data the whole time. We've cracked the Khanate encryption, so all the comms traffic, all the signals—" He nodded toward his display. "It's in here."

Her focus went back to her display. "You're thinking there's going to be a trail that points somewhere. Maybe a code base you could tear apart and see where this tech came from."

"*When* it came from. If it really is the same branch of research, it's older. Or maybe there's something we can exploit."

"Yeah, but if you know where the software came from—"

"*When*. What version."

"—then you have an idea of when it was stolen."

"It's a starting point. Captain Benson wants to have investigations into how our tech secrets are showing up in Azoren and Khanate ships."

Taylor slowly nodded. "I'm with you now."

"So, would you mind kicking off Beta when I kick off Alpha?"

"Two simulations, same data, looking for deltas?"

"Or maybe looking for no deltas at all. The idea is to re-run exactly what happened, then run a series of what-ifs, then pull out what should, in theory, happen."

"And to match the output against different versions of our software?"

"Yeah."

"That's gonna take a while."

"Twelve hours. If you can help me dig through the analysis, I think we can cut that in half."

She rocked in her chair. "I'm going to need some coffee."

"Once we launch the simulation, it'll be a couple hours before we have anything to do. I could…escort you up to the mess and we could…grab a drink?"

"Okay. Ready?"

Parkinson tapped a button, and a counter appeared on a small display mounted on the wall over his desk. When it reached zero, they both typed in the commands to launch the simulation, then worked through the prompts to direct the computing pads through the process.

When the big engineer pushed back from her terminal, Parkinson did the same. "Ninety-nine minutes."

She yawned. "Long enough. Not something I say very often." Taylor guffawed.

Parkinson froze, then realized she wasn't glaring at him or anything. She was actually stretching and heading to the exit from his office.

He followed after her, caught between relief and surprise. In the time since she'd been in his office, he'd come to sort of like the cherry perfume. And it wasn't so bad being a little shorter than her any more than it was a big deal that she filled out her coveralls a bit.

In the passageway outside engineering, she turned toward him, eyes narrowed. "What're you looking at?"

"Hm? Oh. I was just curious."

"About?"

"You said you'd…fucked cuter than me, but you're—"

Taylor snorted and leaned in close. "More than you could ever handle."

Parkinson blushed. It sounded like a challenge. Was it a challenge he was up to?

11

____

Gray skies and a steady, cold rain welcomed Faulk to the heart of Paradies. When his car parked across the street from Primary Health Institute One, one of his men rushed from the trailing Night Leopard with an umbrella. That was good, as Faulk's hands were still shaking from the earlier ambush and subsequent purge. Things had gone to plan, but the sharp smell of expended gunpowder clung to him, and the screams of the dying still rang in his ear.

How odd that was. Normally, an enemy's death gurgle was thrilling—a reminder of how well he'd done. Even Karlson's shocked look when he'd pointed his pistol at her...

It's just the cold. Nothing but the cold.

He squeezed his eyes shut and nearly stumbled over a crack in the road, splashing loud enough to be heard over the downpour and staggering without a hint of grace.

Then there was a hand on his arm, supporting him. The commando's voice was a hiss. "The roads show damage from battle, Field Marshal."

Faulk nodded. "I shall see to it they are fixed."

That was something he could say now, stomping up the slick marble steps gone a sickly, enervated gray, leading the unquestioned largest single force in the military, holding the most senior title and the last promotion given by Supreme Leader Graf.

"You will be my legacy, Child." The old man had managed a rictus smile with some effort, atrophied muscles tugging his lips wide and showing dull teeth.

Those words had been spoken to many of Faulk's brothers in the past, and none of them were alive to talk about it.

He didn't need their counsel. The meaning was plain enough: I will use you until nothing remains, then I will support the next bright young thing to rise up, and you will be another nameless corpse in a mass grave.

The man holding the umbrella could easily be the one to put a bullet in Faulk's head. Doing so would lead to a promotion, at least based on history. That had been the first step to Faulk rising above, after all.

Supreme Commander Graf values initiative.

Guards stopped him and his escort at the private entry on the side of the building. They were dressed in the same black uniform but proudly wore the red skull of the supreme leader's elite bodyguards. Beneath the crisp uniform jackets, a thin layer of armor protected their muscular bodies from small arms and knives. Drugs kept them alert, their reflexes lightning quick. Their eyes were genetically modified to not only detect heat anomalies and minor tics but to be sensitive to aberrations in human behavior—sweating, heavy breathing, blinking.

Yet assassins had twice come so very close to killing Graf.

It was hard to celebrate that. After all, Faulk hoped to have these men guarding him within a year, once the old man finally succumbed.

And he *would* succumb at some point.

After checking and re-checking credentials, Faulk was waved through. His bodyguard was directed into a waiting area just inside the side door. There was no fear or anger in the young man's blue eyes. They were emotionless, almost dead.

Faulk's boots squeaked on the black marble, leaving behind thin streaks of water. He saluted each of the Red Skull bodyguards manning every intersection in pairs, alert eyes darting, evaluating his threat posture.

He was directed up to a surgical theater that looked down onto a green-tiled room. Nurses shuffled around, setting out trays and testing gear. No one paid attention to him, even when he powered on the console that showed a high-resolution video of the surgical station that held everyone's attention. The silvery glow of the display brought on a hint of nausea, so the field marshal turned it back off.

What he needed to know, he now knew. The Kedraalian doctor was moving around in the surgery room below, talking with the people he'd be working with. Dressed in pale gray scrubs, the man was just another instrument in the Azoren surgical kit now.

The old doctor's head bent low, then he nodded and looked up toward Faulk. "Field Marshal Faulk?"

There was a button on the console somewhere, a way to turn on his own microphone. Ah. There. "Doctor Dietrich."

"Come to oversee the surgery?"

"I am."

"Have you ever seen spinal cord surgery? Do you have any idea what it will look like?"

"I *am* a combat veteran, Commander."

"That's nice." There was a smirk in his voice, which the mask covering his face couldn't hide. "It's tricky work. The equipment you have here is primitive. I might as well be using a meat cleaver and a heated poker."

"That would not end well for you."

"My point, Field Marshal, is that I could do better transporting the supreme leader up to the *Valor*."

Faulk thought of the steely-eyed Red Skull guards and chuckled. "No, Doctor. That isn't an option."

"Then get me Ensign Kohn. He's worked with me on this sort of injury."

"The Jew?" The field marshal laughed. "Even less likely."

"You throw that around like it's an insult. Why not call him 'the genius' or 'the doctor'?"

"Because he *is* a Jew, Doctor Dietrich."

"You're a despicable, nauseating monster who has sipped poison and cancer from the teat of a beast your entire artificial life. You're worthy of nothing but scorn and revulsion."

"Really, now. You've put more venom in your description of me as a genetically engineered person than I feel for your Jew."

"My hatred isn't because you were created in a lab. It's because of what they did to you after."

"I see. Is that your professional opinion, Doctor?"

The decorated Kedraalian surgeon looked away. "I've made my professional opinion known. Ensign Kohn's presence would greatly increase the odds of success."

Pain shot through Faulk's jaw—he was grinding his teeth. The doctor had maneuvered cleverly, his words forcing the issue. "I will get you your…" The field marshal licked his lips. "I will get you your *genius*, Doctor. And I will personally shoot him if Supreme Leader Graf expires on that surgical table."

Faulk exited the surgical theater with a smirk and slowly descended the stairs. Despite the surgeon getting his way, things were actually going to plan. How much better could the situation be? He almost laughed but stopped short when he opened the door at the bottom of the stairs.

Two of the Red Skull bodyguards were waiting for him, cold, dead eyes unblinking. Their submachine guns weren't pointed at him but were positioned at the ready, where it would take no effort at all to bring them up and fire.

He could call for his people to storm the hospital, but that would be a bloody struggle, and he would likely die before they could reach him.

The field marshal straightened. "Yes?"

One of the guards blinked slowly. "You will accompany us, Field Marshal."

Not a request. No salutation or hint of respect. He was the third most powerful man in the Azoren hierarchy, yet here he was, staring powerlessly at those who might be planning to execute him. Saying no wasn't a realistic option. Then again, if they'd wanted him dead, they could have shot him before he entered the hospital or at any number of intersections.

Faulk gave the slightest bow of his head. "Lead on."

They moved through hallways with a steady, quick pace, neither acknowledging their fellows on guard nor being acknowledged by them. Nurses and doctors stopped at the thud of the boots, stared wide-eyed, then scurried away, seeking offices or tasks that might make them seem unimportant.

Like vermin hiding from the predator.

Finally, they turned through a pair of stainless steel doors that swung open without a sound. The sharp smell of detergents and bleach; the bright polish and swirl of well-maintained stainless steel tables; the chill of an environment meant to preserve the flesh; the scrape of hard soles on the sloping, tiled floor. And the tall, lanky man—stooped with age—who had created Faulk and his brothers: Purity Minister King.

Father.

The old man stalked the edge of the room, long, bony fingers hooked around each other at the small of his back. His gait was lengthy and slow. The man was known for his patience and perseverance. How else could he conquer the mysteries of DNA, creating the most perfect version of the human race ever imagined?

At the farthest corner, he stopped and turned, fixing piercing green eyes on Faulk. "You've visited the surgical theater?" His accent wasn't like most of the Azoren. It said "outsider," yet he'd risen to where he was through hard work.

"I have."

"What is your impression?"

"This is a highly decorated surgeon. He has no lack of eccentricity, but his record is remarkable. Our own surgeons deferred to him after hearing his diagnosis of the threat the injuries pose to the supreme leader."

The old man squinted. "Hm."

It wasn't a challenge but an acknowledgment and a signal that some thought on the matter was required. There must have been new data in Faulk's words, something that intrigued or surprised his superior.

That realization made Faulk tingle. This was a father pleased by his son.

Such a rare delight, surprising someone so intelligent and wise. The piercing green eyes, the soft features that could have been equally at home on a strong woman, the unflappable, calm voice…

How could such a man not have been created in a lab, same as his children?

Now the old man strode closer, spider-like arms coming around, the left one slowly descending over the field marshal's shoulder. A minty huff almost blocked out a trace of days-old sweat, as if the simple uniform—a white jacket, black pants, and a black tie—had hung off the bony shoulders for a while. "He has requested assistance."

"He has. I was preparing to send a team to retrieve his student."

"Very wise. He forced you to accept an uncomfortable situation; you reversed it onto him by framing the implications of an unfavorable outcome."

"That didn't seem to worry him."

"A surgeon of his skill cannot conceive of failure."

The long, wiry arm pulled free of Faulk's back, and the pacing resumed. After a minute, the second most powerful man in the Azoren hierarchy came to a stop and looked around, as if he might have suddenly remembered something. One eye widened. "You've killed your counselor."

"Colonel Karlson was…a negative influence."

"The war has them stretched thin."

"Of course."

"You are functioning without her guidance?"

Faulk's breath caught. Thoughts compressed his chest: her gas mask being placed against his face, unleashing its intoxicating fumes; her inhuman flesh pressed against his: her cold voice whispering reminders of doctrine and propaganda. "I have no need for a…counselor at this point."

"That is reassuring. And you can maintain such independence for the duration of this war?"

"Of course. I intend to resolve it quickly."

"Wars are rarely won quickly."

"You know my capabilities."

"I do. A bright, bright star. You make us proud." The old man stalked the room a bit more. "You have one hundred thousand soldiers in orbit. Keeping them fed each day strains our capabilities and those of the fleet."

"We will launch soon enough."

"Then you must have talked strategy with your Kedraalian counterpart."

"Today."

"I see." The lanky scientist stroked his chin. "I've summoned them already. Meet them in the cafeteria. Develop your plan with their input. Be ready to launch."

"I worry for my father—Supreme Commander Graf. He faces a very uncertain and risky surgery."

Long arms stretched out, and the old man's big hands settled on Faulk's shoulders. For someone so old and thin, there was strength in the grip. "*I* am your father. Waste no time worrying for me."

"I meant the father of our great Azoren nation."

"Supreme Commander Graf lives, or perhaps he dies. This outcome changes nothing. Your concern is beyond our space—the Moskav and Khanate threats. End those threats, and that will leave only the minor annoyance of the Kedraalians to contend with. Do this, and you will take the seat of power uncontested."

Faulk puffed out his chest. The look of pride in the other man's eyes threatened to bring out tears. "I will do this."

The old man gently patted Faulk's cheek. "You will, my son."

There was a twinkle in the old man's green eyes when he turned, as if he, too, might be feeling the sort of pride Faulk was. The pair of Red Skull guards who had earlier acted as escort fell in on either side of the scientist and exited, leaving Faulk alone in the cold room.

Once again, the old man had made clear that he had no interest in the power that he would have a rightful claim to. Graf had appointed the old man second in power years ago, when the success of the program had been undeniable.

Why would any man not pursue such power?

Because, Faulk realized, the old man could have the power without the responsibility. The scientist had if not dictated then heavily influenced Azoren policy for years, using the doddering supreme leader as a convenient front.

Faulk tugged the ends of his coat sleeves. "Well, Father, that will end when your favored son takes command. Careful that I don't consider you too great a threat."

It occurred to Faulk that he'd been given orders.

The Kedraalians. Discussing strategy. The cafeteria.

Although it was an annoying development, there was inevitability to it. If they intended to launch an attack at some point, they had to have agreement on what that would look like.

He breathed in deep, then held his breath. The chance to prove himself, to seize power—it was coming.

When it came, the heavens would burn.

12

Benson wrapped her arms around herself, feeling terribly out of place. She was still dressed in the flannel shirt and jeans, and Thiessen still wore the simple field worker clothing he'd worn back at the manor. The clothes were too warm for the stuffy cafeteria, where they'd been deposited by more of the black-uniformed men. Everyone who had come into the big room since the two of them had settled in the back corner wore uniforms of some sort. There were the gray jacket and pants of what apparently belonged to the typical soldiers, and there were the black jacket and pants with whatever trappings designated company or battalion or—

She really didn't know how the Azoren structured their military. No one knew anymore.

Thiessen took a seat on a plastic bench so that his back was toward the service area and the few pockets of people eating. "I think I've had enough of the staring."

"And all the whispering." Benson rested her elbows on the table and massaged her forehead. "I think I'd be hungry if this headache would go away. At least it's dark in here."

"You okay? You seem to have headaches a lot."

"Oh. Since I was a kid. It's nothing. The medicine they gave me for the concussion aftereffects is actually making things worse."

"Well, that food smells pretty rich. It could be bugging you."

"Sausages of some sort, I think. Spicy, whatever it is. I'd love it."

"The food we had when I was a kid was either simple and meant to keep you from starving or greasy and meant to celebrate."

Benson frowned. "I'm sorry."

"Don't be. I'm not. I'm alive."

It was a refreshing perspective. "I'll try to remember that. Any idea why they brought us here?"

"It's a hospital of some sort. I saw doctors and nurses."

"All the differences we have and all this time living apart, but we're still mostly the same."

"Yeah. It's the same language, isn't it?"

"Except for some colloquialisms and new words that pop up. Well, discounting the Khanate."

"Do they actually speak a different language, or do they just have that goofy alphabet and the weird prayers and..." He shrugged, but the meaning was obvious: their strange outfits, their personal grooming habits, the way their names all sounded alike.

She'd heard they went as far as changing names to whatever their titles were. How would it feel to be named *Captain*?

The thought only worsened her headache. "A common language should be enough to bring us together."

"Is that so?" The corner of Thiessen's mouth ticked up in a smirk.

"A lot of misunderstanding comes from differences."

"You remember when that blast brought the ceiling down?"

"I'm not forgetting that anytime soon."

"The old general who survived on the side of the room with me? Weber? I had a chance to talk with him after the shock wore off."

Benson leaned closer. "He *talked* to you?"

"Oh, yeah. Once he shook off the effects, I couldn't get him to shut up."

"Faulk wanted to kill everyone. He shot a couple of his rivals. I think he would've shot Graf if Dietrich and Kohn hadn't been there. Kohn said

Faulk had this psychotic gleam in his eyes, like there wasn't even a mind working."

"Yeah, that's it exactly. Weber was terrified."

"Faulk couldn't get through that wall. He didn't even want—"

"Not of Faulk—*all* of them. The ones he called Children."

"If they're all psychotic murderers, it makes sense."

"They must be something. He was terrified. Comatose, barely breathing, paralyzed—he was still scared. He told me he would shoot them all dead if it wouldn't lead to his execution."

"Faulk's still alive."

"That's another thing that's the same everywhere, isn't it? Different rules for different people."

Benson glanced past the Gulmar captain at the pockets of Azoren soldiers watching them. The humans in gray seemed to shoot furtive glances at the Children in black as often as at the two off-worlders. "They're a strange group, aren't they? Outsiders, even among the people they fight alongside."

"Animals. Weber called them demon spawn. He said they came from a place called hell."

"They're certainly predators. I can't imagine people care for that."

Thiessen leaned in. "He begged for us to rescue him."

"He asked us to—?"

"Well, I don't mean that he *said* it. It was in the way he looked at me. You know?" The handsome Gulmar captain's eyebrows rose in a question.

"Are you...asking me to scheme to sneak a senior Azoren officer off this planet?"

"Could we?"

She sat back and closed her eyes, again rubbing her forehead. Weber was a member of the High Command, as senior as General Guderian, assuming he was still alive. There weren't many more high-value targets in any of the rebel powers. His intelligence value would be incalculable. The damage he could do...

Benson shook her head. "It would push the Azoren into war."

"A war that—"

Faulk marched through the entry, neck craning and eyes squinting.

Searching. Benson waved for Thiessen to be quiet and nodded toward the field marshal.

The Gulmar captain groaned softly, then turned, stood, and waved the other man over. "Field Marshal Faulk."

It took a moment, but the Azoren officer straightened, then made a beeline for them. His eyes were focused on Benson. When he reached the table, he barely nodded at Thiessen, then took a seat at the end of the Gulmar captain's bench. "Captain Benson, how good to see you."

She caught the color in Thiessen's cheeks and his narrowed eyes, but the reaction came and went. Jealousy? Her own cheeks flushed. "It's a relief to know you're alive."

"I will outlive my Azoren comrades, Captain. Trust me."

That seemed an odd boast and maybe even misplaced, but she wasn't in the right condition to question it. "We weren't hoping for anyone to be dead."

"Of course not. The two of you live fortunate lives where there are alternatives."

Thiessen spread out slightly, setting one elbow down closer to the other man, then leaning a chin on the upraised hand. "There are only two alternatives on Himmel? Is that 'dead' or 'alive'?"

Without turning to acknowledge Thiessen, Faulk smiled coolly. "Something along those lines, yes."

"A lot of people where I grew up lived in between."

"As well for your people, Captain Thiessen. There are only two states: in power or dying."

The words dug into the Gulmar captain, who blushed and looked away.

Benson wanted to hold him, assure him things would be better soon. It was a silly, maternal feeling. Well, not *maternal.*

She shook her head to clear it, then frowned at Faulk. "I have a question."

"Yes?"

"The way we've been shuffled around—"

"For your own safety."

"Fine. Thank you. But, well, we came here as diplomats seeking an alliance."

"Of course. You have made this point."

"I feel more like a prisoner."

"Unfortunate but necessary. You see, Captain, things have become a little more unpredictable of late. The timing of your arrival has been either fortuitous or terrible, depending upon your perspective."

"Terrible, I think."

"Is it? For me, it would seem fortuitous. You offer options we seek."

"Options? You don't even have a High Command to make that assessment."

There was something of a pout on the field marshal's face for a second, but it twisted into a triumphant smile at the mention of the ruling body. "Ah! But you see, I *am* the High Command."

"You?"

"With Supreme Commander Graf ready to undergo surgery and no other members yet appointed—"

Thiessen wheeled back around. "You killed General Weber?"

"Not yet." Faulk's lips curled down just shy of a frown. "He has, however, suffered an unfortunate accident."

"Oh?"

"Yes. It is only a matter of time now, sadly. His service will be missed."

Benson swallowed. "And General Guderian?"

"A tragic fatality of the blast."

The Gulmar captain shot a look at Benson that said he was done with Faulk. She was, too, but they had a mission.

She bit her bottom lip. "Field Marshal Faulk, it might be better for us to return to our ships until Supreme Commander Graf has recovered from his surgery."

"You would leave your two brilliant surgeons behind?"

"What?" Her heart seemed to lose any semblance of a rhythm.

"Your Commander Dietrich and the…*genius*. They operate on Graf at this very moment."

"Dietrich's doing the actual surgery?" It was a stupid question. She'd known all along he would oversee the old man's recovery.

"At his insistence. Our own surgeons are unfamiliar with the proposed method of approach. Spinal injuries leave people crippled, and we have no room for the weak, so this is not something our medical system has been built to support."

"Ernie—Dr. Dietrich is as good as it gets, but—"

"Good, then! If Supreme Commander Graf survives, so do Commander Dietrich and his aide."

There it was—the psychotic ultimatum she'd been dreading. "They came down as diplomatic advisors."

"Your doctor should have reminded himself of this before inserting himself into situations such as he has. Now, it is time we begin discussion of the strategies you would pursue against this Khanate military that has arisen out of nowhere."

"Any discussions really should include Commander Dietrich."

"Captain." Faulk's lips spread wide, as if he might distend his jaw. "Your doctor is no strategist, and that is our concern. Now…please." He tilted his head, as if inviting her into a cozy tea room.

She slipped her hands under the table and balled them into fists. The man really was a monster. "All right. You've had a chance to read the initial plan—"

"I have. It has the flaw of exposing Himmel and our other holdings to Moskav attacks."

Once again, exactly as she'd expected. "Our understanding is that the Moskav fleet consists of nothing more than cargo ships. Those are unarmed and can't possibly threaten even a modest defense force."

"The same was understood about the Khanate, was it not?"

"But you've been fighting the Moskav for years now. You would know their—"

Faulk held up a finger. "Here are our requirements, Captain. The Moskav must be broken before we assist you against the Khanate threat. They must be broken in a way that leaves their planets and much of the existing infrastructure intact for us to exploit."

"There will be other claims to the resources—"

He wagged the finger. "Ah, ah! These are our *requirements*, you see."

Thiessen scowled but did nothing else. The Gulmar leadership and the

Kedraalian parliament might accept turning a blind eye to blowing the Moskav out of existence, but neither governing group would accept the Azoren taking over the planets freed up by the massacre.

She'd known from the start that breaking the Moskav would be the most likely Azoren demand. Breaking them so that the Azoren could simply waltz in and claim the planets? They weren't even particularly good planets, but like most that had been settled, they were terraformed and offered Earth-like conditions or near enough to be valuable, mineral reserves or not.

Benson drove a knuckle into her thigh. "How would you propose doing this?"

The field marshal smacked his lips together. "The Moskav have a planned economy, primitive and anemic as it is. Every aspect of their governance—food growth, harvesting, and distribution—begins and ends in their central government planning committee."

"I'm familiar with that."

"Yes. Your own parliament follows a similar model, does it not?"

She gritted her teeth. It was that or correct him. "You want to disrupt or bring down their central planning—?"

Faulk again wagged his finger. "Captain. No."

"Then—"

"I want you to approach them with the same proposal you have made to us. Promise them alliance and financial aid and who knows what else. Your imagination is limitless, it would seem. Whatever temptation is necessary, have them bring together their group of leaders. When you do that, we strike."

"Strike? Engage their military?"

"Yes. Where it matters. There, in the capital. And we bomb their leadership."

"While I'm negotiating a treaty?"

"We secret you out, of course. Your only purpose is to wave the white flag and offer the alliance. Once that draws the roaches from their hiding places and brings them together to discuss war, we eliminate them and the military committed to their protection. After that, the rest is a small matter of seizing key points in the capital, destroying transportation infrastructure, and holding out until the populace starves to death. It would be a matter of weeks, and the damage done would be irrevocable."

"But there are tens of millions—"

"When food is a requirement for survival, and you eliminate its availability, the problem becomes elementary."

The civilians. He intended to kill... "There would be disease. The capital—"

"My logistics people have run the models. The secret is to round up the surviving civilians and turn them into a workforce to clear the dead. Burn the corpses. As the civilians die, the remaining survivors gather up the newly dead. By the end, the remaining corpses would be in manageable numbers."

"You've...run models?"

"Oh, yes, Captain. We've only not executed this plan because we lack the capacity to draw their governmental leaders into a single place that we can attack. Since the war began, they've hidden like cowards, dispersed in the city sprawl and in smaller settlements. With you presenting the idea of an alliance..." He spread his hands wide, almost like a hug. "We can finally strike."

"That would be...lying. Dishonorable—"

Faulk chuckled. "That is war, Captain. Whether they die by bomb or starvation only matters based on intent. My people want those worlds without destroying them."

She couldn't meet Thiessen's eyes. The deception was on her. "How would I know you wouldn't do something to get me killed?"

The field marshal slid out from the table and looked down at her. "Why, you will have my word, won't you?"

***

Rain pounded the night-black windows of the Patel Dramoran mansion. It wasn't a steady drumming that might relax McLeod's nerves but a machinegun burst that would go silent only to begin again a few seconds later. Still, he looked up from his fragrant Mulligatawny soup with a smile, letting the hot coconut milk wash over his tongue while the curry settled. Across the long, pale wooden table, seeming almost regal in her bright magenta robes, Devanshi Patel seemed focused on her own bowl. As much as dinner alone with her felt like a deadly sport, he could at least enjoy the quality of the food her staff served.

He slurped another spoonful, crunching on the lentils. "It's quite good."

The Patel matriarch nodded. "Sridevi has her skills."

Thunder rumbled, and it felt as if a giant hammer were being smashed against the ground outside. The chandelier over the table swayed, crystals jangling delicately, and the furnace laboring to keep the palatial building warm sputtered, then stopped.

McLeod cocked an eyebrow at her. "Is this a particularly bad storm?"

Her shoulders rode up in her robes, then settled back down. "They can all be bad. We have a generator should it become a problem."

"That's resourceful."

"Necessary. Our business is too demanding to go long without power."

"I could see that."

She pointed her spoon at him. "What about you? Your business is critical as well, is it not?"

"It is. I spent the day catching up."

"Amazing they could afford to lose someone so vital to a trip like this."

"The military's pretty robust, actually."

"Not the Group for Strategic Assessment. Samir was always going on about how SAID was ten times the size of the GSA."

"We might be a little more careful about our spending."

"I see. Sometimes, actually having the money to spend makes for greater effect."

A young man came out of the kitchen door to McLeod's left and gathered the bowls onto a silver platter. Everything was polished and extraordinarily expensive looking. Authentic. He knew the money behind the Patels. He knew *money*. He'd grown up around plenty himself, but they had it to spare and didn't so much flaunt it as...present constant reminders of its presence.

The old woman leaned back as another young man came out of the kitchen with a tray. He set a plate out in front of her, then a smaller plate, then a small bowl. Sweet and spicy steam rose off the orange sauce and meats. After setting McLeod's food in front of him, the young man returned to the kitchen.

Spices. Coconut milk. Meat. Vegetables. All of it was expensive, brought in from another world where Earth products could grow and animals raised without expensive localized solutions.

It was a show for McLeod.

He tore a piece of naan. "I don't think I ever had the chance to tell you just how sorry I was about Samir's tragic loss. It simply hasn't been the same since his passing."

"No." A quiver ran through the Patel matriarch's cheek. "It has not."

"To lose Srisha, too. Have you been holding up okay?"

"A mother never truly recovers from the loss of her child. Your mother must have told you that."

McLeod dabbed at the sauce and unclenched his jaw. It was a good shot—effective. His mother had never recovered from his...reputation being dragged through the mud. "We don't talk anymore."

"The same as loss, isn't it?"

"It certainly feels like it."

"Well, it's reassuring to see that your career survived yet another scandal."

"Some things are worse than others. Rational people can see this."

"Rational seems to me a curious word."

"For some people."

Devanshi took a sip of wine, then patted her lips with a napkin. "I assume your father hoped you might come back and take over the business."

"He's past that point now. They don't need me."

"Was it you who decided on that, or did you leave the matter to them?"

McLeod took a sip of his wine. Like the food, it was good—dry but not to the point he couldn't enjoy it. "Has someone risen up to replace Samir when you retire?"

"No one could replace Samir, Avis."

"That's true. It's reflected in his decorations and commendations."

"Neither of those comfort a mother at night." She poked at her chicken. "What brings you to Dramora?"

"I've always wanted to see it in winter."

"It's an ugly place all year 'round."

"The thought of seeing it covered in snow was tempting."

"We don't see snow here. Not in the city."

"One can hope."

The old woman lifted her wine glass, then set it to her lips. Her eyes remained locked on him as she finished the fluid. She set the glass down. "You've never been one for travel. Why would that change now?"

"Old age, I think. It makes us seek adventure, doesn't it?"

Her eyebrows crept up. "Old age brings wisdom, actually. Would you truly consider it wise to come to this planet?"

"It's duty. Nothing more."

"Duty gets people killed, you know." Devanshi stabbed a piece of chicken.

"We know that when we sign on."

"I would imagine you do." She chewed quietly.

One of the young serving men rushed out with another cup of wine, then hurried back into the kitchen.

I'm afraid of her, McLeod realized.

If she were ready to act, killing him in the remote mansion was as good a place as any. Better. She could have her staff poison him with the meal, then dump his body out in the desert. No one would ever be able to even make an accusation. No one would try.

Fortunately, that wasn't really her style.

While he could, McLeod focused on the tasty meal and the shelter the mansion offered.

When the last of the plates had been taken away and black, earthy coffee had been set in front of him, he patted his belly. "Thank you once again, Devanshi. That was better than any meal I've had in some time."

"Of course it was. You spend your days in that hideous little Ministry of Defense building, eating what they pass for food. That's no comparison."

A jolt of concern jogged his heart. She had a spy in the building. She had a spy in the building to watch *him*. "Fortunately, it's far too long a flight, or I'd impose on you more often."

"Tell me something, Avis."

"Yes?"

"Have you sent an assassin after me? Because if you have, they won't succeed. And if they try…" A malicious grin spread her lips. "Well, my retaliation won't be as sloppy."

She knew, or at least she suspected. Maybe she was behind Stiles's death. But if Devanshi had been certain Stiles had been an assassin, then the connection hadn't been solidified.

What mattered, though, was that there was at least suspicion.

He sipped his coffee. "The GSA doesn't have assassins, Devanshi."

"Neither do I." Her dark eyes were like ice.

He needed to locate Stiles's body and get off Dramora, and he needed to do it fast.

13

Satrap stirred a spoon through the bowl of rice, olives, and spiced meats. His stomach was acting up again, threatening to turn at the scent of anything richer than rice porridge. Even the advanced nutrients fed directly into his bloodstream couldn't stop the digestive nightmare once it started. All he could do was breathe in the aromas and watch Ikhama's look of pleasure as she indulged in the delicacy. Dressed in her thick, white robes, she sat to his right at the table that had, only a few months before, hosted captains who eventually conspired to kill them both. It was all because those commanders wanted blood, and their commander wasn't delivering it quickly enough.

That and the fact that they were undisciplined rabble raised on the notion that the only way to rise was to tear someone else down.

He was in command of feral monsters concerned only with mayhem and murder.

A soft hum came from the equipment that kept Satrap's shriveled, broken body alive, and a cocktail of medicine tingled in his veins. He was hauled from place to place in the service of the Great and Glorious Khan, suffering through pain and crippling disability thanks to that same depraved old man. Satrap might never understand exactly what had provoked the twisted leader of the Khanate into such violence. Fear, perhaps. Self-loathing for what he had done to the child Satrap had been.

His cheeks burned at those memories.

Ikhama set down the glass of lemonade she'd been sipping at. *"To rise, one must first fall. The greater the fall, the higher the climb—for the strong."*

Her words were tiny daggers of shame. Institutionalized lunacy and corruption. That was how his condition was even possible. Hers was no different. She had been a victim of the old beast, yet she embraced the religion that turned him into the manifestation of the originator of the sick and twisted mess they were cloaked in.

Satrap let his spoon slip from shaking fingers. "How can you sleep at night knowing what he did to you—even worse spread his poison?"

Her wrinkly, gold skin took on an unhealthy ashen tone. "Survival."

"That's your excuse?"

"Yours is different, Satrap?"

There. She'd said what needed saying. He was just as complicit, choosing service as the supreme commander of the largest and most deadly fleet ever launched rather than having the temerity to stand up to the beast back on Azh Shivan. "No different. At least I..." The broken man sagged. "No different."

At the entry to the dining facility, the hard-eyed man who had taken over the Jakkara bodyguards who protected Satrap took a step, perhaps sensing Satrap's anxiety and self-loathing as a threat.

He waved the man away. Chemicals and surgical procedures were slowly turning the bodyguard into the sort of fearless warrior who would kill and die in service to his master. For now, it was equally the oath taken and the fear of repercussions against all he loved that created the loyalty.

Worthy punishment. The man had been part of the assassination attempt that had nearly cost Satrap and Ikhama their lives.

Satrap stared into the bowl of food. "We will be finished soon."

The captain of the guard returned to his post, his ochre robes rustling over the red armor plates that could protect him from small arms fire.

But they would be useless against the ship weapons of his own fleet.

What had happened in that failed coup had stolen the last shred of confidence and hope in Satrap. He had told himself that leading the fleet was the cost of one day being free of the Khan and his sick empire. Nearly being slaughtered by those who were ostensibly subordinates?

I will never live to know freedom. I will die out here, victory or not.

Because treachery was the way of the Khan and his followers.

Ikhama pushed her bowl away. *"Trouble dimples the brow of the king, dreaming not of empire but a walk in the meadows and the kiss of his love.* What troubles you?"

"An excess of metaphorical nonsense."

"The universe exists despite such a travesty."

Satrap smiled. "That almost sounded like humor."

"In effort, there is as much reward as in success; yet only success grants the ultimate victory."

He waved surrender. "You win."

"That does not address your pain."

"Now you are my doctor?"

"A salve for the soul might act—"

"That's enough. My pain is the anxiety of the impossible."

"Your task?"

"My task, combined with what passes for help from the mentally deficient—"

"In all the heavens, none shines as bright as the Grand and Glorious Khan!"

Satrap bit his lip. "Those who operate in the service of the Khan but who fail to execute his vision. I spoke of those. They conspire against his dream of serenity."

Ikhama bowed. She had developed a higher tolerance for his indiscretions since surviving the mutiny, but even she had a limit. It was the hardware installed in her. It would capture heresy and transmit it back to Azh Shivan unless she managed to suppress the systems. Some things couldn't be left to her discretion, though.

It was the illusion of freedom they all endured.

She slowly twisted her lemonade glass on the tabletop. "What have the bureaucrats done now?"

"We've spent weeks in hiding, effecting repairs, implementing workarounds. In that time, I've identified what we can't repair or replace.

I've also made modifications to the strategy and tactics doctrine based on our resources and what we've learned."

"And your work was brilliant, Satrap."

"This morning, the first wave of reinforcements and resupply arrived."

"Our Khan knows no limits. His bountiful wisdom and mercy—"

"At least I thought it was the first wave. Apparently, it was the *only* wave."

The old woman folded the fingers of one hand over the other. "I see."

"You act as if I'm trying to test you."

"Our Khan and—"

"Our Khan, our officers, our soldiers…" He bunched a hand into a small, feeble fist. "You do recall that your faith and purity did nothing to keep you from being targeted. Right? You were seconds from death, same as me."

She covered her face with a hand. "Your task—"

"Yes. My impossible task, you see. Conquer those who would threaten us, and slaughter the heathen. With what? With doctrine?" He held up his spoon. "With this? I need ships of war. I need systems upgrades. I need a simple, clear reminder to be sent to the officers who tried to kill us. What was sent? More suicide pilots. More tenders full of the mush my soldiers and engineers and technicians must subsist on. Delicacies like this—" He struck the bowl with the spoon, producing a soft ring. "—for those same mutinous officers. *Not* the destroyers I requested. Not assurances that the deceitful and venal captains would be made to understand that their role was to follow me, their Satrap."

"Work proves most fruitful when it comes through clever efforts rather than undue exertion."

"That is perhaps the most criminal of all the parables and observations."

"It is no less true."

"We now have nearly four hundred more terrified boys to strap into life-sign-monitoring harnesses that will detonate bombs that will tear them and their fighters into pieces smaller than the tip of my thumb."

"Three dozen virgins await all who die in the service—"

"Ikhama, if you've suffered the way these people have suffered, they aren't going to want a virgin."

She bowed her head. "The pleasure of the new life comes from singing the praises of the Khan, not from exploiting the flesh."

"There is no hope of victory."

"What of the special missile designs sent with the reinforcements?"

"It would take a miracle for those to make a difference in our engagements."

"Miracles are the work of our Khan."

Satrap leaned back in his chair, wincing when a needle dug deeper into a vein. He missed his humanity—the ability to enjoy the touch of food on his tongue, the gentle whisper of cloth against his flesh, the taste of a woman—taken from him for no other reason than the curse of brilliance. Why had he been burdened with intellect when it was something largely bred out of his people?

They aren't my people.

It was a trick of circumstance that trapped him in this environment, on this ship, in this moment. Now he must do inhuman and superhuman things or die.

Ikhama coughed. "The Khan sent a message with the reinforcements?"

"Wisdom for the ages. He said that my task remained as unchanged as the mountains and as certain as the tides of the seas."

"That is wise." She bowed, as if authentically impressed.

Satrap held back a laugh. "Might I interject a point of trivial tactical observation?"

"Against a thousand armed with metal and gunpowder, I rode out on steeds of sinew with no metal of my own except the sabers crafted by Xenu. And with only three hundred, I slew them all."

"Victors write history. Even more importantly, the delusional reimagine events that might share less than an atom with reality."

"Xenu fashioned weapons from the stars."

It was too much for the crippled leader. "You asked what troubled me, and I tried to tell you."

"I listen, Satrap."

"Do you *hear*? Every time I try to point out that we've been giving nothing to stand against this Kedraalian captain, you offer up that—"

She shook her head—just enough for him to see. "Wisdom."

"Wisdom. That fleet should have, by all rights, been shattered in a single strike, same as we saw against the Gulmar. Obviously, someone has lied to us about the capabilities of these stealth systems."

"Yet you said that they worked against the Gulmar."

"Yes. But Gulmar ships are nothing compared to the Kedraalians. That's even more true for the crews. If we had succeeded against the Kedraalians, this war would already be on its way to a quiet, inevitable conclusion."

"Mistakes were made."

Satrap snorted. "Take your pick of them. Incompetent and mutinous officers. Infighting. Refusal to follow orders. There was no shortage of error."

"Rectify the failures, and assert yourself anew."

"You do understand that our systems were nearly overcome by the Kedraalian systems, don't you? They *saw* us. They *attacked* us. We were assured we could strike from the shadows, tearing down our enemies with ease."

"Rectify the failures—"

"Ikhama, our strategy and tactics derive from the promised capabilities of these systems. There is no rectifying. They aren't failures. We were sold a counterfeit bill of goods."

The old woman closed her eyes. "Adapt."

"That was what I tried to do. That order for six more destroyers was adapting. With more firepower to support our suicide bomber-fighters, we have a chance to overwhelm them. With a simple upgrade to the systems provided, we might be able to sneak in just a little closer before they locate us. It's a matter of centimeters to move us from a close battle to outright victory."

"Our people have done what they could. Time matters."

Not my *people.* "A few months to wait for ships to be converted or constructed isn't going to change—"

"Time. Matters."

Satrap slumped. She *had* seen the message from Azh Shivan after all. "Of course it matters. So I've made a change that will work around the limitations we face."

Her wispy eyebrows rose slightly. "This is good."

"My mandate is the timeline—the conquest of our enemies within the next year."

"Entirely plausible."

"If I receive my requested reinforcements." He held up a hand to stop her before she could interrupt. "Absolute destruction of the enemy. But I also have to satiate my bloodthirsty underlings."

"Glory to the Khan."

He couldn't tell if she was being ironic. A few weeks ago, he wouldn't have believed that was even possible. "What I need from you, Ikhama, is support."

She tilted her head, confused. "I have given nothing but support."

"Compared to my officers, you're a mountain. I speak of the future, not the past. My needs are for you to be there when I introduce our new course, just as you were before."

"Your new strategy?"

"Yes. I've taken liberties with the doctrine, modifying things to adjust for our diminished capabilities."

"*Our strength is as the highest wave of the sea.*"

Once again, he signaled surrender. "Our differently capable force."

That brought a small, satisfied grin to her face. "You kept us alive, when the universe seemed ready to allow us to die. I will support you."

I will support you. The words took an unimaginable weight off his chest. "Thank you."

Satrap swallowed, then pulled a data pad from his robes, set the device on the table, and connected to Captain Zohar, the commander of the *Might of the Khan*, the fleet's flagship. "Captain, do you have a moment?"

Zohar's face resolved on the pad's screen—younger than Satrap, with brown hair swept back from a high forehead. He had a hooked nose and protruding chin. His green eyes sparkled with irritation. The irritation didn't come from the call but from the defeat suffered at his superior's hands. "How might I serve you, Satrap?"

"I'm sending you coordinates."

On the screen, the captain looked away. His lips curled down, disapproving. "This change—"

"Comes from me."

"And not from the Khan?"

"From me, as I said."

"Why?"

"Why the change? Because we have a strategy and objectives, and this is the only sensible approach to implement those."

"But it isn't what—"

"Captain, did we by chance receive any cruisers? Any destroyers? Carriers? Anything to better our chances using established tactics?"

Zohar straightened. "We did not."

"No, we didn't. And so, this is our mandate. This is our only hope of success until sense wins out and the things I requested from Azh Shivan are sent to us."

"And you think this new course will give us a chance of success?"

"It will give us our only chance. You will have your killing and victory, Captain. You will have the opportunity to strike against bitter enemies. That should be all you and your peers care about."

Zohar's eyes narrowed. He had become something approximating an ally since the failed mutiny. It was a truce between sane and professional men, but Zohar was the one with his back turned to the other conspirators. He still commanded the flagship. He still had the most senior rank, the most powerful among equals.

The captain bowed slightly. "I will inform the fleet."

"Thank you."

Before Satrap had finished, the connection ended.

Ikhama pursed her lips. *"A champion must ever be victorious, but a wise champion knows the value of brothers and allies."*

Satrap grunted. He was too tired. Maybe he was letting bitterness get to him. Ikhama was right: Zohar was necessary, and Satrap might have gone too far, antagonizing his last ally.

There was work to do repairing bridges, and there was time, but how much?

14

W hen Benson and Thiessen finally left the cafeteria, a completely
different group of Silver Wolf soldiers was waiting for them. The
sun was setting, darkening the gray that seemed a permanent fixture in
Paradies. Fog had replaced the rain, hanging at the tops of the tires of the
Night Jaguars parked beside the hospital building. She and Thiessen
smelled like the rich sausage meal that had been served up the entire time
they'd been inside. The smell had been so strong, it saturated the last
notes of bitter tea she'd finished off as Field Marshal Faulk declared their
strategy session done.

She pulled her flannel shirt closer around her as they descended the
steps, where the fog could swallow them. "Did you get anything from that
meeting?"

Thiessen's head twisted around to get a look at their escort. "The
message that our *ally* already has his own strategy planned out."

"My first assignment—well, not really an assignment. A short training
run. Anyway, it was aboard an old frigate. The *Sao Paulo*. It was barely
space-worthy."

"I know that feeling."

Their escorts held up hands, then strode over to the waiting vehicles,
where they quickly fell into a conversation with the drivers.

Benson blew into her cupped hands to warm them. "The commander was this old lady who seemed stuck in that gray zone between service and retirement. Every morning, she looked like she'd just slid out of bed. Her hair was a mess. She was falling apart physically."

"Um?"

"Yes?"

"Retirement?"

"You don't have a system where you reach a certain age and…well, step away from full-time service?"

"Wow. That sounds nice. But, no. We're expected to work until we die."

Corporate government. How could she be surprised? "You really should consider coming back to Kedraal with me." She stiffened when the last two words sneaked out. She had no idea where they'd come from.

The Gulmar captain snorted. "At this rate, I may end up throwing myself on the mercy of your people."

"I'd welcome you with open arms." She'd done it again—made it personal and uncomfortable. "I mean, we could use another good captain."

"I don't know that I'm a *good* captain, Faith."

Her belly seemed to warm at the way he said her name—intimate, like an old friend. "From what I've seen, there aren't that many. Not anymore. In our navy, that is. A lot of the good ones died recently or retired when the military was gutted. A lot of high-potential officers bailed back then, too."

"I distracted you from your story. About the retiring captain on your first training ship?"

"Oh. Yeah. Lieutenant Commander Odetta Ludvig."

"Ouch. Sounds like she should've been here."

"The name? I guess so. Anyway, she would always pretend like she wanted to get my opinion on a command before giving it. Except she'd already made up her mind. Every time. She would listen to my questions and suggestions, nod, then say we were going to do it her way this time."

"Maybe some of her genes slipped in to our field marshal's vat?"

"That's not genetic. It's a learned behavior. You have to see yourself as more valuable than everyone else to be that way."

Thiessen bowed his head, as if embarrassed. "The task force he's offering up—"

"I know. I was expecting more. It barely matches yours."

"It doesn't sound like the ships are particularly new, either."

"We all have to leave a defensive force behind in case the Khanate fleet tries another attack."

"What makes you so sure they won't?"

"They have to be thinking the same thing we are: Prowling around in the enemy's home systems will make them sitting targets, relatively speaking. And it consumes resources. We don't know if they're carrying reactor fuel in those tenders or if they're being resupplied. But if they hit a world and flee, like they did with Radetta, it's not quite as effective."

"Effective enough. There's not really much left."

"To be thorough requires staying around for a week, maybe even a couple. When they hit Radetta, their fleet was vulnerable. If my fleet had struck..." She shook her head. Tuleyev had missed a golden opportunity, and maybe she was partly at fault for that. It had seemed more important to keep the fleet hidden and safe.

One of the men escorting them waved through the fog. "Captain."

Benson squared her shoulders. "Time to go."

Thiessen was loaded into a Night Jaguar first, then the doors closed, and Benson was led to another. Her escort opened the door and waved her in. Once she was seated, he got in and closed the door, and the engine hacked a few times before growling to life.

When her escort settled across from her, he actually smiled. It was almost lost in the dark interior. "There has been a good deal of violence. The field marshal is concerned for your safety."

That seemed a change. Did that mean the threats and intimidation were behind them?

She filed the information away.

The vehicle lunged, throwing her sideways in her seat, then settled into a steady acceleration. Aggressive turns tested her buckle, and a few times, her head banged against the wall. Not only were they driving faster than she could recall, but they seemed to be taking a different route.

Benson cleared her throat. "Are we expecting trouble?"

"Everything will be fine." Her guard chuckled, or at least he tried to. It seemed to be something he wasn't comfortable doing.

"This doesn't feel like the route we've been taking."

"A precaution. The convoy has been split in two."

Like the trip out from the starport. That hadn't ended well.

A small panel opened in the wall separating the driver compartment from the back, and a disembodied voice said something that barely rose over the thundering engine. It sounded like it might have been a time estimate—ten minutes, perhaps.

Her guard patted the wall, and the panel closed. "You see? Ten min—"

His words were lost in the thunderclap of an explosion and a momentary burst of heat. At the same moment, the dark interior was bathed in an orange light that immediately faded. Benson was thrown forward, toward the driver compartment, then she was bounced around, as if a giant machine had punched the front of the vehicle with a claw, then clamped on and shook it.

She realized her ears were ringing, and the headache she'd only just gotten rid of returned with a vengeance.

The Silver Wolf guard didn't seem much better, blinking and shaking his head.

Heat emanated from the front—less intense than before but constant.

Somehow, she'd missed that her bodyguard had gotten up. He seemed a little wobbly, but he had his weapon raised. He was on his feet, and his mouth was moving. Was he telling her to remain calm?

Orange light glowed in the seams of the wall separating vehicle compartments.

The rear door burst open, and before the guard could bring his weapon around, a human-shaped form of black was in the opening, head covered in some sort of mask, draped in the night and fog. Light flashed, revealing a hand and in that a pistol.

For an instant, the bodyguard stared, as if confused, then he collapsed.

He has a hole in his head. Was that always there?

More of the dark forms with masks burst into the rear compartment. The distant crack of automatic gunfire hinted at mischief somewhere far away.

Hands grabbed at Benson, as if hoping to tear her clothes off. She swatted them away, then realized they were unbuckling her seat belt. For the life of her, she couldn't remember buckling it.

Then she was out in the fog, being hauled along roughly by a couple of the forms. That distant gunfire grew louder, and one of the men hauling her along made a strange noise and fell away, swallowed by the fog.

She was shoved to the ground, and the other man dropped on top of her.

Dead?

No. Pressing her down. Protective.

Black shapes rushed out of the night, and she heard a couple short cracks. It took her a second to connect the flash of light and the cracks and to realize the man lying on top of her had a pistol and had shot a couple men in black. The man pressing against her wore gray.

Where had she seen the gray uniforms before?

She was up again, now being helped along by the man in gray uniform and mask. He wasn't being gentle, his right hand moving from her hip to her back to her ribs and breast. She kept slipping and sagging, and he kept adjusting. They were almost running, but he was doing all the work. There was the faintest smell of sweat and rubber and smoke coming off of him. And damp clothing, with a hint of mildew.

Far behind them, the crack of gunfire continued. When she risked a look back, the orange glow was a vehicle burning.

Then the headache eased a little, and a light—two lights—flashed.

A vehicle. A small one. Angular lines. Low to the ground. It was black, and it murmured like a stream heavy from rain.

The man with the pistol pushed her into the small back seat, taking nearly as many liberties as Halliwell had the last time they'd made love, then hopped into the front seat.

An alleyway, she realized. They'd been running down an alleyway. In the headlights, she could barely make out cobblestones, the faintest shape of a wall, a dark shingled slant of roof, then—

Their vehicle shot forward, the pregnant stream now a rising roar.

More explosions came from the area they'd just vacated, and when she twisted to look up into the sky, she caught a stream of fire rising above the door or back of the car she was looking at.

Car. She processed that. It was a car. Fast. Noisy. Agile.

The headache returned—pounding, piercing. She'd suffered another concussion.

Neither of the men in the front said anything to her, but they did chat with each other. The one with the mask had actually taken it off at some point, revealing an older face—middle-aged, wrinkled, narrow, and pointy. He wasn't looking at her, but back the way they'd come from.

Sounds were resolving, but all she could hear were the murmur of private conversations and the reverberation of the engine.

When she poked her head up, they were out of the city, moving down an empty highway. On either side of her, tall grass grew, swaying above the mist. How many centuries back had Himmel been terraformed? Had any of those architects and engineers ever dreamed that their work would be witness to such a terrifying and backwards scene of violence?

At some point, the man who'd worn the mask turned around again and gave a curt nod, then the corner of his mouth rose. "You are unharmed."

Not a question. He must have checked her during the fondling. She nodded.

"Not long now."

He turned back to the front. His behavior, the way he spoke—it all felt...human.

And his promise proved true. The vehicle downshifted and turned onto a dirt road. Benson thought she could make out a few big, bulky buildings standing around an open area, and off the largest of the buildings, what looked like a huge field.

The vehicle lights went dark, and they slowed even more, coming to a stop in front of the largest of the buildings.

An old farmhouse, Benson realized. The shape of it, the dark and dreary nature—it felt used yet abandoned. And the building they were in front of?

A barn.

They were at least an hour out of the city. How many kilometers? One hundred?

Her—was he a rescuer? Yes. Her rescuer jumped out of the car and darted to the front of the barn. He poked his head inside, then disappeared. A few uncertain heartbeats later, he returned, pushing the door open.

That was the signal for the vehicle to enter. It slipped inside quietly.

Kerosene lamps hung from a few posts, providing just enough light to make the place seem even more creepy. Shadows mostly hid farm tools, an old tractor, and empty bushels.

Spiderwebs. Dust. It was all very reminiscent of images of Earth.

A small form stepped from the shadows, hunched slightly, hanging back from the middle-aged man with the sharp, hatchet face.

The driver hopped out and lowered the passenger seat so that Benson could get out. That's when she realized the driver was a woman. Shorter than Benson, with puffy cheeks and pale hair tucked into a cap. The woman was probably the same age as the man but didn't wear a uniform. Instead, she had on pants and a shirt that could have been made of the same material as the uniforms. Her leather jacket could be mistaken for something a pilot wore.

No one was pointing a gun at Benson. She found hope in that. "Hello?"

The small form stepped from the shadows, revealing a rustic wool jacket, a heavy scarf, and the sort of pants a farmer might wear for chores. He was gaunt, almost rodent-like, with bugged-out eyes that were barely still blue in the lamplight.

Benson found herself blinking in surprise. "Ambassador Manshaus?"

He bowed slightly. "I must apologize for this, Captain."

"I had no idea—"

Manshaus shook his head. "Please. Wait a moment." The little man pulled something out of a jacket pocket and held his hand out for her. "He'll answer your questions."

The driver, the man who'd rescued her, and Manshaus seemed locked into place as Benson examined what she'd been given.

She ran a thumb over the surface. "A data pad?"

"Activate it." Manshaus's eyebrows were raised.

The device was the same sort of design she was used to; she thumbed the spot that would be coded for biometrics.

The screen glowed. A connection request fired off.

Before she could ask if that was expected, the connection was accepted, and an old, fat man in an almost sky blue uniform looked at her. His head was bandaged and bruised. After a second, he squinted, then a thin smile stretched his pale lips. "Captain Benson. How exciting."

It was the officer Thiessen had been with on the other side of the collapsed ceiling. Weber? That sounded right. "General Weber?"

He nodded. "I apologize for the violence, Captain."

"I'm getting used to it."

"How terrible that things have come to this."

She brushed hair back from her face. "I'm not sure what..." Her eyes drifted to the other three watching her.

Weber squinted, as if trying to see what she was seeing. "You wonder why I reached out to you?"

"I guess."

"Because the Azoren—the true Azoren—need you."

"You...need me?" She wished the headache would go away. "How?"

"You've witnessed the work of the Children. You've seen the butchery of Faulk. This rampant terrorism represents not the doctrine we all embraced years ago but the diluted and corrupted ideals of a small group of people. Rather than accepting the superiority of our people, we have been obsoleted by monsters."

He doesn't disapprove of the message, just the messenger. "What do you want from me, General?"

"I lead a small but powerful faction that has come so very close to assassinating Supreme Leader Graf. With his fall, his bastards would follow. But we require assistance."

"Assistance? General, we're here as diplomats, not conquerors."

"Yes, obviously. And your diplomacy—you seek to annihilate a threat that endangers us all. I applaud this."

"That's good to hear." At that moment, it was a refreshing dose of sanity, actually.

"Tell me, Captain Benson—has the field marshal obsessed over the Moskav?"

"Obsessed?"

"Has his demand been that you assist him in eliminating the inbred troglodytes?"

Benson winced. Maybe *sanity* was a stretch. "He wants to eliminate the Moskav, yes."

"It is a task my fleet has already done."

"You run the fleet?"

"As I said, my faction is quite powerful. I've planned naval operations for the last fifteen years, working closely with Admiral Dönitz before his assassination and taking over after that. The problem has only been in finishing the job on the ground. I wouldn't need Kedraalian complicity in removing the last of the vermin. What I *do* need is help eliminating the Minister of Purity and his retched Children."

"I see."

"Return to my people what they believe in, and we shall come back stronger."

"That doesn't really answer my question." *And it doesn't sell me on this idea.*

"What is it that I require of you?"

"Yes."

Weber nodded at someone not visible to his camera. "My fleet is actually commanded by loyalists to my cause. Most of the fleet, at least. There are some senior officers who are Children. I need you to keep those officers preoccupied."

"Preoccupied how? Attack your fleet?"

"Preferably not, but how it happens is up to you. The distraction need only allow my people to take command of the final fleet assets. Once that happens, the forces we've pulled back from Moskav space will be ferried down to Himmel. With their assistance, we'll overwhelm the field marshal's forces. That will be the first step toward righting this aberration and making the federation what it was envisioned to be."

Benson shivered at that. What the federation had been meant to be was a terrible thing, with or without the Children. "What about Supreme Commander Graf?"

"He is old and frail, and he represents our ideals. He can be spared the blood of this fight. After all, Faulk wants *all* humans removed from power."

"Does the supreme commander know that?"

"He does. It's the demon he made a pact with. Fortunately, the field marshal doesn't have the numbers yet. For now, he thinks fear is enough to exert control."

"That's the reason for all this violence?"

"The rebellion? That is the result of Faulk and his brothers persecuting humans. He can't even wait for the corpse to go cold."

Benson shuddered. Faulk was a frightening person—ally or enemy. But Weber wasn't coming across as some warm and kind grandfather. "I'll need to talk to my officers."

"That is understandable." Weber smiled. "Captain?"

"Yes?"

"Do keep in mind that the field marshal will betray you the second you have proven of no further use. You'll know what I mean when you see the *Warsaw*."

"The *Warsaw*?"

"A light battlecruiser. He plans to make it his flagship. There are very few alternatives. My people control the ship."

"I'll take that under advisement, General."

"Very well. When you are ready to commit to my plan, please do reach out to the ambassador."

Weber's connection closed, and Ambassador Manshaus held a hand out for the device. Simply setting the device back in the little man's hands sent a shiver of disgust down her spine.

Manshaus nodded at the driver. "She will return you to a safe section of Paradies, Captain. From there, you may ask for help, and Faulk's men will find you. You are a fortunate survivor of an ambush, nothing more."

"And you?"

The little man slid the data pad back into a pocket. "I await your call."

As Benson slid into the vehicle passenger seat, she struggled with the throbbing headache. The one thought that kept running through her head was that she was caught between two twisted and terrible groups engaged in a battle that would eventually destroy them both. She might be little more than a pawn, yet it was possible for a pawn to not only survive the battle but win it.

If she intended to try for that outcome, she had a lot of work to do yet.

———

Parkinson's terminal glowed a soft blue, the data from the completed simulations occupying the main window. He'd run several analysis scripts against the output, but no matter how he looked at the gray-white text, there was no sense to make of it.

Chief Taylor leaned in closer to his left, her warmth passing through the rough material of her jumpsuit when she stretched to tap the side of the display on his right. "What's this?"

"What's—?" Parkinson squinted, annoyed by the way she was distracting him. Somewhere in between the return from coffee to the simulations finishing, he'd started to notice her perfume. It wasn't the cherry syrup scent, which he'd actually come to appreciate on its own. That must've been her soap. Instead, the perfume was a subtle undertone, like delicate blossoms. And her breathing was like the whisper of a breeze rustling those flowers, the swell of her uniform on each intake like the stems dancing.

Not right. She shouldn't do that. I have a job to do.

She tapped the screen again. "This? It looks like another..." She rolled her eyes and tapped the link, opening another window. "See?"

Heat colored Parkinson's cheeks. "I see it. I don't...know..."

When she turned to look at him, there was an annoyed look on her face. "You've been staring at my boobs for the last hour. Focus on the data for a bit."

The heat spread, and Parkinson's eyes flew wide. "I—"

Taylor crossed her arms over her chest, almost as if to say he couldn't even admire her curves until he'd done his part. "What's that report mean? Did you even read it?"

"Not yet."

He ducked his head down, fighting back the urge to tell her to go back to her own terminal if she didn't want him looking at her. Getting up into his space, huffing coffee breath at him, shoving her big butt into his face.

And telling him he couldn't handle her. What the hell did *that* mean?

A dull pain ran along his jaw. He was grinding his teeth.

Dammit!

As he read the report, he massaged his jaw. There were problems in the analysis, indications that what he'd *thought* were solid snatches from the enemy systems actually weren't. Except that he'd pulled back binaries. The systems had confirmed it then, during the attacks, and they'd confirmed it during the simulations.

Taylor brushed his hand from his cheek. "Stop it."

"Huh?"

"You're going to irritate your skin."

"I'm not scratching; I'm massaging."

"Jeez, remind me not to ask you for a massage."

He froze. *Was* she asking him for a massage? Thinking about it? How had she gotten into his head? "Chief, look, I'm really annoyed. Okay? This report—"

"The one you didn't notice before?"

"Yeah." He opened his mouth to stop himself from grinding his teeth again. "It's saying we've got problems with the software we used for the simulation."

"Isn't that the standard system test rig?"

Parkinson let a withering glare slip out, then turned back to the screen. "Standard test rig. But I'm running our software and replaying our data for the blue side, and I'm running the software modules I captured from their ships, and I'm inferring data for the red side."

She squeezed the bridge of her full nose. "And something's not right? Isn't that sort of obvious, then? You didn't really hack their systems."

"Except that I did."

"When?"

"Throughout the battle. It's something we've got plugged into the signals ships. We don't just eavesdrop and scramble. We're also constantly plucking anything and everything we can from enemy electronic counter-measures—ECM *and* ECCM."

"That's not gonna get their software modules, Will."

His spine tingled. Even with spite dripping off it, he liked the way she said his name. It was almost like having her tender cheek brush against his. "When we get into their systems, we're running hacks. And I was *right* there during the battle. I did some hacking of my own. I mean, well, I helped our systems along when the automated attacks started. Their networks—their *systems*—are just like ours. And I don't mean that in a good way. It's all our hardware and software."

"No shit." She leaned close to the display again and tapped through the interface. "Where's the binary repository?"

"Ours or theirs?"

"Both."

Parkinson reached around her, surprised when she didn't move aside as his fingers danced over the display. But she wasn't looking at him with a teasing, playful face. She was completely focused on the data being shown.

He waved his hand at the software repository interface. "*Voila!*"

She fiddled with the data. "The checksums don't match."

"They wouldn't. Not to ours. We're running the last production release. That's not even six months old."

"I thought you said they were all Kedraalian hardware and software?"

"It has the same functions. I feed it data and it operates exactly like—"

Taylor tapped the screen. "This report. It can query the software library, right? The catalog? It can tell you if these checksums match anything from the code base?"

"Well—"

"Did you bother to see if this is actually the same code, or did you just assume?"

"It's the same—"

She tapped the report button, and the entries for the Khanate software modules all flashed red. A frown stretched her lips. "Not our code."

"It has to be. It's the same functionality. What they're doing…"

"Yeah. Could you have pulled down a partial or corrupted binary?"

"Nope. I was able to get into their systems clean. The simulation confirms what we saw happen could have happened using the software. Those binaries are completely functional. They're legit."

"Then?"

Parkinson pushed back from his desk, brushing against her hip without meaning to. She didn't budge. "Then they aren't running something from our code base. They're running a duplicate or something completely new."

She turned and settled on his desk, legs spread slightly, shins on his knees. But her eyes were closed, her head was lifted slightly. "The Khanate? Do they even have system engineers and developers?"

"Not like ours. I've heard their education system is backwards."

"Didn't think they would. Then how did they duplicate our capabilities without actually using our code?"

Parkinson's eyes locked onto a tiny coffee stain on Tyler's thigh. It was hard to concentrate with her pressed against him. "It doesn't take much difference in code to foul up a checksum. Even a few lines added or dropped—even a single character—can do it."

"How big is it?" Her eyes opened to slits. "The binary."

"Um. Well, big enough. It has—they have all the capabilities we do."

"You sure? We got lock-on, didn't we?"

"So did they."

She shrugged. "Okay. So they've got the same basic software as us, just like you said, except it's different. And the odds of them writing it on their own are pretty slim."

"And there's no way they built the hardware. I still can't figure out where this stuff comes from. I've asked around, and it's really, really locked down. This isn't a navy project."

"Then one of the skunk works groups?"

"And black box funding. Even that, though—" He looked away, half of him excited to have her so close, the other half annoyed that he couldn't stay focused. *This was important.* "I've seen the hardware. I've torn into it. It all makes sense when you think about it, but it's a huge progression over anything I've ever read about."

She nudged his thigh with a boot and winked. "Probably been working on it in the dark for a long time. You know how good things can get in the dark, right?"

The wink. She *was* teasing him. He swallowed. "Um. So, yeah. But I don't think that's what it is. I think we found this tech somewhere, and we've been reverse engineering it."

Her body tilted forward a little. "No shit?"

"No shit."

"And the Khanate just happened to end up with some version of it?"

"I can't see them creating it on their own."

"So we've got spies?"

"Has to be. But this code…it can't be just stolen, or we'd find it in the code database." He should have thought of that before she did. She was really doing a job on him.

She slid down from the desk and yawned, stretching until her coveralls looked ready to burst. Then she frowned at him. "You know what, Will?"

"What?"

"I agreed to come over here and work with you because no one else wanted to."

"You said that."

"I did. But I intended to show you what it was like to have someone make you uncomfortable, the way you do a lot of ladies."

"Oh." He blinked. She'd been pushing so far into his head, making it hard to think of anything else, even though he never would have given her a second look before. "I don't mean to."

"Sure you don't. You're not someone who means to be an asshole."

"I—"

"No. I mean that. You're an egotistical jerk, but now that I've had a chance to work with you, I realize that you're just an insecure smart guy. Everyone else thinks you mean to be abusive, but you're just acting out."

Parkinson's throat tightened. "Are you making fun of me?"

"I'm telling you I feel sorry for you. You've made a mess of things, and you never meant to."

That sounded worse than being made fun of. He looked away, feeling the heat in his face. "I didn't do anything wrong."

"Not intentionally, no. You see a cute girl, you hit on her, and if she doesn't understand how awesome you are, you try to help her figure out how good it is to be one of your conquests. You're not a predator, but it ends up being the same."

His breathing became jagged. His eyes stung. "I'm not a predator!"

"I just said that, Will." She put a hand on his shoulder. "I actually kind of like you."

That made his heart skip a beat. "You do?"

"Enough that I'm gonna offer you some help."

So, not sex. "Help?"

"I'm going to head back to the *Seattle* and give you some space back. You dig into this problem, and when you've figured out what we're looking at here, call me. I'll get the commander to approve me coming back over, no worries. And then we'll tear things apart again. Deal?"

Parkinson parsed that. She *liked* him. He *wasn't* a predator. He was just a *smart* jerk. Wasn't that what he'd always realized about himself on his darkest days?

He smiled. "I'd like that."

She squeezed his shoulder. "Just leave the cute girls alone, okay? Keep your focus on your peers. Play your cards right, maybe you'll get a chance to prove me wrong."

"Prove you—" Oh. That he couldn't handle her. "Okay."

His heart raced, even after she was gone. How had that even happened? She wasn't the sort of lady he'd ever pursued, yet she'd twisted him around and left him gasping.

Later. Figure it out later.

Right now, he had a problem to solve, and being alone again, he could finally do that.

He pulled up the software repository catalog and began working his way through it. Without the source code and management system, he couldn't conduct experiments on how the code had changed, but he could still see how the binaries and checksums had changed. The hash used to produce the checksum meant there weren't any real methods to correlate those changes.

Then what? The Khanate had pirated software, but it was modified.

How could he turn that into something meaningful for Chief Taylor? No—for Commander Benson.

Taylor had him all turned around.

Parkinson got up, shook his head, and paced. It sucked being stuck in a position like this. He liked having parts that fit together. He liked being able to impress people with his intelligence. This situation?

Dig in. Find something. That's all he could do. No pressure.

After all, it was probably the key to defeating the Khanate.

15

———

The *Ollie*'s shuttle rattled and clanged as the drop gear pushed the atmosphere-capable craft out of its shaped hollow at the belly of the ship and maneuvered the small vessel for descent. Caville had trained for shuttle drops in his youth, and he'd ridden in a few since entering the field as an agent, but the fear produced by the process was something you couldn't train out. If your body was fine with being flung from a ship, through space, to a planet speeding around in its daily cycle, then there was something wrong.

Still, nothing was going to go wrong. At least, it never had before.

He was in the first row of seats, behind the cockpit and ahead of the small cargo hold that held some sensitive crates he was supposed to ignore. The *Ollie*'s co-pilot, Talia Leung, was wrapped in her augmented-reality headset, running through the flight checklist. She was almost certainly still fuming about losing the draw to the *Ollie*'s pilot and getting stuck with the mission. Neither looked forward to traveling down to Azh Shivan, but Talia—with her fluorescent pink mohawk, wiry muscled-arms covered in tatts, and love for big sidearms—was as close to an allergen for the Khanate's people as there could be.

Caville smiled inwardly at what was coming, but the pleasure almost instantly faded.

Blood was coming. Murder. The only question was how much.

In the silence between mechanical arms extending the shuttle farther out and angling it downward for launch, the whisper and crinkle of cloth caught his attention. The noise came from Denise Gallo's robes—a coppery red with bright green cuffs and hems. They'd shared a spicy breakfast of flatbread and bean paste just a few hours before, and she'd giggled and chattered like a schoolgirl. Now those spices seemed to ooze from her pores as she plucked at a loose thread, eyes frozen wide and locked on the display in front of her. Those eyes held a mixture of fear and anxiety.

He reached over and squeezed her hand. "You okay?"

She shook her head. "I feel like I've made a terrible mistake."

"This kind of launch is a lot safer than you'd imagine."

"It's not the launch but the destination."

Azh Shivan certainly looked like an ugly smear rather than someplace a pilgrim might return to. It had been terraformed long before Caville's birth, but now it looked like a muddy brown, spinning ball. The oceans seemed like afterthoughts—blips of blue that barely registered. At least the skies were clear of pollution. Supposedly.

Gallo squeezed back and blinked away tears. "I spent years on Kedraal, hiding my belief and identity. I would wear this robe at night, in my apartment, telling myself this is who I really was."

"You have a different name now?"

"I will. When I go through my confirmation ritual."

They even have to give up their names. "Do you know it?"

She quit tugging at the loose thread. "No."

"Is that what scares you—the unknown?"

"The known, really." A melancholy smile softened her face. She brushed a hand over the sleeve she'd been picking at. "This robe…"

"What about it?"

"There's an attraction to what it means—the colors and textures. Even the design has meaning. The number of layers and the creases and the height of the hems. Back on Kedraal, I was expected to compete for every-thing and to be productive, just like anyone else. I had to throw elbows and shout and snarl like a man. Here, in these robes, I'm expected to be quiet and to accept the words of my…betters." She almost choked on that word: *betters*.

It was a tough thing to reconcile, the woman he'd come to enjoy the company of in the weeks of travel and the idea that she was about to give up everything she'd been to find her place on the dusty-looking hellhole below them. "You think these people are your betters?"

"Not people. Men. All women must be subservient to men."

Caville fought back a smirk at the thought of Stiles hearing such an absurd claim. His sister would have been driven into a rage at the idea. Were there men who were faster, stronger, or smarter than her? She might have conceded that point. Better?

Gallo's eyes narrowed. "Are you laughing at me?"

"Laughing at my sister."

"You have a sister?"

"I don't talk about her much. My family is—" *What had they been?* "—peculiar."

"What made you think of her?"

"The idea that men are better than women." Caville kissed Gallo's knuckles. "You might check with Talia up there for her opinion."

Gallo winced. "I think I already know her thoughts about men."

"Hit on you?"

"A few times."

"You should've given it a go. You'll never be sure until you try."

"You…tried…?"

"No. But I'm not even a little curious. You sounded like you might be."

The young woman's eyes widened, and she looked away. "I'm just confused."

"Lots of people are. You confused about what you're supposed to do here?"

"I guess not. Here, I'll just be another woman waiting at the foot of some man."

"Can you do that? You used to hold a position of power and influence, didn't you? This job you had back on Kedraal."

"Yes."

He slipped his hand free of hers and ran his fingers inside her robe sleeve, brushing the soft flesh of her arm. "And this? Your flesh? You can give up what we had?"

She pulled his hand free, face pinched. "There won't be any shortage of sex. It just won't be something I do for my own pleasure."

"Make a man happy. Give him some babies?"

"Y-yes." Her eyelids fluttered, as if that idea might be worse than giving up her power.

"Does having kids mean giving up everything?"

"I don't know. It seems like it."

"You could always go back to Kedraal. Plenty of people have families there and still have careers."

"I was a spy, Darien."

"No one knows that. You could always start a new life, a new identity."

"They'd find me."

"They'd have to be looking for you. Be someone else. Be *something* else."

She bowed her head. "My faith is supposed to walk me through all of this. I should be free of questions. Our holy book is full of parables and gems of wisdom to answer our prayers and alleviate doubts."

"Does it?"

"For some." She sank lower in her seat.

"Not for you."

"This has all been a huge mistake. The spying, this faith. It all seemed so romantic and noble, but now that I'm so close to actually doing it, becoming..." She waved a hand over her robe, as if it might represent every ill she'd described.

"Give it a try. If it doesn't work out—leave."

"That's not how they work. Once you're within the Khanate, there is no leaving. As a woman, I won't even own anything. My husband will own it all."

"Sounds tough. But this is your family? They're down there?"

Gallo's small hands bunched up, the smooth caramel skin reflecting years of pampering inside a cooled office environment. "My mother."

"You lost your father?"

"No. He...he didn't want me to follow this path."

"Why not?"

"His faith is weak. He says that belief is a way to frame the universe, not a way to paint your life. He encouraged me to pursue university, to focus on my studies. Every time I talked about the Khan and his way, my father told me that the universe would accept me for who and what I was."

"Unlike the Khan?"

She nodded. "He said that humans need strong and independent people, regardless of their sex."

"Sounds like a smart man."

"That intelligence would have put him in danger here."

"A lot of people are afraid of intelligence. It's easier to manipulate stupid people."

"Prime Minister Zenawi said the same thing. He often hired firms to test the best messaging. It's amazing to see how changing a few words can get people to support something that's actually against their own best interests."

"I can only imagine." But Caville had actually seen the tactic in action.

"Seeing what Zenawi did sort of pushed me the rest of the way."

"You were considering not coming here?"

"At one point. I started getting worried. My handlers were sending me messages. Everything went from encouraging and helpful before I smuggled out my first bits of intelligence to having an undercurrent of threat."

"Did they suspect you were getting cold feet?"

"I think it's just that they knew they had leverage. My mother's down there. My aunts."

"You talk to them?"

"Not directly. They've sent written messages, but I don't think they're real."

What mother would tell her daughter to live such a life? A hateful one. Maybe. Maybe parents weren't such a great thing after all.

Leung turned around in the cockpit. "Cargo shuttles inbound. We've got clearance."

Gallo stiffened in her seat. "H-how long?"

"Ten minutes. Let me know if you change your mind by five."

"Five minutes." Gallo sagged again. "That's not long to change your course, is it?"

How long had it taken Caville to shoot Stiles in her head? Seconds. But that wasn't changing course. He'd been on this path for years. "Long enough."

The young woman tugged at the loose string again. "My handlers?"

"Yeah?"

"Those messages I told you about? They said: Do your job and everything will be fine."

"That's threatening all right."

She grabbed his hand once more and placed it inside her robe, stroking her flesh with his fingers. "Would you be offended if I told you I used you?"

"It was the good kind of using. I think we both enjoyed it."

"I did. I had to know what I was giving up."

"You said you'd have plenty of—"

"I'm giving up what I *want*. You understand? Freedom?"

"So you're going forward with it?"

"They could hurt my family otherwise."

It always seemed to come down to family, whether the manipulation was a threat to their safety or a call for you to provide safety to them. Maybe his background wasn't so different from Gallo's.

He massaged her tender, warm flesh, and she relaxed, head pressed back against her seat.

Then Leung threw up a thumb. "Here they come!"

Two dots on the screen quickly grew into discs, then those turned into winged tubes with rockets pushing fire back toward the planet. The wings grew wider and clearer, then the tubes resolved into thick, streamlined structures. The cargo shuttles were bigger than their craft, with wide cargo bays. Goldman and his crew would be able to empty the *Ollie*'s hold easily.

Leung flipped a switch and tapped a few buttons. "Better be strapped in. Launch in five, four, three—"

Caville checked Gallo's harness, then his own.

"—two, one!"

He was thrown back against his seat, the cushioning going soft to absorb the press of his body. Leung piloted them away from the shuttles, pointing the nose of the craft toward the planet. It was an unnecessarily aggressive approach and also extremely like her. Her voice was lost in the rattle and creak of the shuttle and the bass thunder of the rocket, but Caville knew she was screaming at the top of her lungs. That was also extremely like her.

They hit atmosphere, and the shuttle shuddered. The pilot was on the intercom, prattling on about angles and velocity and other things that concerned only her. What he heard that mattered was the estimate to their destination: Shod Madieu. The capital city.

They didn't have much time now.

It was another meaningless name to anyone outside the Khanate, but it supposedly meant something like Flowering Light of the Guiding Star.

Whatever. In his head, it meant the center of hell. The source of death.

He'd spent a decade preparing for this moment. He'd shot his sister in the head. There was no way to count the bodies he'd left in his travel to this place, to position himself for this moment. Someone had known years ago—before his birth, even—that this was the place that would need to be eliminated, that there would need to be a bullet fired here one day.

Now Caville was that bullet.

Was he up for the task, or would he face the same sort of fate as Stiles?

Pale blue skies. White, thin clouds.

They had moisture on the planet. They had atmosphere. There were fewer than fifty million people here, and only a handful of cities, yet the planet was an ugly sore.

Some of the blame could be placed on the Khan. The first one had brought violence with him. He'd used bombs and fires to lay claim to the world. He'd recorded mass murders to terrorize the decent folks and to break the spirit of the original settlers. Crops had been destroyed or left to rot in the fields. Someone like the Khan wouldn't care about starvation. He would live in luxury the entire time.

But that wasn't enough to explain the devastation.

Had the various Khans ever asked why? Did they have the intellect to even be aware of this change? Maybe they were more comfortable simply accepting it as the universe oppressing them. It was how they structured thoughts, after all. Here, accept our views. If you don't, you're taking away our rights, you're persecuting us.

But they were the ones who put people to death. They were the ones whose views and freedoms were defined as the absence of opposing views and freedoms.

He glanced at Gallo. Tears flowed down her cheeks. Her bottom lip trembled.

Fear. If she hadn't felt that, he would've been worried.

The intercom crackled, and Leung's voice was in the air again. "Starport in sight. Give it a look. This is your home for the next few days."

Gallo palmed the tears away. The display in front of her seat showed the same angle on the starport as Caville's. It was a series of concrete runways, a disc of that same concrete with more strips radiating out to a group of larger concrete discs, and everything flowing back to the tarmac in front of a series of buildings and hangars. A tower looked down on the tarmac and the strips that were meant as runways.

Sand covered large swaths of the whole thing, and the buildings looked ancient, not so much white as drained of color.

Leung whistled. "Can't wait to work on my tan."

If she could have heard Caville, he would have made a wisecrack about the robes protecting her from the sun and the locals. Then again, he wasn't sure if she actually planned to stay on the planet. Once their cargo was offloaded, she was headed back up to get the rest of the crew. Maybe she'd volunteered to watch over the *Ollie*.

They settled on one of the empty discs radiating out from the hub, then the engines powered down.

The pilot went through a series of switch flipping and button taps, then pulled her helmet off, shook out her mohawk, and turned around. "Welcome to Shod Madieu. I think it translates as Shithole."

Her words dripped with her typical sarcasm.

Caville undid his harness, then helped Gallo with hers. Her hands shook, and she licked her lips over and over. He helped her to her feet, then out of the airlock and down the ramp.

Outside, the air was dry and blistering hot, a steady wind carrying the grit of sand toward the city. It felt like early afternoon, the sun still a blinding light high in the sky. From the direction of the terminal, an open, wheeled vehicle rumbled toward them, kicking up a spray of sand to add to what the wind already carried. Two men sat in the front section, one behind a steering wheel, the other cradling a weapon—an assault rifle. They were in robes, but unlike Gallo's, theirs covered everything but their hands and faces.

The vehicle came to a stop at the bottom of the ramp, and the driver shouted out something unintelligible. Their language. They were drifting further and further away, then.

After a second, the driver spat, then said. "In back." He jerked a thumb at the rear bed of the vehicle.

Caville helped Gallo onto the flat bed, then placed her hand onto a strap anchor that she could use as a grip bar. He settled beside her, grabbed an anchor with one hand, then wrapped his other arm around her hip. The gunman scowled when Caville nodded that he was ready, then turned back to the front.

They lurched forward, and it was all Caville could do to keep Gallo on the bed. He was already missing the feel of her skin and her scent, and knowing that she was walking into this twisted world out of fearful obligation didn't make that pain any easier to accept.

At the back of the terminal, the vehicle stopped, and the gunman hopped off. He waved the barrel of the gun at them. "Go." A jerk of the chin indicated that they were to head into the terminal.

Stepping into the building, Caville realized just how hot it had been outside. The terminal wasn't much better, but when the heat was so intense, even little differences mattered.

They passed through a security check where a robed man studied them with blue, inscrutable eyes.

And then they were at the front of the terminal, looking onto a dusty road.

Gallo swallowed. "A terrible mistake." She barely whispered.

"Let's find your mother."

He couldn't connect to any sort of network, so they settled for hiring a car much like the one that had taken them from the shuttle to the terminal. Their driver deposited them at the front of a tea shop, or at least that's what Gallo said the sign indicated. Caville had never mastered the odd mixture of blocky and swoopy characters used in the language. The GSA didn't have complete records on the language, which was apparently undergoing changes the longer the users were away from the merged English, Hindi, Mandarin, and Spanish that made up Humana, the language used by everyone else.

Standing on every street corner within sight was a gunman like the one who'd sent them into the terminal. Their robes were a faded ochre, their faces locked in a scowl.

From inside the tea shop, he caught snippets of friendly chatter and the clatter of ceramic.

Gallo looked pale and wobbly. "I think this is goodbye."

Caville wanted to hug her and tell her everything was going to be all right, but he didn't feel like lying. "You stay in touch."

She laughed, then when the closest guards glared at her, winced. "You know where you're staying?"

"Right here for now. When I find someone who can point me to the hotel, I'll be at The River Flows With Life."

"It sounds beautiful."

"I'd kiss you if I didn't think those goons would gun us down."

"I'd like that. I'd like more than..." She bowed her head. "Goodbye, Darien."

Her wave felt like Stiles lowering her head for the shot.

It was the job. There were no other options.

16

———————

Riding up from Himmel on an Azoren shuttle felt wrong to Benson. She should have been able to use one of her own. She should have had a detachment of Halliwell's Marines. Not an army but a few—three or four led by Grier would be enough.

Faulk had refused to consider the idea. "This is nothing more than an inspection of the *Warsaw*, Captain. Once you see my flagship, I believe you will have a greater appreciation for what the Azoren have to offer."

The *Warsaw* was the ship General Weber had said Faulk would choose.

A light battlecruiser with a focus on defensive capabilities, it had protected Himmel for decades and was solid if unimpressive.

And it was crewed largely with Weber's loyalists.

The shuttle bumped and rattled like a car running over a piece of debris, then the air recycler groaned, and the cabin lights blinked, but no one reacted. She could still breathe the stale, sweat-tinged air, even if it was a little stuffy. That made sense with the way all the seats were filled with Silver Wolf commandos.

But it wasn't a good idea to bring my Marines. Right.

Benson smiled at Thiessen, who sat to her left, back against the bulk-head-mounted seat. Like her, he was in uniform again, which seemed to have improved his mood. He'd been tense after her return, maybe even a little protective. It was a nice feeling, having someone care about her. Some of her girlfriends from the academy would roll their eyes at the idea of swooning and going weak at the knees about a man protecting them, but the truth of it was, she enjoyed the idea that another senior officer cared more about her than about sabotaging her career to advance his own.

It didn't hurt that Thiessen was handsome.

Faulk sat directly across from her, a pleasant smile pasted on his face, as if that might convince her that his little, rattling shuttle wasn't an odd choice to show off just how impressive his fleet was. "You are comfortable?"

It was a challenge. If she complained about how the shuttle seemed overtaxed and on the edge of collapse, she would be showing weakness. "We've had to use mothballed ships before." *I've seen worse, thanks.*

He chuckled, but it was a forced reaction that quickly gave way to rapid blinking. "The *Warsaw* is our most capable ship. In the home defense fleet, at least."

Although she nodded, Benson wasn't so sure about the truth of the field marshal's words. Weber hadn't said it outright, but he'd hinted that the *Warsaw* may have been their best ship—period.

Would the *Warsaw* even be comparable to a Kedraalian cruiser? Certainly not to the *Valor*. The Azoren ship's age alone ensured that.

Green lights flashed in the cabin, then Faulk's smile returned. "Ten minutes."

She would know soon enough, then.

They fired maneuvering thrusters, braking gently and adjusting. There weren't displays in the passenger cabin space, probably to maximize their ability to haul cargo. Faulk's men had strapped light cases and duffel bags to the anchors running down the center of the shuttle, so that Faulk was hidden from the waist down. She would've rather he be hidden completely.

To the pilot's credit, Benson only realized they'd landed when the green light that had flashed earlier did so again, and Faulk popped his harness.

Thiessen unlocked his and leaned close to her ear. "Here goes."

She tried not to shudder at that. Weber's people were ready. The courtesy call she'd been allowed with Chopra had been enough to arrange a task force maneuver that would get the attention of the Azoren fleet at the appointed time. Everything was in motion, just as planned. She could send a signal from her data pad, and Chopra would begin the maneuvers.

A quick check confirmed that her data pad was still connected to the Azoren network.

Here goes, indeed.

They were hustled into the hangar bay, which held several shuttles, a few of them modified as attack craft: bulked up armor, modifications to their drives, and a roof-mounted railgun.

Faulk beamed at the gunships. "You have noticed the modifications."

"Have you found them effective?"

"Oh, yes, definitely. Most of our engagements are against Gulmar pirates."

Thiessen smiled. "How odd. We face the same problem. Most of them work for the Azoren, though."

"Criminals like this—they will say anything to save their necks."

"They know better. Piracy only has one penalty, whether you're flying for the Azoren or for yourself."

The Azoren field marshal shrugged. "Narratives are meant to be believable."

"I don't do narratives, Field Marshal."

Faulk led them out of the hangar bay and into a narrow but clean passageway that reminded Benson of the *Sao Paulo*. Older warships had been designed with an eye toward nothing but basic functionality, ignoring the value that some minimal comforts provided. An extra meter width in the passageways added space and maybe a little bulk, but that was hardly a problem. They weren't facing drag or paying for a hangar somewhere. Reactors could handle the load to heat and light that extra space, and life support systems could manage the small atmosphere load.

But the *Warsaw*...

Before Benson could ask Faulk how old the ship was, she spotted a crew of technicians hauling a black crate coming toward them, then turning down an intersecting passageway.

Her mind returned to the *Lyon* and the Khanate spy who'd nearly crippled the ship in the middle of battle. She sped up, nearly bumping into the field marshal as she passed, just before they reached the corridor.

The engineers were far down the hall, already setting their crate down.

She froze for a second; Thiessen bumped into her from behind. "Faith?"

"Oh." She adjusted her uniform, barely registering his hands on her hips. It felt right, but he pulled them away. "I'm sorry. I got distracted."

Faulk's eyebrow arched. "Impressed, are you?"

Benson pressed her lips together. "I—yes."

"Did you think while escaping from the terrorists down below that you would live to see something as grand as this?"

"I was in a daze, actually."

"Yes. So many bombs to survive. The medications have helped with your headaches?"

"They have. Thank you." She pointed down the corridor. "Is it normal to have maintenance going on during an inspection?"

"Maintenance?" He leaned past her to look down the way, then straightened and grinned. "Upgrades. We are always undergoing upgrades. That is how you stay ahead of the enemy. We study data from engagements and adapt."

What she had seen didn't look like upgrades. The technicians had been moving quickly, as if time were short. Upgrades usually went on at an almost leisurely pace. After all, installation was the least time consuming of all the work. Testing, adjusting—that's what took forever.

She glanced down the passageway again. Now the duo had panels removed from the bulkhead. A hatch was open, and shouting came from inside it. The words were distorted, but the way everyone moved when they went in or came out, she was sure it was an engineering compartment.

What made her stomach flutter wasn't the work, though. Maybe it *was* an upgrade. In fact, she was sure it was. The *type* of upgrade was what ate at her.

The crates the men had been carrying were the same black crates she'd seen aboard the *Pandora* in the secure storage area.

Those had contained armor, weapons, and…other equipment.

Had it been meant for the privateers who'd taken over the *Pandora*? She'd never been given a clear answer. Stiles had been digging into things, and the last she'd said was that the problem ran deep and everything was complicated.

And dangerous.

Thiessen had said the Gulmar built advanced systems for whoever paid, even the Azoren. Did he know about this shadow technology?

Faulk bounced up and down. "The inspection, Captain?"

She nodded absently. "Of course. I'm sorry."

He moved forward, now turning around occasionally to flash his wolfish grin. "There is another hangar bay on the port side. We will find the officers assembled there. Keeping them waiting would be rude. Even a field marshal must respect his subordinates."

Benson's heart hammered. Something was wrong. This was Weber's plan. Her part was just a distraction for the Azoren fleet, a simple set of maneuvers to spread her ships out from the Gulmar ships. It would be enough to raise suspicion among the Azoren bridge staff, maybe to have them go to general quarters and to demand guidance and answers. But it was ultimately harmless, something explained away by a lack of formalized communications channels between the forces.

But the upgrades? The technicians?

Weber hadn't said anything about them. If the Azoren were installing stolen shadow technology…

Benson stopped. "Field Marshal Faulk?"

Faulk glanced back, then frowned and stopped. "What is it, Captain?"

"Those upgrades—could I see what they're doing?"

"What?"

"Well, this is going to sound crazy, but we had Khanate terrorists aboard our ships. Infiltrators."

"We have no such concern here. Our people universally hold those animals in low regard, you see."

"I understand. But it's just…" She looked back the way they'd come. "I feel anxious."

Thiessen's eyebrows went up. "They planted bombs—right?"

"Yes."

"There were spies on Radetta, too. They caused a lot of damage."

Despite the field marshal's soft features, his jaw muscles bulged. "I see." He waved the two of them to proceed back the way they'd come.

Benson had put him in a tough spot. Deny there could be any way the men could be Khanate spies, and he would come across as irrationally confident, maybe even appear to be hiding something. A quick look at the work wouldn't really put them behind schedule, so he couldn't use that excuse, either.

They squeezed down the narrow passageway and came to a stop a meter or so short of the workers, who barely acknowledged them until Faulk pressed past Benson.

The field marshal's presence brought the men to their feet. "Field Marshal!"

He waved for them to relax. "At ease. Our guests wish to see the upgrade work."

One of the engineers squinted at Benson, then whispered something to Faulk. While they were engaged, she sneaked a peek into one of the tool cases.

Guns were pressed into some of the foam slots. A silver wolf head gleamed from a folded, black jacket in another.

She looked at the men again, this time actually seeing them: gold hair so pale it was close to white; blue eyes that were nearly gray; a uniform appearance to their faces that hovered close to boyish.

They weren't technicians.

Or at least they were technicians attached to Faulk's unit rather than the regular navy.

Something more than a simple upgrade was going on.

He turned around, pouting lips and sad eyes. "Unfortunately, this team is far behind schedule, Captain. They are, however, *not* Khanate spies."

The stern-faced engineer nodded.

Benson did her best to smile warmly. "That's all that matters."

Faulk clapped the engineer on the back. "Return to work, Chief Schmundt."

They headed back to the first passageway and once again hurried forward, their steps a steady thump in the empty space. At the next passageway, he turned in, heading to port. His pleasant chatter was gone until they reached the next intersection.

"Ah." He pointed a little way ahead, then strode to a large hangar hatch. "Our officers await us."

He tapped in a code, and the hatch opened. Inside, a large group of men and a few women, all dressed in pale blue uniforms like Weber's, were assembled in a sharp formation. At a shout from one of the officers inside, the others snapped to attention.

Faulk clapped his hands and laughed. "Thank you, Captain Doughty! This is most wonderful!"

Doughty was a short, skinny, dour-faced man at the front of the assembled officers. He had a sidearm holster on his hip, as did many of the officers. There were several chiefs and security men assembled outside the main formation. They had submachine guns.

All of them looked hard and cold.

They were ready.

Numbers. Opportunity. Willingness.

They could eliminate Faulk. They could change the scope of the war, at least for a little while.

All she had to do was signal for Chopra to cause a distraction.

Doughty squinted at her. Nodded. *We are ready.*

But the Silver Wolf engineers. Their upgrades. Their weapons. What did it mean?

They're ready. I can't let them miss out on this opportunity.

At her side, Thiessen leaned in close. "Quite a display."

He was ready, too.

She pulled out her data pad. "Excuse me for a second."

Faulk raised a hand. "Captain Benson, if you might have just a moment?" He marched toward her, eyes slitted and going from her to Thiessen until close enough to whisper. "Do be careful which side you choose at this critical time."

Doughty raised a hand slowly, attention locked on the field marshal's back. Some of the loyalists reached for their weapons.

Several Silver Wolf commandos stormed through the hangar bay hatch, submachine guns raised. The stern-faced engineer was at the front. He started to say something, then the thunder of gunshots filled the hangar bay.

Thiessen tackled Benson to the floor and covered her with his body.

Bullets cracked nearby, and she lost track of Faulk and anything else beyond the exchange of gunfire. A part of her mind thought how nice it was to have Thiessen's weight on her, although she would've preferred they be on something more comfortable than the deck of a hangar bay. Another part of her mind screamed that this was absolute insanity, that she was being used by her own government and by Weber and by Faulk and maybe by the Gulmar and Thiessen.

Then the gunfire stopped.

Thiessen rose and helped her up. She grabbed her data pad and stuffed it into her pants.

Doughty was down, blood darkening his uniform jacket and pooling on the deck. Several others from his team were down as well, including all of the security group. The rest had dropped their weapons and raised their hands.

Among Faulk's people, only the stern-faced engineer was down. Faulk himself held a bloody hand against his shoulder but didn't seem to be bothered by the wound.

He turned back to Weber's people. "I commend you for your bravery and for your astute observation of the hopelessness of your situation."

One of the women straightened. She was tall and thick, and she had a long face crisscrossed with wrinkles. "What now?"

"I will need to consult with my own security team, Commander." Faulk jerked his head at Benson and Thiessen. "In the passageway, please. I have a call to make."

Benson let Thiessen guide her out. She was shaking, her guts twisting. Had she just let Faulk use her? Was the *Warsaw* inspection all a ruse to draw Weber's people out?

Just beyond the hatch, she stopped.

Manshaus was there, head down slightly, bugged-out eyes avoiding hers. "It is good that you survived, Captain. My heart was heavy enough."

Heavy enough. Without my death. But—?

Faulk came up behind them, boots scraping, clearing his throat. "Do continue into the passageway, Captain. Your present location is ill advised."

Thiessen pushed her farther in, until she stood beside the little ambassador who still wouldn't meet her gaze.

With a stomp of boots, the last of the Silver Wolf commandos stormed out of the hangar, and Faulk slammed a hand against the access panel, leaving a bloody smear on it.

The hatch closed, even as gunfire resumed within.

Benson's stomach flipped. Lights flashed over the hatch, and she imagined the sound of the alarm within the hangar bay, as the gears opened the belly panels that would allow shuttles in and out.

Air would be evacuating, the shooting stopping. Or maybe someone would turn their gun on themself rather than go through the horrible end that vacuum offered.

Manshaus shivered and let out a small, pathetic noise. "My family, you understand…"

It was hard to even imagine him having a family, although she knew better. She wasn't the only pawn, then. Other people were being used to inflict death and ruin.

Her gorge rose, and she fought it back. She wasn't going to give Faulk the victory.

The amber warning light continued to cycle.

How long would it take for someone to die in vacuum? Seconds if they were exposed to it fully and weren't ready. The people in the hangar bay knew it was coming. They were navy professionals. Would they exhale and curl up and try to last as long as they could? She couldn't be sure how she would react in their situation.

It was hard to breathe and hot.

Someone had bandaged Faulk's shoulder. He patted Manshaus on the back. "Very well done, Ambassador."

The little man almost crumpled beneath the touch.

Faulk's eyes sparkled, then he crossed to the porthole on the hatch. After a second, he cackled and turned back to Benson, clapping his blood-caked hands. "And now I must give you my thanks as well, Captain

Benson! It would seem a good many of my brethren have just been promoted."

A dark loathing clutched at her stomach. "We're diplomats."

"Of course you are. And you have no worries. I have no intent of harming either of you. What happened today was necessary, if tragic. General Weber has been a true thorn in my side, and now he has given me all that I needed to complete my purge of his people. It's a glorious day. And more importantly? We have no further need for a boring inspection."

The field marshal chuckled and waved for them to follow.

Thiessen hooked his arm around her waist. "Don't give him an excuse."

Benson let the Gulmar captain guide her after their inhuman ally but wished she'd blasted the Azoren fleet to bits when she'd had the chance. They were every bit the animals the Khanate were.

And now she was sure she'd tied her people to an alliance that would forever erase any hint of moral superiority.

Assuming they survived.

17

One thing Faulk had to admit: Supreme Leader Graf had taste. The rustic manor house that was now home wasn't just safe and removed from the gloom of Paradies but was peaceful and calm. The exterior had the look of a giant hunting lodge that might have stood in as a fortress, with brooding, gray stone and dark, heavy timbers meant to withstand time and the aggression of man. Inside, everything had a comfortable polish and clean finish. Kerosene lamps and glowing fireplaces provided most of the light and heat, although a squint out the thick windows might catch the faint reflection from Himmel's small, twin moons. In the library, those windows were hidden behind heavy, maroon curtains.

He finished off the hard slice of bread slathered in plum preserves, then washed it down with two sips of the bitter tea that filled the larder.

Not everything the old man loved was wonderful.

Faulk shrugged off his black coat, hooking it over the back of the heavy wooden chair, then loosened the tie at his neck and unbuttoned the collar. It wasn't truly dark yet, not like it would be in an hour or two, but sleep was already making its demands. He yawned, then turned his attention back to the data pad on the desk in front of him. The screen snapped back to life with a touch. Its pale, blue light reflected off the polished desktop. That light—the device itself—seemed out of place, meant for a more sophisticated and dangerous place. That was his place, his true home, but for now, he needed a respite, a chance to recharge and restore.

Reports were still coming in on the latest terrorist activity. Weber wasn't yet defeated. In the time Faulk and his guests had spent in space, five different barracks had been attacked, one of them completely destroyed. The losses were unfortunate but not crippling. In a war of attrition, Weber might win out.

Faulk had other plans.

Rising to Supreme Leader didn't only require Graf's death. It required Weber's elimination. It required dismantling the network of support that made Weber possible. After all, Weber wasn't the real threat. He was a pawn, a tool used to weaken the existing leadership, same as the bombers and snipers and terrorists living in the wild.

The real threat was the power behind those pawns. For as long as Faulk had been aware, there had been infighting. Graf had survived hundreds of assassination attempts, although most had never come so close as the one that had sent him to the hospital in the care of Kedraalian doctors.

Investigations were necessarily sloppy. Assassins rarely surrendered or survived. One faction or another ultimately was exposed, purges were ordered, and the problems disappeared.

Temporarily.

But the whole process was wasteful. It drained resources and created a paranoia that poisoned what should have been an invincible fighting force. How often had efforts on the Moskav front crumbled—hard-fought victories washed away in the fire of bombs that should never have penetrated the perimeter?

Weakness. That was the obvious problem. At its core, the leadership appeared weak. How else could someone possibly view an ancient, frail man who only appeared to his troops over video for fear of an assassin?

What everyone needed was a sense of invulnerability and power. They needed Faulk.

And he needed to root out the vermin bent on destroying Graf's dream.

For the dream to live, the dreamer must die.

Faulk chewed on his knuckle. How could he get to the old man? How could he finish the dark deed started by others? And would that finally draw the traitors out into the open so that the pawns could be swept aside and the real power behind them toppled?

A knock at the door brought the field marshal's head up. "Yes?"

The door opened, and one of his bodyguards leaned in. "Purity Minister King is at the front gate. He wishes to speak with you."

"Alone?"

"He has a driver."

Of course he would have a driver. The minister hated driving, especially at night. If he'd come with a small group of bodyguards, maybe he would have been projecting a message. With a driver? "Send him in."

Although the library was warm, Faulk would need his jacket. There was an image to project. He had just cinched the tie when the library door opened wider, and the minister walked through.

The old man nodded but hurried to the fireplace, spidery arms extended. "Winter comes early."

Faulk grunted. "It kills off the weak and sick."

"Is that what I am, Dietmar?"

"Only you can answer that."

"That is a truth." The minister chuckled. "Supreme Leader Graf survived the operation. He is stable and is quite likely to live."

"I see."

"The older surgeon—Dietrich? He was quite impressive. Our doctors hope they can learn from his work. They were also quite taken with his young aide."

"The Jew."

Minister King twisted his torso around and looked Faulk up and down. "Is that really the mind of one of my Children?"

"You expect me to ignore our teachings?"

"I am a man of science. I pursue data to wherever it might take me. Genetics teaches many lessons. The fact that you and your brothers can exhibit so many differences despite drawing from a limited design should speak volumes to you."

"The variances are within controls, are they not?"

"What we field—you and your brethren—are the desired results, but the human genome is not so pure as you might think. Our ancestors share common roots with any number of people who would be considered inferior based on ideology. Your hair, your eyes, your skin are all the result of inbreeding within a specific group over thousands of years."

"Inbreed—"

King raised a calming hand. "For a moment, listen, please. I don't speak of some incestuous arrangement but the result of isolation and societal norms. Your ancestors became somewhat homogenous in appearance, and they told themselves that was what their society found attractive. This isn't wrong. It merely *is*."

"You skirt close to treason."

The old man's bony shoulders rose and fell inside his pale gray jacket. "My research has always been controversial. People prefer not to hear what brings discomfort."

Heat rose in Faulk's face. "So our supreme leader lives. In what capacity?"

"His doctors believe he might walk again."

"Walk? His spine was damaged."

"And the Kedraalian doctor has dealt with such trauma. This shouldn't surprise you. You've been dealing with the Kedraalian captain. Does she leave you so unimpressed?"

Faulk snorted. "More than unimpressed. I find myself wondering what their game is sending someone so unqualified to lead. They look weak and foolish."

"I see. My impression was that she had earned her position by proving herself in battle. The communications we received from our…informants in Kedraalian space point to several successes in engagements, not just excellent scores during training."

"That has to be weighed against the caliber of her competition. The Kedraalians embraced a blend of mud people—"

"Mud people?" King made a tut-tut sound. "She seems of flesh and blood to me."

"Teasing is unbecoming."

"Blind rhetoric is even worse. You do recall that she was part of the group that defeated one of your brothers, don't you? Two, if the reports are correct. We can never know exactly what happened on Jotun, but from the Kedraalian side, all indications are that she held out with a small force against a former rival."

Eric Knoel. From a younger brood. Ambitious. He'd created a reputation for his Black Lightning unit. Jotun had been his chance to prove himself, a stepladder before the climb into the hell of the Moskav front.

But as far as anyone could tell, Knoel had died. He and his men had gone completely silent on the giant, icy moon.

Faulk returned to his desk and resumed his seat. Sweat had moistened his shirt. "We need to know what happened out there. Not just the Kedraalian story. What really happened can only be found by searching that cold surface."

"The Kedraalian Front Command—when we had such a thing—lacked the resources to investigate. Things have gone silent, which would only happen if they all died."

"That is no more reliable a line of thinking than it is to accept that Morganson's task force truly was hunted down and destroyed."

"Your brother's ship transmitted their status. You believe he lied?"

"The *Spear of Destiny* could have suffered a malfunction."

"Or it could have been hunted down by older, less well-equipped ships, and destroyed. If so, this notion you have that the Kedraalian captain is nothing to be concerned with is misguided."

Faulk waved the old man's words away. "What I've seen does not merit—"

"Misguided as your decision to claim Supreme Commander Graf's manor as your own. He might question that in the same way he might question how only you survived the blast. General Weber notwithstanding, of course."

That sent Faulk forward in his seat. "You survive."

"I wasn't there, Field Marshal. And I have never had my eye on running the federation."

"We all have an interest in ruling."

"Serving our ruler has been my role since the day of my arrival. It will be my role until the end."

"Could someone get to Graf?"

The scientist strolled from the fireplace. "An assassin?"

"That term sounds brutish. Consider my question that of a concerned observer. Maybe an accident undoes all the hard work of the Kedraalians."

"They watch over him like a hawk, even though they have no love for our views. He is their patient."

Faulk pinched his lip and realized he actually needed to shave. He could usually go a couple days without, but the stubble was an irritation now, bristling against his fingers. "Graf's strategies for the Moskav front are partly at fault for where we stand today. If he resumes his position, it's not only me who stands at risk."

King bowed his head. "I am nothing more than a scientist."

"My brothers, our dream of empire—those are what matters."

"More than you taking the throne?"

"Of course. The war against the Moskav has become a bottomless void. When it chewed up only the first Azoren people, it was unfortunate but necessary. Now my brothers are at risk of facing that same pointless approach."

"You have a better plan."

"I do. The strategy you insisted I speak with the Kedraalians about— that is my means of completing the work of the original architects but with a guarantee of success."

"Dropping rocks on the planet?"

"Nothing so crude. I'm well aware of the desire to lay claim to the resources without destroying everything."

"Then?"

"You want to know my strategy?"

"Consider me a sympathetic ear yet an honest mouth. If your plan provides concerns to someone lacking even an iota of strategic under-standing, then you will know. Did the Kedraalians raise alarms?"

"That wasn't their place. I did not seek counsel but provided the course."

"I see. And you fear I might not be so willing to remain silent about faults, should they exist?"

The field marshal smirked. "You created me. I value your thoughts."

"Then share your ideas with me. Let me consider potential problems."

Faulk stood, buttoned his uniform coat, and hooked his thumbs over the back of his hips. "Our one requirement is that the Moskav planets be in a state that allows for occupation and exploitation. There are no requirements regarding the people."

"They are beneath you. Perhaps they could be turned into shock troops."

"We have people of our own for that."

"Then you have other plans for the Moskav populace?"

"Fire." The field marshal wheeled around. "And ash."

"Burn the planet—"

"Just the mongrels themselves. The planet will remain intact."

"Ambitious."

"We use the Kedraalian captain to extend the invitation, same as she did us. The cowards who run their government must finally come into the light to hear her offer and discuss it. When they do, we strike."

"And the Kedraalian captain? She will be on the planet?" The scientist almost loomed, pulling up to his full height, green eyes twinkling as if he might find fault with the specific plan for the pretty woman.

Faulk shrugged. "She is necessary in the fight against the Khanate. If she can be saved, we will do that." He wanted to mention how she'd fallen for the trap set for Weber, but it seemed a petty thing.

"And the Khanate. What are your plans there?"

"Lure the fleet out, let the Kedraalian task force suffer the worst of the blows, finish the Khanate fleet, then finish the Kedraalian and Gulmar ships off."

The minister turned back to the fire, shoulders slumped. "And then?"

"Then we consolidate our gains. We'll have more than enough growth ahead of us. Planets to expand to, an era where my brothers can find so much to take for themselves. And after these systems, the galaxy. We will be unstoppable."

"The galaxy is vast." The old man's voice was soft, wistful.

"We will conquer it in time. Continue breeding my brothers. Template them on me so that I can make them all a part of the Silver Wolf group and bring an end to this struggle to prove superiority. I have done that."

"That you have. Even so, not everything is meant to be conquered."

"You hold a human's thinking. My thoughts exceed the bounds restraining you."

King turned his back to the fire. "I see."

"Your skepticism is apparent."

"Good." The old man's eyes closed. "As you know, you are not the first batch to be attempted. My efforts go back years, predating even my time here on Himmel."

"That is how science works—iteration until success."

"Not everything succeeds. Not everything is an iteration. Often, many lines are run in parallel. It was through a parallel testing line that I discovered the means to accelerate your aging process. It was through another line that I discovered the means to slow it again."

"Yes. This is all good."

"My point is that your assumption of superiority, the idea that you must naturally be meant to rise and conquer because of design and ideology—the galaxy is so far, far beyond us. It represents a million, perhaps a billion of these iteration and parallel test lines. As good as I can make you, as good as the human body can be, there will always be things that are superior."

"We will proceed with an eye toward that."

"You can't merely—" The old man twisted the ring that he sometimes wore on his left pinky. It was a silly, worthless piece of jewelry, perhaps more a matter of sentiment than anything else. Certainly, he hauled it out during times of stress, like a toy meant to relieve anxiety. "Dietmar, what exists right *here*, right in the worlds that we know of, might offer threat sufficient to eliminate us."

"Then continue your work to evolve us. Help me in realizing our potential."

"Your potential may already have been met."

Faulk stretched his neck. "No. Graf has been an impediment, a leash long past its intended use. I'll remove him. By the time I depart, I will be supreme leader."

"Will you?"

"Yes."

"And what would you risk to make that happen?"

"Everything."

"I see. Very well. I believe I've provided you with distraction enough for the night. I'll leave you to your strategizing."

A few minutes later, the old man was bundled up and back in his car, seated behind the driver who had no fear of the night or the dangers of the terrorists and whatever else it was that troubled the Minister of Purity.

Faulk stared after the receding automobile lights until they were gone. He had hoped killing his father meant only striking down Supreme Commander Graf. Now it seemed Minister of Purity King would be a problem as well.

The road to empire was never an easy one to tread.

18

———————

Since their return from the *Warsaw*, everything felt raw and dangerous to Benson. When she paced her room, the dark boards creaked, almost whispering a threat to her: He knows you're moving around. The wood in the fireplace popped and spat embers at the screen, making the light unsteady, untrustworthy. Her clothes—the ones she'd taken as her own now that she was out of uniform again—scraped and scratched against her skin. Things as harmless as water and the simple fruits she'd eaten after settling back into her prison room tasted bitter and on the edge of spoiling.

It had been the execution. Faulk had bragged about the numbers. Nearly three thousand tossed out airlocks. Their bodies floated in space, clinging to the sides of the ships like lost spirits seeking to return home.

"A reminder of the folly of betrayal, Captain."

When Faulk had said that, the words had actually felt venomous.

Benson had sat upright in her seat aboard the shuttle, swallowed, and waited for one of the Silver Wolf soldiers to yank her or Thiessen or both out of their seats and drag them to the airlock. When that hadn't happened, and she'd realized the animal respected the protections of diplomatic immunity for the moment, she'd done the only thing that had made sense.

She'd challenged him. "What grants you any more legitimacy in our negotiations than anyone else? Surviving a bomb?"

The wicked man had laughed at that. "The strength to conquer, taken from birth."

And that had been it.

History was full of people who proclaimed divine right. The idea was that some being provided protection and strength beyond the available mundane weapons and armor. That belief alone could sometimes lead to amazing feats and unbelievable successes. Ultimately, though, mortality won out. People discovered that there was no divine intervention awaiting them when the inevitable failings caught up.

Faulk apparently had spent his entire life following this belief. It was built into the twisted teachings he'd been inculcated in. And Benson was pretty sure it was wired into his DNA. That or it was part of some chemical treatment external to the DNA.

She almost didn't hear the knock on her door, it was so soft. After a second, she slid across the floor on thick socks, hoping that might be enough to keep from alerting their overseers that she was still awake.

Her hand hovered over the door latch. It couldn't be one of the Azoren. They didn't know how to do anything so subtle as a soft knock. "Who is it?"

"Floyd." Whispered. Quieter than the fireplace.

Floyd. What a strange name.

The door squeaked open, the hinges groaning like a wounded animal. He slipped through the opening, smelling like the rough soap bars that rested on polished steel trays over the sinks and bathtubs, then pressed a hand on hers and slowly closed the door.

When she started to speak, he held a finger up to his lips and shook his head, then pointed to the bathroom door beside the fireplace.

She led him to the door, then opened it. He sat on the edge of the bath and turned the water on, motioning for her to close the door. She did, then sat beside him on the edge of the heavy tub. "I already bathed."

Thiessen smiled but sagged a little. "You smell nice."

"Thanks, but—"

"I don't know if they've bugged the rooms. I'm beginning to think they have."

Of course they had. She took his hand. "What Faulk did up there…"

"I know. It was a setup from the start."

"Manshaus was in on it."

"I don't think so. Obviously, he was working for Faulk, but—"

"You don't think he wanted to?"

"He said something about his family. I know from years of interactions, he thinks the world of them. He's never said it before, but I always had the sense we could have flipped him. For all I know, maybe Leona did. She didn't confide that sort of thing."

Hearing Trang's name hurt. It must have been the memories of all the death and destruction her arrogance had caused. At least, that was the only sensible reason Benson could come up with. "I still don't trust him. I can't."

"No. He wouldn't want us to."

"So what do we do? I don't think Faulk's going to just let us leave."

"I can't see it. Do you still have access to their network through your data pad?"

"They shut it off after…"

"Yeah." A frown twisted his handsome face. "We sure could use that engineer of yours."

"Chief Parkinson?"

"The little guy who keeps looking at you like—?" Thiessen's frown narrowed. "That's not fair. Most guys look at you that way. But he bugs me."

Benson blushed, although she couldn't be sure what was at the root of it. She'd never really given any thought to Parkinson looking at her any particular way, but now it appeared other people noticed it, too. But the way Thiessen had said it…

Does he—? Is he jealous?

He twisted around, the heavy pants he wore rasping against the white enamel of the tub, then splashed his free hand in the water. "In case they're listening in."

She nodded. Being a prisoner, being spied on, the idea that someone out there might be watching her the same way she'd been watched and recorded by a sailor and never known…

They weren't going to control her. She wouldn't let them.

"Wait here." She pushed up from the tub and creeped back to her uniform pants, which were still draped over one of the chairs. The data tablet was still inside, still with most of its charge. There wasn't much reason to use it, not without the ability to talk to the *Valor*.

Thiessen splashed some more as she sat down beside him. "You have a connection?"

"I know a little about networks and security. I'm nowhere near as good as Parkinson, but aboard the *Pandora*, I had to manage a lot of our systems."

"I…might be able to help." He blushed. "I hacked a little before…"

Before he became respectable. She patted his knee. "You have nothing to be embarrassed about. We don't control our birth. Anyway, I'll take any help I can get."

He leaned in close, looking over her shoulder. His breath was fresh and warm. "So, let's say you get on their network."

"Okay."

"Let's say you reach the *Valor*."

She had the network interface up. Previously, she'd used her own identity to get in, meaning they'd created it in their own security, which meant things were still mostly compatible, despite decades of separation between their people. That meant they were all mostly operating off a similar if not identical architecture.

Benson looked up, caught the concern on Thiessen's face. "I'm listening."

"I was saying, let's say—"

"That I reach the *Valor*. I heard." She held the device up. "I'm still locked out."

"Can I?"

She pressed the device into his hand, then took the opportunity to lean in close to him. It was nice, feeling his heat, hearing him breathe. "I was thinking, maybe we don't have to actually overcome their security. There should be a way to—"

"Use public resources?"

"—use public—" She looked up at him, smiling. "Okay. Mind reader."

"I wish I could. I think I could learn a *lot*."

Her eyes widened. "I don't—"

"About your command training, I mean. I haven't had anything close."

"Oh." She blushed. What had she thought he'd meant? She focused on the data pad, realized he'd found a public network signal and was about to scroll past it. "Wait."

He froze and let her swat his hand away. "You want to try that signal?"

"It's weak, but sometimes an access point like that might be less secure. There were farms in that valley. It could be something set up for them."

"Right. Farmers like that wouldn't care about high-speed networking."

"Is that sarcasm?"

"Just an observation." He twisted and splashed the water some more.

"There." The connection request popped up. The network was so slow, even the prompt took a moment to complete drawing on the screen.

Thiessen dried his fingers on his pants, then squinted at the screen. "Well, I guess I shouldn't be shocked, but that's a really, really old system."

"You recognize the version?"

"Right here." He tapped the corner of the prompt. "Version 21.10."

"That's old?"

"It was old when I did my hacking."

"What kind of hacking?"

"The kind that let me get into security training when the opportunity arose."

She raised her eyebrows. "Were you a Gulmar spy?"

"More like a counter-spy. Half the job was finding out what was threatening the corporation I worked for. The other half was trying to threaten rival corporations."

"Does that seem…silly to you now? With Trang and the others dead?"

"Yeah. Pointless." He tapped in a user ID, then a password.

The prompt closed, and the system signaled that it was trying the credentials out.

Benson shifted, moving so that her hip pressed fully against his. "Let's go back to what we were talking about earlier: What do we do?"

"If we connect?"

"I think we could request evac."

"That would probably be considered a provocation. They could hold your doctors as leverage."

"So, not an option. We can't risk war."

"We can't risk war, or we can't risk a war we could lose?"

"Meaning?"

"I'm not impressed. The *Warsaw*? It's an old ship. It's big enough. I'm betting it would be a tough bone to chew for my destroyers, but our task forces combined? It'd crack like an egg."

"That's *one* ship."

"It's their best ship. You think Faulk's ego would let him use anything else? He really is proud of her. Remember, he hasn't actually seen the *Valor*. I doubt he's even asked his naval people for an analysis of our forces."

"Are you saying we should attack the Azoren fleet?"

"Here's the thing: We knew for years that the Azoren fleet wasn't what it once was. They lost ships fighting the Khanate, and they lost more fighting the Moskav. They patrol their borders more aggressively than anyone, but they don't have a lot of ships committed to it. We got word a couple years ago that they were putting big money into an upgrade of some sort. I think we helped them build part of that."

"The fleet that attacked Kedraal."

He bit his lip, then nodded. "Probably."

"But they still have this fleet here and whatever is out on patrol."

"Don't you think it's an option? Take these ships out, the threat's over."

She glanced at the water in the tub. It looked inviting. "They'd kill us."

"That's always a possibility. Unless we tore through them quickly enough and threatened them with missiles."

"Or threatened to lob asteroids at them." She shivered. Annihilation. "It's not my first choice."

"Not mine, either. It needs to be on the—" He pointed to the device. "You're in."

She took it from him, barely noticing the way he didn't pull his hands free immediately. As she worked her way through the interface, he kept close, sometimes taking her hand and guiding her finger to the right selections. It was intimate and sweet and with the steam rising from the bath, it was quite distracting.

Finally, they landed on a screen that prompted them for a message and destination.

She put in the routing that would get the message to the Valor, then stopped. "Starting a new war with our potential allies isn't option one. What other choices do we have? I was thinking maybe we accept the offered terms, get back to our ships, then make a real decision."

"That's a good choice. That real decision could include blowing them up."

"It could."

"Or we could just say no and leave. We hunt down the Khanate fleet and hope we figure them out. Assuming we have a way to hunt them down?"

"I think I do."

He smirked. "Then we have another option."

"There's…also the possibility of agreeing to go along with their plan."

Thiessen scowled. "Wipe out the Moskav and give those planets to the Azoren military?"

"Then go after the Khanate."

"You trust them? You don't think Faulk would double-cross us the second he gets a chance?"

"Do you trust them?"

"Not for a second."

A loud knock came from the bedroom door, and Benson nearly dropped her data tablet into the tub. She powered it down as Thiessen hurried out to the bedroom, finger once again pressed to his lips. He pulled his shirt off as he went, then tossed it on the bed. Benson pressed the bathroom door against the jamb until there was only a crack she could watch through.

Thiessen opened the bedroom door a crack. "Yes?"

The door was pushed wider, and one of the commandos poked his head inside, turning to the bed. "Captain Benson?"

"She's finishing her bath."

"Tell her to be ready in the morning."

"Ready?"

"The field marshal will speak to you. Both."

"Well, there goes my night." Thiessen made a noise like a bear growl and closed the bedroom door.

Benson pulled the plug on the tub, turning to catch the Gulmar captain frowning at the bathroom door. She stiffened. "What?"

"That's some lousy roleplay. I thought you'd at least go through the trouble of stripping." He chuckled, but it didn't hide his anxiety. "Showtime."

"Do you think they heard us?"

Thiessen shook his head. "I don't know. We'll find out soon enough."

A knot formed in Benson's gut. Would Faulk kill them? Would he order an attack on their fleet? Had she missed her opportunity to steal the initiative? The questions left her shaking, but delaying wasn't going to stop betrayal. They had to know where they stood with Faulk, and the only way that would happen was by facing him.

McLeod's data pad buzzed angrily—a reminder that he was hours late going to bed. His hotel room smelled like late-night East Kedraalian stew, something that came close to Indian but with Filipina influences. It had been too much, or at least he had indulged too much. The spices were cooking his gut, and the sense of fullness bordered on discomfort.

But that wasn't what was keeping him awake.

He popped an antacid pill and scrolled through the reports on his main data pad window. Somewhere out there, Lieutenant Brianna Stiles's body was waiting for its final disposition, and his inability to find something so precious was perplexing.

Thirst pinched his throat. Rather than hot tea, he switched to water. After a few sips, he stretched, twisted, and ran through a few katas—just him in his nightclothes looking ridiculous in a dark, quiet room. The way his joints popped and his muscles ached after so little was embarrassing.

He could lie to himself that he deserved a little slack after dying and coming back to life, but it wasn't funny.

He was growing old.

That was something Stiles would never have a chance to experience.

Now he could add breathlessness and heartache to his list of maladies. None of that could explain why he was having such a hard time finding where the message about Stiles had originated or where her body had been moved to. Those failings were completely his own rustiness in digging through data and figuring out the labyrinthine mess of a network that connected not just cities but continents and planets spread across multiple star systems. He didn't just have to work out where on Dramora the message had come from but which Fold Space routing system.

So, start with the transmitting station.

He had that much, because it was tracked on the Kedraal Fold Space station.

His data pad had the software to tear apart routing bundles, but it was meant for internal GSA messaging, not something external. Still…

The software processed for a few minutes. He stretched to pass the time.

A window popped up on the display: complete.

McLeod checked the output. The message had been sent by the main Fold Space station here in the city. That was reassuring. It meant Stiles had been processed through somewhere close by, somewhere on the planet.

More digging, more tearing apart.

Routing could go through so many layers, bouncing from one internal network to a larger external one to the official one that connected everyone together. Everything left a fingerprint. This was no different. In this case, there were thirty-five fingerprints. Thirty-five bounces. It was the source he wanted.

An internal network. Small. A business but not a big one.

He looked up the address. Chen Funeral Services.

They had a directory site: *economic burial services; treat your loved ones to the proper burial without bankrupting your family; the human touch you'll appreciate.*

Yet it listed a single employee: Evan Chen, proprietor, licensed embalmer.

Automated, then.

McLeod connected to the site and requested an estimate on service. A video popped up of a middle-aged man with sorrowful wrinkles and an epicanthic fold that almost hid his dark eyes.

"Thank you for reaching out to me in your time of sorrow. Although we are still experiencing a significant backlog due to the Daley Mine tragedy, we are holding our standard rates steady. Please keep in mind that we value the well-being of your loved ones, and we will process them with the same respect and care you would expect of us. The current wait time for burial is down to—" Another voice spoke over the recorded message, indicating three weeks. "I look forward to discussing your situation with you."

Chen Funeral Services was cheap, but it was also backlogged.

A quick check confirmed that the facility had a significant solar capability and drew heavily on the grid. That pointed to refrigeration and probably robotics. Discount burial services often managed what amounted to mass grave sites, burying bodies by the dozens. Chen wouldn't be called in to deal with bodies until they were ready for final processing.

Who would have used such a service for Stiles? It seemed petty and cruel.

One good thing about a low-cost business like Chen's: It wasn't likely to have much security.

McLeod poked around the site's interface until he located other services and their costs. Putting a hold on Stiles's processing would cost nearly as much as the service itself. Arranging for a transfer cost double that.

It was an inconsequential price to pay to assuage his soul. He would take Stiles back to Kedraal and take care of her himself.

19

———

Fog hung over the field separating the supreme commander's manor from the woods. If Faulk squinted, he could barely make out the faintest shape of the nearest trees, black and thick, rising above the ground ten meters or more. The mist was wet and cold, quickly coating his uniform and lending a heaviness to the air, pressing the smell of dead grass against him. Weber's people and the local terrorists were hiding out there, or maybe they were taking cover in the valley among the farmers. Wherever there were shadows, there would be assassins and violence.

Someone cleared their throat at the manor's front door—the husband of the woman who ran the place. "Field Marshal? We have coffee."

Warm. Bitter. It would be safe and refreshing, the right way to shake off the effects of a long night. Faulk gave the woods another look, wondering how long it would be before the sun burned the ghostly shroud away. There were things that needed to be taken care of in the city, and driving through that soup was out of the question.

Pebbles scraped beneath his boots as he crossed through the courtyard, throwing hollow echoes.

No one was going to sneak up on the manor.

He laughed at that idea, the noise drawing a curious glance from the guard watching the front gate. Faulk waved, then headed inside.

Once he was settled at the sturdy dining table outside the kitchen, the old woman brought out a cup and dish as well as a steel percolator. Steam drifted from it, trailing the rich aroma. She filled his cup, and her husband brought out cream and sugar and a plate of cookies. He set a cloth napkin before the cookies. Faulk took one of the treats, even though he'd eaten breakfast just a couple hours earlier. These were hard and dark. They tasted like molasses—ideal for this particular brew.

The guard who watched over the security station off the main kitchen pushed through the door. "A call just came in, Field Marshal."

"From?"

"The hospital."

Faulk straightened, trying not to appear too hopeful. "Something has happened?"

"Minister King has informed our people that Supreme Commander Graf is being transferred to an ambulance."

"Ambulance?" *Not dead then.*

"He will be here in an hour."

King had provided the worst scenario possible: Graf was going to live, and he was returning to reclaim his winter home.

Faulk finished his cookie. "Inform the others that we'll be returning to our barracks in the city this afternoon."

The guard brought his heels together. "Field Marshal."

There wasn't a coffee bitter enough to match Faulk's mood. Things were progressing, but he was no longer the one choosing the course. Graf's plans would diverge. He would question or perhaps simply overrule the strategy to deal with the Khanate fleet. Maybe he would demand everything be abandoned until the Moskav situation was resolved, ignoring the intent of Faulk's plan.

Let more of my brothers feed the Moskav fields with their blood.

He needed to bring the Kedraalian captain to heel. With her behind his plan, Graf might concede the strategy. He had a weakness for pretty women, even those who didn't match the Azoren ideal.

Faulk finished his coffee, wiped his hands on the cloth napkin, then marched up the stairs, each step as slow as trudging through a bog. His steps made the wood groan. His breath was deep and heavy in his ears.

The Kedraalian captain and her Gulmar dog should be coming down to the table, kneeling before the field marshal, not hosting him in a room.

Had the two of them truly been planning intimacy, as his guard surmised? Animals. Rutting and cavorting, even in the face of danger.

Or did that mean they didn't really consider the Azoren dangerous?

The field marshal stopped outside the Kedraalian captain's door, teeth grinding so hard his jaw ached. He was owed respect and fear, perched as he was atop the pile of dead who had been his cohort.

Of course, Supreme Commander Graf might disagree with that assessment.

A problem for another time. Faulk knew how to handle such things.

He coughed softly, bowed out his chest, and knocked. "Captain Benson." Not a question. Command dictated a certain protocol.

After a moment, he thought he might have heard wood creaking, then the door latch rattled.

Her hair was down—brown and lustrous. Color darkened her cheeks. She filled her uniform in a distracting way, which was only made worse when she leaned against the open door. "Field Marshal Faulk. I thought we might discuss your strategy plan this morning over breakfast."

"I've already eaten, although we can talk while the two of you eat."

"That would be nice. I thought I smelled bacon."

She took a step, then looked at him with something approaching a warning until he stepped back. He stayed close behind her until she knocked on the Gulmar captain's door. It opened immediately, revealing the smiling fool. He had a ridiculous joviality about him, a way of thrusting out his chest and angling his bearded face that must have been meant to project an air of roguishness. How else would someone who came from a culture of pirates and thieves behave?

Faulk pointed to the stairs with his chin. "Breakfast, Captain Thiessen."

Benson took the scoundrel's arm. "We'll have the opportunity to talk strategy."

Rather than wait to hear their prattle, Faulk headed down. The woman who ran the manor poked her head out of the kitchen, glanced at the two captains, then disappeared from sight. Even the help seemed to be marginalizing the most powerful man on Himmel.

Almost the most powerful man on Himmel. Almost.

For the moment, Faulk settled at the head of the table. It wouldn't be his rightful place much longer. He waited until the captains were seated, and plates and coffee were set out before them, then signaled for another cup for himself. It was best to make it seem like they were sharing the moment as equals, at least if he wanted to secure their help.

They tucked into their meals, complimenting the old woman and her husband, as if there were challenges to their simple fare. Children could fry eggs and bake biscuits.

Faulk let it pass. "The supreme leader should be here soon."

Benson looked up, green eyes sparkling. "He's all right?"

"He has survived every attempt against his life. He is charmed."

"That's good. It provides stability." Her words were jabs.

"Stability and wisdom, yes." Faulk felt his jaw jutting out and feigned a yawn to suppress that bit of petulance. The she-cat of an officer was getting under his skin. "He will want to hear our plan."

"Your plan?"

"We are in agreement."

The captains exchanged a look, then the Gulmar officer cut a biscuit in half. "We still haven't heard you acknowledge that the offer of alliance has been accepted."

He was a dog, sniffing after his bitch. She had such complete control over him.

Not Faulk. He considered his coffee. "Of course, we would be allies."

"If we accept your plan?" The Gulmar captain glanced at his counterpart again.

"The strategy I proposed gives everyone what they require." Faulk smiled, but he put a little threat into it.

Benson bit off a chunk of bacon. "I think we might want to hear that from Supreme Commander Graf."

Such audacity! With the proper implements, he would work that out of her. "You would hunt the Khanate fleet down on your own?"

"If we don't feel we have the proper plan."

"*Your* plan? Hm?"

"Any plan that will eliminate the Khanate threat quickly. Keep in mind that Captain Thiessen and I have no doubts about the danger that threat poses."

"Yes."

There wasn't enough time to break the stubborn woman. In fact, there wasn't enough time to get to the bottom of her newfound backbone, although Faulk was sure it had to do with Supreme Commander Graf's imminent arrival. Or perhaps that had only reinforced her determination to push back. After all, she'd seemed ready for a scrape when she'd met him at her door.

His data pad vibrated: Minister King's convoy was running ahead of schedule. Supreme Commander Graf would be at his manor in minutes.

Too late to hope for a small rebellion group attack or an unfortunate mine. Those were things that could have been arranged with a little more warning. King would have known that, so the lack of warning gave clear indication of where he stood regarding Graf.

Without time to humble the Kedraalian captain or even to put her in her place, the need for a meeting was over.

The field marshal stood. "I hope you will excuse me."

Their eyes followed him to the kitchen, and it seemed like they might follow him out of sight, drilling into his back when he closed the door to the secure room.

Rinnan, the man on duty at the moment, looked up, steel-gray eyes attentive. "Yes, Field Marshal?"

"Show me the convoy."

The commando transferred focus of one of the road cameras to the main screen, revealing four Night Jaguars bracketing two speeding cars. "They move too quickly for foot units to react. No one could have known they were coming, so this is sound tactics."

"Thank you, Sergeant. Tell our people to prepare their bags."

"Yes, Field Marshal." It was said without hesitation or question.

Why couldn't everyone be so thoroughly imprinted? Fighting against the smartest plan was wasteful.

Yet the purity minister was doing that, wasn't he?

Faulk let himself out through the kitchen door to the garden, walking among the statues of Graf that had been set alongside the stone walk.

There was Graf the Philosopher on the left, beside a fountain, hands clasped behind his back and brow knitted in thought. Then Graf the Leader across from that, one hand raised above his head, his mouth open, in the middle of a fiery speech. Some meters past that, Graf the Father, kneeling and laughing to welcome imaginary children who didn't warrant statues of their own. Graf the Scientist, Graf the Judge, Graf the Spiritual Guide...

Every imaginable role for the people of the federation, all filled by Graf.

The title of supreme commander didn't seem adequate to capture his greatness. Now add his ability to survive a bomb that had laid low so many others who had been younger, healthier, more vibrant and vital.

Something had happened. Perhaps there truly was something to the belief of the Khan zealots, that a Guiding Light and a divine hand truly protected some.

Engines roared in the distance. When no explosion silenced them, Faulk settled on a stone bench, ignoring the moisture that seeped through the material of his pants.

Eventually, the outer gate clanged as it was thrown open. Brakes squeaked, and the roaring engines drew closer until he could make out the gurgle of each as it idled, then died. After a few heartbeats, metal doors slammed open. Boots scraped in the courtyard, just as Faulk's had earlier. Voices called out, and the heavy boom of wooden doors opening filled the courtyard.

He could have been there, putting on a smiling face and welcoming both of his fathers—the ideological one and the scientist who'd snipped the perfect genetic template from billions and billions of samples.

But Faulk didn't have the energy. He'd grown tired of the struggle, especially after suffering another setback. His destiny eluded him.

Sunlight burned the fog, and the dampness dried from the stone bench, then his trousers. It warmed, and the hardy flowers that had been grown in the same manner as Faulk and his brothers released their muted fragrances. They were sweet and soft in the autumn morning. Maybe they would be stronger, more intoxicating and alluring in the summer. More likely, they would always be muted. That was the cost of being self-sufficient, engineered to a specific task. The insects and animals brought to Himmel didn't care to take part in perpetuating the unnatural plants, so one living design had engineered away the need for the others.

Sergeant Rinnan hurried out of the kitchen, booted steps louder than normal. "Field Marshal?"

Faulk turned, wondering if Rinnan might be holding a pistol, ready to carry out the order to eliminate his superior. But no—neither a pistol nor a look of concern. "Yes?"

"Supreme Commander Graf will see you now."

Of course, he wouldn't *request* a moment of his most senior commander's time. "Thank you."

Only after Rinnan had returned to the kitchen outpost, blinking in confusion because Faulk didn't spring up and run in to see his commander—only then did Faulk actually push up.

Blood rushed from his head. His limbs trembled.

Benson and Thiessen could have moved from the kitchen to the entry and stopped the old man in the hallway, ingratiating themselves and maybe complaining about how incompetent and brutish Faulk was.

As he passed through the kitchen, he nodded at the old woman who ran the manor, for the first time realizing he'd never bothered to ask her name. No matter now.

People hurried in and out through the entry area: loading and unloading.

His boots left brown grass on the stairs, wet and flaccid. Red Skull bodyguards stared straight ahead as he passed.

Had the staff put down fresh linens? Had they opened the window to let out Faulk's scent? That seemed as much professional behavior as a favor to compensate for his own incompetence for not specifically requesting it.

Rather than wait for a knock, the door opened, and the major of the Red Skull detachment—Pétain?—waved Faulk in.

Pillows propped Graf up in his bed. The sheets, the blankets—all new. The curtains had been tied back, allowing in the strengthening daylight. There was a chill in the room that must have come from the windows being opened, and a new fire struggled to life. Someone had even returned the annoying mechanical clock to the room, its pendulum grinding a loud but steady reminder that time marched on forever.

Tick-tock. *You are just a passenger.*

Tick-tock. *The universe laughs at you.*

Tick-tock. *Not relevant.*

Faulk moved forward, always with momentum, always with direction, but the universe favored no single vector. It expanded outward from an eons-old blast, creating and destroying in a cycle that would continue long after he was dust.

I moved too quickly. I lost sight of my objectives.

A pretty, young nurse with long blonde hair and alabaster skin stood beside the bed. Despite her tight uniform, he hadn't noticed her until she handed the supreme leader a glass of water. His knobby fingers—some still raw and bandaged—closed around the glass, and his cold eyes locked on Faulk. The old man sipped, then returned the glass to the woman.

Graf waved, and the nurse exited the room, trailing a perfume of alcohol and lilac.

The major stepped out after her, then returned with the two visiting captains. "Your guests, Supreme Commander."

Benson beamed, an almost authentic look that made her green eyes sparkle like gems in the light coming through the windows. "Supreme Commander Graf. What a pleasant surprise."

Exactly as expected, Graf's eyes drank her in. Even broken by a bomb, he couldn't hide his nature. "You are absolutely enchanting, dear."

For just a second, the Kedraalian's facade crumbled. She was repulsed. "Thank you. Th-this is Captain Floyd—"

Graf's dead eyes barely moved to the Gulmar Captain. "Captain Floyd Thiessen, yes." Graf looked ready to tear Benson's uniform from her. "Are you sure we haven't met before, Captain Benson?"

"I've never been to Himmel."

A dry chuckle escaped the old man's throat. "Perhaps not in the flesh. How unfortunate."

She straightened. "We had hoped to talk with you about the proposed alliance—"

"Your proposal has been accepted."

"Our proposal?"

The old man licked his thin lips, then turned away to squint at the windows. "This Khanate threat is exactly as you have described. Fail to stop it, and no one will survive."

"Then you—"

"I saw your proposal to operate as a combined fleet? Yes, Captain. The Azoren Federation is ready to commit three tenders, six destroyers, and the *Warsaw* to your hunting pack. Field Marshal Faulk will see to it that the troop transports still in orbit are put to effective use as well."

Faulk clapped his heels together. "Of course, Supreme Commander!"

"You will see to it that you launch soon, won't you, Field Marshal? Those soldiers must be quite tired of doing nothing but eating and sleeping in orbit. They want the feel of soil beneath their boots, not the composite of our ship decks."

An admonishment. It was better than an order for the Red Skull major to drag the field marshal out and execute him.

So, Purity Minister King wasn't working against his favored son after all.

The realization nearly stole Faulk's breath away. "I will see to it immediately, Supreme Commander."

Faulk bowed and backed out of the room. Halfway down the stairs, Benson called his name. He nearly stumbled but recovered enough to turn with a hint of control. "Yes, Captain?"

She didn't speed up but moved like a cat, almost prancing. "A minute?"

He tried to control his breathing. "Yes?"

Rather than stop to talk, she continued past, still moving slowly, hand skimming the thick, wooden bannister, forcing him to follow her. "All the activity out front—are we leaving?"

"You heard the supreme commander."

"I heard it all from my bedroom window. I thought it was his arrival, but it sounds like our departure, too."

"It is." *Our* departure rather than just his, as he'd thought.

She continued on toward the front door. "I hope we can put all this maneuvering behind us and find a way to work together now that—"

"Now that I've been given my marching orders?"

Benson hesitated in the foyer, nearly washed out by the sunlight coming through the front door. In the courtyard, doors were slamming shut. A motor rumbled to life. Her eyes slitted, and she drifted to the door, freezing for a moment, as if she'd seen something incomprehensible.

Her hand drifted up to her face as tires scraped against the pavement and an engine grew louder. "Who—?"

Faulk moved just quickly enough to see the car speeding out of the courtyard but not so fast she might mistake it for running. "What?"

She pointed toward the disappearing car. "Who was that?" Her voice was choked.

"In the car?"

"Yes."

"Jack King—our Minister of Purity. He's the father of our genetics program. In a sense, he is my father. Why?"

"Oh."

"Is everything all right, Captain?"

She leaned against the door jamb, as if she might need it to keep her feet under her. "Yes. It's just that I thought I…had seen him before."

It was a silly idea, but Faulk said nothing. The captain was obviously shaken. Based on her appearance, she was in her mid-thirties. King had been running the genetics program on Himmel for nearly as long and had never left.

They have spies, Faulk remembered. The Kedraalians knew who many Azoren leaders were. It explained how quickly she'd connected with Weber.

Still, it might be wise to talk to Minister King before they departed.

Perhaps the scientist had his own thoughts on why the pretty captain might have reacted so strangely to a glimpse of his departure.

20

———

By the time Goldman was headed down to Shod Madieu, the sun was a deep red blister sinking beyond the horizon, and Caville had the local network hacked. There was no shortage of security vulnerabilities, but the clunky interface the Khanate's people had put on the outward-facing piece with its alien alphabet almost acted as an impenetrable defense for outsiders. Fortunately, Caville's data pad managed the interpretation without trouble.

It was cooling quickly as he strode past the tea shop on his way to the starport. The shop's aromas—fresh spice cakes and complicated herbal teas—floated out of the opening, carrying the chatter of customers ready for the night. Their voices were pleasant, but it would have been nicer to hear laughter.

Except that there was no joy here.

He was halfway across the street when he heard a soft voice. "Darien?"

Caville spun. "Denise?"

Her bright and decorative gown was gone, replaced by one of the plain ochre robe outfits, which was cinched mid-waist by a sash. The flesh of her collarbone and neck were hidden behind a hideous, cream-colored piece of cloth, so that only her face was revealed. There was an impossible sorrow there, a network of wrinkles that spoke of fear and anger as well. "I need to walk with you."

"Sure."

She matched his stride, material slapping softly against her with each step. "Thank you."

"Goldman's on the way down."

"Good."

"You all right?"

"No. I need to talk to him." Her voice shook, and it wasn't from trying to keep up. She was breathing hard, but it was the sound of someone fighting back tears.

"I'm listening."

A subtle shake of the head, eyes darting around...

She needed him to shut up, to let it go. He did, drifting closer to her. The guards on the corners stood beneath pale lights, watching the foot traffic, scowling at Caville.

At the starport, they were refused entry but were allowed to wait where the cars gathered. Gallo stayed in the shadows, keeping Caville between her and the armed men. They were too far away to see the front of the terminal in the night, their vision fouled by the street lights, but they were in her head.

Overhead, an arc of fire plunged toward them: one of the robotic shuttles. Its roar started as thunder, then built until it was a vibration in Caville's core. When it disappeared behind the terminal, the sharp, chemical taste of its exhaust settled all around.

Time dragged. Caville brushed sweat from his brow with a swipe of the back of his hand. In his mind, he replayed the terminal security he'd gone through earlier—the lazy glares of suspicion and dull pace of bureaucratic tyrants with no schedule. He could imagine where Goldman was inside.

Finally, the pirate exited the front, face twisted in anger, duffel bag over his shoulder. At his side, Theo was surprisingly sober despite bloodshot eyes that glared at the floodlights mounted on the building front.

Caville waved. "Lev!"

The pirate searched around, then returned the wave. He whispered something to Theo, pointed toward one of the cars, then hurried over. "You get a room yet?" The question could have been intended for the young woman, too.

Gallo pressed herself against Caville, hot in the cooling air. "Captain Goldman, do you have a moment?"

"Maybe." Goldman shot Caville a look, the question obvious: *Do you know what this is about?*

Caville shook his head.

After straightening and looking around, Gallo stepped closer. "I need to get off this planet."

Goldman snorted. "We all do."

"I made a terrible mistake. This isn't my home."

"Well—" The pirate massaged his jaw with a thick hand.

"I have contacts. I can arrange payment. Get me to Dramora. I'll—" Her voice caught. "I'll do anything."

"You might have to."

"I can't live here."

Goldman squinted at Caville. "I don't know how anyone can."

Something was…wrong. Goldman was fearless, or at least he was resigned to things being a disaster. Now? He sounded scared.

Caville twisted around to be sure Theo was still at the car he'd gone off to hire. "Where's everyone else?"

"Talia's in orbit. They made us send the others down in one of the other shuttles. We lost track of them once they landed."

"I can get you onto the network." Caville waved for the other man's device.

The pirate handed his data pad across. "Won't do us much good if the rest of the team isn't on."

"You didn't arrange for a rendezvous?"

"The hotel."

"Any reason they wouldn't be there?"

"Same reason they came down before us: This isn't normal."

Caville tested the device's connection to the network by sending it a message from his own device. He handed it back to Goldman. "You're on. They won't be able to detect you, if you keep your traffic low and stick to comm discipline." That meant piggybacking off existing innocuous message communities, creating innocent sub-channels, and talking in code. As an SAID operative, Goldman would have experience at it.

After poking at his data pad for a bit, the pirate captain grunted. "All right." He didn't look up from the device. "Miss Gallo, if we can get you off Azh Shivan, we will, but I'm not risking my crew."

She thumbed tears from her cheeks. "Thank you."

Goldman waved for Caville to follow, and a few meters away from the young woman pulled him by the shoulder so that his ear was close. "I hope you know what you're doing."

"She's scared." But Caville wondered if that was true. "I'll keep an eye on her."

"Do that."

The pirate released his grip on Caville's shirt and gave a gentle shove, then jogged over to the car Theo had grabbed and climbed inside. They sped away with a spray of sand and rock that clattered against the sidewalk.

Gallo crept up on Caville, hand softly pressing against his back. "I… don't have a place to stay."

He glanced around, but no one was nearby. "I'll get you a room."

She pressed her hand into his—hot, damp, trembling.

Rather than hire a car, they walked back to the city, her drifting closer as they went, until he could smell her sweat. It was dark as they neared the main thoroughfare. Beneath the street corner lights, the guards cast pale, gray shadows that watched suspiciously.

The young woman pulled her hand free now that they would be more than shadows within shadows. "They're tyrants."

"The guards?"

"All of them. This place, their doctrine—this isn't me. It's not my world."

"You never lived here, right? You said you grew up on Kedraal."

"I've never been here. But this isn't shock. I can't adapt to it."

"How would you know that?"

"What I saw at my mother's home and the other homes. Everyone but my mother is terrified. The others whispered warnings, as if there were bugs installed everywhere. Spies. No one can be trusted."

Caville found himself thinking of Stiles's look of defeat, the way the blood misted around her head when he pulled the trigger. "No one."

"I mean it. Even my mother."

"You can always trust your mother." Couldn't you? Human mothers were notoriously protective, almost delusional, weren't they?

"Her sisters say she's a spy. She made me wear—" Gallo waved at the outfit.

"For your own protection."

"She threatened to turn me in if I didn't change. She's nuts, Darien. She's not the woman I remember. This religion destroyed her."

They reached the road, and the two nearest guards separated from the side of the buildings where they'd been watching, angling lazily toward the couple, then picking up speed when Caville pretended to not notice them and changed direction.

Gallo choked back a sob.

The guard directly in their path was short and stocky, with a round face and a shaggy, brown beard. He smelled like spice cakes and sweat. When he came to a stop a meter short of them, he held up a hand and mumbled something meaningless. After a second, he edged closer. The other guard, taller and with an oversized head, was behind the Genesis agent, weapon held low ready.

Caville shrugged. "I don't speak—"

"This one—" Short and Stocky pointed at Gallo. "—is a danger."

"Danger?"

From behind. "Bomb. She could have a bomb."

Gallo gasped, and Caville realized Big Head had moved close enough to put his hand on her butt.

Short and Stocky glared. "Danger. See?"

Big Head pressed up and down Gallo's back, squeezing enough to bring tears to her eyes. He backed away, then Short and Stocky moved forward. He ran his hands all across Gallo's thighs, up to her belly, then her breasts. The whole time, Big Head had his finger on the trigger guard of his weapon.

When Short and Stocky stepped back, a smile slid across his face. "No bomb."

Despite his training, Caville shook with rage. They would interpret it as fear and impotence, which was fine. What he felt... "We're going to the hotel."

Short and Stocky shook his head. He reached for Gallo's elbow. "No."

Big Head hissed. "Stay away from foreigner."

Caville took her arm. "She's my wife. We married before our trip here."

Short and Stocky looked past Caville, at Big Head, then sneered and stepped aside. "Go. Keep her under control."

That was exactly what Caville did, pulling the former Khanate spy along with him.

Once they were a few steps past, she squeezed his arm and began to cry. "I'm sorry."

"Don't you apologize. That's their problem, not yours."

There was only one real hotel in the city, and the place was as sad and desperate as everything around it. A few floodlights showed from the lobby entry, highlighting the dun facade and brown-tinted windows. It was isolated from the rest of the city by a sand-covered, kilometer-long road. The walk gave Gallo time to recover.

The people behind the registry desk scowled as Caville signed in, repeating the story that the two of them were newlyweds. In the small tea shop off the lobby, a man who was obviously part of the same security apparatus as the guards back in town watched the process with feigned amusement.

In the lift, Gallo leaned against the back wall and covered her face. "They're going to figure out that you're lying."

"How?" He pulled out his data pad. "They really don't understand technology. At all. You seal yourself off from the outside, you don't have any idea what's really happening."

"They'll know I arrived on the *Ollie.*"

"Will they? If they had, they should have had a car there waiting for you."

"But—"

"They know about Goldman, because he's been working for them for years. He's cooperating, and they've probably got spies tracking him while he's down here. You?" Caville shrugged. "Look at the way they treat women. Once you left Kedraal, you probably became irrelevant to them."

She dabbed at her eyes with the sleeve of her robe. "You're not what I imagined a pirate would be."

"I don't consider myself one."

"But you're in Goldman's crew."

"I'm a mercenary. I've guarded cargo, rode shotgun on a couple convoys, been muscle during negotiations—nothing that would technically make me a pirate."

A smile broke on her face. "I think you lied to me to get into my bed."

"Did you enjoy it?"

She covered her face again and made a sound that was part laugh, part sob. "I messed up everything."

"We all feel that way at some point."

The lift finally chimed, and the door opened. Their room was at the far end of the hall, past several on either side. A mirror stood on top of a small table halfway down. There would be a camera embedded. Caville spotted two others.

He hooked his arm around Gallo and kissed her cheek, which was salty from tears. "They've got cameras all along the hallway."

She tensed, and her head turned slightly, then she stiffened. "In our room?"

"Most likely. These people are so uptight, they probably need to get their kicks remotely."

"I—I don't know—"

"You just traveled on a pirate ship for several weeks. You're too tired. It makes sense."

Their room was modest: nightstands bracketing a bed with rough linens; a bathroom with toilet, sink, and bath; a standing cabinet; two chairs.

No display. No refrigerator.

He tossed his duffel bag onto one of the chairs and waved to the bathroom. "You can go first."

Gallo disappeared through the doorway—there was no door. After an awkward silence, the bathwater started. He turned his attention to the data pad and began rummaging around in the network, searching for more vulnerabilities, more opportunities to launch attacks when the time came. There were no obvious resources to research the city's history or to find video or imagery that would give him a sense of the layout. Maybe it had all been lost in the internecine wars with the Azoren and Moskav. Then again, there wasn't even a simple map to show tourist sites or holy areas or whatever it was the Khan valued.

But there was the hotel network. It had a simple protection layer that was easily disabled, and doing that opened everything else: the registry system, the billing system, the security system.

There were two cameras in the bathroom and four in the main room, including one over the bed.

It took Caville several minutes to get through the interface, find the history, then loop video that replayed him and Gallo walking around in the bedroom. Whoever was stuck monitoring them would grow bored quickly.

A part of him observed that Stiles would have finished the work in half the time. Another part told him to let that go.

He crossed to the doorway, staying just out of sight of the bathroom. "How well do you know this area?"

Over the sound of the water running, he thought he caught a gasp. Gallo came back into the room, her robe undone but still covering her. She looked around the room sheepishly. "Is it safe to talk?" She whispered that.

"They're getting a very boring look at the two of us walking around the room."

"Oh." She dropped the robe to the floor. "Maybe we could talk in there?"

Caville had no compulsion against mixing pleasure with business. It was how he'd operated from the first day in the field. If anything, this was more pleasant, not requiring him to influence the young woman at all.

When they lay on the bed later, sheets thrown back, cooling after finding a heat of their own that was much less miserable, he kissed her cheek. They hadn't really talked, not about what he needed answers to. He'd been more concerned with helping her deal with the anger and resentment that came from believing something you'd been told was true from childhood.

He pinched a strand of her hair between his lips and traced a finger over her soft belly. "When did you turn?"

"I think I was twelve. I was going through changes. My mother had sent messages back for years. I hadn't really listened to them. Not *listened.*"

"Do kids ever listen?"

She blinked rapidly, then sucked air in with a whistling sound. "I was… fat. Ugly. Awkward. My father couldn't understand what was wrong. But my mother, when I sent her a message about how terrible it was, she understood. She told me that the Khan saw the inner light. He didn't care if someone was fat or skinny, smart or stupid."

"That does sound good."

"She said all the things I needed to hear at that time. A woman didn't need to think for herself, not with the Khan. His words were the path to follow. When I struggled with studies, I could tell myself that. The Khan had words, and I only had to listen."

"Your father—did he know this was going on?"

"I think he had a sense. He still pushed me to study. It was hard to believe him when he said I was beautiful and smart and it was all up to me how far I went. There was someone all-powerful out there talking to me through these comforting parables and…"

"It's easy. That makes it comforting. We all prefer easier."

She pressed a hand against his chest. "You don't believe in anything?"

"Right and wrong, I guess. Basic decency. Honor. All the usual things."

"Is that really usual?"

The way she squinted at him left Caville feeling a little less certain for a moment. "I think so. It's down to the individual, though."

"You were asking me a question earlier."

Could he trust her? He didn't really have a choice anymore. Working alone would be slow, and things seemed to be coming apart around him.

"I'm looking for a place: ruins. They'd probably be off limits. There might be guards around."

She rolled onto her side. "The Place of the Fallen?"

"Maybe? Can you describe it?"

"No. But I know that if you go there, you die."

"How many guards are there? Weapons systems?"

"Not like that. I don't know if anyone would be willing to guard it."

"Then how—?"

"It kills you. No one has been inside it and lived. Not even the Khan."

"Denise, I need to go there."

"You can't!"

He cupped her face in his hand. "I have to."

Tears welled up in her eyes but didn't fall. She sniffled. "I can ask around."

"Discretely."

"Yes."

The soft blue glow of his data pad caught his eye, then came the rumble of its vibration. Gallo rolled off the bed and padded to the bathroom. It was hard picturing someone long and slender as she was as ever having been the fat kid she described. That was the terrible power of the mind.

Caville sat up and grabbed the data pad, knowing before accepting the connection that it was Goldman. The pirate captain was in the dark, the light of stars in the sky far overhead, moving. He was walking. In the blue light of his device, muscles moved along his jaw.

He looked heavenward, then back at the device. "Darien? Where are you?"

"In the hotel." The sound of running water came from the bathroom. "Where are you?"

"Come on out the back. I'm about half a klick west of the kitchen."

"The connection's about as secure as we're going to get. What's up?"

Goldman came to a stop, and the image shook as the device camera adjusted. "The Khan."

"What about him?"

"He just double-crossed me. No hostage release."

A chill ran along Caville's spine. "You delivered everything?"

"All of it. Exactly as agreed."

"That's not good."

Sand rattled against the SAID agent, forcing him to close his eyes. When the breeze died, he sucked in a breath, then exhaled. "I think he's going to kill us. All of us."

21

———————

Returning to the *Valor* was both jarring and comforting for Benson. There were the familiar patterns of life, the sounds of air recyclers and people rushing across deck plating that always seemed dull and filtered like the air, but there was also the absence of the chaos and violence that had so quickly come to define Himmel. It reached even her departure, with the escort vehicle erupting in fire and launching two meters into the air not fifty meters in front of her own vehicle. The shuttle crew had caught the entire thing on high-resolution video on descent and shared it with her once they were airborne.

That was the world Supreme Leader Graf had created, ripped from peace and stability decades before and deposited into a ravening whirlwind of hatred and megalomaniacal conquest.

Had she really chosen monsters to fight monsters? Had that really been the suggested alternative laid out for her by the prime minister's advisors from the start?

She sighed and pulled her uniform jacket on, welcoming the looser fit of the blue combination. Her days of diplomatic negotiations—a laughable term—were behind her now. A final tightening of the covers on her bunk, a brush of fingers over imaginary dust on her foldout desktop, a light spray of perfume on her wrists, then she exited her cabin.

Although the ship's lighting was meant to match what human eyes had come to expect, there was no replacing the air she'd breathed on Himmel. She missed the sweet smell of the cultivated woodlands and pushed aside memories of the stench of gunpowder and burning vehicles. Some impressions from the planet would be slower to forget.

Chopra greeted her with her *Pandora* drink container—cool to the touch—when she passed through the bridge hatch. "Welcome back, Captain."

"Thank you." She nodded to the bridge officers, who smiled before returning their attention to the command console that held their frenetic work. She made a point of nodding at the Marines protecting the hatch, even though they wouldn't acknowledge her.

Rather than wave her to the raised command station, Chopra clasped his hands in front of him. "We are laying in Fold Space jump plans."

That meant they were making final adjustments to match the Azoren demands. She'd warned everyone how petty Faulk and his people would be. Rather than argue, she'd asked for appeasement. For now. "Any concerns?"

"Only with their tolerance for inefficiency."

"We'll survive."

His eyebrows ticked up, perhaps questioning that assumption.

She opened the drink container's inbuilt straw and took a sip. Cold fluid trickled out, cooling her tongue with its bittersweet tang. It wasn't the rich, authentic coffee they grew on Himmel, but it had a buzz of its own.

Benson stepped in close to Chopra. "Take the command station."

He rose on the balls of his feet. "You are—"

"I'm focused on the combined fleet, and I'm pretty sure that's more than I can handle."

"What about Alexander?"

"Commander Tuleyev will direct the task force. I need you running the *Valor*."

For a moment, she thought Chopra might protest, then he adjusted his jacket so that it de-emphasized the potbelly that had grown back in the time she'd been on Himmel and climbed to the raised station. His hands shook until he gripped the support railing encircling most of the station. "Lieutenant Konrath, could I have a status, please?"

The young man turned so that his hard profile was silhouetted by the glow of the console. His blond hair had been shaved until barely a centimeter rose from his scalp. "Course programmed in. Ready to launch, Commander."

Benson took a communicator headset from her pocket and slipped the device over her ear. She attached to the bridge comms, tilted her head at her XO, then opened a connection to Thiessen, Tuleyev, and finally Faulk. "Gentlemen."

Tuleyev cleared his throat, almost stepping on her audio. "Captain Benson. Kedraalian task force reports ready for launch."

Silence. It was the awkward, unspoken negotiation between Thiessen and Faulk, the dynamic being established now that the field marshal had been ejected from his home world and into the more fragile world of starcraft and the cumbersome protocols of navies.

Finally, Thiessen made a clicking noise—maybe the sharp clap of teeth. "Gulmar task force ready for launch, Captain."

Another stretch of silence, then the extended intake of breath, and finally the field marshal. "The Azoren Strike Fleet launches into Fold Space in five minutes."

There was nothing to do but bow her head and tell herself that at least she hadn't opened a video connection. No one could see the color rising in her cheeks. "Enter Fold Space in…" She checked the countdown that showed on the *Valor*'s giant display. "One minute. Best of luck on your travels. Remember your assignments once we reach our destination. We'll be exiting at the point Azoren ships have identified as safest from detection."

She disconnected at that point.

Fifty-two seconds.

Fifty-one.

They had weeks in Fold Space ahead of them, an opportunity to get separated or find themselves caught up in who knew how many dramas if they didn't coordinate their operations. Fold Space might be a fractional representation of the universe, a place where distance could be rendered down into percents of normal space, but it was still huge. It would take nothing to drift too far apart for radio operations to work.

The Azoren ship commanders had to know that, and they had to know the risk involved if they didn't maintain fleet pace. Dealing with Faulk was their concern.

Benson pulled the headset off and returned it to her pocket, then leaned against the command station. "Thoughts, Dinesh?"

Her XO twitched, then looked down. "We've all worked out the process."

"You don't think the Azoren will be trouble?"

At the helm station, Konrath's head came up as if he might want to contribute an opinion, then his shoulders slumped and he returned to studying his station. His background had been vetted. His psychological profile was solid. There was shame for his family's involvement with the Azoren, and there was anger toward that faction, but paramount was his loyalty to the Kedraalian Republic.

He wasn't a concern.

Supposedly, they didn't have any worries about conflicted loyalties among any of her crews anymore. That was something she needed to be doubly sure of, though.

When the strange blip of nausea and the accompanying sense of disorientation hit, and she knew they were in Fold Space, Benson drew herself up. "Commander Chopra, you have the bridge. If you need me, I'll be going over task force security."

"Yes, ma'am."

There was a moment where Benson thought Lieutenant Mahama's dark head might have twisted around, his black eyes might have narrowed, then she realized he was going over the weapons systems data on his console.

Spies. Bombings. Betrayal. It was getting to her.

Benson had always imagined the Azoren were a monolithic culture, people of one mind about the human species. Discovering that they were just as riddled with splinter factions as anyone else was refreshing. It meant they weren't quite the dangerous force she'd expected, but that said something about the human—and other than human—condition.

She exited the bridge at a good clip and checked her data pad to locate Halliwell. He was in the port hangar deck with his Marines.

Partway down, she changed her mind and swung by the medical center. Dietrich and Kohn were back on duty, and the conversation she'd been meaning to have with them had been put off long enough.

Once through the hatch, she shivered at the familiar smells of detergents and medicine. Those should have been comforting, but they always reminded her of death and pain. She caught the glance of the young, dark-eyed woman who'd replaced Lieutenant Stiles for Kohn, then followed her nod to the surgical bay, where Dietrich and Kohn were caught up in another of their heated exchanges. At least the commander had the sense to hide his shouting behind the glass wall.

Benson didn't announce her presence but let herself in.

Dietrich's face was red, and the last snatches of his raised voice clung to the stainless steel ceiling. He set his shoulders, flashed an annoyed look at Kohn, then set that same look on her. "Captain. What brings you to the medical center? Another near-corpse for us to salvage?"

"Actually, I wanted to take a moment to thank both of you for what you did on Himmel. Your work made this mission possible."

Kohn had maintained an unreadable mask since turning at her entry, something that might have been pained or annoyed. That slid away, and he blushed. "Thank you, ma'am."

But Dietrich frowned. "More bodies being smashed into pieces. I'm not sure that's something I appreciate being thanked for."

It was typical of the surgeon, but the words were like a hot poker just then. "I thought we had an understanding."

"An understanding that war is a pointless waste of life?"

"I won't argue that it's a waste of life, Ernie, but it's tragic, not pointless."

"Tragic meaning necessary. I can't agree with that assessment."

"You're going to have to, so long as you remain in the navy."

Kohn bowed his head. "Was it really worth it, ma'am? The Azoren?"

Something coiled in her belly. "I don't think we'll ever have a good answer. I can tell you that, without the Azoren, any engagement against the Khanate force is going to be worse."

"They seem pretty twisted."

"We're not here to convert them, and we're not going to help them, either. What they did—attacking Kedraal and killing all those people. We can't forgive that."

"But we can work with them?"

Benson saw a smug smile beginning to spread on Dietrich's face. Part of his teaching apparently included his thinking about the military and war. She spread her feet apart slightly. "Ensign Kohn, did you know any of the people who died in that surprise attack on Kedraal?"

"I went through tech training with a few."

"Did their deaths hurt you?"

The young man's thick, dark eyebrows bunched up. "Yes."

"And the people who died on the *Pandora*? On Jotun?"

"I think that's pretty obvious, ma'am."

"All I'm trying to do is find a lesser pain. When we fight the Khanate, right or wrong, I want the Azoren to be the ones to take the brunt of the attack. I want people who aren't us and who have reprehensible views to be the ones sucked out into space or burned to a crisp."

Dietrich's smile drew into a pinch. "All human life—"

Benson shook her head. "I don't have time for that, Doctor. We're allied with people who define our ensign here as less than human. Do I want to kill them for that? No. But if people are going to die—and they are—I'd rather it be people like that."

Kohn nodded. "I understand, ma'am. I'm not really sure I agree with being paraded around in front of them as proof that their views are wrong, though."

That pulled Dietrich's attention back to his student. "You proved exactly—"

Benson cleared her throat. "I actually think the commander ultimately had a good point."

The surgeon thrust out his chin. "Thank you."

"We're all being used in a broader operation. Having you down there was more than a message that the republic represents ideals contrary to those of the Azoren. It shows that our views are *right*. You helped save their leader. Is there a stronger refutation than that?"

It went silent, then the ensign shook his head. "I guess not."

She smiled. "The two of you were as brave as you were professional. I worried they weren't going to release you, and it seems like they came close to keeping you down there. That's going to be noted in my report."

Dietrich was surprisingly quieted by that, something she took as a positive sign. She ducked out before he could spoil the moment.

As she approached the hangar bay hatch, all the good feelings from her short interaction with the doctor and his prize student were sucked away. Marines were filing out of the hatch, their T-shirts and shorts dark with sweat. They nodded at her in passing, the smell of their exertion hanging around even after they were gone. Inside the bay, Halliwell and Grier stood, also in workout gear.

They were close to each other, discussing something softly enough that Benson couldn't hear their voices. It was just an officer and his reliable sergeant chatting, but it looked so…intimate.

Just familiar. They're friends. They've served together for years.

Benson tried to make her stride seem natural, the product of momentum from her speedy exit out of the medical center, as if the Marines would have known she had just been there. "Lieutenant Halliwell?"

He turned, lips twisting. "Captain."

Grier nodded in a way that said she would've snapped to attention if she'd been in regular uniform. "Ma'am."

It was only fifteen or so steps to reach them, but with each of those steps, Benson felt the difference in age and fitness became more pronounced. They were both vibrant, their faces flush and moist from their workouts. She'd come to talk about security, but she felt like an intruder.

Even smiling took serious effort. "I saw your report on the last round of background checks and inspections—"

Halliwell hooked his thumbs on his hips. "We've gone through every—"

"I know you have, but we're on the hunt again. We have a little while before things get messy, and I want to coordinate one last set of inspections."

"My people are already stretched too thin."

Grier looked away, lips squeezed tight, body sunken in enough to signal her discomfort.

That signal…

Benson nodded to a spot somewhere away from where they were. "Could we talk over there?"

Halliwell sighed. He seemed ready to say no, but he followed her, his steps quiet only because he wore sneakers. Still, he came up short of where she'd indicated, drawing his own line in the sand. "Faith, this is too much."

She looked around to be sure there weren't maintenance people working on the shuttles. Alone. Just Grier watching. "And this is unprofessional."

"Is it? Me standing up for my Marines? Then what's professional?"

"Maybe a little respect? Is that too much to ask?"

The Marine rose up to his full height, so that he was looking down into her eyes. "You know I respect you. I'm telling you that you're pushing my people too hard. We're not getting enough sleep—"

"I know."

"—and we're falling behind on training—"

"I know. Clive, I know. It's not ideal. And after this last inspection, I think we can start cutting guard teams in half. *After* this last inspection."

He let out a grunt. "This professional thing…the respect?"

"It's just how things look in front of—"

"Yeah, I get it. So, let's make things a little easier, okay?"

"Easier?" Benson's heart stuttered.

"I don't want anyone thinking we're not being professional. So we need to keep things that way. Captain, lieutenant. That's it."

She tried to breathe. Still anchored to the deck where they'd left Grier, the sergeant covered her mouth to hide her laughter.

No. She bit her knuckle. Was there pain in her eyes? Sympathy?

Benson's knees seemed ready to buckle. "O-okay."

Old. She felt old. Old and unwanted, even as memories of her time with Thiessen down on Himmel hung in her mind.

Halliwell spun around and hurried away. There hadn't been any obvious malice in his voice, although she wanted to imagine it. He actually seemed hurt. Maybe. Or that could have been her imagination.

She waited until the two of them were gone, sucked in a breath, then took a step.

Then another.

Until she had herself under control.

Her stride was controlled and her breathing back to normal when she reached Parkinson's office. The place felt hot after the cool of the medical center. Or maybe it was still the pain from what Halliwell had just done.

What was overdue...

She crinkled her nose against the smells of lubricant and cleaning fluids, then knocked on the bulkhead, drawing the chief engineer out of whatever he was watching on his desktop terminal.

The little man spun around, locked onto Benson for an instant, then turned back to the display. "Hey."

Benson froze. She hadn't come for the thrill of Parkinson's hungry eyes, but after the way Halliwell had broken things off, the engineer's complete disinterest was almost as annoying as being mentally undressed. It was ridiculous. She was in command of the largest—and probably the *only*—combined fleet in Kedraalian history. She'd escaped the destruction of the Gulmar center of power and negotiated an alliance with one of the most loathed people in the galaxy.

She didn't need a man to appreciate her.

But Parkinson's behavior *was* odd. That meant something. "What've you got for me, Chief?"

"Well..." He sat back and crossed his arms over his chest. "Not exactly what I wanted, and I'm really annoyed about it."

She stepped over to his chair. "This is about the Khanate stealth technology?"

"Yeah. Greta just about had it figured out, but the last little bit..." He shook his head.

"Greta?"

"Oh. Sorry. Chief Taylor. She figured out that their systems aren't really using the same code as ours. It's the same code *base*, sure, but from way back. Like, older than the system we had installed on the *Pandora*. And whoever gave this to them made a lot of modifications."

Benson rocked back on her heels. Was he giving credit to another person? It was as unlikely as him not being a twisted wreck because he couldn't figure something out. "So, it's our tech, right? This shadow tech?"

"Our tech, but not as good. I think."

"That's good news, right?"

"If you like unknowns. How do we know they don't have improvements that end up making their systems better than ours?"

"But we managed lock-ons."

"And they managed lock-ons to our ships." Parkinson rested his elbows on the desk. "We're flailing in the dark, and without the actual source code and a team of software engineers to dig into it, that's not going to change."

That wasn't what Benson needed to hear. "You were going to run simulations…"

"We did. All told, about twenty of them."

"But they didn't tell you anything."

"Well…" He tugged at the little patch of whiskers beneath his bottom lip. "We know *how* they use their systems. That's something. It's crude, like someone who takes a hammer from a toolbox and thinks that's the only solution available."

"That's not the system itself?"

"Don't think so. It looks like a very simple set of tactics built around basic functionality."

"Like they don't know what they're doing?"

"Oh, they seem to know what they're doing. But…"

"The hammer analogy?"

Parkinson nodded. "Might be their other technology limits them. Those fighter craft they're launching like missiles? That design is very limiting. I can't figure why they wouldn't just use missiles. They *have* missiles, so why bother with these fighters? It's not efficient. It's like they're trying to make a point, but I can't figure out what."

"History's full of bad military decisions built around cultural and political pressures. It's easy for us to look at this from the outside and wonder what's behind it."

"Well, without knowing the *why*, it's impossible to solve the puzzle."

"It's something, Chief. What about their capital ships? Can we exploit anything with them—overwhelm their defenses?"

The little engineer shifted. "Maybe."

"If you're worried that it's not airtight—"

"I'm—we're—working on it."

We. This other chief he seemed to respect. Benson suppressed a smile. "You've got this time while we're in Fold Space."

Parkinson grunted. "I don't know if *years* would be enough."

She fought back the urge to remind him that the enemy would change and improve in that time, that striking now was their best chance at crippling the enemy they hadn't even realized was a threat until it revealed itself by destroying the center of power of the Kedraalian Republic's best potential ally. What mattered was that they had an alliance *now*, and they were aware of who the greatest danger was.

At least, she hoped that was true. But the strange crates she'd seen aboard the *Warsaw* left her wondering just how much she knew about Azoren capabilities. Maybe they hadn't actually gained knowledge about shadow tech from the Jotun ruins, as some within the military suspected. If the crates had come from someone inside the Kedraalian military…

That was something she would have to think about later. She had to focus on one enemy at a time, or their mission was doomed.

The Patel headquarters building was in the heart of the Asilo business district, an ugly slab of red that must have been ten kilometers to a side. Buildings there were mostly squat and sturdy, using the same stone or sand that went into the sidewalks and roads. The windows were thick, a greenish filter that distorted the interiors so that McLeod couldn't be sure what was inside as he passed. Not even the blinding light of the morning sun could fully penetrate the glass.

His car found a parking spot in the small side lot reserved for VIPs. He sucked in the cool air, like a diver about to leave the protection of a diving chamber. When he opened the door, the heat rushed in. Sweat beaded the back of his hands by the time he reached the lobby.

A bubbly young woman with a broad smile and hair colored like a nova waved him over, passed a pre-credentialed card to him, then pointed a manicured finger to the lifts. "Miss Patel is waiting for you."

He tried the nearest car, but it warned him he would need to use the one that went to the top floor. Six stories, but only one way to the very top.

Devanshi was at her office door when he stepped out. "Avis. Do come in."

His data pad buzzed a warning—it was disabled. Not just off the network but disabled. Up here, he was invisible, lost.

Golden wood paneling, brown-red marble, and polished bronze trim gave the hall and office fronts a warm, welcoming feel. That disappeared the second he passed through her door. Her office took up the entire eastern end of the floor—the office proper with its desk and small confer- ence area; a bathroom; a small gym; and a bedroom...all labeled. Incense drifted from a niche built into the north wall, where a multi-armed bronze statue rose from a black stone base. A river rushed over rocks somewhere—ambient sound that didn't so much soothe as irritate.

She settled behind her desk and pointed him to a chair directly across from hers. "You've been busy."

McLeod took the proffered seat, vaguely noting how little padding there was to it and how it lacked armrests. It was another thing meant to agitate, to keep people off balance. "I told you I came here for business."

"You did." She nodded toward a desktop-embedded display. "But this..."

He stretched his neck out, as if that might be enough to see what she was looking at. "This?"

"You've been poking around. It's an unwise thing to do."

"I've been doing GSA work."

"There's GSA work, and there's sticking your fingers in holes where they shouldn't go. You know we conduct very sensitive business. Digging around in dark corners—not even your connections can save you if you make trouble with me, Avis."

"You're threatening me?"

"It's not a threat. I'm explaining to you that you face a choice. You can keep doing what you're doing, or you can stop. One of those choices will leave you very, very dead."

McLeod crossed his leg and rested his hands on his thighs. "You have a lot to hide."

"I run a business. Either you have the stomach to oversee unsettling things, or you don't. If you don't, the business doesn't last long."

"And I serve the people of the republic."

"Don't delude yourself. You run a black ops group of assassins and spies for the military. Samir told me about all the special tricks your people could do with their guns, the way you could tear a weapon apart and reassemble it blindfolded or swap a bullet out in a weapon without anyone seeing."

"Exaggeration."

"Don't lie to me."

"We do what we do for the Kedraalian people."

"Keep doing it with me, and I will have my people chop you into tiny, little pieces and spread you across the desert."

"When I saw your invitation this morning, I thought it might be about this."

"I've lost two children when you were involved. No one can prove that you were responsible, but I don't need proof. And with my business, I'm much more protective."

Tingling ran down McLeod's arms. "I'll be leaving tonight."

"Good. Keep your nose clean, and you'll be just fine."

He leaned forward slightly. "I am curious, though. Your family has had connections to the government for decades. You've been called out as patriots. Do you really care about the ideals of the republic, or has it always been about the money?"

She clasped her hands before her. "I told you: I run a business. Money is all that can matter."

"I guess that's not surprising." He stood. "I can go?"

"This was your last warning."

At her door, he paused, perhaps expecting someone with a weapon to meet him. Devanshi was already concentrating on whatever she'd been working on before he'd interrupted her.

He took the elevator down, returned the credential card to the young woman, then headed out to the waiting rental car. His shuttle left in ten hours. It was time enough to grab a meal and resolve the situation with Stiles's body. If he were even ten years younger, it might have been time enough to track Devanshi down on her way between the office building and her mansion and show her the dangers of making threats.

But he wasn't. He was old and out of shape and still recovering from resuscitation. If he was killed here, there would be no return from the dead—not this time.

Caution was the watchword, then. Caution and patience. With Stiles gone, taking down the Patels would require a focus on the long game.

He could only hope things were going better for other operations.

22

Faulk never had the stomach for the navy. It wasn't just because of the sense of helplessness that came with floating in space, waiting for a single missile or rail gun round to kill you and the hundreds of people around you. Or the idea of breathing in the air someone else had just breathed out or drinking water that had just been evacuated from someone else. The problem was that he was a man of action—pragmatic and sensible. If fifty cases of ammunition needed to be redeployed to a forward operating position, then fifty cases of ammunition were loaded onto a trailer and sent high-speed to that position. In the navy, there were regulations and traditions and a million other reasons to *not* actually accomplish something.

For that reason, he left control of the *Warsaw* and the task force to Captain Leopold Hart, someone content to be a follower rather than a rival. Faulk's brother was quite close in height, with paler skin and a hint of red to his thinning hair. Hart's cheeks were softer, and his nose was less pronounced.

But he was still a brother.

That made it possible for Faulk to feel something approaching sympathy when standing on the *Warsaw's* cramped bridge while the captain dealt with his subordinates. As far as Faulk could tell, there were four commanders who got under Hart's skin. Apparently, everyone knew when he was talking with them, because the bridge would go silent, leaving only the captain's pained, patient voice.

"Exactly as I said, Commander Pelham." Clipped, followed by a sigh.

"That is how Fold Space works, Commander Adel." A smothered groan.

"The brilliance of mathematics is that it works the same for all of us, Commander Baden." The pop of teeth snapping together.

"Yes, Commander Brummell, your sensors require power to detect ships." The head bent forward so the temple could be massaged vigorously.

One such exchange had just ended, leaving the captain swearing under his breath and close to tears. The chatter on the bridge slowly resumed, with the young officers moving between the control stations, offering each other suggestions and pulling up online manuals. Something about the moment felt vaguely annoying, or perhaps even worrisome, to Faulk, but these were Hart's officers and problems.

The field marshal gave his captain a moment to compose himself, then stepped over to the raised command station, boots scuffing in the warm air. "Problems, Captain?"

Hart shook his head—just a few millimeters. It looked as if more might have been enough to cause his skull to explode. "We have yet to suffer a fatality."

"Your report painted a dire situation."

"An inexperienced crew. Funding cuts for training. Nothing more."

"You have weeks to learn the new systems provided by our friends."

"Not—" The captain straightened and tugged down his tight-fitting jacket. He had eschewed the black uniforms of the Children, choosing instead the baby blue of Weber's navy. Brummell cleared his throat. "Our staff lacks rudimentary knowledge of command fundamentals."

"Then you have weeks to ingrain those into them."

"We have lieutenants in slots meant for commanders, and ensigns in slots meant for lieutenants, and their only qualification is that they came from one of our breeding batches."

"Which makes them superior candidates. Exploit their potential."

The captain bowed his head, as if he were dealing with one of his problematic subordinates. "It's not just the lack of training. These ships were weeks behind on basic maintenance."

"We faced budgeting shortfalls. Hard decisions were made. Fighting the rebels and terrorists consumed more resources every month."

"One system failure, and we could lose hundreds of sailors. Or many more of your soldiers."

"Do not let a system fail, then."

Vigorous massage made the captain's face redder. "What can I do for you, Field Marshal?"

"The complaint you logged about the new systems my men installed."

Somehow, the captain managed to nod without stopping the massage. "As I said in the message, we lack expertise, training, or fundamental training materials."

"Read the manuals, then."

"The manuals cover only the most basic functions under normal conditions. Things in battle are never anywhere close to normal conditions."

"Then you must improvise."

"Improvise? Field Marshal, we have no baseline from which to create the idea of improvisation. We don't know up, because we haven't the ability to define down. We can't zigzag without knowing what a straight line looks like."

"You make excuses, Captain. At this time, I am looking for solutions."

"Yes. Exactly as you say." The other man frowned. "There is no one with actual experience using these systems?"

Faulk smiled. "We'll have an opportunity for live fire usage soon enough."

Hart made a snapping sound with his teeth, as if he'd literally bitten back a reply. His shoulders sank. "As you command, Field Marshal."

"How are we performing in Fold Space?"

"I made a point of assigning two officers to each ship's bridge crew with at least three trips through Fold Space."

"Excellent! That is doing more with less."

"It has been my lifelong dream to find solutions to impossible problems."

That came across almost sarcastic, but Faulk thought the captain might simply have a strange sense of humor. "You will find ample opportunities here."

Faulk spun on a heel and exited the bridge, his two bodyguards close behind. When the hatch closed, he raised a hand and turned on the two men. They might have been younger brothers or children from his own loins. Their backs were straight, their black uniforms as crisp and clean as his. Their gray eyes were fierce and hard.

Lines formed on the brow of the one to his left. "Field Marshal?"

"Remain on the bridge."

"The bridge?"

"I have the concern that our captain requires a reminder of the sensitive nature of our operation. His focus on excuses is inappropriate in front of junior staff. Your presence should act as a reminder of what is acceptable and what isn't."

The bodyguards stood even more erect, then returned through the hatch.

How would Hart react to their taciturn stares? It was something Faulk would have to determine later. For now, preparations for the ground assault against the Moskav capital awaited. His systems had finally completed assembling a composite map of the most current imagery of New Lenin, drawing from every source known. Strikes could be made with an accuracy of one hundred meters, which would be meaningful for the weapons in use. Putting high-yield explosives down at the four corners of the Bureau of Policy building would pulverize everything inside the strike zone into a fine powder.

Faulk chuckled at the thought of that. Leveling key points in the city, eliminating the leadership, crippling the command structure—it was guaranteed to shatter the last resolve of the Moskav animals.

With an attack plan that couldn't fail, all that was required was actually gathering the leadership into their places of power.

Could this Kedraalian captain do that?

Already, she had shown that she had sufficient charisma and sincerity.

Her combination of vulnerability and confidence had a way of charming people. Even the supreme leader seemed enchanted by her. And her offer of alliance against the Khanate? Naïve but also the exact sort of thing that would draw out the Moskav leadership. They had troop transport ships hidden somewhere, always out of reach of the shrinking Azoren navy. An offer from a substantial task force to escort those ships would be irresistible.

Would this Captain Benson be ready for the Moskav demand that the destruction of the Khanate be followed by an attack against Himmel?

No. She had probably been briefed by her own government to seek out exactly such a deal.

Had that been her intent all along?

It was actually an intriguing puzzle. According to Ambassador Manshaus, she had originally come to the Gulmar with her task force to seek out a mutual defense alliance. Or perhaps it had been meant as a step toward destroying the Azoren Federation.

Then the Khanate had attacked.

Manshaus's tale of absolute destruction was absurd, but he'd been the main architect of intelligence gathering in that domain for nearly a decade. Since his return, the Gulmar network had gone dark.

Faulk drew up short as he approached the lift. Two techs who could have been from the same batch squatted in front of the open hatch, their gray coveralls stained with grime and grease. Broad-shouldered, hair tinted slightly red, soft faces… Hart's people.

They had toolboxes opened and several brown cardboard boxes—parts—spread before them.

One turned and offered a dull-eyed smile. "Good morning, Field Marshal!"

"The lift is inoperative?"

"Yes, Field Marshal. It is nothing we cannot fix."

The other technician held up one of the boxes. "These relays and control elements go bad under significant stress. The new crew coming aboard—it has been exactly that sort of stress."

It was the same sort of thing Captain Hart had complained about. Was this his doing? An inconvenience meant to drive home his request for…

What *had* been the idiot's intent? Cancel the attack, return to Himmel, and spend months in training?

Faulk puffed out his chest. "How long?"

"Until it is fixed, Field Marshal?" The technician holding the box looked at it. "We have yet to determine which part is defective."

The other technician nodded. "It might be best to replace all the parts."

All the parts. There were gears and belts visible atop the lift car.

Hours, then.

A groan slipped free, and Faulk dismissed the two with a flip of his hand. "I will take the stairs."

"A good choice, Field Marshal!" The dull-eyed one beamed like an idiot.

It was criminal, being surrounded by inferior people, even if they were his brothers. Faulk wasn't asking for everyone to be as capable as him, but the Minister of Purity could at least acknowledge he had finally found the perfect design and start mass-producing true brothers for the field marshal, who was destined to lead the Azoren Federation to its final destiny.

He stomped into the stairway, making a mental note to talk to Hart about prioritizing critical systems maintenance. There should always be one functional lift for the senior officers. Time was critical, after all. Being forced to use the stairs was fit for enlisted and junior officers. On such an old ship, the narrow steps required careful and slow movement. Someone might be injured. There were mismatched sections on the walls where the paint was just a little off or the skin bulged out slightly following serious repair work. It was like fresh scarring layered over older scars, reminders that the *Warsaw* had seen many battles and never really been repaired adequately.

Other booted feet echoed in the area that ran between the decks. It sounded like they were coming up from below. Whoever it was, they would be in his way.

Exactly as he had feared. A functional lift would have avoided this.

The men whose steps he'd heard came into view on the landing below: two more of the dull-eyed, red-haired men who belonged to Hart's little family of imbeciles. They wore the same sort of coveralls as the technicians but didn't have tools or parts. Instead, they had goggles of some sort pushed to the top of their heads and odd pouches hanging off the front of tool belts. The pouches seemed to have lenses on the front.

If those were tools, Faulk couldn't recall seeing their like before.

"Good day, Field Marshal!" It was the one on the right, offering a gap-toothed smile. "Taking a stroll?"

The man's companion smiled—dull-witted and…

It was an oddly menacing look, actually. There was no respect or fear in his blank eyes. His coveralls were unzipped halfway down his chest, and there was a slouch to his shoulders, almost defiant in the way it didn't match the erect posture of the Children. His comrade's coveralls were also unzipped.

Faulk's eyes narrowed, and he came to a stop. "Sailor, your uniform is—"

As one, the men grunted, smiled, and took the next step closer. They reached into their coveralls.

A strange buzz filled the stairwell, followed by a pop, then the lights went out.

It wasn't coincidence. A smell like overloaded circuits hung in the dark air.

"You are all right, Field Marshal?" Their voices were unchanged —menacing.

They mean me harm. "Stay where you are."

A cackle came from below, then their steps—rushed stomps —rolled up.

Faulk twisted around and took a step back up but misjudged in the dark. His boot caught on something, and he went down with a gasp. Instinctively, his right arm shot out to catch his weight but instead banged against the edge of a step with enough force to send a bolt of jagged pain through him.

He rolled off the wounded limb and howled.

Then the sailors were on him, making gibbering sounds that echoed.

Something scraped along his back—cutting. A knife!

Another pain, piercing and dull.

He'd been stabbed before, in his youth, caught on the end of a Moskav bayonet when ammunition had run out. There was a natural, subconscious disconnect that came with such wounds. The body registered the soft, meaty whisper of the blade going in an instant before the sharp note of agony.

His right arm was a mess, so he flailed with his other arm. Then kicked.

The reward was a solid resistance against his boot heel, followed by a surprised blurt, and what must have been one of the assailants tumbling down the stairs.

But the other one remained. He'd caught Faulk's arm. Lifted it up. Drove a blade into the exposed ribs.

How could they see? They had run up the stairs. They were stabbing him.

A part of his mind distantly tried to make sense of his own assassination. Night vision goggles. That's what had been on their heads. There was no light in the stairwell, but maybe the devices on their belts were ultraviolet projectors. It was the sort of thing select commando units would use.

Faulk had been a commando in his youth. A good one. And he wasn't dead yet.

He yanked his good arm free of the assassin's grip and shoved him away while bringing a knee up to catch the man in the back of the legs or the small of the back.

Once again, fortune smiled upon the field marshal, as the other man made a surprised yip, and the sound of his tumbling body filled the space.

There were booted steps, too.

The other assassin was climbing back up.

Faulk rolled onto his belly and pulled himself up the step above with his good arm, but he nearly blacked out when his bad arm banged against the hard surface.

A hand grabbed him by the back of the uniform, stopping his climb. Then the assailant fought to roll Faulk over.

Expose the belly, the heart, the throat.

These weren't commandos. They were sailors. Their attacks were brute force, completely free of skill. The hard truth was that skill wasn't necessary to kill a human. It improved the odds and sped up the process. But a knife, enough strikes in the right area?

Anyone could kill.

Another jab into the gut—just one more pain among too many.

Faulk coughed. He was losing blood, weakening. The attacker was nearby, gibbering again, making sounds that weren't words. A madman, then. Someone who'd sucked in a toxic gas and would die shortly after killing his victim.

I am not a victim!

It seemed a ridiculous delusion, but that was something to be sorted out later. For now, the field marshal swung his good arm wildly again, this time hooking his fingers to grab flesh or cloth or—

His fingers closed over something slick and hard: the knife. Mostly blade.

The attacker twisted the weapon, cutting into Faulk's hand. But he held on, desperately dragging the ruined flesh down the blade until he had the other man's hand.

Grab a thumb. Break it. Snap a wrist.

They were the sorts of thing he could do with a good grip, before breaking an arm, and being stabbed several times, and having his hand sliced to the bone. Now?

The assassin punched—not the knife, so with his other hand.

Spots of lights danced in the field marshal's vision.

The lights grew brighter and danced around, revealing the gray walls, the blood-smeared coverall of one of the assailants. He had his free hand raised, shielding goggles. His teeth were bared, and meaningless words hissed between them.

Then gunfire: thunder that shook the stairs and jostled Faulk around.

Hot fluid spattered on his face. The assailant's gray coveralls disappeared from the light.

A body tumbled.

Boots slapped against the stairs above and below. More strange gibbering was overwhelmed by gunfire, then the lights were in Faulk's eyes.

"Field Marshal!" One of the bodyguards. "Field Marshal!"

Their hands were on him, dragging him until he was back in the passageway. Emergency lights glowed amber there. Voices shouted.

Someone screamed for emergency medical attention.

The dull blue glow of a data pad. Voices closer, then farther away.

People were at his side, calling his name. Boots stomped.

It sounded like chaos. Madness.

"What happened?" A voice of authority: Hart.

"Assassins." One of the bodyguards. "The lift was open and tools were there, but no one was around. We heard shouting."

There were more words, but they became muddy and hard to understand.

It was growing cold, and the pain was growing distant. Faulk wanted to tell them about the gibbering. Something about it…

He let the cold wash over him.

23

Despite Benson's best efforts, reports seemed to simply pile up in her queue. Maintenance reports, perishable supplies tracking reports, recycling efficiency reports, weapons testing reports, systems diagnostics reports, personnel effectiveness ratings reports—everything imaginable, rolled up from first line supervisors to section commanders to division commanders, then up to the XO and captains, and finally summarized for her. Getting through those reports required liters of strong stimulant drinks that left her jittery. She had to take breaks to hit the treadmill, running until her lungs seemed ready to fail. Her final option to push through was cold showers.

She was back to coffee now, fighting against the acid gurgle threatening her gut. The first hints of nausea created a chill that countered the drink's heat.

There were antacids in her drawer, but she needed something more.

A break. Something to clear her mind.

She pushed out from her desk, took off the jacket that felt like it was crushing her ribs, then tugged the clasp from her hair, which she shook out.

Then she stretched.

Just a little. Just enough to get the blood flowing and the muscles to loosen up. It broke the monotony of the reports.

At her level, it was about the summaries. And looking for patterns. Were there training blind spots? Had a failed system failed in the previous three months? Six? A year? Were exercises and simulations highlighting the same shortcomings over and again?

Simulations. That reminded her.

She settled back in her chair, closed the analysis on the perishables consumption and spoilage rate, and opened a message to Chief Parkinson. It had been a week without an update, and she needed something—anything—to give her guidance on the Khanate systems.

"Chief, I know you're keeping busy, but if I could get an update on your Khanate simulations, I'd appreciate it. You and—" What had been the other chief's name? Taylor? "—Chief Taylor had some pretty promising results last time around. Anything new?"

She sent the message, letting it queue up. It wasn't something worth poking the bear over. Then again, Parkinson had actually been civil the last few times she'd interacted with him. In fact, in their last conference call, he'd been downright respectful to Taylor, deferring to her a few times and never talking over her. That wasn't like him at all.

Was he changing?

Benson smiled at that idea.

The smile faded when her data pad lit up with a priority incoming call from Chopra.

She accepted. "Something wrong, Dinesh?"

His chin came down, emphasizing the small double chin and jowls that had settled on his face in recent weeks. He needed to get back to exercising. "Very wrong, Captain. Although…" He shrugged.

"What is it?"

"Commander Tuleyev received notice from the *Warsaw*. Captain Hart reports that Field Marshal Faulk has been wounded."

"Wounded? How? Is it bad?"

"Apparently, it's quite serious."

A coup? That was an inconvenient possibility, given the bloodthirsty nature of the Azoren. Then again, Faulk had assured her that he'd put *his* people into command positions after Weber's failed assassination. This Captain Hart wasn't supposed to be a problem. "Did Captain Hart say how this happened?"

"He sounded a little unsure, but it would appear—" Light from the bridge command station reflected off the XO's bald scalp. "It would appear it was an attempted assassination."

"Well, that's not so shocking, really."

"So you've said. But this was different. They believe it was Khanate assassins."

"Khan—?" She tried to process that idea. How? The Azoren were genetically engineered. They were brainwashed from birth. Where would an outside influence have an opportunity to take root? In all the violence and chaos? Could even the Azoren Children be driven to alternate philosophies? "They need to begin security sweeps."

"They've identified the four assassins, apparently. And it would appear that will be the extent of the investigation."

"There could be bombs. They have to vet the crew."

"The field marshal seems to disagree. From what Alex said, Captain Hart wouldn't discuss whether he agreed with the field marshal. It would seem, though, that this is considered an aberration, a small group of what they call defectives. Captain Hart assured Alex that this is something their Minster of Purity warned about. The percentages appear to be quite small, but it's not unheard of."

"This doesn't seem possible. How small a percentage are we talking? And it happens now, when they're fighting against the Khanate? Have they seen this before?"

"Defectives?"

"Khanate spies. They seemed reluctant to believe the Khanate were even a threat at first."

Her XO frowned. "Weren't the Azoren engaged in a war with the Khanate?"

"Years ago. From my briefings, I took it they abandoned that to focus on their war with the Moskav. And us."

"They do seem to enjoy their wars."

"That's exactly it, though—they love war as much as they love themselves. That's their religion: their philosophy of purity and hate."

Chopra nodded. "Would you like to talk to Alex?"

"Please. Ship-to-ship only. Full encryption."

"One moment."

A soft buzz came over the line when Chopra's face disappeared, then a louder one when he reappeared. Another window showed a grainy image of Tuleyev, still fiddling with his headset, which seemed stuck in his thick gray head of hair. His lips were pursed, his forehead bunched, then he had the headset in place and relaxed, his jowls quivering as he shook his head slightly.

Tuleyev's eyes focused more clearly. "Dinesh?"

"Alex, thank you. Captain Benson wanted to talk with you about the situation with Faulk."

The commander of the *Lyon* growled. "Very much a problem, Captain."

She let out a sigh of relief. If *he* saw it, then it wasn't just her. "Does this sound like a coup, like something this Captain Hart could be behind?"

A low rumble shuddered through the connection, and Tuleyev bowed his head. She could imagine him clasping his hands in front of him, just under his belly. "It is possible, this idea. They have a history of such things."

"But you don't think that's what's going on here."

Tuleyev lifted his head and jutted his chin out. "This captain, this Hart —he seems content to command his fleet. His concern for the field marshal, this had a sincerity to it."

"I was afraid of that."

"Also, the captain said they found necklaces on these assassins."

"Like the ones we've identified?"

"The same, yes."

Benson ran fingers through her hair. "They've been compromised. The Khanate has spies—they've converted even Azoren Children."

"It would seem to be the case, Captain."

It felt warm in her cabin now. Had she really been bored looking at reports just a few minutes before? How was that even possible? "Do you think there's any chance this Captain Hart might look a little deeper into this?"

Tuleyev's bushy eyebrows rose, and his gray eyes took on an almost whimsical light. "It is my impression that this captain is one to follow orders."

"And the field marshal has declared this resolved."

"Exactly that."

Faulk was a perfect storm of misguided confidence and unbridled contempt. The only way Benson could imagine him reaching such a position of power was an unmatched history of successes combined with a determination and endurance that exceeded human norms.

Or luck. That could definitely have played a part.

She sighed. "We need to go through another round of security inspections."

Chopra and Tuleyev grunted at the same time.

Benson cocked her head. "You disagree?"

Tuleyev looked away, signaling exactly that. "Your Marine commander assured us that all inspections were complete, did he not?"

"Comprehensive inspections can never be comprehensive enough. Dinesh?"

Her XO puffed his cheeks out. "They have been pushed hard."

And they've had a few weeks of rest. But, the commanders were right. There were only so many times she could make demands of the under-staffed Marines before their effectiveness broke down.

"All right." She braced her elbows on her desktop and propped her chin up. "Let's run another analysis of crew through systems searches. Look for patterns of the people previously identified. What commonalities did these people share? Talk to the two we have in the brig. See if we can draw anything out of them."

Tuleyev raised a hand. "This I will take as a priority tasking."

"Do you have some systems people who could help with the queries?"

"Two very good and reliable people, yes. One was close with Chief Tucci."

Benson caught the pain in Tuleyev's eyes. He had also been close with his chief engineer. "Thank you."

"This threat—I feel bad for missing it before. I will not miss it again."

The admission was more than enough. It was time for the wound to heal. "I'm sorry, Alex."

He nodded. "Tactically, there is an advantage here, yes?"

She bit her lip. It felt morbid bringing this up, but it was true. "I agree. Whether Faulk authorizes the sort of search he should or not, he's going to have to keep watching over his shoulder now. You can't ignore an assassination attempt."

Chopra stroked his chin. "This makes them less effective, though."

"It does." Benson's gut rumbled. "Officially, we're allies. We have to treat the Azoren that way. Unofficially, we need them to take the brunt of the attack when we find the Khanate fleet. If this makes them sloppy or sluggish, if it costs them a few ships, it's ultimately for our good."

"Because you expect to face these ships as enemies one day."

"Because—" She leaned in closer to the data pad, as if that might make their conversation even more secure. "—I expect to face these Azoren ships as enemies the second they have an opportunity to turn on us."

"Hm." Chopra blinked rapidly.

In briefings before travel to Himmel, she'd touched on the strategic need to use the Azoren but not to trust them. She'd skirted around the particulars of actually exploiting their potential allies, choosing instead to emphasize the history of Azoren betrayal by way of analyzing their tactics.

Now? They would have to be more specific at some point.

"Dinesh, the idea of betraying trust is reprehensible. It's something I find almost impossible to stomach. But we're dealing with a group of people who've made clear their intent to destroy us. We have a mutual enemy, and that enemy poses a greater threat to both of our nations than either of us do to each other. Once that threat is eliminated, do you really believe the Azoren are going to honor the terms of our alliance?"

"Is it about them honoring the terms or about us doing so?"

"When it means risking lives, it's about doing the right thing."

"And that is?" The bald man looked away slightly.

"We'll have to see. For now, let's be sure we have a thorough review of their force composition. Take the data you gathered while I was on Himmel. See what you can assess based on how they perform in Fold

Space and once we get to Moskav. Get with your weapons officers. Put some simulations together."

"To what end?"

Tuleyev cleared his throat. "To know where we stand with our allies once matters with the Khanate are resolved, Dinesh. The captain is right. Blind trust of a viper that crawls into bed with you—this is the same as injecting the venom yourself."

Chopra closed his eyes. "It seems a betrayal, whether we act or not."

"This is preparation, nothing more. Is this not so, Captain?"

Benson nodded. "I'm hoping the field marshal surprises me, and we part ways on good terms."

Tuleyev chuckled. "They will turn on us."

"I know." She had no illusions about what she had gotten them into. "For now, though, let's do all of this analysis with an eye toward where sabotage is most likely to happen. When we're in battle, same as what happened with the Gulmar task force. Where would bombs likely be planted? What would that mean to Azoren maneuvering and firing?"

"Yes. Would guns be compromised? Are their missiles vulnerable to explosives?"

That would be a real danger, and she hadn't thought of it. "When we were aboard the *Pandora*, an Azoren destroyer boarded us. Someone took that ship out, and it's quite likely they did so by planting bombs on the missiles. That could be a vulnerability in their operational security."

Chopra's eyes widened. "Should we alert them to this potential vulnerability?"

"No." Benson swallowed. "We need to prepare as if the Azoren aren't actually here to help us but to be targets. Like Alex said, we've aligned ourselves with monsters because we're fighting worse monsters. Even so, the Azoren can't be counted on, whether because they intend to betray us or because they refuse to look for spies and saboteurs."

Her XO nodded, but it came across almost like a bow. "I understand."

"All right." She rubbed her forehead. "So now that our day is ruined, I need to contact our Gulmar allies and update them."

The right corner of Tuleyev's lips twisted up. "Captain, if I might?"

"Yes?"

"This inability to trust the Azoren—it is sensible, maybe wise. Should we see the Gulmar as so different? After all, what was done during the War of Separation…" He squinted. "It was more than just the Azoren."

"It's a good point. Let's keep it in mind."

She disconnected and considered the data pad.

Khanate terrorists aboard the Azoren ships. It was hard to accept, until she thought through what Chopra had said: The Azoren had spent years fighting the Khanate. Mostly, they had broken their fleet, but they had also left blood on the soil of Khanate worlds. No one in the Kedraalian intelligence services knew exactly how long the fighting had gone on or how many had died, but there was no doubt about the war.

People could be changed by fighting. It left some damaged—hyper-violent, maybe nonfunctional despite medical technologies. Could it leave them damaged enough to become like their enemies?

Absolutely.

This revelation opened a whole new set of questions. What if some of the rebellion elements weren't people fighting to claim power alongside Supreme Commander Graf or weren't locals unwilling to go quietly into the garbage bin of history. What if some of those rebels were people who had been turned to worship the Khan?

Azoren help became even more problematic if there was a chance Graf might fall only to give rise to something worse.

At least she could trust Thiessen and the Gulmar.

Or could she? Their navy had apparently been thick with spies and traitors. Those should all be dead now, though. Except…where you found one spy, you were probably missing two others.

There was only one way to know: She called him.

Connecting to Thiessen's ship took time. Her data pad indicated protocol mismatches, which seemed odd. Then, quick as it had happened, it was gone. One of Thiessen's bridge officers—a bearded, hefty, middle-aged man who looked in need of sleep—accepted the connection, then passed her on.

Thiessen accepted immediately. He also looked tired, the slightest hint of purple under his eyes. His beard and hair needed a trim, but his smile was still as warm as a summer sunlight. Sweat dampened his brow. "Faith! I hope you're doing better than me right now."

"What's wrong?"

He shrugged, and she caught a glimpse of his shoulders: lean but muscular. There were scars there, too. "No one knows. Systems keep misbehaving, one after the other. Our engineers are digging through the diagnostics, but so far they've got nothing."

"Would you be offended if I offered help?"

"I don't think there's anyone aboard who feels like we're in an ideal situation. If so, they can stick their pride in a locker."

"Can you have your lead engineer contact Chief Parkinson?"

"The…cranky one?"

"Actually, he's doing better right now." Benson pulled up the personnel file on Chief Greta Taylor. The woman wasn't quite the type Parkinson tended to go for, but there was a mischievous gleam in her eyes. "I think he might have found what he needed all along."

"I'm not going to ask. When we're done, I'll have Yuri connect, if that's all right?"

"Perfect. And let me know if Chief gets out of hand."

"Absolutely. So, what's the reason behind this pleasure?"

His words caught her off guard, and she blushed. "W-well—"

"Oh. Sorry." He laughed, an embarrassed sound, then brushed his hair back. "I'm a little punch drunk. We've gone three cycles without air conditioning."

"That's not good."

"Trust me, it isn't."

She licked her lips and wished she could get a better look at his cabin. There'd never been a chance to visit long enough to take in everything about his ship. "So, bad news."

"*More* bad news? There needs to be a legal limit."

"I'm sure we're not there yet."

"Noted."

"Faulk is wounded, and it's apparently pretty serious."

"I'm still waiting for the bad news."

Benson fought back a smile. "It looks like Khanate assassins."

"Khan…" The Gulmar captain bowed his head. "Okay. That *is* bad."

"It doesn't sound like he's in danger of dying, but…it got me thinking."

His head came up again. "About?"

She checked the connection once more to be sure it was fully encrypted and ship-to-ship. "About what we discussed before. The way strikes might need to be prioritized? Targeting might need to be considered? How the heat of battle would inevitably change things?"

Thiessen squinted, then his eyes lit up. "Oh. Yeah. Fortune favors the bold."

"Exactly."

"Well, it's hard to argue with the idea. An assassination attempt…" The Gulmar captain twisted his head slightly, giving her a look at an even more handsome angle. "They're searching for bombs, I assume?"

"No. That's just it. Faulk apparently dismissed the idea that this was anything other than…he called it an aberration."

"That's not good."

"If we rely too heavily on their ships, we might find ourselves in a situation where we're exposed."

"Or worse. Someone gets into their weapons control, they could open fire on us."

She nodded. This sort of thing would be so much easier to do face to face, but moving between ships in Fold Space could be risky. She wasn't even sure the Gulmar were trained for it. "So, my own officers might be reluctant to follow this line of strategy."

"Hm." Thiessen leaned closer, and it looked like he was now resting his chin on his hands, his long fingers scratching his beard. "That could be a problem."

"The thing is, once we commit to a course like this—"

"*We* being *me*."

"Y-yes." *Like a pawn making the first move.* "Once that happens, we're *all* committed. We're forced by agreement to continue forward." *Firing on the Azoren.*

"Well." He smiled. "That's good to know."

She bowed her head, uncomfortable beneath his probing gaze. "It's something we may want to talk about more closely, once we've concluded this Moskav deal."

"I think that's a great idea. Maybe over dinner."

Again, she blushed. "Let's…do that."

Thiessen laughed—deep and warm. "Looks like we really need to get this place in order, then. I'll put Yuri in touch with your chief."

"Thank you."

She disconnected, "Floyd" half-formed on her lips.

This was the absolute wrong time to start a new relationship. Even if she weren't on the rebound from Halliwell, the task force was in the middle of a very fluid and dangerous situation. Yet there she was, feeling like one of those old videos where the star was unable to ignore the spurning of a lover or to keep from fooling around with another officer's spouse. She remembered a particularly old classic where two navy men had risked their careers—even their lives—over relationships. There had been a scene with one of the men and his forbidden love on a beach, kissing as the waves washed over them.

Thiessen would look good like that—holding her in his arms.

Her data pad beeped. Another report had entered her queue.

The life of a fleet captain never ended.

24

A few days in Fold Space could feel like an eternity. Three weeks helped Benson gain a better understanding of torture. It seemed that the Gulmar ships might disappear at any moment, either being thrown out of Fold Space with the failure of a drive or be tossed into a different dimension with the malfunction of the controlling systems. And the Azoren ships were worse—older, even less well-maintained, crewed by junior personnel in over their heads, and...

Still not checked for bombs.

That might have been the thing that hung over her head the most. A refusal by Field Marshal Faulk to accept the possibility that a saboteur might have rigged one of the nuclear warheads to blow.

So, she spent each night lying in bed, waiting for sleep that wouldn't come, going over everything she *could* do to protect first her ships, then the Gulmar from potential rogue Azoren ships.

But all those nights were at an end now, leaving her frazzled and gummy-eyed as she stood on the bridge, sipping the cool, bittersweet drink she so desperately needed for a boost. A tart, lemony aroma came off the container when she raised it to take a sip. That scent was what she equated to caffeine, to getting through this last, uncertain moment. After that?

Get out of Fold Space, effect repairs, and go over their plans one last time.

Chopra's bridge crew moved through a haze, bathed in the glow of the broad command console, murmuring softly as they prepared to return to normal space.

The lone Marine now assigned to the bridge stared straight ahead. He was a boy barely into manhood, Benson was sure, with the same sort of soft features as the Azoren Children.

Her fingers trembled, and it seemed like her breath caught every other intake. This wasn't dangerous. They were expert sailors.

And yet…

Her XO twisted around, tugged down his gray jacket, and smiled hopefully. The light from the console reflected off his polished scalp. "Exit in five minutes, Captain."

Five minutes. Everything could hold together just five more minutes. Couldn't it? This was safe, an exit point used by the Azoren numerous times. "Thank you, Dinesh."

A countdown timer appeared on the giant display at the front of the bridge, daring her heart to race it. It didn't decrement evenly but accelerated, sprinting toward the uncertain moment.

She rubbed her eyes.

There was time to go back to her cabin and change out of her jumpsuit. There was time to prepare for the post-exit meetings she was dreading. There was time to assemble her plans.

So much needed to happen.

Parkinson had found bugs—old, mismanaged systems code—in the Gulmar ships' systems. He'd put aside time that was supposed to be dedicated to solving the Khanate shadow tech puzzle, and he'd done everything possible, but the Gulmar navy had been run like a business, focusing on savings and efficiency instead of effectiveness. She wondered if the leadership team had enough time for a moment of regret before the Khanate attack had obliterated them. It seemed more likely those last thoughts had been about the inefficiency of the attack.

Chopra climbed up on the raised command station, and Benson realized she'd been so absorbed in her thoughts, she'd missed four minutes of the countdown.

The timer raced down to the last fifty seconds.

Benson pulled out her data tablet and ran through the last list of reports. They were green on every ship. The automated checks on the crew had completed with no more findings.

She'd done everything possible, yet her stomach felt like a block of lead.

They needed to prioritize exactly what they would do once they exited Fold Space. The face-to-face meeting with Thiessen was near the top. Planning her trip to Moskav and subsequent rescue was up there as well. Establishing a deployment strategy—especially when it came to the Azoren ships—might be their first priority.

It all came down to how they came out of Fold Space. What would her combined fleet look like?

And then, the counter dropped to zero, and she was hit with the strange sense of a lurch, of time and space adjusting back to normal. The giant display flickered as the ranges and the universe around them reset to a prime reality.

The bald XO leaned close to his own display, then pumped a fist. It was a small motion, meant only for him. He smiled at the comms officer. "Lieutenant Nuñez, do we have status reports yet?"

A smile cracked the young woman's square face. "All clear, Commander."

Chopra raised his eyebrows at Benson. "Captain?"

She exhaled. "Status on the Gulmar and Azoren ships?"

Nuñez rubbed the end of her blunt nose. "No reported impacts or failures. We've come through clean. Everyone's reporting green or amber."

Benson checked the status dashboard for the amber ships and thumbed through those. "Let's get everything to green, please, Dinesh."

The XO bent over his display, swiping and tapping. "Yes, ma'am."

Lieutenant Mahama stepped back from his station, caught the XO's eyes, then nodded toward the weapons station. The young man's cheeks seemed flush. "There's movement on the long-range scans."

Benson stiffened. "Movement? We're at the edge of their system."

"It could be asteroids, ma'am."

"We're below the ecliptic. This should be dead space."

The weapons officer's beady eyes blinked. "It's…nothing critical, ma'am."

"Keep an eye on that, please."

Mahama nodded and returned to his station.

Chopra came down from the command station to stand beside her. "You're concerned?"

"How old is our intelligence on Moskav space?"

"From the time of the War of Separation."

"And the Azoren didn't offer any updates. That could be debris, or it could be minefields, or it could be sensors."

"They said this was safe."

"They did. But they're also saying those Khanate spies aren't a thing."

"Should we launch probes?"

"I think that would be prudent." She groaned. "After I've talked with our *allies*."

The XO drifted over to the comms officer and whispered to her. He looked dumpy next to her lean body. When he turned back to Benson, it was with a nod: She had a connection request in to the *Warsaw*.

After a moment of hesitation, she pulled her headset from her pocket and slipped the device over an ear. And waited.

It didn't take long for Field Marshal Faulk to accept. "Captain Benson. You look terrible. Is that really your uniform?"

"Thank you, Field Marshal. You continue to look less like a corpse each time I see you. They let you out of the infirmary?"

"My health is as a young man's."

So is your ego. "We need to—"

"I am glad you contacted me, actually. I have an idea to rearrange the deployment of our ships—"

"Field Marshal—"

"—to take advantage of the more agile components of my force, positioning them—"

"We have—"

"—with the Gulmar ships."

Benson clenched her jaw and counted to ten. "Let me try this again."

"You said something, Captain? Because I was discussing ship placement."

"We'll get to that in a moment. Right now, my concern is with movement at the outer edge of sensor range."

"Movement? What kind of movement? There is nothing here."

"Yes, I realize that's what your intelligence stated. We're too far out to know what this is just yet."

"Any heat to indicate rockets?"

We would've said so. "No. Do you have historical scans of this area?"

"Ah, ah, Captain. The Azoren have labored long and hard in Moskav space. What we know, we've earned."

"Can you at least tell me if this is a known debris field or if there are known bodies that pass through this area?"

Red bloomed on the field marshal's pale cheeks. "This is dead space."

"Then I'd like to send a gunship or two out to check on what we're seeing."

"First, we must discuss my plan to place my destroyers—"

"Field Marshal, you have a cruiser. It needs to be on the front line, the same as the *Valor*."

"Ah, but my destroyers must be deployed to protect the *Warsaw*."

"On the front. The Gulmar task force doesn't have the armor the *Warsaw* does. We—"

"That is exactly my point, Captain. We are agile *and* provide defense. It is ideal for the lighter Gulmar ships to be near us. Your task force can operate in the front when engagement occurs."

Heat ran along Benson's back. "This is a discussion that should involve Captain Thiessen."

"Truly, Captain. The Azoren operate with very clear rank structures. As field marshal—"

"We're a combined fleet. Supreme Commander Graf agreed to my proposal, which put your task force under me."

Faulk's chin came up in defiance. "This is not how the Azoren operate."

"Your supreme—"

"We should be spread out here, in dead space, operating silently, drive systems off."

She wanted to point out to him that the Azoren ships were the ones bleeding the most heat, that they were so old and poorly maintained that they would be easily detectable if the Moskav had the ability to pick out infrared and happened to be looking in the right place with their sensors. Neither seemed very likely based on the briefings she'd received. Interminable war with the Azoren hadn't quite knocked the Moskav back into the Stone Age, but trivial things like satellite networks and telescopes weren't likely priorities when food and weapons were the key to survival.

So Benson grinned. "We *are* running silent."

"And now is the time for deployment."

"*Now* we should be talking about getting ships repaired. We should be going over the final plans for my message and the timing of my evacuation."

Faulk held up a finger to stop her. "*This* is the ideal place to exit Fold Space, Captain."

"That's why it was selected."

"Good."

"And it's why we need to have our ships ready. We need to have maintenance—"

"No one is going to threaten this space, Captain Benson. The Moskav have no fleet. The Khanate have no reason to come here."

Benson felt ready to explode. "The Moskav and Khanate have a history."

"Zealots slaying zealots. Our focus must be on destroying the Moskav."

They would go around in circles forever if she allowed him to run the conversation. "I'm sending a gunship out. If you want to send a ship of your own—"

"We have nothing so small as your corvettes."

Except for the armed shuttles, he apparently thought she'd forgotten about. "Fine. We'll keep you updated about what we find."

The field marshal dismissively waved a hand that was glossy with fresh skin. "Asteroids."

"We'll confirm that." She disconnected, surprised at the abruptness.

Or maybe happy with it.

Maybe letting the field marshal think he'd gotten under her skin was good. She was done wasting time, and that true motivation was what mattered.

Benson powered down her headset, strolled the width of the bridge, then powered the device back on. "Lieutenant Nuñez, if you would connect me to Captain Thiessen, I'd appreciate it. Ship-to-ship, full encryption."

The communications officer adjusted her own headset, pushing aside her short, brown curls. "Connecting now, Captain."

Out of the corner of Benson's eye, she saw Chopra fidgeting, as if he wanted to ask her something. What could possibly be bothering him?

The gunship!

She covered her microphone. "Dinesh, could you have one of the gunships—?"

He nodded rapidly. "Immediately."

Thiessen was in her ear then. "Faith?"

It seemed appropriate for her to make this a more private chat. She pointed her data pad at the hatch to signal Chopra that she was stepping out, then hurried into the passageway outside. "Floyd. Sorry for the delay."

"I didn't even notice."

"We've got a couple things going on."

"Does one involve everyone's favorite field marshal?"

She sagged against a bulkhead and nearly laughed. Thiessen seemed to have a magical effect on her. "He's trying to make this fleet his."

"I don't recall that being the agreement."

"I know. But it was inevitable. On top of that, he's trying to cut you out of the decision-making process."

"Hm. And I take it this locked-down communication is the result?"

"We're pretty sure one of his destroyers has signals intelligence capabilities."

"We are, too. The *Danube*. And what we saw on the *Warsaw*."

"Yes. So, the second thing: movement at the extreme edge of sensor range."

"Oh? We didn't detect any."

"The *Valor*'s systems are the best available. If we see something, it's real."

Thiessen made a ticking sound. A quick glance at the video revealed his tongue moving against his teeth. "Okay. I thought this was supposed to be dead space."

"He confirmed as much."

"Want me to send a ship to check?"

"We've launched a gunship."

"Then that leaves our little bundle of joy. You know, this might be the ideal time to take care of those problems we discussed before. No time like the present. That's what no executive on the leadership team ever used to say." Thiessen smirked.

Destroy Faulk and walk away from the Azoren alliance? It was tempting, certainly, but it would mean immediately returning to Azoren space and eliminating the remaining defense force. They couldn't do that. Not yet.

"I don't know, Floyd. It would slow down the hunt for this Khanate fleet. We've already lost so much time."

"And we'll lose more with this Moskav action. I see it as time regained."

It would be. And it would mean not betraying someone she was promising an alliance to. But it would be one betrayal replacing another.

She *hated* dealing at this level—lying while smiling.

"Let's see where the task force stands, first. A couple of your ships came out of Fold Space showing amber. Is that accurate?"

"More system failures. My teams are implementing the process Parkinson gave us. He did a good—"

The bridge hatch opened, and the bald XO poked his head out, searching around.

Benson pushed off from the bulkhead. "Problems?"

Chopra's eyes widened. "It's the gunship."

"Did it find something?"

"Actually, it's reporting little visible to passive sensors."

"Asteroids or debris, then?"

"Yes, quite possible." The bald man hunched slightly. "Except—"

An alarm klaxon sounded, and the two of them jumped. Benson followed the commander back to the bridge, where a warning light strobed.

Mahama's face was pinched when he turned. "That movement, Captain. The masses have fired up rockets and are accelerating."

Missiles!

Chopra pointed at Nuñez. "Battle stations. Pass that along to all ships."

Nuñez let out a surprised gasp. "We've lost contact with the gunship!"

Benson shook her head. It didn't make sense. She remembered vaguely that she was still connected to Thiessen. "Floyd—?"

"I heard. We're going to full alert."

"Those are missiles. But the Moskav don't have a fleet."

The XO scowled, perhaps thinking she was talking to him. "Yes. I understand." But he clearly didn't.

Mahama's small eyes flew wide. "More rockets. Closer. We have impacts being reported."

It made no sense. "Impacts? From missiles? We just detected them."

"These were closer in, Captain. Not moving, not detected."

Shadow technology? With missiles? "Which ships have been hit?"

"The *Sinclair*, the *Castro*. The *Tojo* sounds bad. We can't raise the *Mao*."

That was their signals ships. Were they targeted? They had to have been.

Chopra hovered beside the command station, uncertainty on his face.

Benson bounded past him, settling behind the command station console. She set her drink container in a mesh holder. "Lieutenant Nuñez, inform everyone that we are under attack by missiles—stealth missiles. Lieutenant Mahama, none of those remaining missiles get anywhere close to any of our ships."

The two lieutenants acknowledged the order. Chopra was already standing beside Konrath, the helm officer. There was no mistaking the tug of the drive and maneuvering systems firing. Her XO would work with Tuleyev to get the task force moving, pushing out evasion packages.

That left it to Benson to focus on the real problem: the signals ships.

She connected to Parkinson. "Chief, are you getting all this?"

"Battle stations, right?" He sounded winded, as if he might be running.

"Stealth missiles. And regular missiles. They targeted our signals ships. No signals intelligence, no counter to stealth technology."

"Shit. That's a problem."

"A big problem."

"Special targeting. That's new. Anti-radiation, locking onto our electronic warfare systems."

That was almost impossible to believe. Where would the Moskav come up with such technology? "We need those ships functional. The *Mao* is unresponsive. It sounds like the *Tojo* is seriously damaged, too. Who are our best engineers?"

Parkinson snorted. "Me. And Chief Taylor."

She'd expected him to volunteer a couple other people. "I need people who can get on those ships."

"That's me and Taylor. She's good."

"All right. Get to the hangar bay. We'll get you to the *Mao*."

"On my way."

Benson almost pinched herself. This was *Parkinson*? What had Taylor done to him? "Lieutenant Nuñez, I need Commander Karras. Now. Connect Commander Tuleyev, too."

Seconds passed, then the communications officer tapped her headset: Benson had her requested connection.

Tuleyev spoke first. "Captain—"

Static.

She pressed her headset against her ear. "Alex?"

"—missiles—"

He was still there. Maybe the *Lyon* had taken a hit. She checked to be sure Karras was still connected. "Commander Karras, our signals ships are seriously damaged. I'm sending Chief Parkinson to the *Mao*. I'm going to need you to send Chief Taylor to the *Tojo*."

Karras coughed. "We're under attack, Captain."

"And Chief Taylor has a good team to handle damage control. They don't need her *there*. Without those signals ships, we're going to have a *lot* of damage to contend with. We need them up and running *yesterday*."

"I can't give up my—"

Tuleyev's connection hummed, then cleared. "Commander Karras, the captain is not requesting this. Put Chief Taylor on a shuttle and get her to the *Tojo*. Do so immediately, please. Thank you. Is there anything else, Captain?"

There was so much else, but this was when Benson had to prioritize. "Make sure the chief has an escort."

"Yes. A Marine, please, Commander Karras."

"Thank you." Benson disconnected. She needed to see to it that Parkinson had an escort as well, but that meant talking to Halliwell.

No time for hurt feelings in combat.

T he instant the battle stations klaxon triggered, Grier knew things were going to get ugly. It was a flutter in the gut, an intensification of every sound and scent—that's how she was sure. Even if it were merely a ship-to-ship attack on the combined fleet, at some point the captain was going to have to talk to her Marine contingent commander, and the breakup was still raw.

That's one of the reasons they discourage us from having relationships.

Yet here they were, Grier and her direct supervisor, doing exactly what he'd just undone with *his* boss.

And when Grier jumped from her chair in their shared office and rushed over to Halliwell's desk, sure as shit, he had his headset on, and he was already grinding his teeth.

He waved her closer, then squeezed his eyes shut. "I understand they're valuable. So are my Marines."

Uh-oh. Grier came to a stop in front of his foldout desk so that her thighs just barely pressed the rugged material of her pants against the desk edge. She imagined the lieutenant was giving off heat she could feel, but that was just the cramped shared space. Like her, he was down to his

T-shirt because of that heat, revealing scars and fresh scrapes. His cologne and sweat were a subtle masculine musk.

Halliwell shook his head, eyes still closed. "We don't know that Parkinson can do anything. If it's not responsive, it could be slag metal."

Shit. Something was hit? If Halliwell would look at her, she'd raise her eyebrows. He was too pissed, though. That meant it was probably the captain on the other end of the connection.

That made everything just a little bit more terrible.

Grier might not know exactly what was going on, but she could figure the basics out.

A ship was hit. Parkinson was involved, probably being assigned to save the galaxy, because…Parkinson. And he needed an escort. Marines. Other than the klaxons and a minor maneuver or two, it didn't feel like they were under attack yet, but everything said they were.

She hurried over to the even smaller foldout desk she used and pulled her shirt off the back of the chair. If there was going to be an escort, she was the best option, even if Halliwell wouldn't admit it. And her gut instinct said she was going to need to armor up.

The Marine weapons and armor lockers were right next door.

She knew her armor so well, she could get it on in a few minutes. It was snug against her muscles—a second skin—and held her familiar scent despite all the times she'd cleaned it. A quick check confirmed the oxygen reserve was at full. At the weapons locker, she pulled a carbine and three extra magazines, which she squeezed into external thigh and hip pouches. Better to be over-prepared.

Her office was close to the starboard hangar deck, which was where the armed shuttles were kept. A quick check confirmed a pilot—a young lieutenant named Espinoza—was en route.

Shuttle-712. Not just armed—a stealth model.

Parkinson was already there, pushing a rolling toolbox up the ramp.

She sprinted up, bumped his hip with hers, winked, then helped with the toolbox. "Whatcha planning to do with these big tools of yours, Chief?"

"The *Mao* is down." No humor. No annoyance. Weird.

"How bad?"

He pushed the box into a corner, locked its wheels, then pulled securing straps from the bulkheads. "Can't raise it. It took a missile hit."

"Yikes. Lieutenant Espinoza's on the way."

The chief engineer took an environment suit from a locker and unzipped the front. In all the years she'd known him, he'd been timid and anxious at the thought of going out. Now, he was focused like a laser. He had the suit on in no time.

She waved him over. "Let me check you out."

Parkinson raised his arms and spun around slowly while she tugged on his seals and checked the suit's external readouts. He performed the same checkout on her when she was done.

Grier was just about to slap him on the butt when she heard clomping on the ramp to the airlock. Instead of Espinoza, it was Halliwell.

He had his gun and most of his armor in his hands, so he jerked his head back toward the hangar deck. "We need to talk."

Rather than a slap on the butt, she flashed a thumbs-up at Parkinson.

Halliwell was pulling his armor on at the base of the ramp. "I need you to get back to the office and ready the—"

"Whoa!" Grier shook her head. "You're the Marine *commander*, Clive."

"I got that. And I'm commanding you to—"

She shook her head even more vigorously. "No. Stop. You need to think of what you're saying."

His head came up. "I know what the hell I'm saying, *Sergeant*."

The outer hatch opened, and Espinoza jogged in, black hair wet and matted so that it looked less like a tight shag cut and more like a swimming cap. His flight suit clung in spots. "I was in the shower!"

Grier smiled. "We're ready when you are, sir."

Once the pilot had darted up the ramp, Halliwell leaned in close to her. "This isn't a discussion."

His anger was up. The captain had gotten to him. How would she defuse him, though? She was always better at it than Grier could ever be.

Logic. Reason. Calm.

Grier held up a hand, palm out. "Clive, will you give me just a second?"

He glared.

But it wasn't a no. "We're under attack. You're going to be coordinating actions across all the ships. The captains are going to want to hear *your* voice. Hell, you're not even fully recovered. If the chief needs something really physical done, you might push too hard. Who's that going to help?"

Halliwell's jaw worked, then he took his chest armor off. "Okay."

She leaned back with a satisfied grin. It was *that* easy? "We'll be careful."

"Damn right you will." He glared at the ramp, then back at her. "And don't do that again."

The shuttle's systems whined as it powered on.

"Do what?"

"That thing. Acting like her. I don't like it."

"You mean don't argue?"

"No. I mean…" His brow furrowed. "I mean argue like *you*."

Was that meant as an insult? "I—"

He grunted. "Look, I was wrong, okay? You could've shown me that. Doing it like Faith…hurts."

Grier swallowed. That was…unexpected. "Gotta go."

Halliwell shrugged, turned, then stopped. His head dipped down. "You come back in one piece. That's an order."

She ran up the ramp, a lump forming in her throat. When she got back, they were going to talk, and it wasn't going to be pretty.

Every rattle, every bump, every imagined hiss of air—Parkinson felt them. He smelled the air going stale in the shuttle passenger bay, which meant they were suffocating. He felt the heat building, which meant the environment was failing. He heard the stutter of the engine, which meant the reactor was on the edge of shutdown.

He squeezed his eyes shut and told himself it was going to be fine.

In all their years on the *Pandora*, Martinez had never made Parkinson go on risky missions. It was an understanding they'd shared.

I'm too valuable.

What was it Taylor had said over coffee? "Everyone's valuable, Will."

It was true. She was good, maybe as good as him, at least in some ways. But she was fearless. She was powerful and strong and smart and…

"You just have to suck it up." She'd slurped her coffee after saying that, teasing.

Everything she'd said—she was right.

This wasn't just a job. He'd signed on to protect the Kedraalian Republic from enemies foreign and domestic. He'd taken pay and banked credit toward a government retirement and lived a decent life, all in the name of the navy.

People die doing their jobs. I'm no different.

He shivered as the *Mao* grew larger and more distinct on the computing pad strapped to his thigh. The shuttle's belly camera adjusted as the little craft turned. There were scars along the signals ship's port side: pockmarks and black smears where fire must have spat out when atmosphere vented.

An ugly missile hit. And more were coming. *Lots* more.

How do they do this? How can they all be so brave?

He connected to Taylor, swallowing hard as the long seconds dragged by. His tablet had to negotiate with the shuttle's communications system, ride on a degraded channel, then find the other shuttle. Then she had to accept—

Her face began as a small square, then filled the display. In the moment where the image distorted, her nose seemed comically long, her cheeks ridiculously narrow and drawn. It wasn't as if she was pretty even without the video doing what it was doing, but she had the most amazing eyes and smile. There was so much surety and strength there.

"Will?" She tilted her head. "You okay?"

"No." His eyes jumped over to Grier, who was absorbed in something on her own tablet. "Scared shitless, actually."

Taylor snorted. "You'd be crazy not to be."

"*You're* scared?"

"Sure. Nothing wrong with that. As long as you do your job, no one cares."

"Oh." He relaxed a little. "So, I hope you don't mind that I told the captain that you're the best for this?"

"Are you kidding me? This is what we do, right?"

"Yeah." The *Mao* was so close now, he could pick out lights coming from one of the holes. "Not long now."

"We're about to connect to the *Tojo*."

Parkinson's tablet chimed. "Same here. I mean, for the *Mao*."

Fire bloomed along the larger ship's hull. A seal must have ruptured. Or maybe a secondary explosion had—

"Will?" Taylor's voice sounded scratchy and stretched.

"Oh." Parkinson recoiled from the display as the shuttle's light tracked over a charred body. "Uh. Yeah?"

"You're going to be okay."

"Sure. I—I've done this before." *Never in the middle of a battle.*

"I have to go. We're getting connection requests from the damage control team."

"Okay. I'll—" He was thrown against his harness by a hard maneuver. "Be careful!"

"You, too."

Taylor disconnected, just as Espinoza twisted the shuttle into position.

The pilot turned around, knuckling a bloodshot eye. "Hey, Chief? You ready?"

"I—what's wrong with your eye?"

"Shampoo. I couldn't rinse it all out. Damn."

Parkinson held his helmet up. "Ready!"

They slammed against something, then the passenger bay went dark.

Espinoza whooped. "We've got a seal."

Grier popped her harness. "Let's go!"

She closed her helmet, and its interior lit up, washing her face in soft, blue light. It made her even fiercer looking than normal. Parkinson sealed his own helmet, then followed her to the airlock.

It was a miracle they'd managed a good connection with the signals ship. The *Mao*'s hull was warped, even in the area not directly hit by a missile. It looked like a rib of the frame had poked through the outer hull, the gentle curve now a sharp angle. Damage control teams moved frantically beyond the airlock, coming into view through the porthole as the air cycled.

Inside, the klaxon sounded wrong—distant and weak. It could be the thin air, or it could be the environment suit blocking out a lot of sound. Emergency lighting was all they had to work with.

Grier waved to get his attention. "Damage control's working to seal off that damaged section completely. They just had another explosion."

"Saw it on the way in."

"Okay. We're clear to get you back into Engineering. They've got this section sealed off."

She grabbed the front of his toolkit and headed aft, hooking hands into wall grips. He stuck his foot into the same grips and pushed, realizing the first time a corner banged against a bulkhead just how spoiled he was by the *Valor*. The passageways on the signals ships were narrower, the layout more crude. Their suit lights caught gray paneling that seemed lifeless and old, and that wasn't just because of the emergency lights.

At the Engineering hatch, the Marine pulled up. The hatch bulged and looked discolored. A quick check confirmed there wasn't any atmosphere on the other side.

Grier opened the toolkit and took out the pry bar, braced, then drove the flat tip into the hatch crease. While she wrenched the hatch open, he pulled out a brace. They worked together to get the entry open wide enough to accommodate the toolbox.

She ran her light over the bulkhead and equipment. "Ouch. A fire?"

Everything was soot-stained. Systems had been blown from shelf mounts. The Marine squeezed under a fallen section of shelves, then pushed up until there was room for him to get by.

He wished he had her calm.

What he wanted was the control console. A chair was squeezed in close to the desk. Someone—one of the ship's engineers—was crushed beneath a piece of debris that had been blasted in from the crumpled ceiling.

Parkinson fought back nausea and pulled the corpse free, then took the chair, careful to stay clear of the sharp edges of the frame that had killed the other engineer. Spiky knives of hull segments glinted in his suit's light, blocking the way to the aft bulkhead that bordered the reactor room. "Um, so, priority one is power."

Grier pushed herself down beside him. "Kinda need that. What about gravitics?"

"Low priority. Fuel cells and batteries. It wouldn't last long."

"And the reactor?"

He searched around. "Online. There must be something broken somewhere."

"Okay. I'm going back for another brace. I'll get this ceiling off you."

"Thanks." But the engineer was already focusing on the problems in front of him. The control console used the same battery power, and the diagnostics reports it was throwing weren't pretty.

He connected with Taylor again, running through the diagnostics while he waited for her.

"Will?"

Parkinson smiled. "Hey! You in?"

"Almost. They took a pretty good hit here. Engineering's a complete loss. It's open to vacuum. I'm connecting a remote terminal in the secondary coupler."

"Wow. The *Mao*'s not much better. They were targeted, right?"

"Like, anti-radiation weapons?"

"Did they have countermeasures powered on yet?"

"I..." It was almost like Taylor made an audible shrug. "I'll ask. I think some are always powered on, right?"

"Yeah. Hey, you have any idea how long before the other missiles get here?"

"Not long."

"Great." He flipped through a few more diagnostics reports, then spotted something and flipped back. "Hey! Reactor online but no power. Sensor packages all show a hard down, but they're not even receiving power. That sound to you like the primary conduit might have a short?"

"Could be. Or it could be you've got a cut bundle between the main breaker panel and that power input line."

"Yeah!"

Parkinson squeezed around Grier and the brace, then pulled a screwdriver and multimeter from the toolkit. The conduit ran forward, stopping just shy of the bulkhead and feeding four couplers that carried power to assorted distribution panels that fed to the ship. It was closer and easier to check than the main breaker panel aft.

He popped the cover, tested for voltage on exposed surfaces, searched around for any obvious cuts in the cable bundle, then peeled back the protective cap and probed the test sockets for power.

Nothing.

That meant it had to be the main breaker panel.

Getting to the panel required crawling under a twisted and collapsed set of shelves close to the jagged bulkhead, then slithering over a raised section of the deck and beneath a warped segment of ceiling.

Sure enough, he found the sheared cable just beyond that point.

"Hey, Greta?"

Taylor sounded like she was straining, maybe moving something big. "Yup?"

"You were right—cut cable. There're other cable segments beneath the deck. They're not rated for this level of current, but we're not talking about a long-term solution. What do you—?"

"Do it. They're within tolerance. We're only worried about getting the sensor arrays up right now."

"Sensor packages and the shadow tech."

"Same-same."

They were, now. The signals ships could listen in on enemy comms. They could spit out noise and confusing signals and overwhelm enemy sensors. But the biggest benefit was the shadow tech systems, which fed sophisticated masking systems and more importantly countered the most advanced mundane countermeasures systems.

He pried a deck piece up, found a burned-up cable segment, then moved to the next section. There, the segment was intact, but the insulation showed signs of heat damage.

Good enough.

It took care not to short anything while plugging the cable in, but Parkinson had mastered that sort of work in his early years.

He crawled back to the test sockets and checked: power!

"Greta? I'm heading back to the console. We've got power."

"Nice. I'm a little more screwed here."

"Okay. If we get this running, maybe I could come help."

"Wouldn't say no, Will."

A comforting warmth ran through his belly. He ducked under the braced ceiling and ran through the control console's interface, bringing first enough power up to get the engineering systems running, then to the ship itself. Once that was done, he brought up the sensors package interface and rebooted that and the shadow tech systems. While those rebooted, he fired up the comms array.

Grier leaned in. "How're we looking, Chief?"

"We'll know in about five seconds." He pointed to the system reboot trackers.

Sensors went a pale amber, then a sickly green, followed a moment later by the shadow tech indicator doing the same thing. It ended a little closer to a healthy green. Comms was a solid amber, but it had enough bandwidth to handle feeding the critical data to the *Valor*.

Grier clapped him on the back. "We got it?"

"Almost." Parkinson wanted to let Taylor know that they were almost done, but he worried the comms system might fail.

He poked through the sensor array interface, which brought up everything fully and showed a clean connection to the shadow tech systems. Those indicators looked a little flaky but operational. He sent that output to the *Valor*.

Parkinson smiled. "All we need now is to see if it's really working."

There was a cracked display on the deck. He propped it on top of the desk and fiddled with the connector until an image started to glow and come into focus.

He laughed as the ships of the combined fleet flickered and took on shape—green for the Kedraalian ships, blue for the Gulmar, gold for the Azoren.

Grier pointed to a band of red triangles. "What're these?"

"Missiles." Parkinson frowned. The triangles were moving closer, but they weren't coming from the right direction. "Wait a second. That must be an error."

More triangles appeared, these from the section of dead space where the gunship had been destroyed.

But these other triangles were coming from sunward, coming down from the ecliptic. How…?

"Oh."

Grier shook him. "What?"

His gut flipped. The last thing they'd programmed into the system had been… "Those aren't missiles. They're *ships. Khanate* ships."

25

Caville found Goldman in the back corner of the tea shop just off the main street. The pirate captain was hunched over a steaming cup, the aroma of mint coming off it was almost eye-watering. White crumbs dusted his lips as he chewed on what looked like thick sugar cookies.

After exchanging nods, Caville ordered a cup of tea at the counter, then took the seat diagonal from his boss, shifting the chair enough to keep the front entry in view. "Not even sunrise for an hour, and it's already getting hot. How do they live here?"

The other man's cybernetic eye scanned the room, wrist twisting to shrug with the cookie. "You get used to it, like anything else."

"If you say so."

"I do." Goldman finished off the treat, then took a sip of the hot tea. "Why'd I call you?"

"Right. That was going to be the question."

The pirate grunted. "Because I was right. They seized the cargo about three hours ago, then his Glorious Fuckface summoned me to his palace to inform me that the terms of the deal have changed."

"Let me guess: They keep all the gear and systems, no hostage release, but you get to walk away alive."

"Maybe. You really think they'll stick to their end of the bargain?"

"No. This is why you don't deal with psychos."

"Yeah, well, I always have a backup plan. Always."

Caville leaned in close. "To get out, or to get the hostages out?"

"Both, if at all possible."

An elderly woman in the same sand-colored robes Gallo had been forced to wear shuffled over and set the cup down. The woman brushed back blonde hair mixed with silver, then returned Caville's bow before shuffling back to the counter and out of sight.

He blew steam off the yellow liquid, breathed in the mint, took a sip, and nearly yelped. The fluid was blisteringly hot. "You need my help?"

"That's why I paid you. This is going to be risky."

"What isn't in a place like this? Look around you. They're all terrified."

"Sure." The pirate waved his cup around to take in the people in the shop. "But they signed on for this insanity. They breathe it in. You can't be completely innocent when you don't turn away the poison."

"What about Denise? She wants out of here, too."

"She was a passenger. No way I can trust her."

"If I can get her to you before you go?"

Goldman's fingers rasped over gray-flecked stubble while his cybernetic eye locked on to the younger man. "Nothing gets in the way of this rescue."

"Absolutely."

"You're in? Even if she has to stay behind?"

"What matters is those hostages, right? That's what you said."

"Okay." The pirate tossed back his tea with a wince, then set the cup down. He took one of the remaining cookies and handed the other to Caville. "Let's go."

Caville had his tea transferred to a thick paper cup, then met Goldman outside the shop. The nearest guard was already watching the pirate without turning, head angled just enough to keep the foreigners in view as they walked toward the main thoroughfare, then to the right.

There were hints of something floral as well as something herbal in the cookie, which turned out to be more like a dense cake. Whatever was mixed in with the flour made the treat filling.

Goldman didn't say anything until they'd walked past the road to the starport and turned off the main road onto another broad avenue that pointed them east, away from the airport and toward the first light of dawn rising over the simple, low buildings that must have been residential. People were shuffling out of doors to sit on steps, benches, and chairs all around the road. The buildings were sturdy and ugly concrete, the sort of things that might be built after a few invasions.

The pirate bit his cookie in half. "This is what they do, most of them."

"Sit around all day?"

"And gossip. Argue about the meaning of some of these dumbass parables. Maybe whisper regret to someone they think they can trust but most of the time can't. You know how many people are disappeared here every year?"

"A hundred?"

"Tack on a zero. And that's a good year."

"How do you know that?"

"Because I've seen the big prison where they torture them before putting a bullet in them and dragging them out into the desert. The Khan thinks it's something to brag about."

Caville squeezed his eyes shut over the memory of the defeated look in Stiles's eyes just before he shot her. It hadn't been torture, not like the SAID agent-turned-pirate captain meant, but it sure hadn't been humane or even necessary. Stiles could've been shipped down to Dramora with Patel.

But it was how Goldman had made it this far. It was just odd that he couldn't see that this Khan would use the same excuse.

A couple of the locals waved, and Goldman waved back. He didn't seem to hate the people, but he clearly hated the Khan.

The two of them covered a couple kilometers, turning down alleys, then up new streets, then heading into buildings to wind through basements that were quiet and cool. Finally, they turned north onto another major road that could handle traffic several cars wide, even though Caville couldn't recall seeing more than a couple cars at a time since arriving.

As the sun turned up the heat and long shadows stretched across the road, their likely destination came into view.

Goldman didn't slow. "Don't stare at it."

"Right."

But it was hard to look away. About half a kilometer ahead of them, the street widened out into a huge, orange-brick plaza. Sitting in the middle of the plaza, surrounded on all sides by metal posts connected by thick rope, was an old cargo hauler.

Not just any cargo hauler, but the one that had been abandoned decades ago during the failed rescue.

The thing was at least twenty meters high, probably half again as wide at the center, and maybe seventy-five meters long. It was dust-coated and had a few holes in the outer hull that might have come from heavy weapons fire or explosives. Sand had stripped away paint and left everything an angry, red color, but it otherwise looked completely intact and authentic.

Caville sipped his tea now that it was a little cooler than molten rock. "A statue?"

"The real thing. That's the *Charlemagne*."

It seemed impossible, but the closer they came, the easier it was to believe. "They kept it here all these years?"

"It's actually functional. Flew here on its own power. The Khan likes to keep it on display in the city. His predecessor had it buried in the sand. This current Khan? Used the hostages to dig it out, then had his engineers get it running, and..."

"Like an operational statue."

"A reminder of the great and glorious—" The pirate grunted. "You know."

They strode around the thing, a couple tourists who were already past the gawking stage. Winds dashed the spacecraft with sand, the howl nearly loud enough to drown out the scratching impact.

Goldman squatted to tie a boot string, and Caville hunched low to shield himself from the sandstorm. The pirate leaned toward the younger man. "You see them?" It had to be shouted, but no one else would have heard it.

Rather than respond, Caville flashed two fingers, then pointed at the recessed doorways on opposite sides of the plaza. They could have passed for emergency or maintenance exits on the side of the buildings, except for the obvious reinforced frames and the reflective glass, neither of which were visible anywhere else they'd gone in the city.

When the wind died back down, the pirate pushed up and resumed his previous pace, slowing only after they were winding in and out of alleys and headed west again.

They stopped in one such alley maybe a kilometer out from the tea shop. People had been driven off the streets by renewed wind, even the guards.

Cybernetic eye glowing brilliantly, the pirate pulled Caville in close. "This takes two operations run in parallel."

Caville nodded. His fingers were itchy with anxiety. "The *Charlemagne*."

Goldman jabbed a finger into the younger man's chest. "That's you."

"And you?"

"I know where the hostages are imprisoned, remember?"

"A breakout?"

A firm nod answered. "We've worked this out a couple times in the past. It's feasible."

"That ship's going to be empty. The rockets might work, but how good do you think the life support system's going to be? What about food and water?"

Goldman held up a hand, signaling to slow down; he had answers. "One, we can get food and water aboard with the hostages. That's part of the rescue. Two, we don't need to last too long. A week in Fold Space gets us to a rendezvous point. All we have to do is get it out of atmosphere, hook up with the *Ollie*, get some scrubbers and filters transferred, and go."

"These guys have ships."

"And atmospheric fighters. I know."

It was an insane idea, and it sounded worse by the minute. "How many guards in those stations off the plaza?"

"I've only ever seen two."

"So plan on four."

"That's smart."

"You mind telling me how you plan to deal with the aircraft and space-craft issue?"

"I kind of have to, since that falls on you."

It was late afternoon when the text came over the data tablet: *Paladin.*

The code word to go. The special knights who served the king, *Charlemagne.*

Caville pulled his duffel bag out from under the bed and began unzipping hidden compartments. Steam came from the bathroom doorway, along with the occasional splash when Gallo moved. She seemed content now, staying in the hotel, wearing only the ridiculous undergarment her mother had forced on her. The thing somehow magically connected all of the people to their Khan. It was probably a literal thing—a tracker or bug or camera must be hidden somewhere in the heavy material.

But Caville figured it was better than the robes.

Spices from dinner still lingered on his breath, even after cleaning his teeth. It was like the planet insisted on leaving its mark.

He set the contents of the hidden compartments on the bed: boxes. They acted as structure for the bag, but inside each box were ceramic and plastic pieces that could be snapped together. It was training that went back years, to childhood—disassembling and assembling guns; loading and unloading magazines; changing out ammunition. He had the weapon assembled in a minute.

A small pistol—cold to the touch, smooth, and unimpressive. It wasn't terribly accurate beyond twenty meters, and it only held three rounds, but it could slip through almost any security screening.

Now that the storm had died, getting to the plaza was maybe a ten-minute stroll. People had seen him wandering the streets a couple times already, so he wouldn't draw too much attention.

But once he left the hotel, it was done. He was committed.

And that meant leaving Gallo behind.

He leaned against the bathroom doorway, admiring the way her warm, brown skin glistened where it rose out of the bubbles.

She turned, smiled, then squinted. "What's wrong?"

"Trust."

"What's that mean?"

"It means I've got a problem, and it comes down to whether or not I can trust you."

"I told you where the Place of the Fallen is."

"You did. In general terms."

Gallo twisted around in the tub to look directly at him. "Are you leaving?"

He tensed, then realized she meant was he leaving *her*. "Depends."

"I don't have anyone else, Darien. I'm not marrying one of the brutes they want me to give myself to."

"I know."

"So stay with me. Let me figure out how we can get off this dump. I think there might be a way to get enough money so your captain can sneak me off—"

"You were a spy for the Khan."

"Well…yeah. I believed what I was told. I was a kid. I know better now."

"Do you?"

She squinted. "You think I came here to spy on you?"

"No. There were enough spy devices in this room that they wouldn't need a human operative to listen in on me."

"Then what?"

He shrugged. "I just need to hear it from you. Do you want to leave?"

"More than anything. I—I'd even be willing to face trial for what I did." Her eyes fell away from him.

Every single bit of body language was authentic. Her voice was right. If she was lying, she was the best he'd ever run across.

He grabbed her towel and held it out horizontal to the floor. "Time to go."

She dressed without a word, and followed him out, hand on his hip, smelling of the sweet spicy soap. They kept their pace casual, and he kissed her a few times in public. They were newlyweds, after all. That, and he was sure she had no idea what she was about to get herself into. He needed her calm and trusting.

When they approached the cargo hauler, she grimaced. "*That* is hideous."

"It is."

"Why would someone put that in the middle of the city?"

Once again, she sounded completely authentic. He pointed to the guard shack entry on the west side of the plaza. "Let's ask."

Her brows rose in confusion, but she followed him. When he handed her his duffel bag, she took it. "What—?"

He shook his head, smiled, then knocked on the door.

It opened, and one of the perpetually angry guards popped his head out, scowling around a bushy, red beard. Despite the facial hair, the man was young, with a chubby face. Maybe the beard was meant to make him feel more manly. His assault rifle was slung over his shoulder, but his hand hovered over a pistol holstered on his hip. "Yes?" Humana, not the local language.

Caville chuckled. "My wife and I were wondering why that ship is parked there."

The guard's scowl deepened. Behind him, a voice snapped something in the strange language of the Khanate. Red Beard snapped back, then whipped around to glare at the annoying tourists.

Caville shot the young man between the eyes, the gun barely making a whisper, then caught the falling body and lowered it to the ground.

Gallo's eyes were huge, and her mouth was wide, but she said nothing.

There was a small room beyond the door, a hallway to the left, and a larger room. Heat and light came off that room, which was full of electronic gear. Two men were seated in front of terminals, neither watching the displays. Instead, they were arguing heatedly. The closest of the two was old, with skin burned almost black by the sun. His robes clung to pudgy shoulders. Beyond him, a younger man with bright pink skin and gold hair shook his head violently.

Then he stiffened as he saw Caville.

An instant later, the younger guard fell back, blood gushing from a hole in his throat.

The black guard turned around, confusion twisting his face. "You—"

A soft buzz, a pop, and the final bullet tore through the guard's left eye.

Caville returned to the outer doorway, grabbed Gallo by the hand, and yanked her into the outer room. "Listen to me. Are you listening?"

Her eyes were still locked on the first guard's body, but she nodded.

"We're getting out of here. Do you understand?"

She nodded again. "What—?"

"No questions. Grab his gun. The pistol." Caville took Redbeard's assault rifle and the spare magazine tied to the belt, then hurried back into the main room.

She followed, pistol in her hand. She stared at the weapon while he searched for the console he was looking for. "What are you doing?"

"There's a control system in here. Centralized security. It's all sloppy and lazy and cheap, so I guess it makes sense. Here." He pushed the pale corpse aside and settled in the now-available chair. The guard had actually been logged in.

"You're going to…?"

"I'm going to get you out of here. That's what you want, right?"

She sobbed. "Yes. I didn't want more killing."

"With these people, we don't have a choice."

Tears streaked down her cheeks. She rubbed the back of her hand across her face, then seemed to realize she was holding the pistol and switched to her other hand. "I can't believe. I mean, I don't understand how I ever believed. My father was right: It's not like the parables and teachings."

"Nothing's ever like it's advertised." Caville pushed away the feeling of shooting Stiles—shooting his sister.

On the console, he brought up all the major security systems and disabled them—cameras placed throughout the city; secure communications systems from the Khan and his leaders to the dispersed security facilities; the giant network of sensor bases. It would be minutes before everything shut down completely, and they wouldn't stay down long, but it gave them the time they needed to execute their plan.

Maybe.

He sent the text back to Goldman signaling this leg of the mission was done: *Charlemagne.*

Caville grabbed the assault rifle leaning against the desk, then picked up a spare magazine and pistol off the pale kid's corpse.

Gallo blinked. "What now?"

"Now we see if that cargo hauler really is functional, or if we've been played all along."

"That cargo hauler? You're getting off this planet in that junk heap?"

"Not if we stand around and argue." He pushed the fresh pistol into the space between his belt and the small of his back, then tossed his depleted pistol into his duffel bag. "You still want off this rock?"

She exhaled. "Yes."

"Then let's move. We don't have much time."

26

Satrap was deep in the data, swimming in a sea of black, tracing the lines of sapphire and green, red and yellow. His plan had been simple, but the data flowing in always held complexities. It was simple just *reading* the data. Interpreting it? *That* special ability was what made him so valuable to the Khan.

Diving into the data revealed so much more than the projected casualty rate, which he could already see was going to be even better than expected. It showed actual strike locations, blast radii, temperatures achieved, targeting efficiency, and up-to-the second follow-on effects.

Every aspect of his stratagem was right there in front of him, ready for analysis. That analysis was like a salve against the agony in his bones. It was freedom from the dying flesh, release from the stench of his own weakness.

Here in the data, he was free from Khan and his terrible creations: Ikhama; the senior officers with their scheming and bickering; the constant pain of a body broken out of spite.

Free.

So, of course, Satrap wasn't in the least surprised when a sharp sting bit into his awareness: a priority message.

He shook off the wonder and thrill of interacting with data, which never betrayed or failed or argued pointlessly. Data was data. It had no artifice. The systems were the one thing he knew to be pure.

But, like him, they served a greater power, and that power apparently needed immediate attention.

Passageway lights silhouetted the captain of the Jakkara, who stood in the entry to the darkened cabin that kept the fleet commander safe and isolated from the rest of the fleet. When Satrap blinked away the sleep that gummed his eyelids, the other man bowed. There was concern in his eyes.

Satrap worked the numbness from his hands. "Something has happened?"

"Captain Zohar sent an alert. You will want to see it."

Now fully aware, Satrap realized his body had been about to wake him on its own. It was time for the evening nutritional cycle, and he had a choice to make: the bio-feedback signals could simulate a Mediterranean meal or some Americana fare, both from old Earth. Those were memories and sensations that weren't his at all and they served no greater a purpose than smelling someone else's meal.

He chose neither flavor, and the nutrient regulation system pricked him, as if angry that it had been dismissed.

The first hint of energy fed into Satrap, and his awareness ticked up slightly. Tiny beads of sweat were on the back of his hands. Even before pulling up the data Zohar found so critical, Satrap could feel what it was: maneuvering. It was a barely noticeable tug and sway.

He leaned against a bulkhead for support. "This is an attack?" It didn't seem possible.

"Not against *us*, Satrap. We move to attack."

The ghastly captains should have been reveling in the fire and smoke, not seeking out more destruction. Rather than ask who could possibly threaten them now, Satrap pulled up the data attached to Zohar's alarm.

Impossible.

The Kedraalian and Gulmar task force! And…

Azoren?

It had to be. The ships that had been engaged previously were red triangles on the display, but nearly a third of the force had gold triangles with identifiers matching Azoren ships, including the *Warsaw*.

Who could ever have imagined someone seeking out the Azoren as allies? And then to come *here*? To know where to go to find the Khanate fleet?

Satrap balled his hands into small, baby-soft fists. "The odds of them finding us here were too small to even consider."

The Jakkara captain hesitated, then bowed. "Captain Zohar, Satrap?"

"Yes. Thank you." This wasn't the bodyguard's fault, so being unpleasant toward him was petty and rude—something the Khan would do. Satrap connected to Zohar. "Captain. Tell me of the glory of the *Might of the Khan*."

Zohar's brown hair was a little less smooth and put-together than normal. Redness spotted the tip of his hooked nose, as if he might have been pinching it. There was the slightest tremor to his prominent chin. He squared his shoulders. "If you worry that we might have suffered damage in an engagement while you toyed with your data, you will be pleased to know that the fleet has yet to be engaged. We are closing on the enemy force, though."

"Closing? They have ships we have yet to even identify."

"Azoren ships. The *Warsaw* is the only threat among them."

"You trust your sensors?"

"I do. I trust the received transmissions even more."

"Transmissions?"

"Spies. They have confirmed fleet composition and await orders to strike."

Spies had survived among the Azoren. It had always been hoped for—the recruitment through outreach on Azh Kali and Azh Shivan; the diplomatic missions to Himmel meant for nothing but reaching out to such elements; the occasional rumors of secret Fold Space transmissions.

How could such people succumb to the Khan's nonsensical ramblings? They were rumored to value rationality.

People needed to believe. It was a flaw in human wiring.

Fine. It was something he could exploit at the moment. "The readouts show damage to ships already. They flew into the anti-radiation defensive missile network?"

"On the edge of it. The rest are firing toward them."

Which meant those damaged vessels were the problematic signals ships. Perhaps there truly was some sort of blessing for Satrap in the universe. "How long before we have full fighter and missile capacity?"

"Within the hour."

Satrap scanned the current inventory: seventy percent for fighters, sixty-five for missiles.

It was a dangerously low level if they intended to engage a force the size of this combined group. Then again, it was three different forces, and the Azoren were notoriously inept at cooperation, even when the groups were all Azoren. It was why the Khanate still existed.

This *could* be an opportunity to further sate the bloodthirsty needs of his captains. More importantly, it could be the opportunity to break the Kedraalians.

Plus, Zohar had already committed the fleet. Turning away without giving his captains at least a chance at this enemy could be the act that pushed him away as a reluctant ally.

Satrap dabbed the backs of his hands against his robe. This wasn't the best time to engage, but there would never be such a thing. "Launch fighters."

Zohar's face registered surprise and for a moment gratitude. His calculation had apparently been less certain than expected.

He bowed slightly, then disconnected.

On the data readout, waves of fighters fell from the carriers. Almost immediately after, the frigates accelerated. The tactics hadn't changed, because they hadn't been the problem when engaging the Kedraalians before. What had turned the battle had been the captains and their ill-conceived betrayal. Now, Satrap had what he needed to keep them in check, at least for a little while.

Following the frigates came the carriers, protected by the cruisers, including the *Might of the Khan*. They were too far out to manage any sort of targeting, so this stage was all maneuvering and shaking out the systems. It was a test of enemy determination as much as a preparation for engagement.

The enemy showed no signs of fleeing.

It could mean that they didn't fear the fleet, or it could mean that the Kedraalian commander wasn't going to leave wounded ships behind.

Without those signals ships, the task force would be easy prey.

Still…

Satrap ran potential retreat scenarios: which ships to send away first, which to cover the rear, what coordinates to head to through Fold Space. If Zohar proved right, and this was the engagement to seek out, then the planning would be a few moments wasted. Time was plentiful just now.

Rather than slip back into the data, Satrap activated the giant displays embedded in the walls of his room. The gulf of space was a black void between the green of his fleet and the red and amber of the enemy. At full acceleration, that void would slowly shrink.

Then he would have the firepower to test this new combined force.

To his surprise, the Azoren held position, deploying ships around the *Warsaw*. As the distance closed, the amber symbols transitioned to red: confirmation that this wasn't a ruse, that the spies were real.

Fortune favored the Khan.

One of the Jakkara was at the hatch, escorting Ikhama.

Satrap motioned for the old woman to come in and take a seat on one of the pillows, but his mind was absorbed in the coming battle now. He was barely aware of the woman's soft groan as she lowered herself onto the largest pillow.

Rather than keep quiet, she sighed, then glanced at the displays. "Battle again so soon?"

"What we did before wasn't battle but slaughter. This will be a test."

But even as he said that, the Azoren ships broke off from their previous maneuvers and surged forward. They were going after the fighter craft.

Hadn't the Kedraalian captain warned these allies of the danger of such a maneuver? The Azoren ships were old. Perhaps they'd undergone a refit? There was always a chance that technological advances could make the engagement successful.

At this point, there were theories and questions—nothing more. Let the fighters seek out targets, let the frigates pick at the edges of those seeking to engage the fighters. The most obvious targets were the crippled signals ships, at least so far. Maybe that would change once the *Might of the Khan* was a little closer, and its sensors could provide a better understanding of the opposing forces.

Some of the data that Satrap had previously glossed over now drew his attention.

Although marked in red, some of the enemy ships weren't meaningfully labeled. He drilled down into the data on them.

Ships that must have been Kedraalian reinforcements.

Ships that were Gulmar but not in the records.

And other ships. But these had profiles and signatures that were in the system. There were prompts offering to populate the blank records. He approved the prompts, and the data on the ships populated.

Azoren. TT.

Troop transports? They had brought along troop trans—?

Satrap blinked. Then he chuckled.

Ikhama turned from the display. *"In the whirlwind, there is fire. Take from this the strength to mock your enemy."* She sounded unsure of the parable.

"This is not strength but an enemy's foolishness."

She nodded. *"In the heart of an enemy, the pool of resolve may reflect weakness. Take from this strength, for it is the will of the Khan."*

He hated the mindless prattle of the Khan Kabal. "This force that leaves the others behind? You see it?"

After a moment, the woman nodded. "I do."

"They are Azoren. I thought they might be testing a new tactic or weapon. Instead, they move to protect those ships at the rear of the main group. You see?" He highlighted the TT-labeled vessels. "Those are troop transports. Lightly armed and armored—they will be full of soldiers."

"This means that the enemy force is even smaller than it appears."

"What it means is this combined force didn't come here to confront us. It came here to attack the Moskav."

"The opportunity to flee, the opportunity to stand—which is wisdom, and which is folly?"

"We could flee. I considered it. We might yet. But what this presents us with is an opportunity the likes of which we haven't seen before."

"Unprotected ships?"

Satrap rubbed the aching crease of his thigh. "All but defenseless."

He connected to Zohar. "Captain, at only seventy percent capacity, our fighters will need to be used at maximum effectiveness."

One of the older man's eyebrows arched wryly. "A wise observation, Satrap." The sarcastic tone bit.

"Had you seen these?" Satrap highlighted the troop transports.

Ah! Now the captain's dismissive glare faded. His eyes narrowed, then he stroked his chin.

"Troop transports? To attack a fleet?"

"Azoren troop transports. They don't move with the rest of the Azoren ships, though."

"Then—?"

"They came here for a ground assault, not to seek us out. And those transports are a stone around their necks. That is why the Azoren ships have leapt forward: to engage our fighters."

"It cannot be done. Their systems—"

"Exactly. So now we must use this to our advantage. Have the remote operators maneuver the fighter craft in such a way that they keep the Azoren ships between them and the rest of that combined group. The ultimate goal is the troop transports. If they cannot be reached, then attack the wounded signals ships."

"But these transports present no threat. Their weapons—"

"Their weapons are small, defensive, short-ranged—" Satrap waved the protestations away. "Those vessels represent something more valuable: resources the enemy will do anything to protect."

"But their value is nothing. They have no use here."

"You and I know they hold no value. The enemy does not. And that means they will make costly mistakes defending them."

Realization seemed to settle in the captain's eyes. "I see. This will be passed along."

"Thank you."

Minutes ground by, then the swarm of fighters changed course. The

Azoren ships adjusted as well, moving between the bulk of the enemy ships and the closing Khanate ships. Perhaps the Azoren captain was inexperienced. Certainly, he would never have seen Khanate tactics and would expect them to be crude and simple. That was how the Azoren saw all their enemies.

The fighter craft maneuvered again, and the Azoren matched.

Satrap couldn't have asked for a better tactical mishap. He brought up the missile information, then laid out the targeting array. With the Azoren acting as unwitting shields, missiles could be launched at the *Warsaw* and then sent right past, into the ships beyond. For the Kedraalian and Gulmar ships to fire, they would have to risk hitting the Azoren. Do that, and even a strong alliance would falter and collapse. He couldn't conceive of a strong alliance between the Azoren and anyone.

Fortunately, Zohar didn't question the orders for the missiles. He was smart enough to see the intent.

Now there was nothing more to do but wait.

After a few minutes, the fighters were at the edge of the Azoren weapons range. Khanate frigates fired not at the Azoren ships but beyond them, into the ranks of Gulmar and Kedraalian ships anchored down by their own wounded targets. There weren't any significant hits, but what mattered was that the enemy was now engaged, and they were limited by the actions of one of their own.

On the display, the faster and more agile fighter craft dropped below the Azoren protective ships and came up and around, screaming toward the troop transports.

Now the Azoren ships risked firing on their allies, who were limited in their maneuvering. In fact, some of the Gulmar and Kedraalian ships seemed committed to protecting the defenseless Azoren troop transports.

A few of the fighter craft winked out. The "volunteer pilots" wouldn't even be aware that they had been killed. They were dead the second they launched, whether or not they found their targets. If the fighters didn't crash into their targets and obliterate the pilots, they would simply be left behind to die. The chemicals that kept them alive long enough to speed through space at lethal velocities weren't gentle, and the fighter craft were disposable, meant only as high-speed battering rams and explosives delivery mechanisms.

Three of the fighters at the edge of the swarm veered off, one of them flickering—systems were failing, and the pilot was dying. The other two were headed for the wounded signals ships.

The failing fighter ship winked out, too far away from any target to matter, but the other two had a chance. They were going after unmoving targets.

More fighters winked out shy of their targets, but enough were making it through.

One impacted, detonating instantly.

All that mass moving at such a terrible speed—even without the explosives, the fighter craft would punch a hole in the transport's armor. And when the explosives inside the fighter detonated…

Sensors caught enough of the outcome to show the transport as wounded.

Then another fighter found that transport.

And another.

Its signal disappeared.

How terrible and desperate the crew must have felt. Maybe even the soldiers knew in the moments before they were set ablaze or torn asunder or hurled into the void of space.

Satrap could understand exactly how a captain would feel knowing that this fate awaited his soldiers. It was terrible to exploit it, yet…

Something chimed, drawing his attention from the battle: Another group of fighter craft had been completed. Four more volunteers were being strapped into the tiny cockpit, prayed over, medicated, then hooked to monitoring gear.

In minutes, those fighters would launch.

But already, the Azoren were causing as much chaos and terror for their allies as any group of remote-controlled fighters ever could.

Lights flickered on the screen.

The carriers and cruisers were in range to open fire on the closest Kedraalian and Gulmar ships.

There would be no fleeing for the enemy, not until the signals ships were destroyed. Satrap could almost feel sympathy for this Kedraalian captain, who had done well before. Now? After stumbling into a trap that had only been left behind as a result of adapting to the new gear, there was no hope.

Satrap had the enemy right where he wanted them. Now he only had to execute on his mandate.

All praise the Khan!

27

Getting into the cargo hauler was harder than Caville had expected. It was so old and weatherworn that he had to search around with his fingers in the gloom beneath the ship's ass for the remnants of the airlock access panel. That panel was a rusty, scraped mess of cracked composites and metal. But the real problem was that the contacts had receded and were unresponsive. Fire from the fumbled hostage rescue decades before had charred away the panel labels and fried the friendly interface beyond use. At some point, someone had pried away most of the glass cover to get to the electronics underneath. So close, all that wear and the damage gave off a smell, like rusty andirons covered in ancient ash.

Gallo's back was pressed against his, warm and damp through her robes. When he shot a glance over his shoulder, she was looking past one of the thick landing gear struts, staring at the door to the security station opposite the one they'd cleared. Her breathing was irregular, broken by sobs and gulps that rose above the eerie quiet.

His thumb worked against an uneven, round plate, which he was sure had to be the activation button, although it wouldn't budge. "Not long now."

"Okay." She barely managed to gasp that between sobs.

"I'm sorry you had to see that."

"Piracy is…barbaric."

"That wasn't piracy." *It was espionage, like you did, except you used a system to send people to their death, while I get my hands dirty.*

"It was terrible."

Something cracked, and the plate gave. Little pebbles rolled past his thumb and into his shirt. He caught a couple and sniffed them: rust.

She turned around. "Did you fix it?"

"Almost."

As if to put an exclamation mark on his lie, the circular plate rasped down from inside the circular channel and fluttered to the ground.

Apparently, Gallo didn't notice. She rubbed the wrist of her robe against her eyes. "If they come out—"

"They won't. They wouldn't have heard a thing."

The contacts were broken, worn through, or corroded. Whatever the problem was, he needed a piece of metal to jam into the channel. If there were still functional leads with current waiting to run through them, a bit of metal should do it.

"Hey." He grabbed the sash around Gallo's waist. "Take this off."

"What?"

"I need the buckle."

"Oh." She handed him the assault rifle, then unbuckled the sash and unwound it and handed it to him.

"Thanks." He handed the weapon back, then bent the buckle prong back and forth until it snapped and fell into the sand. His fingertips were raw by then, making it hard to feel the metal, but he finally fished it out. It took a second to wrap one end in the sash material, which he squeezed tight before jamming the end of the prong into the channel.

A current locked his arm in place for a moment, then a loud, terrible groan rumbled from the airlock hatch, and a grinding panel opened to release a stuttering, clunking ramp that telescoped out to the ground.

Caville took the assault rifle off his back and pushed Gallo down, then moved behind the landing gear. "They're going to hear that."

Sure enough, the door to the security office burst open, and three men in robes boiled out, weapons already rattling around to point to the cargo ship. They couldn't see Caville, but he could see them.

He fired, and the assault rifle bucked.

One of the guards yipped and stumbled, but the other two brought their weapons around to focus on the muzzle flash.

Now that Caville had a feel for the weapon, he targeted the largest of the standing guards and tried another short burst.

The guards returned fire, and bullets banged off the hull.

A dull pain ran through Caville's right foot, but the guard he'd shot at collapsed.

Caville put a burst into the last standing guard, who had flipped his weapon to full auto and sprayed the overhanging hull and landing gear providing cover.

Then the final guard fell.

Before Caville could finish off the one he'd winged earlier, a single shot rang out from behind.

The final guard pitched forward, and Caville spun around.

Gallo knelt at the bottom of the ramp, staring down at the rifle in her hands, as if she couldn't believe what she'd done. Her bottom lip trembled.

He rushed up, grabbed her robe where it was bunched at the center of her back, and hauled her up. "Don't think about it."

"I—" She looked ready to vomit.

"You've killed a lot more people than that. All that's changed is that now you've seen what you've done all along."

Her eyes bugged out, then she spun away and retched.

While she got that out of her system, he sprinted over to the fallen guards and gathered their weapons and ammunition, which went into the duffel bag.

The young woman was still hunched over, moaning softly. He limped up the ramp, his foot now aching. Past the airlock, the huge cargo bay was like a tomb, barely lit by a few dull lights embedded in the bulkheads. What had once probably been dull, gray sheets of carbon weave covering the metal-and-composite inner hull were now blue-black in spots, and patches were worn through all the way to the ribbing and plating. Columns of foldout bunks with ratty cargo straps dangling down ran from the entry to the hatch that separated the rear cargo area from the central one.

In the central cargo area, there were more bunks and the silhouettes of cargo crates, which had probably held food and water when the rescue had been aborted and the hauler abandoned. Two small heads—a sink, a toilet, a crude shower—were built into the bulkhead connecting the two cargo areas.

Someone should take the time to check the ship: hull integrity, atmosphere recycling, gravitic systems, water drainage and recapture, the bunks and cargo secure points.

He didn't have time. Either the reactor and engines worked and they launched, or the mission was a no-go.

A ladder took him up to a catwalk, and from there a narrow passageway took him past a handful of private cabins and another crude head, then to the bridge.

There were three seats on the bridge: pilot, copilot, and a navigation station, all curved around the roughly 180-degree sweep of the nose. Even those seats looked ancient, the covering ripped and burned and gashed. Impact-absorbent gel had dripped from the co-pilot seat and gathered on the deck, turning into what looked like a spiraling turd of grime and sand.

Caville dropped the duffel bag on the deck with a loud thump and settled into the pilot's chair, blinking hard and trying to find calm. He'd been trained on the basics of starship operation, but the trainer had been a standard design from the last couple decades. This…?

All consoles followed the same basic concept. There would always be an operations section, an engineering control section, and a flight control section.

He ran the side of his hand over the console, brushing away sand and grit. Under the console, there was a raw spot of twisted metal and cracked polymers where the military security modules had been torn free. That meant there was no need to fight with card readers and privileged codes.

It also meant he needed to figure out how to trigger the battery systems. Without batteries, there would be no firing up the reactor, and without that, there would be no engines.

Someone had flown this beast out from the rescue site. They'd dug it out of the desert. They must have replaced or recharged the batteries.

A closer look revealed that his console had been less grime covered than the co-pilot console. And there were cables in still-glossy black insulation running along the curved bulkhead to the bottom of the console.

Caville ducked under the console and spotted a small, metal box behind the spot that had once held the security system. A thin strip of plastic covered the box bottom. Feeling around that strip located hinges and on the opposite side, a thumb-tip sized lip that jutted beyond the box.

He pulled that lip down, probed the inside of the box, and found a button.

One press, and the bridge lit up dully. Then his console did the same.

Slow steps rang from the passageway as he dropped into the pilot's seat. Then came a soft, trembling voice. "Darien?"

"Up here." The chair creaked when he spun it around to check on Gallo.

She stepped through the bridge hatch opening, looking gray and weak. "I—"

"Navigation." He pointed to the seat across from his, beyond the co-pilot seat. He didn't like having to keep his back to her, but he didn't want her on a seat without protective gel, and he didn't need the distraction of her haunted face. "Strap in. If this goes right, we're airborne in a couple minutes."

It was like looking at a robot, the way she shambled over to the other seat and melted into it.

Shock affected people differently.

He found the engineering section of the console and triggered the reactor startup. There was no time for a graceful warmup and safety check. If the Khan's people had left fuel in the reactor but hadn't given it a safety inspection, the rescue ship wasn't going anywhere.

The reactor indicator glowed amber, as did the batteries. That was actually good: power wouldn't be drained from the batteries if the reactor wasn't viable, and getting enough energy from the reactor to show it was powering on the rest of the way meant it was operational.

"Once this reactor indicator gets a hint of green, we fire up the engines, then we lift off." He turned to look at her, realizing for the first time she'd left her rifle behind. There was no time to recover it. He cycled the airlock closed.

Seconds ticked by, then the reactor indicator showed a hint of green, and the batteries started to recharge. It wasn't enough to run the ship in space, but it was enough to get it off the ground.

A tap on the console transferred power to the engines, and Caville twisted his head around. "We're a go."

Rockets rumbled, and a deep shudder ran through the hull as dust and sand bloomed around them. That was probably the least of the damage. Windows would shatter all around the plaza, he was sure. It was further proof the Khan was an idiot.

Caville grabbed the controls and pulled back, getting the ancient hauler airborne. Warning lights flickered on the console. That was to be expected.

"Denise?" A quick twist confirmed she was still there and strapped in.

They were several meters up. He didn't have to look at the camera feeds to see the rooftops, but he did anyway.

Goldman needed to know.

Caville pulled out his data pad and connected to the SAID agent. Their decision to create a backdoor inside the Khanate's crude network seemed prescient now. With the main security apparatus offline, sending the simple code was overkill but still wise.

Stick to the mission.

After a few seconds, Goldman sent back confirmation. His mission was a go now, too. Caville had a rough idea of the target, but without a network of positioning satellites, he was going to have to wait for a crude signal to know exactly where to land.

For now, he got a basic heading using the hauler's inertial navigation system and tested the engines.

Everything rattled, filling the cabin with a thick clatter.

Even over that, he heard Gallo's ragged breathing.

It would've been easier to keep his focus on the ship, but they were en route, and everything was either going to hold together or it wasn't. Showing a little decency wasn't going to add or remove any risk.

He filled most of the display with the belly camera, which captured the sandy world whipping past beneath them. "You need to talk?"

"No." She sniffled. "What you said—it hurt."

"Sorry."

"It hurt because I realize it was true."

If they hadn't been in the middle of the mission, he would've pulled her to him and offered her reasons why what she did wasn't terrible. People died, even if you weren't a spy feeding information to the enemy. "You did what you thought was right."

"And I was so wrong. It was my father who was right. I think—" She gagged. "At some level, I knew that. Or suspected."

"Kids are born to disappoint their parents. A mentor told me that a long time ago."

"Mission accomplished." She gulped and gasped, half-laugh, half-sob.

"Okay. Let's see if we can't accomplish *this* mission."

She turned her chair around and craned her neck. "Where are we going?"

Even if she were a spy, there was nothing she could do to stop him. "There's a prison. The Khan keeps the last of the Kedraalian hostages he took there. We're taking them home."

It took a moment for that to set in, then she slowly nodded. "You're… here for the hostages. You've been trading weapons to the Khanate all along for—"

"The hostages. Yes. I think Zenawi was angling to use the rescue to make his case as prime minister for some time now. Maybe it rescues his career."

"I never understood his fascination…"

"Political capital. A better person would say it was the right thing to do, but he's not a better person—he's a politician."

"You're not a pirate."

"Hired gun, just like I told you."

A brilliant flare glowed orange against the darkening sky, then headed down toward a shallow, wide valley. Beyond the flare, there was the glow of a fire.

The prison.

Goldman.

Caville angled the cargo hauler toward the valley. The ship's clatter changed tone, then settled back to its previous pattern.

As they drew closer to the ground, lights danced in the gray gloom: headlamps.

How many hostages were still alive? How many could they safely move?

Beyond the front group of six vehicles, more headlamps glittered like tiny stars. Either Goldman's team had gotten separated into two groups, or he had pursuers.

The latter seemed more likely.

Caville set the hauler down in the valley with all the grace of a boulder hurled by a tsunami. Nothing exploded or went to red, so he considered the landing a success.

He slapped the airlock release, then unbuckled and gathered up the weapons and ammunition that had spread across the deck. "You can stay strapped in if you like. It's going to get ugly out there."

"Ugly?"

"Goldman's rescue didn't go unnoticed. I think he's got some guards on his tail."

Gallo unbuckled, stood unsteadily, found her balance, then grabbed one of the assault rifles and a magazine. She'd wrapped the sash around the robes, but the way she'd tied the material, it bunched below her sternum, lending her the appearance of a strange sort of heft.

She followed him out and up the side of the narrow valley where they were able to dart across the rim until they reached a small opening that must have long ago been a river. Goldman's vehicles were speeding toward that.

The SAID agent's six vehicles looked like four buses and a couple cargo trucks. Figuring twenty per bus, that put the rescue operation shy of a hundred.

Would that qualify as a success or a tragedy?

Success.

Tragedy would be getting even one hostage this far and not taking off.

Thinking like a politician, this was a black eye for the Khan. Thinking like a human, this was a long-overdue attempt to free innocent people from a lifetime of wrongful imprisonment.

A voice in the back of Caville's head questioned whether he had the right to consider himself human. He felt like one at that moment.

He found a rocky protrusion that looked down onto the dry riverbed and set his assault rifles down. When Gallo settled beside him, he began checking the magazines and swapping in fresh ones.

She did the same, stopping occasionally to squint at the nearing lights. "Are they going to have time to get everyone aboard?"

"No."

"So we're fighting them here?"

"Yes."

"And those other vehicles are…?"

"Personnel carriers, probably. I'm guessing twenty or more guards."

"That's a lot."

He dropped to a hip, propped himself up with an elbow, then pulled his wounded foot closer. There was a blood-darkened hole in his boot, right where his little toe had been.

She settled onto her belly, a welcome pressure against his side. "I think I'm better shooting just one bullet."

"One bullet kills just as well as two." He kissed her cheek as the front bus rumbled by below, tossing a cloud of sand into the air.

A form jumped out, a submachine gun dangling from a strap. Before the next bus could enter the valley, the form darted to the opposite side of the opening and scampered up the sand wall, grabbing stone where it poked out.

The other vehicles groaned and squeaked as they slipped through the pass. In the glow of one of the truck cabins, Theo's face was a bloody, wrinkled mess of determination.

Caville whistled, and when the form on the other side stopped climbing, waved.

Goldman.

He'd already spotted a perch of his own and quickly settled into it.

Three against the world. It was the mission for now.

Gallo breathed in deep. "Who should I target?"

"Can you target the driver of the lead vehicle?" Caville motioned with the nudge of his chin, even though she wouldn't be able to see it. "Upper chest, if you can. I've got the guy riding shotgun in the second vehicle."

"So if I get the driver—?"

"Second shot is his buddy."

"Why are you going for the second vehicle?"

"Fifty-fifty chance the driver comes around the lead vehicle and exposes himself to me or Goldman. If the guy brakes, the guards get out farther away. Good for us."

She grunted, then her weapon roared, and the lead truck jerked sideways.

It became a chaotic muddle after that.

Weapons fire echoed down into the valley and out the other side. The Khanate guards showed the sort of poor discipline Caville had expected, some running out into the desert in a panic, others climbing under vehicles. A few were killed when they darted in front of the third vehicle, which was apparently driven by someone absolutely determined to get to the fleeing buses.

The driver died when Goldman sprayed the side of the vehicle.

There weren't as many guards as Caville had expected, but there were still enough to make things ugly. A spray of gunfire knocked Goldman from his perch, and Gallo screamed before crawling back on the ledge.

But Goldman got back up and hobbled for the spacecraft, and Gallo returned to the ledge, shouting what Caville assumed was an explanation.

He never stopped firing.

Then, after an eternity, the shooting stopped, and it went silent. After a bit, a few low moans came up from below but no gunfire.

He had a half-empty magazine left and the pistols. One pistol went into a pocket, and he kept another in his hand. Blood trickled down the side of Gallo's face, but she seemed fine.

"A rock." She was shouting, but he could barely understand her. She whipped fingers past her head, maybe meaning to show that a piece of rock had grazed her.

Caville jumped, then slid down the sandy slope leading out to the vehicles. In the valley, the buses were still unloading. They would be for a while. The dead and wounded Khanate troops were spread out for twenty meters or more. One of the officers had a flashlight, which gave off bright light after a good slap. A few survivors were curled beneath the trucks, crying.

"Out!" Caville pointed a pistol at them and waved them into the open.

They came out reluctantly, hands held high. After a few attempts, one of them got past blubbering and shouted out a meaningless parable.

Caville put a bullet between the man's eyes.

The other two ran, and he shot them in the back.

He turned to Gallo. "You okay with that?"

She nodded but looked shaken. "What if they'd offered to surrender?"

"That would have told me they weren't elite troops and they could be reasoned with. That's important to know."

"But would you have let them go?"

"We can't. They would either be rounded up and executed or forced back into service. You've seen how this Khan guy operates."

Understanding washed over her face. She brushed away the blood on her cheek, then followed him back to the spacecraft without a word.

Goldman was there, waving for people to hurry. One of his crew was wrapping a bandage around his chest. Blood spread slowly through the gauze. He managed a painful grin. "I owe you a bonus."

Caville shrugged. "Get them home; we're even."

"You're not coming with us?"

"I've got some other things to do. If you could take Denise with you—"

The pirate captain frowned. "I guess I was wrong about her."

"We all make mistakes."

Gallo grabbed Caville's elbow. "What do you mean—you're not going?"

"Like I said, I've got things to do."

"The Place of the Fallen?"

He pulled out his data pad and opened it for her, activating a simple audio capture application. "Dictate the directions in here."

"No."

"I got you a way off this planet. You owe me."

"I do. So I'm going with you." She thrust her chin out.

"You don't need to make up for what you did. You'll have a lifetime to deal with that."

She shook her head. "I'm not leaving my husband behind." A smile trembled on her lips.

Goldman snorted. "We don't have time to wait for you two to figure this out."

Caville stepped back from the ramp. Without her guidance, he wasn't going to find the ruins. He waved at Goldman and the ship, then headed back to the valley mouth. Gallo followed close behind, helping him gather ammunition, canteens, lights, and any other useful gear from the dead. They climbed into the second troop transport, and he backed it out.

Gallo pointed northwest. "Head that way."

He saluted, then pointed the truck as she'd directed.

His mission had finally begun.

28

───────

It seemed to Benson that red filled the *Valor*'s tactical display. Swarms of triangles flitted around the Azoren troop transports, but other triangles slipped off and headed toward the wounded signals ships. What she needed was targeting data, but without all the signals ships operational, the task force wasn't getting enough for lock-on.

She stepped back from Mahama's weapons station, around Chopra, then slid over to Nuñez's station, careful not to trip in the darkened bridge. With the battle stations klaxon off, it was deceptively quiet, almost peaceful. The young woman's eyes were distant, and she was talking to someone in a soft but firm tone. Commander Tuleyev's name was dropped, and Benson relaxed, then signaled for the communications officer to mute.

Nuñez tapped her headset, and the mute light came on. She palmed sweat from her brow, as much the result of stress as the bridge temperature slowly climbing. "Ma'am?" Her breath had the bite of dehydration they were all probably experiencing thanks to the timing of the attack.

"Is that the *Lyon?*"

"Yes, ma'am."

"Put me through to Commander Tuleyev, please."

The communications officer gave a quick nod, then unmuted. By the time Benson was back atop the raised command station, she had the requested connection.

"Commander Tuleyev, I assume you're seeing what I'm seeing?"

"Many targets but no lock-on, yes?"

"Yes. We're getting some feeds from the *Sinclair*, but the *Castro's* systems went down again."

"And the other two ships—any news?"

"Chief Parkinson has power back on for the *Mao*, but their systems took serious damage. It sounds like the *Tojo's* even worse off."

Tuleyev grunted. "One ship to do the work of four. This is not the path to victory."

"We've operated with less."

"Against this Khanate fleet?"

"No. Does that change anything?"

On the command station display, the old commander shrugged. "I had hoped for more meaning about what you referenced, nothing more."

"It was the fight over Jotun. Different ships, same idea: We could've used more capable hardware. I'm thinking we need to have the *Sinclair* focus on these fighters. We've got some making for the *Mao* and *Tojo*."

"Ah. This is a problem."

"The bigger problem is Faulk and his cowboy task force. Even if we get a clean target, we'll have limited firing options."

"Also a problem, yes. Perhaps our maneuvering should adjust for positioning."

"Meaning?"

"The Azoren task force maneuvers do not match ours. They mirror their own troop transport maneuvers. We do not know the particulars of these maneuvers, yet we can work around them."

She saw it then: Even though the fighters had gotten past them, the Azoren ships were moving as a group to shield the troop transports from the closing frigates. When the transports moved up the Z-axis, so did their shield of destroyers and the *Warsaw*. Adjusting the Kedraalian and Gulmar ship maneuvering to counter those moves—up when the Azoren went down, down when they went up—would be enough to get cleaner angles for fire.

Or she could simply order that the Kedraalian targeting systems not to be concerned if an Azoren ship was at risk from weapons fire. Except that would start the battle she wasn't ready to fight just yet.

"Please have our helm team adjust the maneuvering package."

Tuleyev nodded. "And the fighters headed for our signals ships? This is still a problem, is it not?"

"Put the gunships on an intercept course. Scramble any shuttles we can spare."

Although only his upper torso was visible, the older man's body language was such that it was clear he had his hands clasped beneath his paunch. "If we lose our signals ships…"

"I know. I'm already working out what a retreat will look like."

She disconnected. As she worked through which ships would provide cover for the retreating force, she couldn't stop wondering what had happened. The Khanate fleet had been hidden for weeks. It had obviously resupplied, and it was possible it had been reinforced. There were ships too far out for sensors to get a good read, but the numbers looked close to what they'd seen when they first encountered the fleet.

Had the Azoren sold the combined fleet out? Were there spies in the senior ranks somewhere back on Himmel? A Fold Space transmission sent just before the combined fleet launched could have reached the Khanate ships in time for them to prepare the ambush. It would be a messy way for Supreme Leader Graf to eliminate his—

Benson shook her head. The notion was insane. She was letting the paranoia of the Azoren leadership get into her head.

This Khanate captain had to be a genius. That was all there was to it.

Her headset vibrated: a private connection. Halliwell?

No. Thiessen.

She brushed stray hairs out of her eye and accepted the request. "Captain?"

He was focused on something to his left, nodding, then he turned to his camera. "Faith?"

"You connected to me."

"Oh. Right. We're receiving new maneuvering packages—"

"Yes. Sorry. It's the Azoren. We're trying to get around this..." She shook her head. *Incompetence.*

"The fighters are tearing a couple of those transports apart."

She searched for a video feed, hoping a camera on some ship might be able to show exactly what was going on. "Those ships are too slow for us to protect."

"Faulk's going to be livid."

"I'm not happy, either. They're defenseless." She spotted something coming off one of the *Nairobi*'s cameras: a thumb-sized image of fire blooming from the side of one of the boxy transports, then more fire, then the ship tearing apart.

A maneuver made the details harder to make out.

She'd seen enough. Those weren't her soldiers. She wasn't even sure if they were normal humans or more of Faulk's "brothers." Either way, it was a terrible loss of life.

Muscles bulged along Thiessen's jaw. "We have to be ready for him to blame us. He could attack."

Meaning *they* should consider their pre-emptive strike.

Except she didn't have her signals ships. "This was his disaster, Floyd. I'm working on a retreat plan. If we can't salvage the signals ships, we can't stand and fight."

"You're putting together the rearguard?"

Benson nodded. "Destroyers. Two from each force."

He bowed his head. "D-7 and D-11."

"Thank you."

She plugged the designators in, a part of her preferring the simple designators of the Gulmar over the antiquated idea of proper names. It made saying goodbye easier when she had to do what she was doing. Those two destroyers would join the *Ganges* and *Veleka* from her force. The Azoren destroyers—

That fight with Faulk would come later, if the signals ships were lost.

"Floyd, I'm not seeing any more fighters. This may be the extent of it."

"Isn't it enough? We can't stop those missiles without your signals ships, and if they're using anti-radiation systems, just powering up the electronic warfare packages gets you killed."

"Not if we can get our ships coordinated. Those Khanate carriers are too far forward of the cruisers. If we can get our forces on top and below them, we can tear them apart in a crossfire."

"We need those signals ships."

"I know. It comes down to Parkinson and Taylor."

But a quick check of the tactical display confirmed Benson's worst fears: The gunships weren't stopping the Khanate fighters. The targets were too fast and too small without clean lock-on capabilities.

She was going to have to pull the engineers out.

<hr>

Grier's back ached, the pain as deep as the hardest workout she could ever recall. She'd convinced herself that everything being in 0g would mean the work would be easier, but operating the bracing equipment and stopping things when she moved them still required exertion. Mass was still mass, even if there wasn't weight, and once she got a few hundred kilos moving, it was a few hundred kilos with momentum that she had to stop. The same applied when a structure needed to be reformed or deformed by the bracing equipment.

So, she ached. Her uniform was soaked inside her armored environment suit. Sweat beaded on the inside of her helmet until she shook her head, then the moisture would come free of the treated glass and get sucked into the suit's recycling system. It couldn't keep her cool, though, and it couldn't take away the smell.

Her breathing was a ragged, hollow sound inside the helmet, and it left her feeling lonely in the black of the engineering section, where only one uncertain light remained after the missile strike.

At least Parkinson was alive, and he seemed to be making progress. The reactor was mostly functional, and he'd dragged cabling and systems around until he was caged in by equipment.

And the whole time, he was chattering with his girlfriend, Chief Taylor.

It was actually cute, watching the change come over him in the days since they'd first reached Azoren space. Taylor was nothing like the ladies

Parkinson typically pursued with all the grace of a horny tomcat. She was a little taller than him, and to say she was curvy was an understatement. Parkinson had always been more drawn to dainty women, except for Stiles. Then again, she'd been different, using him to complete her mission.

That had to sting. It wasn't as if most folks minded Parkinson taking a hit like that. He could be a little shit to most people.

She pulled herself up to the top of the starboard-side equipment wall. "Chief?"

His helmet twisted around. "Yeah?"

There wasn't much fear in his voice and no annoyance. Taylor had really done a job on him. "How're we doing?"

"Better than the *Tojo*." There was an anxious tone about him.

"Damage control team says they've still got about six major breaches. Maybe fifteen minutes before atmosphere can be restored everywhere." *Well, not here.*

"System's operational when they seal things up." He turned back to his console, which seemed to be working okay despite the crack running down the display. "Bigger problem's the Khanate ships."

"Any luck with the electronic warfare gear?"

There were modules of the stuff he called shadow tech in the piles around him, locked into place by cable bundles and thick plastic ties. Silvery lights glowed along the smooth, black surface of some of the gear, but other modules looked completely dead or had intermittent flashes.

He patted one of the modules. "Soon. There were some fried power supplies, but there's so much redundancy, we should be okay. I'm more worried about getting everything synchronized and having the pattern recognition library load up after all those core dumps."

"Sure." Whatever the hell that meant. "What about a time estimate?"

"We'll have the shadow tech operational before the rockets. In fact, you might want to have the crew get back to their stations, because—"

The silvery lights that had been intermittent went bright, then settled into the same sort of soft glow as the systems that had apparently been brought back to life earlier despite "core dumps."

Parkinson pumped his right arm up and down. "That's enough comms working. We should be able to synchronize with the *Sinclair* and *Castro*."

"And, um, drive systems?"

"A couple more minute—" His head bobbed back, as if he'd straightened his back abruptly. "Shit."

"What?"

Parkinson tapped the side of his helmet. "Captain Benson. She wants us to abandon ship. Hold on."

Abandon ship? Grier was pretty sure there was no fighting the Khanate without the weird shadow technology that had brought nothing but trouble since they'd found it installed on the *Pandora*. It didn't seem likely a couple damaged signals ships could handle the workload, either. Not unless the Khanate fleet had shrunk, and what Parkinson had shown her before the sensors flaked out the first time looked like the same pack of "oh shit" they'd tangled with before.

But Captain Benson was smart. Maybe she'd figured out some way to crack the Khanate's shadow technology. That would be nice. Even if the *Mao* and *Tojo* were fixed, Grier had seen the crew quarters. The *Mao* was maybe at half crew now, and the important people couldn't be replaced with just anyone. Parkinson knew the guts of the shadow technology, but the electronic warfare people knew how to operate the things. They were the experts.

She needed to be sure she saved as many as she could.

Grier connected to Espinoza. "Lieutenant? How's it looking out there?"

"Not good. I'm getting live updates, and my sensors are picking up bogeys incoming."

"What are they?"

"Those fighter-bombers. Sounds like they're trying to take out these crippled ships. So…how long before we bail?"

"I think soon. How many can we fit on the shuttle?"

"If we use the co-pilot's seat, twelve. So you, Chief, me, and nine more."

There were twenty-one survivors. "What if we squeeze people into the airlock? Strap people down to the deck?"

"That's not safe."

"Safer than being on this ship when those bombs go off?"

"Right." Espinoza whistled. "Okay. We can probably double that. Twenty-four. Snug and intimate, and it's going to limit maneuvers."

"Sure. I think folks will understand. I'm going to let people know."

"Don't be long. We've got minutes."

"Understood."

Grier couldn't bring herself to interrupt the chief, who seemed to be caught up in some frenetic round of twisting from one hardware module to the next, then turning back to the console and swiping something there. They still had a little time before abandoning ship.

She realized suddenly that without even trying to, she was running an operation. Not with the captain's guidance, and not with Halliwell telling her what to do.

Just running an operation. Who could have ever seen that?

Data streams glowed inside Parkinson's helmet. "Greta, look, you've got to get out of there."

On the cracked console, he'd given most of the display to the shadow tech output, and it seemed like everything was red. Their combined fleet barely registered as a few small clumps of green, and some of those clumps were winking out.

Taylor's sigh was heavy and thick in his helmet's speakers. "Damn near got this figured out. Just this one cable bundle keeps giving me trouble. What about you?"

"We've got power. The shadow tech's up. Drives are coming online."

"That's good enough."

"I wanted to get everything running. It pisses me off when all of this piles up suddenly. *Everything's* a top priority."

"That's how it goes."

"But we should have time to do things *right*."

That drew a snort from Taylor. "Wartime, all we can do is keep things running and hope it's enough for the mission, right?"

"I...don't know if it's good enough to shake these Khanate fighters, though." What he *wanted* to say was that he didn't want to do anything until she was off the *Tojo*, but that would offend her. "Captain Benson said we need to abandon ship."

"I think I can get power operational if I can figure out which of these cable bundles has a short. Power comes online, I got the rest of it figured out. They lost a lot of people in that first missile strike."

"Maybe you should go now. That ship sounds like it's a wreck."

A deep, throaty growl came over Taylor's connection. "Damn! It wasn't the bundle I thought."

"Greta?"

"Yeah. I hear you."

"Well, I think you need to move. We're running out of time." He could order her to abandon ship, but he didn't *want* to. She was a peer, really. "Captain Benson—"

"I *know*, Will." Metal rang, as if Taylor might be stomping on something. "All right. This thing's lost. I'm telling the crew to get onto my shuttle."

"Thank you."

She disconnected, and Parkinson saw a flash of green: The *Mao's* maneuvering drive was online.

He twisted around and waved at Grier, who was talking to someone.

Her eyebrows rose, and she connected. "What's up, Chief?"

"Drive's online. They're abandoning the *Tojo*, but I think we can move."

The Marine drifted over the top of the piled equipment. "You *think* or we can? It's a big difference. I need to tell Captain Benson if we're staying."

Parkinson brought the engines fully online. Everything still showed green. Some other time, maybe he would've waved at the display dramatically to emphasize just how impressive his work had been. Not now. "We just need a pilot."

"I'll let the crew know." There was a click, then silence as Grier talked to someone. She flashed a thumbs up, then pulled Parkinson into another channel. "Lieutenant Espinoza, new plan. We're going to stay aboard. If you could disconnect, we're about to light up."

There was a soft hiss, then Espinoza's voice, which sounded distant. "Retracting umbilical. Should I inform the *Valor*?"

"Already on that."

"Good luck, Sergeant."

"We'll need it."

Parkinson wanted to say this had nothing to do with luck—it was all hard work and know-how, but that would mean Taylor hadn't known what she was doing. He'd gotten lucky that the things broken aboard the *Mao* were easy enough to fix, even if the fix had to be ugly.

Grier dragged him into yet another channel. "Captain Benson?"

"Sergeant Grier, what's going on? You've got fighters inbound."

"Chief got the *Mao* running, ma'am. We're on the move."

Benson was silent for a moment. "Okay. We're seeing your sensor data. We don't have targeting just yet, but it's looking good. You sure you can get out of there? Those fighters are closing on you and the *Tojo* fast."

Parkinson came off mute. "Chief Taylor's team is exiting the *Tojo*."

"They need to get a move on."

"She knows. The *Tojo* had some serious damage, but the *Mao* has enough power to keep systems running." *For now.*

"You sure?" The captain sounded more anxious than anything else. "I'm about to commit everyone to a dangerous maneuver. I don't want to put you or the task force at risk if we aren't solid on this."

"We're rock solid."

It sounded like Benson swallowed. "All right, Chief. Thank you."

Now other voices filled the channel—the crew. It sounded like an Ensign Cameron was the commander and pilot. She ordered people to stations.

It was terrible that the engineers had been killed, but there wasn't really much of a section for them to work in right now. He smiled, surprised at the pride he was feeling for getting the *Mao* operational. It wasn't pretty, and it wasn't something that would last for long, but like Taylor said: In battle, you only worry about getting things done and hope it's good enough.

He texted Taylor: *You gone yet? Captain's worried. Fighters incoming.*

A few seconds passed, then Taylor replied: *Strapping wounded in. Sucks losing a ship.*

There would have been an obnoxious reply in the past, a tease that a *real* engineer didn't let a ship fall to an enemy. Maybe he would've attached an image of the cracked console display, showing green for the critical systems, not counting life support.

Not now. He responded: *What matters is fighting another day. Hurry!*

It felt right. It felt *good.*

She responded back with an image of her scowling. There was mischief in her dark eyes, though.

He tensed. Mischief? Playfulness? It seemed like a trap. With someone else, he would've joked about his prowess, maybe he would've tried to get her to come to the *Valor* for some more coffee and another go at cracking the Khanate shadow tech systems puzzle. It was all harmless if she was in on the teasing.

Was that what she was doing? Was she actually interested?

Cameron's voice boomed in the channel that had gone quiet—surprisingly strong and sure for an ensign. "We've got maneuvering drives and thrust. Thanks, Chief Parkinson. I've plugged in the task force's evasive maneuvers guidance. Strap in. One of those fighters is coming at us awfully fast."

Parkinson's heart raced as he replied to Taylor's text: *You're an excellent engineer, Chief.*

That wasn't offensive, was it? Pedantic? It didn't seem like it.

The *Mao* moved, thrusting him back and causing the piled gear to sway like sea plants in the current. Everything was locked into place with sturdy ties, so long as the pilot kept the ship accelerating and maneuvering at a modest enough rate.

The *Mao*'s commander whooped. "That fighter shot past! We're clear!"

Grier disappeared behind the wall of equipment for a second, then appeared not far away, arm hooked around a now-empty equipment rack.

Taylor replied with another image: tongue stuck out this time. Text followed a few seconds later, a string of letters slowly streaming past: *And here I was looking forward to seeing your*

The rest was garbage, a string of scrambled characters. What—?

It was the connection: dead. He checked the *Mao*'s systems, but they were green.

Cameron groaned. "We've got two impacts on the *Tojo*. Looks like the explosion took out that shuttle. Damn."

Parkinson's heart stopped beating. He couldn't breathe.

That shuttle? Maybe Cameron meant some other shuttle. Maybe…

But Parkinson knew better. Taylor was gone.

29

The fireball from the *Tojo* explosion flooded half of the Valor's main display. Benson had been drilled in, watching the shuttle full of wounded attempting to evacuate the damaged ship. They'd nearly made it, too.

But the Khanate fighters had slammed into the signals ship before the shuttle could get clear.

It was war. People died.

That didn't make the pain any easier to take. It didn't help Benson shrug off the image of the explosion or the one that came from the burning shuttle, spinning away from the larger ship.

Superheated shrapnel had almost certainly pierced the thin hull.

Heat and chills took turns swimming through her gut. She squinted at the command station display, sure that if she just concentrated hard enough the distance to the bridge deck wouldn't seem so vast, and her legs wouldn't feel so weak. Maybe the bridge crew would forget the white-hot glow that was still there on infrared.

At the broad helm station, Chopra twisted just enough for her to see him biting his lip, watching her without actually looking directly at her.

She sucked in a deep breath, realized the air was no warmer than before, despite that distant explosion and the pall of perfumed perspiration. When she swallowed, it was as if those scents sank into her tongue and coated her dry throat.

It took a few tries, but she pulled her drink container from its mesh holder and took a sip of the sweet drink. It was warm now, but it helped.

Benson cleared her throat. "Commander Chopra."

Her XO turned more fully. "Yes, ma'am?"

"Let's get a full display of the battlefield, please."

The bald man reached between Lieutenants Konrath and Mahama, tapped a few command display options, and the giant screen filled with the black of space and the detailed tactical display.

With the *Mao*'s data now coming in full, Benson could actually pick out targets on the *Valor*'s battlefield. It would've been easier, the confidence in where to target would have been higher, if they hadn't lost the *Tojo*, but she would take what she could get—she had eyes, and that's what mattered. And they'd lost the entire crew, along with Greta Taylor, the chief engineer, and the Marine sent with her to try to rescue the ship.

That had been Benson's call. She could have sounded the retreat earlier.

On the display, the large Khanate carriers crept closer. They were putting more distance between themselves and the cruisers and what the signals ships indicated might be specialized ship tenders at the rear.

Or maybe some of them were the source of the anti-radiation missiles.

Benson had already fallen for one trap and lost ships. It was a mistake she wouldn't repeat. "Commander, please open an audio communication with Commander Tuleyev. I need to know his thoughts about the Khanate posture."

"Posture?" Chopra tilted his head as he glanced at the display.

"The way those carriers are edging forward. Was that the last of their fighters, or is this an attempt to lure us into committing prematurely so they can launch another wave?"

"They only had thirty-six, according to our sensors."

"Our diminished sensors, yes. We should talk with Commander Tuleyev."

Chopra nodded, then slipped behind the communications officer's station and began chatting with Nuñez. The young lieutenant blinked

·rapidly but seemed under control. When the explosion had lit up the bridge, she'd let out a loud gasp.

Perhaps she'd known someone aboard the *Tojo*. Even if she didn't, it made sense that she was worried. Everyone had heard their captain send the shuttles out to the wounded signals ships. They had seen her misunderstand the threat posed by the movement of things where there should have been dead space. Maybe they could sense Benson's doubt in her own abilities.

There was a chirp in her headset, then her XO stepped back from the helm station, taking his own headset from his glistening head. It was her call now. "Alexander?"

Tuleyev sighed. "Dinesh? You are still there? This is a dangerous engagement, so I suppose you make a call outside regular channels for a reason?"

Benson cleared her throat. "Alexander, this is Captain Benson. I asked Dinesh to reach out to you."

"I see. There is a problem?"

"We lost the *Tojo*."

"The explosion—it registered on our tactical display. Unfortunate. We are, however, facing many frigates with no ability to target them."

"That's what I wanted to talk to you about. You've seen the way those carriers are sneaking forward?"

"I have, yes."

"And you saw the proposed maneuvers I sent out?"

"It was my assumption that this depended on the *Tojo* being rescued."

His words weren't meant as an attack, but Benson flinched. "We're getting sensor data from the *Mao*. The *Castro* and *Sinclair* are operational."

"You seek my support for a counterattack against the Khanate, Captain?"

"We've suffered losses, but we're still functional."

"Three signals ships remain, but they are all damaged, yes?"

"We would use them to draw the Khanate ships even closer in, keep them at the edge of operational range."

"But, as I have just said, these ships, they are damaged."

She nodded, then remembered they were audio only. "They are."

Tuleyev grumbled to himself. "Against this shadow technology, the networked systems provide power and redundancy—am I correct?"

"That's correct."

"So we are not just down to three of four ships; we are down whatever systems were damaged among all four ships. And they are fragile. Any one ship, it could suffer a failure. This is true also?"

"And we would lose targeting if that happened."

"Captain—" The old man let out an exasperated gasp. "—the risk seems dangerously high."

The bridge hatch opened, and Benson saw Halliwell step through out of the corner of her eye. He turned to the Marine on guard and the two chatted.

Another distraction.

Benson massaged her brow. "Alexander, the real question is about those carriers. They could be moving in to launch another wave of fighters. They could be ready to launch more missiles."

"Then we should leave the field of battle. We are compromised, Captain."

"But we aren't completely disabled. If this Khanate captain believes we can't defend ourselves, this could be our opportunity to capitalize on their mistakes."

Tuleyev grunted. "This is what you believe—they are making a mistake?"

"They've shown reckless confidence before."

"Hm." It was a sound that might have been a concession or a challenge. "And you are sure these damaged signals ships can do as you have said?"

"I believe this is an opportunity to hit back and hit back hard."

"A punch thrown too hard leaves you exposed. This you know."

Chopra's dark eyes went from the tactical display to Halliwell before locking on to Benson. There was a shrewd determination in the commander's gaze. He moved close. "Take the opportunity."

It was whispered too soft for her headset to pick up. She squeezed the supporting bar of the command station. "Commander Tuleyev, I think this is a punch we *have* to throw."

The old man smacked his lips. "Time to send out confirmation of these maneuvers, then."

"Thank you. Please implement immediately. I'll inform the Gulmar."

Her XO grinned and killed the connection. "A strike against this Khanate fleet is long overdue."

"I know. And I'm not letting it slip away."

One of the support braces Grier had put into place where the hull had collapsed threw an alarm. She muttered a curse and pushed off from the rack she'd been using as an anchor. The *Mao* losing its gravitic systems complicated everything. Years of training for 0g rescue didn't make the work easy, just less likely to go haywire. It didn't make it so that you weren't stuck breathing in your own sweat or dealing with sudden chills turning to swampy heat as your environment suit compensated for exertion and relaxation. Cooling fans might whirr so loud that they interfered with your audio, or the sudden silence might leave you feeling unsure of your hearing. You had to use embedded lifeline anchors and handholds to do anything meaningful. You had to take even more care with loose gear, which could turn lethal under a hard maneuver.

And in a ship as damaged as the *Mao*, there was plenty of wreckage to worry about. A penetrated environment suit could mean losing precious atmosphere, or it could mean something pointy getting buried in your gut.

She made herself small, curling in her armored shoulders as she squeezed past the little fortress of gear Parkinson had surrounded himself with and grabbed onto a handhold. The engineering section was already a cramped space. All the gear that had been wrenched from mounts or pulled out to allow for quick access—that was a threat, too.

Grier keyed her microphone. "Chief, you there?"

He grunted. "Yeah. Busy."

Was he just busy, or was he dealing with the fallout from the *Tojo* strike? It sure seemed like Taylor had meant something to the little engineer, but maybe Grier had been reading it wrong the whole time. "Hey, um, I'm getting alarms on one of the braces. All this maneuvering, probably."

"Need help?"

"No. But I'm moving around."

"Let me know if—" He made a sound that might have been a simple inhale or a sniffle. "—you need anything."

"Roger."

Farther forward, there were a couple spots where both layers of hull had been warped by the missile blasts, deforming until the deck bowed up into what should have been the ceiling. She had to swim away from those, drag herself over cracked consoles or squeeze between narrow gaps where control panels had been snapped or shattered. Most of the fine particles from the broken glass would have low mass enough to have been sucked out into space with whatever atmosphere vented, but it wasn't a perfect absence. Her lights sparkled against a few fine clouds that hadn't made it all the way out before they lost atmosphere.

The problem brace was in the corner, holding up one of the sections where a rib from the ship frame had bent hard. Although the brace itself was still functional, a fine cloud of red mist was forming around it.

Hydraulic fluid.

She pulled a deck tile up, braced herself, and waved it through the mist, collecting as much of the fluid as she could. That was sufficient to expose the problem: a small sliver of metal protruding from the tank.

One of the early lessons from search-and-rescue training was to always—*always*—carry a variety of sealants. There were a few multipurpose ones that could handle almost anything inorganic, and there were a couple that could handle anything organic. She had a canister for each purpose. The one she preferred for a job like this was more of a paste, which could be applied to a silicone strip that kept the material from activating. Metal, paint, solvents—those acted as catalysts to harden the seal. She squeezed the paste onto a strip, then pressed the strip against the hole and the protruding metal sliver.

The spray stopped.

Grier pumped her fist. "Mission accomplished."

"Hey." Parkinson sounded surprised.

"Yeah?"

"I could use another pair of hands."

It was exactly the sort of easy opening she loved to turn into a crude comment, but that felt wrong if Parkinson was hurting. "On my way."

"This—" He cleared his throat. "This won't be easy."

"Sure." There was a serious determination in his voice that was welcome, a change from his testy, frightened tones when things turned ugly.

When she poked her head over the gear fortress wall, he was busily tapping and swiping through a series of interfaces. Now he started typing speedily. The way the control software flashed, winked out, changed, then repeated—it was dizzying. He never slowed, like he was just a part of all of it.

Experience. He was smart.

His head came around, the console light reflecting a pale blue off the glass of his helmet. "You get that brace fixed?"

"Yup. It was a leak. What've we got?"

He pointed to the interface on the screen. "The way they designed all these systems, I can access most of the controls through this console here, but I have to access some through my computing pad."

"Saw that."

"Some stuff can't be brought up with either of those, though."

"Why's that? It's all software, right?"

"Yes, but you want separate systems. Air gaps. It protects from compromise."

"Sure." Air gaps. Core dumps. Whatever. "What do I do?"

"The system I need you to deal with is the shadow tech. The advanced electronic warfare stuff?"

"Okay."

"We're getting alerts: failing processors. I'm running some modifications. Load balancing alterations. These systems have twenty processor pair bundles—probably five times the processing power they actually need."

She whistled. "Okay. Do not understand, Chief. Just so you know."

"That's fine. What I need to do is get the power routed to a different breaker panel. That's going to let me pull up another console." He pointed to the other side of the fortress, opposite her. "Over there."

"So, you want me on that other control panel?"

"Yes. To re-route power, I need to get back to the reactor."

"I could do that. Just walk me through—"

"No. The reactor took some damage. The coolant reservoir is leaking steam. Radioactive steam."

"Oh." Grier wanted to get back to Halliwell. She'd fought so long to get him; there was no way she was going to lose him. Spending weeks in the infirmary, going through blood transfusions and maybe even getting put into cold sleep—that would suck.

He crawled out of his fortress and waved her to the console he'd told her about. "You settle in there. When it powers up, you'll see some prompts."

"And you'll tell me what to do?"

"It's easy."

"Great. Anything to keep this shadow tech running. The captain's counting on it."

The chief sagged, but he tried to hide it. "I know."

He crawled over the fortress and out of sight, leaving Grier alone in front of a black control console. Parkinson was pretty useless in combat, and she'd come close to punching him out a few times over the years, but looking at the sort of work he did left her feeling stupid. She knew the basics of systems operations—turning power on and off; lighting up engines; reading sensors. Re-routing power lines? Balancing air-gapped processor whatever load things?

She tapped the black glass of the dead console. "Extra pair of hands, huh?"

Don't you get yourself hurt, Chief. Everyone's counting on you.

L ight throbbed inside the reactor bay. From the opposite side of the safety door, Parkinson could actually see wisps of steam snaking toward an unlit section of the chamber.

That meant a hull breach, despite the extra shielding the reactor chamber had.

The ship's engines thrummed through the hull, radiating through every part of him that touched the deck or bulkhead. He was dangerously close to all that power.

It would've been easier to switch the cable bundle from one panel to another inside the engineering bay, but the area he needed access to was a tight maze of jagged, twisted metal. Pounding the threats back would take too long.

So he took a deep breath of stale, recycled air, checked his environment suit one more time, and opened the safety door.

Everything in the chamber was polished and smooth. The core itself was a stainless steel barrel a few meters across. Pipes, cables—everything was shielded. But the missile that had locked in on the ship's sensor antenna array had blown a hole through the hull and the shielding.

He swallowed, tasting something bitter in his throat. Fear. He was ready to vomit.

Taylor had been trying to deal with power problems on the *Tojo*. That's what had kept her on the ship too long. He couldn't make the same mistake.

Power cables were marked with gold bands. They ran out to capacitors, distribution systems, batteries—

The distribution system he wanted would be labeled EB. There would be one major cable going in, and three lines coming out: EB1 through EB3. Everything was running through EB1 right now, but the breaker panel wouldn't feed the console he needed to work from if he was going to do anything serious on the shadow tech system. His computing pad was simply too small for anything that delicate.

His environment suit lights flashed over power lines labeled for the engines and life support. The EB cables were deeper in, close to where the steam was leaking out.

Parkinson hunched into a ball as he moved deeper in, taking a moment after every cautious push from handhold to handhold to search around for the hole in the ship's skin. When he reached EB1, his light caught the steam rising to the bulkhead not two meters away. An ugly, ragged wound poked inward several millimeters, although the hole was so narrow he might not have spotted it without the steam. From that hole to the source of the steam—

Yeah. Whatever had come through the ship's skin had also cut through the steam pipe.

Bad luck.

"Sergeant Grier, you hear me?" The engineer pushed down to the EB1 cable bundle and unclipped the stainless steel cover, revealing the black insulation shielding the power line.

"Yeah." She sounded scratchy.

Interference. "I'm going to switch these cables around. I've got everything set up so I can remotely power this down—"

"Wait. Won't that kill the systems?"

"No. You've got battery backups in there. We can go without the reactor for several minutes. It's okay."

"A-all right."

"When I'm done, you'll see that control console power on. Okay?"

"Got it."

"You'll need to respond to the prompt quickly, or it'll lock out that console. It's a security precaution."

"Okay."

Parkinson unlocked the other EB cable cover and disconnected the plug. Now came the fun part.

He triggered the power down on the EB cables and unplugged EB1.

The ship shifted beneath him suddenly, and he lost his grip on the cable plug.

Something sounded in his helmet, what might have been the pilot warning that they were taking evasive maneuvers. All Parkinson knew was that he had bounced off a bulkhead—

His head ached. It was hard to focus.

"Chief? Chief Parkinson?" It was Grier. She sounded panicked. The hiss in her connection was bad.

"I'm—" Parkinson wasn't sure how to respond. Fine? His head hurt. His thigh burned. "I'm okay."

"You went quiet. Did you unplug things? Because the lights are going dim."

How long had he been out? He was floating—

He was floating in the flow of steam! He looked down to where his thigh burned and saw a cut in his suit.

Shit!

Parkinson pushed away from the hole in the bulkhead and settled on the deck. He pulled a suit patch kit from his hip. "How long was I out?"

"You were out?"

"The ship maneuvered?" At least he thought it had.

"Oh. Yeah. They're firing at us—the Khanate."

"How long ago?"

"Five minutes? We'll have to maneuver again soon."

Great. He sealed the cut, gritting his teeth when the material pressed against his burned leg. That wasn't good. Radiation. Steam. A cut. Not good at all.

He crawled over the deck to the cables, found a place to brace one boot, then the other, and plugged the cable into the new outlet. That should do—

Wait. He was forgetting something.

His head throbbed. "Did the console power up?"

"No."

Of course it wouldn't—he'd forgotten to turn power back on! It took some effort to concentrate on the helmet interface, but he brought power back on.

"Oh! Chief? I've got that prompt."

At least that had gone as planned. "Good. Here's how you log in."

As he walked her through the process, he dragged himself to the chamber door. He'd banged his head, lost some oxygen, and burned himself. His suit started flashing radiation warnings before he reached the engineering bay.

Not his best moment, but he had the *Mao* operational, and soon he'd have it stable. What was it Taylor had said? In wartime, all we can do is keep things running and hope it's enough for the mission.

It was going to have to be.

30

———————

It was easy for Satrap to fall in love with data. Data didn't have a bias. It didn't bend to the will of a despot. There was nothing about data other than the data itself—no hidden meanings or deception or influence. Data was data.

And what the data said about the combined enemy fleet was…troubling.

He leaned back against a pillow, blinking away tears that told him he'd left his eyes open while darting through the myriad sensor, weapons, and damage control feeds of his fleet. Pain might also have played a role in the fluid dripping down his face. It was why he preferred being shut down, almost asleep, when he reviewed data. His broken body often protested the long dives into analysis that caught him up and took him away from the damage done to his body by the Khan so long ago.

Ikhama still huddled in the far corner, pillow pressed to her chest, eyes occasionally drawn to the giant display showing the battle in brilliant colors. "You look troubled, Satrap."

No parables or prayers? He bit back the urge to snap at her. She seemed sincerely concerned, which meant something. And her concern was warranted. His robes were damp from sweat, and he stank as if his care-taking system wasn't keeping up with the poisons of his body.

Those were data points he should look into. Later. When his fleet wasn't at risk.

Satrap waved a hand toward the display, barely noticing the cramping in his forearm. "Do you believe in illusions? Apparitions?"

The old woman squeezed the pillow tighter to her bony chest. "Magic?"

"Deception. Misdirection." Those seemed to match what he was seeing.

"When the night glows with the silver of the moon, the enemy looks upon the valley and sees only the black grass whipping in the wind. Shadow in shadow, darkness hiding truth. When the sun rises and spills its glorious rays upon the warriors, the true strength of the Khan's host is revealed. Hide strength from sight, waiting for the right moment to show your power."

He wanted to challenge her, to point out that the moon the Khan wrote about didn't give off light of its own but reflected the light of the sun. The thing was, her parable was valid, and the Khan's observation—or whoever he'd stolen from—was correct.

And it was entirely possible the Kedraalian captain had the same idea.

How could that information be conveyed to Zohar and his fellow captains? How could an order to retreat be given without provoking claims of cowardice and incompetence again?

Satrap sighed. "When you look at that display, do you see the red symbols of the enemy?"

Ikhama bowed. "Their nature is small and fragile."

"When we look at the display, yes. But our sensors probe them and the details in our databases take on flesh."

"Knowledge is power."

"Yes. Thank you, Ikhama." Satrap waited until he was sure she hadn't taken offense to his sarcasm—or even noticed it—and pressed on. "There are three distinct groups: the Kedraalian force, the Gulmar force, and that Azoren force."

"Already, the Azoren force suffers terrible losses."

"Of troop transports. Those are the low-hanging fruit intended to slake the bloodthirst of my insatiable captains, if only for a little while.

Those ships held no meaningful defensive capabilities and no offensive capabilities at all."

"*Blood easily drawn with the blade is no less blood.*"

"Ikhama, please. We face a problem."

She closed her eyes. "Yet victory seems so close."

The monitoring system bleeped, then a surge of medicine burned in Satrap's veins. He swallowed a gasp. "Our numbers…seem overwhelming, but the truth is that we are outgunned. The Azoren force is mostly destroyers—old and unimpressive upon first glance. But our ships try and fail to get clean lock-on. There is no consistency in our electronic warfare superiority."

"You destroyed an entire fleet with the gift of the Khan."

"A second-rate fleet run by inexperienced, part-time captains, riddled with security flaws that left half the ships vulnerable to sabotage. A straight-up engagement would have been a greater challenge."

"*We knew victory by its true nature, despite the words of doubters and the poison of traitors.*"

A sigh slipped from Satrap. "The important data here is that the Azoren force actually outguns us. Not on its own, but in combination with any other element of the combined force. Those destroyers? The *Warsaw*? Even with the Gulmar, they're a real danger."

"The Gulmar are dead and have yet to realize it. This was the word of Captain Zohar."

"And he may be right. But those Gulmar ships? Those are newer than the ones we destroyed. They have lighter armor, and there are fewer weapons bristling on their surface, but they have more missiles. Our sensors are marking their missile bays now."

Ikhama squinted at the display. "They offer no resistance."

"The signals ships have been damaged. Without them, they can't manage targeting. None of them can, except apparently the Azoren."

"Then you were wise to strike against them. *Know the enemy who is true—*"

Satrap held up a hand to stop her. "No. Striking those troop transports was the *wrong* thing to do. Taking the easy kill…" He squeezed his eyes shut. "The real threat is still the Kedraalian ships."

"They have fired as little as the Gulmar. *What does not attack cannot kill.*"

It was worse than trying to teach a computer how to cry. "Ikhama, do you understand what you see on the display? The Kedraalian signals ships were not destroyed by the missiles the Khan *gifted* us."

"But one shows that it is dead."

"*One.* There were *four.*" He highlighted the three distinctive shapes that still glowed on the screen. "Three remain."

"And more of the missiles close even now." She pointed to the racing green rectangles.

"Close, yes. If the Kedraalians manage to protect those ships, they will have the capacity to target again at some point."

"Then destroy them now, before the missiles hit."

It seemed to Satrap that his back could no longer hold him up, and that he must rest his head against a pillow and sleep. Ikhama could only see success, and he could only see the potential—the inevitable—failure. If the Khan's anti-radiation missiles had been half as effective as promised, the signals ships would all be destroyed.

To get Zohar to understand the threat, Satrap had to reach the old woman. The message had to be that clear and simple. "Do you see how the missiles we launched with the fighters are slowly disappearing from the heavens?"

The old woman's neck craned until he was sure her bones would pop. "They are not to their targets yet."

"Exactly. And that means the signals ships are operational enough to target the missiles."

"So the special missiles will find them. Our Khan's gift—"

"It's possible, yes. But a commander must see not just the most beneficial outcome but the most likely. That outcome is one where all our missiles are eliminated. At such great distances, with all those ships, the odds of impact are poor under the best of conditions."

Ikhama's wrinkled brow bunched. "But we have numbers…"

"We have frigates. We have carriers that are little more than oversized troop transports until more fighter craft are readied. Our cruisers cannot match theirs for firepower. Our design relies upon the advantage of missiles and fighters on the battlefield, and we're spent."

Her thin lips flattened. "You have so many of these frigates. Attack the vulnerable ships."

It was a child demanding more cake after being told they'd had too much cake already. "It is this simple: If those signals ships survive and become fully operational, our advantage is undone. The odds of them surviving are greater than the odds of them dying. With each missile we lose, our effectiveness diminishes. We came into this fight at exactly the wrong time, despite the advantage of surprise."

And, he thought, they were greatly outmatched despite the brilliant missiles gifted to them by the Mighty and Glorious Khan instead of more frigates or another cruiser, as had been requested.

Her hands slid down the pillow to her lap. "What, then?"

"The Kedraalian and Gulmar ships rise above and sink below us. They slowly stretch beyond the last of the frigates. Do you see? And the signals ships drift farther and farther back, drawing everything toward them, past the ships that extend into the space between our frigates and us."

"The enemy is overstretched. Attack them."

"No. *We* are overextended, not them. That is the point I've been trying to make. This Kedraalian captain knows our tendencies and exploits them. Our captains send their frigates after the promising targets—the signals ships, the isolated Azoren force. They fail to see this threat." Satrap highlighted the Kedraalian and Gulmar destroyers forming spearpoints already parallel to his own frigates.

"This Kedraalian captain uses the Azoren as...bait?"

"It would seem."

"Then eliminate the Azoren. Destroy the bait."

Satrap clenched his teeth. *At least she's set aside the prattle and nonsense of the Khan Kabal.* "The Azoren lead ship—the *Warsaw*—is too heavily armored to destroy without fighter and missile support. This is the flaw in the fleet's design, as brilliant as it may seem." *All hail the Mighty and Glorious Khan!*

"Then these old Azoren destroyers—strike them!"

"Ikhama, *listen*! The longer this fight drags out, the more we are put at risk of devastating losses, perhaps even complete defeat."

"We have—"

"We have nothing. No advantage. No superiority. Look at the way the Azoren ships move now. Their captains adapt. They realize they are bait and move back toward the Kedraalian signals ships, forcing our frigates even closer."

Ikhama's lips moved, as if she might be counting the numbers.

He shook off the torpor that troubled him when the universe reminded him of how stupid the people around him were. "My captains cannot or will not see that they're being outwitted. They send our frigates —their primary weapons platforms—deeper into a trap. Help me. What can I say that can break through such stubbornness and incompetence?"

The old woman's chin shook. "These captains were selected by the Khan..."

"But they *aren't* the Khan." His stomach protested at such a lie; raising the Khan above even the lowest of the captains was a crime. Their incompetence was mostly a matter of birth into power. The Khan was a travesty of imbecility.

She nodded, embracing the branch he'd extended. "Yes. The Khan would see through this."

Satrap pointed to the tips of the spears that glowed on the display— Gulmar and Kedraalian ships drawing closer to the carriers with each second. "They may ignore the frigates. They may attack the carriers, which have allowed themselves to move far too close to the main battlefield. They may attack us."

"The Khan has great pride in his carriers." She whispered something— a prayer. "It is the strength of our fleet."

Finally—the message was sinking in! "What can we say?"

"To reach these captains?" She sounded as if her thoughts were elsewhere.

"Yes. They have broken from my doctrine. They have placed our fleet —the Khan's glorious fleet—in peril. You remember the penalty we faced the last time we challenged them."

Her hands came up to the pillow again, and she rocked back and forth, but her eyes remained focused on the display. Satrap added subtle emphasis to the lead ships at the spearpoint. He brightened the carriers and intensified the dark between the cruisers and the big, blocky ships that were even then printing out aircraft for the hundreds and hundreds of volunteers—pilots.

Ikhama's voice rose and fell, and words floated in and out of audible range: the Khan's grace and blessings; the fruit of his crop; the honor of victory.

Was she suggesting parables to reach these officers who had already conspired to kill not just her but the Khan's own appointed Satrap?

Satrap needed to communicate in a way that didn't isolate. Her ideas had worked before, but now things seemed more tenuous. His captains had been drawn in by the scent of blood. They felt confidence and saw an end to their service to the younger man their Khan had appointed to lead their fleet.

But what was the key to making the message something other than a recrimination?

Before he could ask Ikhama for something more specific, she let go of the pillow and clasped her bony fingers together, working the thick knuckles back and forth. "Pride."

Satrap groaned inwardly. "I can't make it seem as if this is their fault." No matter how much it actually was. By diminishing his role to little more than advisor, the captains had ensured this sort of debacle would repeat until the fleet collapsed.

Ikhama licked her lips. "The fleet is the pride of the Khan, and the carriers offer his stamp—his fingerprint—upon the field of battle."

"All right."

"To crush the enemy, to drive them before us, we must have the power of these brave pilots. It is the Khan's will."

That had never been explicitly stated anywhere in the strategic doctrine provided by the Khan, but it was something implied. Satrap could see the shape of the idea. It was the Khan who had imagined the suicide spacecraft, using "heroes" as detonation mechanisms.

Could the idea be sold to Zohar?

Lights flashed across the display, as the *Might of the Khan*'s systems tracked the crossfire Satrap had been warning about. Energy weapons that pulsed and disappeared at the speed of light slashed through the rear elements of the frigates.

The enemy ships drew closer.

Satrap's gut tightened. He sent a connection request to Zohar, who accepted immediately. When his face appeared in a corner of the giant display, he smiled broadly. "Captain Zohar—"

"Satrap! Calling to congratulate us on our imminent victory?"

Careful. "Actually, I wanted to engage you about a concern Ikhama and I have."

"A concern? This sounds philosophical. Our attention is on destroying this elusive Kedraalian captain."

"*That* is our concern."

"I see."

More lights pulsed on the display. In a small corner of Satrap's awareness, one of the frigates spat out a long trail of amber alarms.

He fought the urge to yell at the captain for not seeing the threat. "Our carriers are still empty. We'll be hours getting even half our fighters replenished."

"What we launched earlier seems to have sufficed. The enemy—"

"Captain, the Khan holds the carriers in special regard."

Zohar's shoulders went back. "And those carriers have made this victory possible."

Satrap took a moment to check the data: The wounded frigate's alarms went from amber to red, then its data feed stopped.

Gone. "Without the Khan's carriers launching fighters, we'll be overextended."

The captain leaned closer to the display. "The Khan cares only about success."

Another frigate threw amber errors as lines flashed on the giant display. Then came more lines. A lattice of energy weapons that would soon shut down any opportunity for evasion.

Why wasn't Zohar seeing this? "Ikhama, perhaps you might...?"

For a second, there was only silence, then the old woman hissed between her teeth. "Captain Zohar, our Mighty and Glorious Khan designed this fleet to sweep the corruption of lost humanity from the skies."

Zohar bowed. "We serve the Khan."

"His gift was the brilliance of these vessels to carry the heroes to their end, all in his name, and as a gateway to a new life for these brave souls."

"I recall, Ikhama."

"Now the ships that carry the Khan's will are at risk. You see that on the display? My eyes are old, so it *is* possible I misinterpret what the Satrap's display shows."

The captain looked away, and with his profile toward them, Satrap could see the muscles moving in the other man's cheek.

Then Zohar flinched. He'd seen it.

He turned back. "A moment, Ikhama."

And like that, the connection died.

Satrap held his breath, then sucked warm air in. His environmental controls should have kept things cooler. He would need to dig into that data, too. For the moment, he cocked an eyebrow at the old woman. "Your eyes are old?"

A grin curled her lips, then was gone. *"Age brings wisdom but also pain and sorrow."*

"Yes."

Zohar reconnected, and any hint of joy was gone. "I have spoken to the other captains."

They didn't listen. Satrap could see it in the captain's eyes. "What do they say?"

"That we are close to victory."

Another of the frigates burped out amber alerts. "Our frigates are caught in a dangerous web of fire."

"They are." Zohar's eyes drifted from the camera to something else—the same battlefield display showing in Satrap's cabin.

"And our carriers will be vulnerable soon."

"I can see the same battlefield you do, Satrap."

"Can you? Because what I see is that we'll soon be overextended and protecting our carriers and frigates will be impossible. I see a battle going exactly the way this Kedraalian captain wants!"

On the display, rather than flashes of light, the enemy fire seemed to be a constant stream. Shields buckled. Armor bubbled and slid away. Frigates threw more and more troubling damage control reports.

Then the flicker of lights tracked to the *Desert Sands*—the Khan's favorite carrier. A handful of systems flashed amber.

Zohar's breath caught.

It all played out in front of Satrap. The data spoke of a complete collapse. In minutes, everything would fail. In every engagement, once a force hit a tipping point, there was no way to salvage things. There was only one option. "Retreat. We must retreat."

"We have them, Satrap! We have them!"

"No. They have us. The tide has turned, and staying any longer will only make the outcome worse."

Ikhama nodded. "The carriers must survive, Captain. These are the Khan's favored vessels."

The captain stared off to his left, then nodded sharply. "I will sound the retreat."

Satrap relaxed. "Another day, Captain. We will have them another day."

But Zohar had already disconnected.

There was nothing to do but hope it wasn't too late, that the tipping point wasn't already behind them.

Satrap saluted the display and the Kedraalian captain who continued to run circles around his incompetent subordinates. It would be nice to meet the man one day, perhaps to share insights into the limitations each faced. Lessons could be learned. Perhaps a friendship could be had. At the very least, Satrap might explain his plight and regain a measure of respect.

It was a quaint idea and also ridiculous. Only one force commander would survive this war.

And that has to be me.

31

———

From orbit, Moskav seemed to Faulk little more than a gray ball, a world of smoke and ruin. He was still waiting for reports back from the *Warsaw*'s shuttles that had been dispatched to confirm what sensors told him, but the static that hissed and popped over their connections were warning enough.

The planet was a decimated ruin, and it was the work of the Khanate.

He paced the bridge, rubbing the light cast that protected his arm, doing his best to ignore the smell that told him he needed to remove the plastic assembly and wash everything tonight. The breaks had been well on their way to healing before a scan detected a problem with the set. That forced a re-break, which was mostly healed now, but he had developed an infection, forcing treatment that left him weak and nauseated most of the time.

It seemed undignified, especially for someone created to be superior to humans. Yet here he was, staring down at the work of simple barbarians. The Khan's fleet had denied Faulk his victory and the glory of claiming the Moskav world. It was supposed to be the event that cemented his ascendancy.

Captain Hart stared down from the command station without making it seem like a statement of authority. His thinning hair glistened coppery in the warmth of the bridge. "A tragedy."

"The rest of the Moskav holdings will fall to us easily now."

Hart bowed his head. "Of course, Field Marshal."

Faulk didn't let the hint of insolence trouble him any more than the other man's perspiration or the faint wrinkles in his coat. "The Kedraalians continue their pursuit of the Khanate fleet?"

"They do. Without our assistance, as you ordered."

After a heartbeat, the field marshal looked up at his task force commander. "You would leave the remnants of our troop transports unprotected to hunt down this enemy?"

Hart straightened. "We suffered terrible losses because of this ambush. Morale would be helped with the destruction of an enemy ship or two."

"We waltzed into a trap because of this Kedraalian whore. Such will not happen again."

The captain bowed and turned his attention to the display mounted to the top rail of his raised command station. It might have been imaginary, but there seemed to be a little color to the man's cheeks. "Do you believe there might be a chance… These saboteurs the Kedraalian captain warns about, could they be a threat?"

"Of course not. This was a handful of our brothers turned to assassins by Weber, nothing more."

"Checking for more such assassins would seem prudent."

"A waste of resources. This discussion is over."

On the giant display, several of the red triangles winked out. Hart frowned. "The Khanate fleet abandons its wounded ships to escape."

"Frigates are easily replaced."

The captain pointed at the display with his chin. "One of the carriers remains."

A carrier. If the Kedraalians managed to take that down, it would be a significant blow to the enemy. There would be a feather in Captain Benson's cap in such a success but also a thorn beneath the skin for the Azoren task force. They had three damaged destroyers and had lost nearly half their troop transports.

How many of their brothers had died in the hell of vacuum? How many were incinerated or torn apart by the impact of the suicide fighters?

And what had the Kedraalians lost? A signals ship—little more than a corvette stuffed with electronics. Those electronics had failed to detect the Khanate ambush, same as his own upgrades.

The Gulmar privateers had lied or been deceived. The equipment was worthless.

Failure wasn't bad enough. It had been failure in front of two forces who should have been impressed. Instead, the two captains he'd had under his control for days now saw that the Azoren Navy was far from infallible. If anything, his task force probably appeared to be a joke.

Faulk placed his hand with cast over it behind his back and held it with his good hand. "We will need reinforcements."

Hart's brows rose. "There are reinforcements?"

"I will send the damaged destroyers home and demand replacements."

"It was my understanding that the supreme commander would not weaken the planet's defenses further."

"You spoke to him directly?" The field marshal glared at his captain.

"No, Field Marshal."

"War is risk. Boldness carries rewards, while cowardice smears you with shame. Supreme Commander Graf will understand this. It is the burden of leadership. Should you reach the High Command one day, this will become obvious to you."

One of the bridge crew officers—not even based on the same genetic template as Hart—snapped to attention. "Captain! The Gulmar and Kedraalian ships begin their attacks on the wounded Khanate carrier."

Hart leaned forward slightly, hands locked on the supporting ring. "What can you see, Lieutenant?"

"Missiles impacting, Captain. They have closed to long range—for our systems. The accuracy of the strikes indicate optimal range is more likely for them."

Exactly as Faulk feared—there was respect in the young officer's voice. Soon, that would turn into fear.

We are being undermined by such short-sighted leadership. This task force should be doubled in size.

Except, of course, there weren't enough ships in the entire Azoren navy to support an operation of such a scale. Everything had been wasted on Morganson's ridiculous adventure and on the fight to take the ruined planet below. What technology hadn't gone into Morganson's expeditionary fleet was years out of date, procured by the same unreliable privateers.

What would have happened if that fleet had succeeded in obliterating the Kedraalians? Would these Khanate savages have turned to Himmel after laying waste to Radetta?

So much of war was happenstance. Even a genius such as his could be undermined by misfortune.

He felt the eyes of the bridge crew on him, even if he never caught them actually looking. They needed leadership, courage—things that a feeble officer such as Hart couldn't provide.

Faulk stretched his neck. "What losses we have suffered will be avenged."

Now the young officers turned from their stations, staring stupidly.

They needed to hear more. "Supreme Commander Graf appointed me to this mission out of appreciation for my experience and keen insights. What I offer more than compensates for the loss of a few ships." A smile seemed appropriate, something that might bridge the gap with younger and less wise crew.

The young men glanced at each other, and one grinned. "Thank you, Field Marshal."

Apparently satisfied, they turned back to their stations.

Without turning from his command station display, Hart's head bobbed. "Everyone better appreciates the value of your presence, Field Marshal."

"Good!"

The captain's head came up, then he stepped down and came to a stop beside his superior. "You are close with the Minister of Purity?"

"We served on the High Command together. I spoke with him almost daily."

Hart stared straight ahead. "What are his thoughts on this Kedraalian captain?"

Faulk's legs locked, and his belly felt tight. "He has no thoughts on her."

"I had the impression this captain spent time with him on Himmel."

"No." Faulk's eyes darted around to be sure no one else was listening. "The assassination attempt on Supreme Commander Graf left only me and Weber in position to speak with her. Without the burden of other distractions, I quickly determined it was Weber behind the bombings. My focus turned to running the government while the minister tended to Graf's survival."

"This is not what I had heard."

"We try to limit exposure to sensitive information. It protects everyone."

"Yes." The captain's blue-green eyes narrowed. "She seems remarkably capable."

Faulk snorted. "She flew us into a trap."

"I provided her the best exit point from Fold Space based on existing intelligence. Our ships have used this opening for years without peril. Moskav ships take a completely different route when traveling to other holdings."

"What are you saying, Captain?"

"This is an observation, Field Marshal. I lack the experience and keen insight to offer an opinion."

"Then what is your observation?"

"By all accounts, this captain has managed success against at least one of our brothers—"

"Morganson was a reckless fool."

"—and has stood against this Khanate fleet. She has done so twice now."

"And you will have the chance to do the same."

The captain acknowledged with a slight nod. "Still, it would seem an opportunity missed if Minister King failed to find time to meet her. He adores exceptionalism, even in the inferior races."

"Exceptionalism is a myth used to generate ill-advised pride. It clouds thinking and distracts from fact. The minister immediately realized that this captain is more the product of good fortune than any brilliance or craftiness."

"He shared this with you? Was this during the time where you were busy running the government?"

Faulk thought there might have been sarcasm in the other man's tone, but it didn't show in his pale features. Those were calm, almost disinterested. "Captain, you may not be as ideal for the High Command as I thought. Our role requires subtle analysis."

"I see." Hart turned sharply and mounted the step to his command station.

Somehow, that simple moment felt like a dismissal.

Faulk realized he couldn't allow the situation to get to him and influence his command and resolve.

With some effort, he flashed a smile at no one and everyone, then exited the bridge. His bodyguards were in the passageway outside and fell into step immediately. After the assassination attempt, he wasn't about to shoo them away. Officially, there might not be saboteurs or assassins in the task force anymore, but he wasn't about to risk his own life to support this notion.

The two men settled against either side of the hatch to his cabin, never saying a word. They were loyal and reliable.

Still, once he was alone, he searched his quarters: lifting the mattress off his bunk; opening the drawers of his desk and closet slowly; peeking inside the shower.

Safe.

He dropped onto the chair set before his foldout desk and brushed his hair back with his good hand. After a few moments, he dug around in his desk for a stylus to scratch the wrist enclosed by the cast. That was a huge relief.

Until he considered Hart's questions again.

Why hadn't Minister King asked to meet Benson? Why had she reacted so strangely to seeing him leave the manor?

King had chuckled at the questions when asked. *"Consider whether this is truly a good way to expend your intellect with war against the Khanate so close, Field Marshal."*

It hadn't been an answer at all. Rather, it had been evasion.

Faulk tossed the stylus back into its drawer. Dark thoughts threatened.

They were the sort of things Amanda—Colonel Karlson—would have helped him deal with.

"You and your brothers are compromised by excesses and eccentricities, Dietmar."

She had always used that as an excuse for the intoxicating gas and the elixirs she'd slipped into his drinks. Her android brain had ever been the extension of Graf and possibly even King—control and manipulation over every imaginable distance. Her flesh had been a minor addiction, something he could break free of with time. And now? He didn't need her any more than he needed Graf or King.

The field marshal tugged his jacket off and tossed it onto his bunk, then pulled his data pad from his pants pocket and set the device on the desktop.

He needed to send an update.

Damage control data had already been compiled by Hart's officers. Faulk gave that a summary walkthrough and added a few comments about the failure of the Kedraalian force to identify the threat when they exited Fold Space. After tapping his fingers on the desktop for a few seconds, he made a private note to the High Command—Graf and King now—about the possibility that this had been an attempt by Benson and her Gulmar lapdog to cripple the Azoren task force, something that might have been intended all along.

Next, he recorded a message to attach the report to. "Supreme Commander. My dear Minister King. I have unfortunate news—" Faulk's throat tightened.

He deleted the message, cleared his throat, and tried again.

"My fellow members of the High Command. I bring good news! The first engagement against the Khanate fleet has gone our way, despite treachery and misfortune. The fleet was waiting for us when we exited Fold Space. They had numerous missiles placed near our normal exit zone. These missiles seem to have locked on to the shadow technology used in the most advanced of our ECM and ECCM systems. Fortunately, the Kedraalian ships suffered nearly as much damage as we did."

Faulk paused the recording, then went back to review the damage report. It was nothing but data. No one had attempted to create a scapegoat by questioning the decision to leave the protection of the Kedraalian task force. And after all, his idea to press the attack against the advancing Khanate ships had probably saved one or two troop transports.

This was not the time for backbiting, after all.

He resumed the recording, smiling now. "While our ships performed admirably during the battle, mistakes were made. To keep morale at an acceptable level, I've assigned some of my most reliable security officers to see to it that officers under Captain Hart's command who failed to live up to expectations are eliminated. It will be a mixture of quiet poisoning for those now in the infirmary and very public airlock executions for those deserving of a grand example. A few bodies floating around the ships will act as a strong reminder of the cost of failure."

His thumb stroked the pause button.

When his heart had settled into an acceptable rhythm, he resumed the recording. "Although we can begin repairs, it is better to send the damaged ships back to Himmel and to have them replaced. Unfortunately, several of our troop transports were targeted by the enemy and lost. Those brave soldiers quite obviously cannot be replaced."

Faulk did his best to look somber and hurt, stretching it out what felt like an appropriate length of time.

"Once I have our task force at full strength, I will turn my attention to finishing this mission with the sort of ruthless efficiency my career has been built upon. To the bold, victory."

"Oh. One other thing." He let his serious look transform into what he hoped might appear to be a practical blankness. "As you must have inferred by this update, the Khanate fleet was here, in Moskav space. It would appear they chose to eradicate the Moskav after the Gulmar, starting by destroying Moskav itself. This could possibly be coincidence, but I now find myself concerned that by pulling me away from finishing off Weber, we might have left a spy capable of compromising the intent and will of the Azoren Federation."

Another smile seemed appropriate, so Faulk put on his most sincere effort. "I look forward to sharing even better news upon my victorious return."

He thumbed the stop button, then watched the recording from the start. A few small glitches needed cleaning up, which took a minute, then he sent the message to the Fold Space transmitter.

Recording the message was nearly as exhausting as dealing with Graf himself. It was stressful living in the man's withering gaze.

When the mission was all over, and Benson and her fleet burned in orbit over the swirling pyre of Azh Shivan, Faulk would have all he ever needed to return to Himmel and finally depose the old man.

And when Faulk claimed the seat of power, the galaxy would follow.

F ire gushed from a hole in the side of the Khanate carrier. Benson almost felt bad that she couldn't interpret the name of the ship from the strange jumble of swirls and squares that made up the fabricated language. There should be some way to know what they were destroying. Then again, as pockmarked and blackened as the hull was, even large blocks of Humana text wouldn't likely be readable.

Chopra backed up to the command station where he bobbed up and down on the balls of his feet. "Four frigates and this carrier. A good day."

"I would have liked to get those last two damaged frigates."

"They may not survive the jump to Fold Space."

"True."

On the battlefield display, computer-generated lines showed shot after shot landing—gouging holes in the dying ship. All three of the bridge crew stared at the images, hands clasped behind their backs. It was as if the fire those thousands of kilometers away was somehow washing across the *Valor*'s hull, heating the bridge, pushing the atmosphere control system until its familiar drone became a loud grind and the air took on a thick, tired mustiness.

Just the systems working under a load.

The bald XO turned toward her. "Will they surrender, do you think?"

"I wouldn't accept if they did."

"There are conventions—"

"We've signed nothing with them, and they've already shown their capacity for mercy, Dinesh."

"Perhaps one day, there will be agreements."

She rubbed her forehead with the heel of her palm. "When we reach Azh Shivan, I don't intend to take prisoners. It's not what we were sent to do."

"If they surrender—?"

"No different than this fleet. You saw what they did on Radetta. It sounds like they did even worse on Moskav. It's in their doctrine: Convert or die. What options do we have when faced with that?"

"But—"

"We're tolerant people, but we have a right to survival. If they have a policy of assimilation and slaughter, there's not really room for our survival, is there?"

"What about the civilians?"

Benson sighed. "If they can surrender, we'll see. People like this have a history of using civilians as shields, so I don't hold out much hope."

Konrath turned from his weapons station as the display shifted from tactical to a high-resolution image of the burning aircraft carrier. "Secondary explosions on the aircraft carrier, Captain."

On the giant display, the hull rippled and blew away in several sections, pushed out by fireballs and debris.

The weapons officer pointed to the line of ruin along the starboard side, where the explosions continued until the ship was down to warped ribbing and twisted plates. "They were carrying explosives for those suicide vessels. I think those must have gone off. That's the last of the ship."

"Intentional?" Benson thought it might be, but wanted the young man's assessment.

"Possibly. All of that going at once? It seems unlikely."

Or more poor design. "Thank you. Please continue firing until nothing larger than a fist remains." She glanced down at her XO, one eyebrow cocked as if to ask if he understood.

He sagged, defeated. "Maybe they will rise up against their leaders."

It seemed unlikely. These people had chosen their belief system at some point.

She cleared her throat. "Lieutenant Nuñez, please connect me to Captain Thiessen. Commander Chopra, you have the conn."

Benson was in her cabin by the time the connection went through. She peeled off her jacket and put it over the back of her chair. Her shirt was damp, and she was breathing hard. "Floyd?"

"I saw it."

She powered on the display built into her desktop. The Gulmar captain's handsome face smiled back. "They're damaged."

"Wounded. I don't think they can recover from this."

"We can't let them." Benson dropped into her seat.

"You look like I feel."

"I feel exactly how I look, so I guess we're both miserable."

"You have a chance to catch your breath, Faith. Take it."

What she wanted was some sleep, maybe a deep-tissue massage. It looked like something Thiessen would be good at. She checked to be sure their connection was secure. "This is going to make things worse with Faulk."

"I know. The way he reacted during the attack…" Thiessen brushed hair back from his forehead.

"I'm going to tell Faulk we're searching the system for stragglers and traps. I'd like you to come to the *Valor* and meet with my staff. I think the two of us need to talk."

"It's a good idea. But, just so we're clear: Whatever you decide on, I'll back your play." His eyes sparkled.

No. She was imagining that. "Thank you. I'll be in touch."

She killed the connection and stripped off the rest of her uniform. They had the tiniest of windows to figure out their next step. If she was honest with herself, she already knew what they had to do.

And that would put them on a course they could never come back from.

32

———————

Benson strolled the passageways of the *Valor* with Thiessen at her side, feeling like she was a schoolgirl again, showing off her boyfriend to the other girls. It was silly, and it pressed against her sense of being a leader and diplomat. She was finally doing the real work of bridging the gaps between allies. With the ship's environmental systems finally back to full capacity, she felt comfortable in her dress whites, and the Gulmar captain was devilishly handsome in his blue-black business suit uniform. Her crew were in good spirits and most seemed genuinely impressed with him.

Victory could undo great harm.

She came to a stop outside the conference room, stomach twisted in a knot. Instinct told her to hook an arm around Thiessen's elbow and lead him in. That was loneliness eating at her. The last thing she needed was to start rumors. Even clapping him on the back and laughing wouldn't be appropriate.

Her key command staff had already assembled—Tuleyev, Halliwell, and Dietrich—and were sipping tea and working their way through thawed fruit spread out on plates atop the narrow table in the center of the small room. Benson's mouth watered at the sweet smell of berries and apples.

Chairs hissed back on tracks as everyone stood. Benson waved for them to sit but waited for Thiessen to take the seat to her right before settling in at the head of the table herself.

Thiessen set a plate in front of her, then helped himself to one as well, plucking a few grapes and marveling at them. "These could be fresh."

Dietrich scrubbed his hands with a moist cloth. "We continue to make advances in almost every aspect of science. Imagine what could be done without war draining resources away from research."

"I was always told that every form of research has benefits, even weapons research."

"If you count profit as a benefit."

Benson poured a cup of tea and slid the saucer over to the Gulmar captain, then poured herself a cup as well. "We're not here to argue the merits of war, Dr. Dietrich."

"That would be a short argument, don't you think?"

She took a sip, enjoying the bitter warmth on her tongue. "We've spent three days hunting for Khanate stragglers."

Tuleyev dabbed his wet lips with a towel. "A goose chase this seems."

"A necessary goose chase. It's given us time to begin repairs in earnest, and it's verified the battlefield has been swept clear of the enemy." She nodded toward Thiessen. "And it's given us an opportunity for a meeting like this without our Azoren allies knowing about it."

"Assuming they have no spies." The old man set his towel on the table.

"We've vetted our crew multiple times. I believe we can trust them."

Veins bulged on the back of Halliwell's hands as he squeezed his towel, eyes locked on Thiessen. "We can trust *our* crews."

The Gulmar captain smiled pleasantly. "And I trust mine, Lieutenant."

Benson shook her head. "The intent of this meeting is to dissect what happened and to plan for the next engagement."

Dietrich pushed his saucer toward the center of the table. "Is it appropriate to have your senior medical officer involved in that?"

"I value your perspective."

"I'm a doctor, not a butcher."

"Ernie—please. Give me a minute."

The doctor leaned back in his seat and waved toward the table: *Be my guest.*

She would have loved to toss a blueberry into her mouth, to pop its skin with a bite, but the meeting wasn't about making a point. "We'll be a few weeks getting the signals ships back to full functionality. Losing the *Tojo* hurt. Fortunately, Captain Thiessen's force has compatible systems installed. We can leverage that technology, implement a few upgrades, and that will make up for our losses."

A smirk twisted Halliwell's face. "Meaning we become reliant on them."

"The Gulmar force is here to help us complete this mission."

"Yeah? Which mission? Weren't we supposed to take out the Azoren? What happened to that?"

Benson glanced at the Gulmar officer, then back at the Marine. "We'll get to that."

"We can't trust them."

"All right. Let's discuss that now, then. We've got an Azoren problem, and we all know it. We can talk about our losses at a later date."

It seemed to dawn on Dietrich at that moment why he had been called to the meeting. His jaw slowly lowered until he snapped it shut abruptly. "Your question is going to be: What did you learn on Himmel, Commander Dietrich?"

"It is."

"What I learned is that their doctors spend so much time coping with a war that never ends that they can't keep up with basic advancements. Amazing the way my point about wasting money on warfare seems proven yet again."

"They have less advanced medical training."

"And facilities. And they struggle to maintain sufficient supplies of even the most fundamental medicines, thanks in large part to our Gulmar allies here."

Thiessen set down a half-eaten slice of honeydew. "I'm a security officer, Commander."

"In the service of a power with a long history of predatory pricing of—"

Benson held up a hand. "That's not relevant."

Her Gulmar counterpart frowned. "And I doubt the corporations will have the capacity to produce even half of what they used to produce."

Dietrich threw his hands up in frustration. "Which means they'll have an actual justification for the pricing."

Inviting the doctor to a meeting was always risky, and Benson was beginning to think she might do better interviewing him separately. He was clearly committed to polishing his firebrand bona fides. "If that's all you can think of, Commander Dietrich…?"

He stood. "Thank you for the fruit, Captain."

Once he had exited the conference room, she turned to Tuleyev. "He's the best surgeon in the fleet."

The old commander pulled out a soiled handkerchief, wiped his nose, then shrugged. "Perhaps such a skilled surgeon should have been left on Himmel."

She couldn't help smiling. "We need to talk about the field marshal."

Halliwell leaned in. "He's a lunatic."

"They all are. The Children, at least. And Graf is a real gem. That's who's running things right now." *And this Purity Minister King…I can't talk to anyone about that—not right now. Maybe not ever.*

Thiessen turned to her. "You okay?"

"Hm?"

"You look…" His brow bunched. "Is this about what happened on Himmel?"

"It is." That wasn't a lie. Not completely. How could she possibly expect him to understand? *She* didn't. "But it doesn't change our situation."

Halliwell's gaze shot from her to Thiessen. "You going to tell us what does?"

"Of course. To begin with, I asked Chief Parkinson to try to tear into the Azoren shadow tech. We've picked up most of the signals they were using during the battle."

Tuleyev stroked the corners of his mouth. "We have ample data from their attack on Kedraal, do we not?"

"Those were top-of-the-line ships. I doubt this task force has the same hardware. More importantly, they were installing upgrades when we went aboard the *Warsaw*."

"Upgrades? You know this how, Captain?"

Thiessen clasped his hands on the conference tabletop. "I think I can answer at least part of that. When we were aboard the *Warsaw* for the field marshal's show of strength, there were a lot of people taking equipment out of fairly distinctive cargo crates."

Benson pointed to Halliwell. "Like the ones in the *Pandora*'s secure area."

The Marine nodded. "Smugglers?"

"Floyd thinks it was probably privateers."

"That—" The Gulmar captain smirked. "—is synonymous with smugglers, though."

Quiet seconds seemed to stretch, then Halliwell popped his knuckles. "Then Parkinson can figure their systems out. What's the problem?"

It was never easy getting through to Halliwell when he was mad, and he seemed pretty pissed off right then. Benson showed her palms: surrender. "Whatever they've got, Chief can't crack it. It's the same problem we have with the Khanate systems. We know it has to be the same technology, but he thinks it's a different branch of development."

"Why?"

"We don't know. For whatever reason, someone forked the research somewhere, and they gave that stolen tech to the Azoren and Khanate."

Thiessen squinted at his clasped hands. "And, indirectly, to us."

Both Halliwell and Tuleyev turned to the Gulmar officer, but it was Tuleyev who finally spoke. "This Azoren shadow tech is something you have, Captain?"

"Like I said: indirectly. Privateers are ultimately businesspeople, and they're notoriously flexible. Ethically, I mean. That's how we saw our first shadow tech. This weird new technology suddenly showed up, and a privateer crew decided there was money to be had selling Gulmar security a first look. Our engineers tore it apart, cloned it, and gave it back. It was a revolutionary advancement in electronic warfare and stealth technology. Then a couple years ago, the Azoren came to us with a request to manufacture a lot of systems for them. Most of it was typical starship equipment, but some of it was these same systems you call shadow tech. Of course, they had us working on it in bits and pieces, but we already knew how it fit together."

Halliwell rolled his eyes. "You built wartime equipment for your enemy?"

"*And* for ourselves. Look, I know you folks do things differently, but keep in mind I wasn't consulted on this. I know about it because I'm part —I *was* part—of the security apparatus."

Tuleyev grunted. "And this is the same? You are certain?"

"No. I'm pretty sure it's not. But your chief engineer apparently feels he could crack the code base to the software if he could get a look at the point where things fork. I think our systems are that point. We still have copies of that old software."

Benson let that sink in for a moment, taking in Halliwell and Tuleyev's faces while she sipped her tea. Finally, she set her cup down. "So, if this proves true, we have an opportunity. Not only could we fully crack the Khanate stealth but the stealth of that Azoren task force."

Tuleyev's bushy eyebrows arched. "They would not be a threat."

"They would just be a bunch of obsolete warships. And when we're done with the Khanate threat, we would be in a position to eliminate Field Marshal Faulk."

"An enemy should be confronted with honor." The old man stared at the tabletop. "But as we have said, these enemies have no honor."

Benson was glad she'd released Dietrich. He was too precious and pure, too sure that the benefit of holding to the moral high ground would somehow compensate for the losses suffered. For him, the sailors killed in ambush by the Azoren and the people working on the original *Valor* at the dockyards were victims of War—big "w"—and the problem was the concept, not the people who refused to accept even the basic boundaries of decency.

"Commander Tuleyev, Lieutenant Halliwell—I'd like a preliminary tactical mockup by the end of the day tomorrow. Assume three potential scenarios: We engage the Azoren at full strength and manage complete surprise; we engage the Azoren at half strength and manage complete surprise; and we engage the Azoren at half strength after they launch first strike."

The two officers nodded, then stood when she did, both muttering "Captain" as she exited.

Thiessen followed after her a few steps, but when they turned down an empty passageway, he touched her elbow. "Hey."

She stopped and tilted her head. "Why didn't I ask you to coordinate with them?"

"No, no. I get that. Security. I'll follow your lead when this happens."

"Oh." Why couldn't her officers be like that?

"The way you froze in there—" He looked around, then moved closer. "Did something happen when you disappeared on Himmel? Did they…do something to you?"

It took real effort not to laugh and cry at the same time once she realized he was concerned about her. "I never did get to tell you everything that happened. I'm sorry. They didn't do anything to me. It was just that request to help them kill Faulk."

"That's it?"

She put a hand over her heart. "That's it."

Although he seemed to relax a little, he was still tense. "Then can I ask what made you freeze up back there?"

How could she tell him? She squeezed his arm. "Later. When this is over."

His eyes drifted down to her hand, which she didn't pull away. "Over dinner? A victory celebration."

"Promise."

He stepped back, a hint of reluctance in his eyes. "I look forward to it. But now it's time to get back to my ship. We don't want the field marshal wondering why our ships came so close together for so long."

They walked to the hangar bay in silence, drifting close enough together that the backs of their hands sometimes brushed, then separating when there were crew in the passageway. The contact—even the close proximity—felt electric and left her shivering.

Thiessen waved from the ramp before jogging into his shuttle.

She radioed Chopra that she would return to the bridge after lunch, but she wasn't going to be able to eat, not now that she'd committed herself to whatever lay ahead with Thiessen.

Her cabin lights flickered to life when the hatch opened. She hurried through and locked the hatch behind her.

Committed. It was the right term.

Anchored on the edge of the shelf, reflecting the lights off its curved surface: the globe that had held her aspirations for so many years. She picked the knickknack up, overcoming the smart adhesive with practiced ease, then stared inside at the holograms that had been dreams for so long.

Becoming captain of the *Valor*.

Being awarded The Republic Ivory Order of Meritorious Service.

Seeing her father again.

She returned the globe to its shelf.

How could she tell Thiessen—how could she tell *anyone*—that all of her dreams had come true now? How could she admit they had all been soured by what she'd seen on Himmel?

How could she believe that her father was this Minister of Purity King, the second most powerful person in the Azoren High Command and the creator of the Children?

Burnt-orange sand disappeared beneath the hood of the truck. That was all Caville could see in any direction: sand. Maybe once in a while, there was a ridge of similar-colored stone rising up at random here and there. If the sun weren't so bright, the sand would be a deeper red. Wind whistled softly through the open windows, but it didn't cool him any more than it sucked away the salty-sweet smell of perspiration. He doubted Gallo was any better off. Her robes clung to her, same as his shirt.

He took a sip of sweet water from a bottle, then checked his data pad. Using the planet's magnetic field and the angle of the sun was as good as they could do without global positioning, and the system insisted he was on course.

The young woman smiled at him through heavy-lidded eyes. "How're we doing on fuel?"

"If these directions are right, we'll make it."

"Make it there but not back."

He shrugged. "Back to where? This was always a one-way trip. You're the one who said everyone who goes to this place dies."

She opened her robe, revealing the ridiculous undergarment that had been conjured up as magical protection by the first Khan. The thick material was dark with her sweat. "I'm free now, so I think I'll live that way."

It took several minutes, but she managed to untangle the thick robes, then untie the undergarment straps. When that was all done, she threw the garment out the window, laughing meekly.

Afterward, she dropped back on the seat, uncaring about the fine sand settling onto the sheen of moisture covering her.

There wasn't anything else to see, so Caville enjoyed the distraction for a while. "Is this all about making up for what you did?"

Gallo squinted through the front window. "Spying?"

"People died."

"I guess so." She scraped the door with her thumbnail.

"Any regrets?"

"About the spying or about this?"

"Any at all."

Dark curls clung to her face as she surveyed the vast desert. "I heard this used to be something. Maybe it was a big, fertile valley?"

"All the major planets were terraformed to the point human habitation was supposed to be comfortable."

"That was the people from Earth, right?"

"Centuries ago."

"Was that terraforming penance for them?"

"For the good ones. I think for the worst ones, it was just a way to spread the disease of humanity to the stars."

"Disease." She nodded. "I like that. It's not an excuse, is it?"

"An explanation."

"I don't care for the idea that what I did killed people, but I think I had a disease of my own back then." Her fingers went to something that clung to her chest: a medallion that was almost lost against the warm brown of her flesh. She lifted the thing, then yanked against the delicate chain.

It snapped, and she studied the medallion for a bit. A closer glance revealed it was one of the Khanate symbols. She tossed it out the window.

Gallo smiled. "Free. Cured."

Caville grunted. Just as he was about to challenge the idea that an emblem was enough to undo everything she'd done, his data pad beeped.

She leaned against him, smiling when his eyes tracked from the device to her, then tapping the display. "Trouble?"

He nodded to the front windshield. "This is supposedly it."

"That's not good."

The vehicle shuddered, then the engine coughed, and finally it died.

"That's the last of the fuel." Caville wondered if that was what this original Khan had felt in his deranged state, wandering a radioactive desert on Earth and imagining his own divinity was talking to him.

Gallo groaned, then pushed open the passenger door and slid out. She brushed sand from her skin, shook out her robe, then pulled it on. Caville was out of the vehicle by then, too, water bottles in one hand, assault rifles in the other.

He handed one of each to her. "You ready to test your conviction?"

She took a long pull from the water bottle. "Do I have a choice?"

They trudged back the way they'd come, until they reached the point where the data pad insisted that they had arrived at the Place of the Fallen. Caville cupped a hand over his eyes, but there were no landmarks and nothing in the least special about the place.

Overhead, the sun actually seemed to grow brighter.

Caville dug a booted toe into the sand. "If they made it off the planet, it could buy us a few days."

"Do you think they did? That cargo ship was a hunk of junk."

"If I can get a connection into the Khanate network out here, I'll see what they say."

"Do we have enough food and water to last?"

"We can probably make it a week out here. You don't want to, though. Desert survival is miserable."

"The teachings all say that the Khan survived in a desert for—"

"A month, right?"

She nodded. "That's just the teachings."

"A month with a bottle of water that refilled each night while he slept, and he woke each morning to find fruit—right?"

"And sometimes a lamb that had been slaughtered."

"Yeah. There weren't any lambs within two thousand kilometers of that desert. That guy was a fraud."

"I know." She bowed her head. "But I'm telling you, the directions were correct."

"The person you got them from has been here?"

"She knew people who had been here. She helped with some of the video work. They may not be able to accept women as equals in the eyes of the Khan, but sometimes they have to accept help despite the teachings."

"A fraud *and* a misogynist. That's a great religion."

Gallo turned away. "It's the only thing I knew growing up."

"You grew up on Kedraal."

"But my parents were believers."

That was exactly what he'd expected her to say. Although he wasn't as good at dealing with people as his sister, his training had covered many aspects of human development, including childhood privilege. People like Gallo—middle class, educated, smart—often found themselves imagining they needed something to make them special. In her case, she chose to listen to her mother's teachings about the Khan rather than her father's. Ideally, there would come a time in her young adult life where she developed critical thinking skills and formed her own opinion based on objective data and observation.

Ideally.

Caville shrugged. "I'll get the rest of the gear."

He stuffed his duffel bag with the water and food packets from the truck cab, gathered up the rest of the guns and ammunition, then trudged back to where Gallo was stomping the ground, as if she could just break through meters of sand and rock to find this mysterious place.

She frowned. "It has to be here!"

"Or it could be somewhere nearby." He pulled a calorie bar out and handed it to her. "Might as well get used—"

Something creaked beneath them, then groaned.

Then the desert floor gave way, and they tumbled into shadow.

Rain hammered McLeod's rented air car as he tried to nudge it down in front of the surprisingly large Chen Funeral Services building. Despite pushing the car to its top speed, the GSA officer was nearly an hour late arriving. Below him, the single amber floodlight mounted on the southern door revealed a dark red car as the sole occupant of the parking lot.

Car. Not air car. The proprietor didn't live large.

Landing proved a challenge, with the vector thrust on the left side being stickier than McLeod had realized. From the scrape that rumbled through his feet, he thought he might have dinged the undercarriage.

He powered down, pulled his umbrella out, then shoved the door open and stepped into the storm. The wind nearly tore the umbrella from his hand, and he quickly discovered that freezing rain was mixed in with the rest. A deep, earthy smell hung in the air, stronger than the stench of smoke coming from the refinery a few kilometers back. That might explain the acidic bite the rain left on his lips.

The facade was corrugated steel, a dark mustard color in the floodlight. Mounted next to a steel door was a keypad with a card reader, and above that was a camera. To the right of the reader was a doorbell.

McLeod rang the bell, then looked up into the camera. "Hello? I'm Avis McLeod. Sorry I'm late. I had an appointment for seven."

There was no response at first, and he wondered if maybe the car wasn't the proprietor's after all. Then a deep buzz came out of the door, followed by the heavy clank of a lock opening.

A quick look over his shoulder ensured no one was watching him from the dark. He let himself in and shook out the umbrella, taking in the small reception area with a desk and chairs, all decorated with tasteful, somber gray and black accents. There were digital image frames mounted about a meter and a half high, and inside those a stream of images played: coffins, urns, cemeteries, tombs.

"Mr. Chen?"

A door opened, and a small man stepped out. He wore baggy pants and a white shirt with sleeves rolled up to reveal hairless, wiry arms flecked with liver spots. Chen had a round face that was older than the one on his business presence site. His black hair was silver-streaked and had receded.

He clasped his small, delicate hands in front of him. "Mr. McLeod?"

"Sorry I'm late. The storm—"

"I try not to use that term. As I tell people all the time, I work with late people every day." The little man beamed.

"Oh. I see. I wanted to arrange for the transfer of Brianna Stiles's body back to Kedraal."

"Body? Not a cremation? It would save significant money."

"Body, thank you. The military will cover the cost."

"Oh. She was military?"

"She was."

The old man nodded, projecting warmth and empathy. "Would you like to see her?"

McLeod shivered. He'd known from the second the alarm had come in that Stiles was dead, and that there would come a time when he'd have to deal with seeing her. Since taking over as her commander, he'd expected her to outlive him. The Genesis 3 children had been created to age more quickly, but they were also created to be more than human, to live longer. It was unfortunate so few had even made it into their teens.

He nodded, then followed Chen through the door. The old man shuffled down a hallway, past an open door on the left where light leaked out: an office. They were headed toward a closed door on the right, opposite another door on the left labeled *restroom*.

Chen smiled over his shoulder. "You said Kedraal."

"I did."

"That's a long trip. She came here to visit family?"

"She was killed in action."

"Ah." The proprietor clucked his tongue against his teeth. "Tragic. I see so many young people. Men, mostly. Miners and risk takers. Some come in torn to pieces, held together by a bag."

McLeod's stomach lurched. "This is a hard world."

"It is. Never fully terraformed. Not like a lot of other places. It takes a certain kind of person to live here." Chen's back straightened, and he held his chin up a little more.

The notion was nonsensical macho rhetoric. Dramora had been terraformed as much as any other settled planet. There was simply a limit to how much could be tamed when the world was essentially a muddy ball of minerals and rock.

Chen opened the door on the right, and a bright, white light flashed on, revealing a polished, white tiled floor, two stainless steel tables, a wall of matching refrigerator hatches, a gurney, and a couple of push carts. Digital readouts glowed on the hatches, and the old man shuffled to one next to the west wall.

Unease worked through McLeod's gut, not just at what he was about to see but at the way the old man knew exactly where Stiles's body was held.

A shaky hand rose, then the old man turned to consider McLeod with a cocked head. "Is it normal for the military to pay to have bodies priority delivered and kept frozen?"

"What?"

"Brianna Stiles—your soldier? I was just now thinking how odd it was that someone would pay what they did to care for a body like this. I suppose her being military, it makes a certain sense. An open-ended payment line—I must admit, I will miss her." The old man tittered, then he opened the hatch.

McLeod stepped back as chill air misted out of the cooler. His throat tightened when he saw Stiles's black hair. As the tray slid out, he could see that someone had washed and brushed her hair and cleaned her up, although there was nothing they could have done about the wound on the side of her head. It was stitched up, but the skin around it was discolored and puckered.

Tears welled up, and it became hard to breathe for a moment.

Chen was too busy stroking Stiles's face to notice. "She must have been beautiful. I mean, she is still."

How could anyone reply to that? It was part of her design? Her job required her to exert control over people? She was far too young to die, but that youth is still there, in her face?

The old man held up a finger. "You might want her possessions, I suppose."

He shuffled over to a cabinet in the corner across from the cooler. He clanged through a few drawers, then returned with two plastic bags labeled: Stiles, Brianna. One held folded clothes, the other held…a resuscitation ring.

McLeod stared at it for a moment, then turned to the cooler. "You said someone paid to have her priority delivered here?"

"Yes. Straight from the starport."

"Did they dictate what temperature to store the body at?"

"Zero."

Impossible. The GSA officer leaned in closer to the wound, now seeing it—really seeing it—for the first time. "This stitch of the wound was your work?"

"Yes. I always clean up any corpse that might be buried. I always expect cremation, but—"

"Can you cut the thread? Please?"

Chen's eyes bugged out. "You want—"

"Hurry. Please."

The old man shambled over to one of the carts and returned with a box of surgical instruments. It was as if he moved through a thick gel, struggling against the universe. His hands shook as he snipped the thread and pulled it free.

McLeod's heart pounded. "Do you have gloves?"

That required another trip to the cart, fiddling with a small box, then an even slower return. McLeod almost snatched the gloves away, then realized he was pulling them over the wrong fingers.

Slow down. It's going to be okay.

Except he was dealing with the *impossible*. No, he was dealing with something he should have thought of all along.

He peeled the skin back from the wound, fighting against nausea and horror. It would only take a moment to confirm his worst fears or his greatest hope, but he had to push through the gore—

Chen bumped against the colonel's side, leaning in to watch. "What is it?"

McLeod gritted his teeth, but he was nearly—

He gasped. The white of bone—

Stiles's skull was cracked but intact. There would be brain damage, but that could be nothing more than swelling. The resuscitation ring would have dealt with that at the time of injection.

An exultant laugh slipped out. He turned on Chen. "Put her back in the freezer. Hurry."

"What?"

The colonel tried to shove the tray in himself, but it was locked somehow. "Put her back in. Now."

Chen grunted, tapped something on the rail, then pushed the tray in and closed the hatch. "What—?"

McLeod pulled out his data pad while waving the other man to silence, then walked back to the hallway, legs shaking. It wasn't until gory streaks appeared on the pad's display that McLeod realized he was still wearing the surgical gloves. He set the device on the floor, pulled the gloves off, then put an earpiece on.

A connection signaled over the earpiece as he picked the data pad back up, then there was a voice in his ear. "Colonel."

"I need a doctor scrambled to my location immediately—someone familiar with resuscitations. Brain trauma experience, if possible."

"Understood."

The connection died, and McLeod felt ready to collapse. Stiles wasn't dead. If he did everything just right, she might not even be damaged. Someone had shot her in the head, but the wound wasn't lethal. It'd been caused by something low caliber or maybe a defective bullet. The impact hadn't penetrated her reinforced skull. And someone had paid to have her kept frozen while the resuscitation ring drugs were in her system.

He would need answers if—when—she came around. What mattered now was that he hadn't lost her. And that meant the Devanshi Patel situation might still be resolved and the work of a lifetime salvaged.

DEDICATION

For those held hostage by tyrants.

ACKNOWLEDGMENTS

Shadow Pawn is the fifth chapter of **The War in Shadow**. Combining space opera and military science fiction, this series captures many science fiction elements I enjoy and find intriguing. I hope that's conveyed to readers.

This novel derives influence from numerous sources, including the paranoia of Cold War spy works and the dark times of Nazi Germany. *Shadow* holds multiple meanings in the series, including espionage and the darkest elements of politics and diplomacy. I think that's most obvious with this story.

If you find this series entertaining, I hope you'll consider posting a review of the books and letting friends know about it. Word of mouth and reviews are invaluable.

For updates on new releases and news on other series, please visit my website and sign up for my mailing list at:

http://www.p-r-adams.com

ABOUT THE AUTHOR

I was born and raised in Tampa, Florida. I joined the Air Force, and my career took me from coast to coast before depositing me in the St. Louis, Missouri area for several years. After a tour in Korea and a short return to the St. Louis area, I retired and moved to the greater Denver, Colorado metropolitan area.

I write speculative fiction, mostly science fiction and fantasy. My favorite writers over the years have been Robert E. Howard, Philip K. Dick, Roger Zelazny, and Michael Crichton.

Social Media:
www.p-r-adams.com
pradams_author@comcast.net

www.ingramcontent.com/pod-product-compliance
Lightning Source LLC
Chambersburg PA
CBHW070820190726

48292CB00006B/2064